2014 √√

D0341100

HOPE AT HOLLY COTTAGE

The future seems rosy for Plymouth schoolgirl Anna Millington as she studies for teacher training college. However, her family hides a cruel secret from back in 1941 the night of the Plymouth Blitz, when Anna aged five cowered in a bomb shelter. Now, in 1954, the devastating consequences erupt again in tragedy, making Anna abandon her aspirations for a successful career.

Leaving behind her dear friend Ethel, Anna escapes to nearby Dartmoor, of which she has fond memories. But will her return to the moor bring her hope?

HOPE AT HOLLY COTTAGE

HOPE AT HOLLY COTTAGE

by

Tania Crosse

Magna Large Print Books
Long Preston, North Yorkshire,
BD23 4ND, England.

British Library Cataloguing in Publication Data.

Crosse, Tania
    Hope at Holly Cottage.

    A catalogue record of this book is
    available from the British Library

    ISBN   978-0-7505-3363-8

First published in Great Britain in 2010 by Allison & Busby Ltd.

Copyright © 2010 by Tania Crosse

Cover illustration by arrangement with Allison & Busby Ltd.

The moral right of the author has been asserted

Published in Large Print 2011 by arrangement with
Allison & Busby Ltd.

Magna Large Print is an imprint of Library Magna Books Ltd.

Printed and bound in Great Britain by
T.J. (International) Ltd., Cornwall, PL28 8RW

For all my good friends and neighbours in the Home Counties, especially Joan and Arthur Gibbs for all their kindness.

And as ever for my husband for being my hero and my best friend.

Chapter One

'Where the hell's my dinner, you lazy slut?'

Upstairs in her bedroom of the little terraced house, Anna Millington lifted her head from her homework, feeling the familiar pulse of anger and fear at the sound of her father's voice. What time was it? Half past eight already? She had been so engrossed in her study of Racine's Greek tragedy, *Andromaque,* that she had forgotten her own problems, but now they flooded back with a vengeance.

The house shook as the front door slammed, making the pencils rattle on the little table she used as a desk. Another crash reached her ears. Her father stumbling into the kitchen, no doubt.

'I told you to have my dinner on the table!'

Oh, no! Her father had been drinking again. The pubs opened soon after knocking-off time at the building site. Doubtless he'd been downing pints ever since. Oh, please don't hit Mum this time, she silently prayed, and suddenly her cold hands were clammy with sweat. She would have to go downstairs and sort it all out – as usual! How on earth was she supposed to get her A levels like this?

'Please, Vince,' she caught her mother's feeble voice as she flew down the stairs. 'We didn't know what time you'd be back and–'

As Anna scudded along the narrow hallway, she was met by a resounding slap and another crash.

11

Reaching the kitchen threshold, she saw her mother crouched on the floor where she had fallen, while her father was towering over her, one hand gripping his wife around the throat while the other was poised to strike her face.

'Dad, no! Stop it! Let her go!'

Anna tugged forcefully at her father's raised arm. He turned his flaring eyes on her and she glared back. But then she saw the hatchet lines of fury on his face first freeze and then slacken before curiously melting away. He turned back to his wife with stricken eyes, slowly uncurling his fingers from around her throat, and as Anna released her grip on his raised arm, he let it flop powerlessly to his side. She watched him feel for the kitchen chair, his anger-flushed cheeks now grey and the great white scar in the deep dent on his forehead fading into his ashen skin.

Anna gulped in a huge sigh of relief. The crisis was over, and she doubted there would be any more trouble from her father that night as she watched him sink into the chair with his head in his hands. She stood back as her mother scraped herself from the floor, swallowing and rubbing her neck, and went to kneel in front of her husband, enclosing him in her arms and rocking him like a child.

Anna turned her head away, unable to witness the pathetic scene. In her opinion, her father belonged in an asylum or some such institution, but he was too proud to ask for help. And he refused to apply for war disablement benefit or whatever it might be called. But his wasn't an obvious disability. Anna wondered if it might not have been better if he had lost an arm or a leg. There was no shame in that. But to have your brain damaged so that you were frequently and unpredictably attacked by a personality disorder that brought on fits of black depression and drunken violence, well, that was something else. It was unutterably hard to live with, and too shameful to admit to.

She went into the scullery that led off the kitchen. There was just room for the built-in washing copper in the corner, the gas cooker on its tall, enamel legs, and the chipped butler sink with its wooden draining board. Anna turned on the stiff cold tap that dripped constantly however hard you turned it off, and ran some water into the aluminium saucepan.

It was one of the few relatively new utensils they possessed. Her mother had often told her how she had dutifully given up all but one of her precious pans to the war effort so that she could proudly watch them fly overhead transformed into a Spitfire in one of the dogfights over Plymouth. Anna remembered when, some time after the war was over and she had been reunited with her parents in their new home, she had gone with her mother to the hardware shop to buy what she hadn't been able to pick up second hand.

Anna had been fascinated. Even the shopkeeper had seemed proud of his rows of gleaming saucepans, and looking back, Anna realised it was because such things were only just becoming available again. The pan wasn't quite so shiny now, despite her mother's efforts with the Brillo pad. Anna crowned it with her father's dinner on a plate, lit the gas beneath it and left the meal to

13

steam. Her father would doubtless feel better once he had eaten.

She crept back through the kitchen. Up in her room, she still had a large chunk of *Our Mutual Friend* to read for her Dickens class the following day. That was if she could concentrate after the upset. No matter how often it happened – and it seemed to be happening more often of late – she could never get used to it. But someone had to stand up to her father when he had one of his 'fits' and jolt him from the demon that overtook his brain. Her mother wouldn't – or simply couldn't, Anna wasn't sure which.

'Your dinner'll be ready in about twenty minutes,' she said brusquely.

She was making for the door without stopping, but her father caught her arm and extricated his head from where it was buried against her mother's shoulder.

'Thank you. And I'm so sorry.'

Anna nodded briefly. Oh, yes. The *real* Vince Millington was sorry *now*, but how long would it be before it happened again? Next week? Tomorrow?

She climbed the stairs wearily. Back in her room, she sat down at the little table, wrapping herself in the blanket again. It was the only way to keep warm. There was a tiny iron fireplace, but they couldn't afford the coal to burn in it. Anna dreaded the approaching winter. Though a hot-water bottle tucked into the scratchy old blanket would keep her body warm, her hands would grow painful from cold and eventually she would be driven downstairs to the warmth of the kitchen.

14

She found it so hard to study down there with her mother creeping about the room. And if her father was there, even in his normal state, he would be rustling the newspaper or cleaning and refilling his pipe. The silence would be palpable, tense, and concentrating would be impossible.

Ah, well, she must get her head down over her book while she could.

It was like living on a knife-edge. As she sat in the classroom, Anna's mind kept wandering back to the Victorian terrace in the old area of Ford not far from the Devonport Dockyards. During the day, her mother would potter about the house making sure everything was clean and tidy, just as Vince liked it. She might turn on the radio, ever so quietly, and hum along to *Music While You Work*. She would do the shopping, so much easier now that rationing was finally at an end – nine years after the war was over! And then she would scuttle back home like a little mouse, never popping in for a 'cuppa' and a chat with one of the neighbours. Not that she was asked anymore. *Stuck-up cow,* Anna's best friend, Ethel, across the street had confided her mother was known as. Freda Millington's only friend was Ethel's mum, Mabel, and as far as Anna was aware, even she didn't know the truth.

The bell heralding the end of the school day started Anna from her deep thoughts. She packed her books into her satchel and made her way along the corridor to her form room. Silent and in single file, keeping to the left. They were like soldiers, she mused. But she supposed when hundreds of girls were moving round the huge school the rules were sensible. And adherence to discipline was what had won the war, or so Anna's form mistress frequently told them.

'Anna, I'd like a word with you.'

Miss Moore's steely grey eyes fixed her with an accusing glare, and she inwardly sighed. Miss Moore was like a sergeant major. Even the most rebellious pupil would cower under her withering gaze, but Anna felt nothing. Her mind sealed to everything but the prospect of what the evening might bring.

'I'll wait for you in the cloakroom,' her friend Maud whispered as she closed the lid of her own desk.

'Afraid I can't,' Pam who usually walked with them added. 'Got my ballet class and I'll be late if I wait for you.'

Anna bobbed her head in acknowledgement and waited patiently in front of Miss Moore for the room to empty. What did the old battleaxe want? Surely she wasn't going to complain about the stain on her gymslip? How ludicrous. And anyway, they couldn't afford a second one, so if they wanted her to come to school in uniform, they'd have to put up with the dirty mark until she could wash the garment over the weekend.

'Anna, your subject teachers have brought it to my notice that your work is slipping,' the tight lips pronounced when everyone had finally gone. 'And as your form mistress, I must warn you that you really must pull your socks up. If you want to get into teacher training college, you'll need good grades in your exams, and June will be here

16

before you know it. And when are you going to fill in those application forms?'

Anna met the woman's ice-flinted eyes. 'I'm not really sure what I want to do,' she answered evasively.

Miss Moore drew in her double chin. 'And what would you do instead? You could go to university if your work returns to its usual high standard. But we all thought you wanted to be a teacher.'

Anna's eyes flashed. She had more important matters to deal with just now. 'I can change my mind, can't I?'

Oh, Lord, she shouldn't have said it like that. Miss Moore would probably give her a detention as well now. But the dragon's face softened as she eyed Anna suspiciously.

'This is most unlike you, Anna. Is anything wrong?'

Huh! No more than usual! But Anna had hidden it all her life, and she wasn't about to spill the beans now. She couldn't remember a time when she hadn't been obliged to protect her mother from her father's violent outbursts. At least, not since the incident that had ruined their lives.

'No, nothing,' she lied. 'May I go now, please?'

Miss Moore's lined forehead pleated further. 'Yes, you may. But remember what I've said.'

Yes, she would. And anyway, Maud would want to know what the 'harpy from hell' had wanted her for. As they walked the mile or so together, Maud was all ears, just as Anna knew she would be. She would have to be careful what she said. Maud and Pam were both good friends, but Maud in particular was apt to spread things around.

17

'I thought you wanted to be a teacher,' she was saying quite predictably.

Anna's mouth twisted. 'Well, I suppose I would really. But to be honest, we can't really afford for me to do the training. So I thought instead of three years at college, I could do a year's secretarial course. I could keep on my Saturday job at Dingles, and then I should get a good job at the end of it. Plymouth's a growing city now. I'm sure I'd get a decent position somewhere.' It wasn't the main reason, of course, but she wasn't going to tell Maud. For how could she tell her she was afraid of leaving her mum to cope alone with her father while she was away at teacher training college?

She set her mouth grimly as she said goodbye to Maud turned off in the direction of her own home. She hurried along the narrow streets, the evening already drawing in and everything, the sky, the rows of houses, the very air, a drab grey. At least in the summer the world had seemed generally brighter, and on warm Sundays she had escaped with Ethel to the frivolity of the Tinside swimming pool and lido, possibly meeting up with other friends and splashing in the water or licking at a mouth-watering ice cream. But it would be a long haul before the summer came round again, despite what Miss Moore had said.

'Mum, I'm home!' she called cheerily as she let herself in.

There was no answer, so Anna assumed her mum had popped out to use the privy in the backyard. Taking off her school gaberdine and the velour hat she hated with a vengeance, Anna hung them on the old utility coat stand in the hallway and went through to the kitchen.

The room struck oddly still and not as cosily warm as usual. Anna went over to the little coal stove that heated the room and provided a constant supply of hot water. She used the tongs to lift the lid, but needn't have done. It was cool enough to touch, and peering in, she could see that the coals had burnt through. Anna frowned. It wasn't like mum to let it go out. She set to, raking out the cinders, relaying and lighting the fire, adding more coal when it got going and adjusting the air vents. Gosh, her mum had been a long time. She hoped she didn't have a funny tummy. And a knot of apprehension tightened in Anna's stomach as she found that the back door was locked.

The creases on her forehead deepened. Had her mother gone out? But she was always there with the kettle on the go waiting to make a pot of tea and chat to Anna for half an hour before she started on her homework. But what if, God forbid, something had happened to her father and her mum had been called away? If her dad had suffered one of his flashes of uncontrollable rage at work – it wouldn't be the first time – he might have caused an accident or brought one on himself.

Anna shot up the stairs. She must focus her thoughts, be rational. It was probably no such thing. She would change out of her uniform, hang it up ready for the morning, and put on her comfortable slacks and the big woolly jumper she had knitted for herself. And by then her mum would probably have come in through the front door with a packet of tea or some other essential commodity she had run out of. A bit scatty like

19

that was her mum.

It was as she pushed the door to her own room that Anna heard the stifled sob from the front bedroom. A lump of ice froze around her heart. So her mum *was* there! Good Lord, whatever could have happened? She tapped gently on the door and poked her head into the room.

Her mother was huddled in the bed, still wearing her blouse and cardigan. Her hair was all awry from its frizzy perm and her eyes were red-rimmed in her pallid face. But as soon as she saw her daughter, she rearranged her expression into a watery smile.

'Hello, Anna, dear.'

'Mum, whatever's the matter?'

Her mother sniffed and wriggled herself into a more upright position. 'Good heavens, is that the time? I hadn't realised. You must have come in quietly.'

Anna bit her lip. Surely her mum had heard her raking out the stove? What could have happened to make her unaware of the noisy rattling?

'Are you all right, Mum?'

She felt herself trembling but her mother nodded her head. 'I'm fine, really. Just a bad headache. One of those migraine types. But I'm feeling better now.'

Anna eyed her dubiously. 'Can I get you anything? Some aspirin?'

'I've had some, thanks. But a cuppa would be proper welcome.'

'Won't be a jiffy, then.' Anna forced a grin, half relieved and half dogged by nagging doubt. Tea was her mum's answer to all ills, and Anna sensed there was more to it than she was letting on.

'There we are,' she announced five minutes later.

Her mother was looking less peaky now, but as she reached out for her cup of tea, her neck stretched out of the collar of her blouse. Anna's insides clenched as she noticed the clear fingermarks from her father's onslaught the other evening. The bruises were turning livid in the white skin, blossoming like a row of little purple roses. And Anna felt the deep, rumbling anger against her father persist in her chest like a stone.

'Mum, look,' she faltered, but she must summon up the courage from somewhere. 'You can't let Dad go on like this. It isn't fair on you. One day he might really hurt you. I know when he has these fits, he doesn't know what he's doing but–'

'No, dear. Your father would never hurt me. Not seriously. He's a good man. He wouldn't hurt a fly, not in his right mind.'

A serene light came into her mother's eyes. Anna knew that look and was beaten. Her mum was going to relate the tale over again and there would be no stopping her. Anna knew it by heart, as if her mother was reciting a revered psalm. There was only one thing to do and that was to wait until she had finished.

'He was a real hero that night,' her mother went on just as Anna knew she would. 'And all the nights before. It wasn't his fault that wall collapsed and crushed his head. And all from the goodness of his own heart. On his way to look out for the dockyard in the raid, him being a dockyard worker all his life. To join his official battalion of the Home Guard. The 17th, it was called. Only sup-

21

posed to defend the dockyard. But when that house was bombed right in front of him – blown clean off his feet, he was – and then he could hear someone calling out from beneath the rubble ... well, he could hardly ignore it, could he? Should have left it to the City Battalion and the ARPs and the rest of them, but he was there, on the scene. My God, what a night that was.'

Anna sat back, knowing she was defeated, and her lips firmed to a mutinous line. She had heard it all a thousand times before. Oh, yes. That dreadful night...

Anna had studied it at school and knew all about it. In March 1941, the city centre and all around the famous Hoe had been blasted to smithereens by two massive Luftwaffe raids. Plymouth's business and shopping area and the Promenade Pier, countless houses, and many churches, cinemas, hotels, some schools and even hospitals had been destroyed, with well over three hundred civilians killed. Despite the gallant efforts of the bone-weary, grime-encrusted and bleary-eyed defence services, blazing infernos had raged through familiar public buildings, shops and private dwellings, lighting the sky like a beacon and filling the air with black, choking smoke.

By dawn, swathes of the city had been flattened. Scores of buildings were burnt-out shells, charred skeletons with steel girders twisted by the heat. Walls tottered and collapsed, and fire hoses were still run out like snakes through the battered, debris-strewn streets. Anna had seen photographs in books, and wondered at the spirit, the courage and heroism of the men and women who had

22

faced the appalling danger, trying to put out the fires, rescue the trapped and injured, all the while putting their own lives at risk. People, she supposed, like her father.

And then, a month later, it had been Devonport's turn, just as Lord Haw Haw had warned with evil relish. For three consecutive nights they came, wave after wave of raiders droning overhead, the incendiaries and flares falling like rain to burn and light the way for the bombers to dive down with their high explosives to blow away what little remained of the city centre and to destroy the Devonport Dockyards, navy personnel and whole streets of shops and civilian houses in the vicinity. The third night, when Devonport had taken the full brunt of the attack, that was the one. And what was more, at nearly five years old, Anna remembered it quite clearly.

'Yes, Mum, I know,' she said softly. 'We'd gone down the shelter, remember? Horrible and damp and smelly, wasn't it? And so cold. I'd taken my teddy, like I always did.'

Her mother blinked at her. 'You always say you remember, but are you sure you're not just imagining it? You were very young.'

Here we go again, Anna sighed to herself. Her mum always said the same thing. Perhaps it was the shock of what had happened both to them and to Vince that night that prevented her from accepting that her little daughter shared the same horrific memories. Anna didn't like to say too much. Her mother, she had recognised long ago, was frail and Anna didn't want to revive the terrible ordeal. But she could hear the sound of it all

23

now, the whining siren that woke her before her mother did.

'Wakey, wakey, Anna, Mr Hitler's coming and he mustn't find us in our beds, must he?'

'Has Daddy gone to look after the ships he builds?' she had answered, rubbing her eyes.

'Yes, he has. So come along, hurry up.'

Anna jumped up eagerly from her bed. 'I'm ready, Mummy, and so's Teddy.'

'Oh, good Mr Teddy! Come along, quickly now!'

They ran down the stairs, grabbing their gas masks and the emergency bag as they called it, and then there was that strange feeling of being outside at night as they hurried down the garden to the shelter. Anna glanced up in fascination. Brilliant shafts of gleaming silver sliced through the darkness as the searchlights scanned the indigo sky, and the shadow of a barrage balloon floated in mid-air like a great whale.

A moment later they plunged into the pitch-dark stench of the shelter, and then there was a tiny click as Freda turned on the torch. The rasp of a match was next as she lit the oil lamp.

'There,' she smiled reassuringly. 'Quite cosy now. I'll turn the torch off. Mustn't waste the batteries.'

Anna climbed unbidden into the little bunk bed. She knew the routine. It hadn't just been the recent devastating raids. There had been plenty of smaller ones before. She cuddled up with Teddy, her coat over her nightie, and Mummy piled the blankets on top of her, but she still shivered with cold.

'Try and get some sleep now,' Mummy soothed.

She obeyed. She only wanted to please Mummy, and so closed her eyes and lay perfectly still, pretending to be asleep. But she wasn't. How could she sleep in the tense, expectant silence?

Which came first, she wasn't sure, the distant hum whining its way towards them, or the staccato rattle of the ack-ack guns pounding skywards. The thrum of aircraft engines overhead grew stronger, deep-throated, followed the dull thud of incendiaries landing all around. Later, perhaps an hour or so when the fires had had time to catch and blaze and turn the night to day, came the shriek of the bombers as they dived down to release their cargoes of death on their illuminated targets. Missiles fell to earth with the characteristic whistle Anna had learnt to recognise, shells burst like a crack of lightning, explosions roared and echoed, and the ground shook, ever nearer.

On and on it went, five or six hours. Anna peeped out from beneath the blankets to seek reassurance from the calm figure of her mother, but all she saw were the whites of Mummy's eyes flashing in terror at another screaming blast. And shortly before it all ended, a great, thundering crash reverberated about them, and the ground suddenly shook with such unimaginable force that Anna was thrown into the corner of her bunk and her mummy, crouching fearfully by her side, was flung against the back wall.

'Yes, I do remember,' Anna said now, her voice tiny as the memories flooded back. 'That blast, it was so loud we could hardly hear afterwards for hours. You weren't sure you could hear the all-clear, and we crept out very slowly just in case. It

25

was still dark, but the sky was orange. And I was confused because our house and half the street just weren't there anymore. And it was all so quiet and unreal. I thought I was dreaming.'

She paused as her mother turned to her with tear-filled eyes. 'But we weren't, were we?'

No, they weren't. It was more than thirteen years ago, but just as vivid in their minds for all that. Plymouth had recovered, a phoenix from the ashes, though without many of its sons and daughters. But on that night when their home had been obliterated from the face of the earth, Vince Millington's head had been caved in by a falling wall as he tried to save another family, his brain damaged in some cruel, festering way so that his life could never be the same again.

'Mum?' Anna was jolted from her thoughts as her mother moved in the bed and drew a wincing breath through her teeth. 'What's the matter?' she asked firmly. 'Not just a headache, is it?'

Her mother melted against the pillows. 'No,' she admitted in a whisper. 'I suppose you're old enough to know. It's a miscarriage.'

'A miscarriage! But ... but shouldn't you have the doctor?'

'No. There's no point. There's nothing they can do. I've had the doctor before—'

'Before?'

Anna's eyes stretched wide, but her mother reached out and took her hand. 'Sit down, dear, and listen. I've had several before, so I know all about it.' She hesitated, meeting Anna's shocked gaze. 'Just don't tell your father. He didn't know I'd fallen pregnant again. He gets so upset, you

26

see. We've wanted another child for so long. I'm sure it'd have made Dad better. He so wanted a son. Always.'

Anna's heart darkened in dismay. A son. Her father wanted a son. And what was she? A girl. Not that her dad had ever shown her any particular dislike. In fact, when something flipped him over the edge and brought that maddened, damaged side of his brain to the fore, it was always she who calmed him down – as a child by her mere presence, and as she had grown older, by standing up to him. Like the other night.

'Promise you won't tell your father?' her mum repeated.

As she stretched up her head to look at her daughter, the bruises on her throat were clearly visible again. In a week, they would have faded. Until the next time. And who could say where it would all end?

Chapter Two

Anna knocked loudly on the front door of Ethel's house. You had to if you wanted to be heard above the din that, as usual, was coming from inside. Oh, come on, someone open the door! It was cold, the first frost of the year, and as Anna hunched her shoulders inside her school gaberdine coat, she noted the peeling paint and the cracked windowpane. Her father wouldn't have stood for that! And yet for all the orderliness of her own home, Anna

27

would willingly have swapped it for the happy chaos that reigned at Number Sixteen.

At long last, the door squeaked open and Ethel's mother stood there in her old slippers. She was wrapped in a stained crossover pinny, curlers visible beneath a bright-orange scarf, and a cigarette, as always, dripping from the corner of her mouth.

''Ello, Anna dear! Come on in. Cas'n 'ave you dithering on the doorstep this snipey weather. Ethel's just in the bog. She won't be long.'

How does she do that, Anna mused for the thousandth time as she was ushered into the kitchen, smile and talk without the cigarette – or fag as she called it – dropping from between her lips? On countless occasions, Anna had seen Mrs Shallaford drink and even eat with the little white stick in place. Perhaps it was glued there? But despite the rancid smell of nicotine that seeped from her, Anna had always been very fond of the slovenly woman.

'Want a cuppa?' she asked, leaning over the table.

'Oi, Mu ... um!' young Billy moaned as he and his little brother and sister slurped at bowls of lumpy porridge. 'Your blooming ash 'as fallen in me breakfast.'

'Yere, don't you bloody well swear at your mother!' Fred Shallaford staggered, bleary-eyed, into the room. ''Ow do, Anna, young maid?'

'Very well, thank you,' Anna replied, and watched as he lumbered into the scullery, leaving the door ajar. Dressed in just a greying singlet and baggy trousers with his braces dangling around

28

his ample hips, he proceeded to lather his chin at the sink.

'You sure you won't 'ave that cuppa?' Mrs Shallaford repeated.

'No, thanks. There isn't really time,' Anna answered, glad of the excuse since the cleanliness of the Shallaford crockery was always somewhat suspect.

'An' you should be down the market an' all, Billy!' his mother declared, whisking away the bowl from which the boy was carefully scraping the ash. 'Mr Riddler'll give the job someone else, an' us could do with that few bob.'

Anna saw the boy roll his eyes and then scoot out of the door, on his way grabbing his torn jacket – a hand-me-down from his elder brother, Davy, who was nowhere to be seen. But, like his father, Davy worked for the railway so Anna supposed he could be on his shift or asleep upstairs. That just left eight-year-old Sammy, and little Primrose who was five, staring up at their visitor from dirty little faces.

''Ow's Freda?' Mabel Shallaford asked casually as she ticked more cigarette ash onto the floor. 'I 'asn't seen 'er in a while.'

Anna felt her heart thud. 'Oh, Mum's fine, thank you,' she lied, and took the opportunity to glance at her watch again. They were going to be late. And just as Billy needed to keep his Saturday job as barrow boy, Anna needed to keep hers in the lingerie department at Dingles. Besides, she enjoyed it, specially handling the more luxurious items of underwear which made her dream of a romantic, happy, uncomplicated life where money

29

was never a problem.

'Oh, there you are!' she snapped as Ethel finally came in from the backyard and went to wash her hands in her father's shaving water. 'We'll never get there on time!'

''Ave to take the bus then, won't us?' Ethel shrugged, ramming the remains of Billy's slice of bread and dripping into her mouth. 'Bye, Mum, bye, Dad.'

'Bye, love. Bye, Anna.'

'Cheerio!'

Outside, their breath wreathed about them in a white halo as they hurried down the street.

'Oh, do come on!' Anna grumbled when she realised Ethel had suddenly stopped behind her. 'We'll miss the bus as well!'

'I've got summat in my shoe,' Ethel mumbled and then, straightening up, she ran to catch Anna up. ''Oo got out of the wrong side this morning, eh? Is ort up?'

'No, nothing's wrong. Just don't want to lose my job. Oh, there's a bus coming!' she cried as they turned the corner. 'We'll have to run!'

They did. As luck would have it, there was quite a queue, and as the passengers gradually clambered on, it gave them time to get there. They had to stand between the long sideways seats by the platform, holding precariously on to the rail above their heads. The journey was uncomfortable with no one getting off, and all new passengers had to go upstairs. Thank goodness she hadn't had to, Anna thought with relief. She hated it upstairs as it was always so smoky, like at Ethel's house, and it made your clothes smell. But at the bus jerked to a halt at their stop, and they were among the first to step down onto the platform and across onto the kerb.

'Got a face like ninepence, you 'as, this morning,' Ethel observed as they walked across the wide, modern expanses of the new city centre. There had been nothing for it after the war but to bulldoze the entire site and start again. Dingles, the fashionable department store where Anna worked on Saturdays and Ethel worked all week, had been one of the first shops to open, but now, in 1954, the rebuilding was pretty well completed.

Anna said nothing, but Ethel wasn't going to leave it there. 'Come on, Anna. Us've known each other since we was tackers, ever since us met on that there evacuation train to Tavistock, an' my mum took you under 'er wing cuz you all on your lonesome an' you was barely five, same as me.'

The memory brought a faint smile to Anna's lips. 'Yes. I'll always be grateful to your mum for that.' But then she added defensively, 'It wasn't my mum's fault she couldn't come. She had to stay in Plymouth because of Dad. He was in hospital for months and she wouldn't leave him. And when he came home, she had to look after him.'

'Yes, I knows that. An' I also knows when summat's wrong. An' you was the same last weekend an' all. So come on. I's your best friend an' you knows what they say. A trouble shared an' all that.'

Anna sighed. Ethel was so different from her in many ways, happily leaving school at fifteen to go out to work, with no ambition but to carry on her life as the rest of her family always had, living from hand to mouth. But there was a directness

31

about her, no beating about the bush or bottling things up, that Anna envied.

'All right,' she gave in, lowering her voice. 'Mum had a miscarriage. About ten days ago.'

Ethel stopped and turned to her, mouth fallen open. 'Bleeding 'ell,' Ethel murmured. 'Oh, I's sorry, Anna.'

'Oh, come on. We can't just stand here,' Anna pressed her awkwardly. 'We'll get the sack for being late.'

'Yes, you'm right. But I really is sorry. But I suppose your mum's a bit long in the tooth for 'aving a babby.'

'They've been trying for years apparently, but every time mum gets pregnant, she loses it.' Anna felt herself flush with heat, despite the frosty morning. But Ethel, as usual, was right. She did feel better for having confessed to her friend. 'You promise you won't breathe a word to a living soul?' she couldn't help adding, though.

'Course not. Not fair, life, sometimes, innit? There's your mum desprit for another babby, an' my mum couldn't stop 'aving them. Mind you, there's only five of us, an' my mum were one o' thirteen. So Dad must've been doing summat right wi' they rubber thingies!' She nudged Anna in the ribs and grinned before finishing, 'Mum says, though, she cas'n wait for the change cuz then she won't 'ave to worry so much!'

As they went in through the staff entrance, Anna couldn't help but smile. Oh, Ethel was so good for her! And she blessed the day, thirteen years before, when she had found herself all alone and frightened on the crowded train, gas

32

mask and label around her neck and clutching a
paper bag that contained nothing but a spare pair
of knickers – since they had lost everything when
their house had been blown to kingdom come.
And then the bustling woman with the loud voice
and the cigarette in her mouth had taken charge
of her, and after that, everything had been all
right and Anna had felt safe again.

'Shall I price up those new suspender belts?'
Anna asked Mrs Woodhead, her boss.

'Please, dear. I'm just popping down to the
storeroom for more of those lacy camiknickers.'

Anna nodded, and began writing out the labels
in her best hand. It was gratifying that Mrs Woodhead would leave her in charge of the department,
but they had been working together on Saturdays
for three years now. Should she tell the kindly
older woman about her distressing situation at
home, Anna often wondered? Discussing it with
someone more mature might help, but it would
seem like a betrayal, wouldn't it? And so she only
ever confided in Ethel. But at times it was unbearable, as if she was carrying the weight of the
world on her shoulders. She was only just
eighteen, for heaven's sake, but sometimes she felt
more like eighty.

For the second time, she made a mistake on a
label and had to tear it up. Oh, what was the
matter with her? She supposed she was dwelling
on her mother and the miscarriages. And the fact
that her father's temper, or rather the depression
that led to it, was getting worse week by week.
Perhaps she should go and talk to the doctor about

it if her mother wouldn't. Find out if there was anything to be done. Yes, she would go one evening next week, though persuading her parents to take up whatever help might be available was another matter.

The thought, though, cheered her up somewhat. Her lunch hour didn't coincide with Ethel's, so they couldn't talk until they were walking home from work through the darkened streets.

'You coming to the flicks tonight? Davy's friend, Bert, you knows the one, 'e said 'e'd meet us outside if I wants.'

'You want me to play gooseberry? No thanks.'

'Oh, come on, Anna. Tidd'n like that. It'd do you good, the black mood you'm in. Thinking of your mum, is it?'

There she went again, Ethel, hitting the nail bang on the head. 'It's not just that,' Anna murmured into her scarf. 'My dad's going through one of his depressed phases and I've told you how he can get a bit violent. I don't know how long it'll be before something really terrible happens.'

'Getting worse, is it?' Ethel's voice was vibrant with concern.

'You might say that.' Anna sighed. She had struggled to hold everything inside, but suddenly the fight had gone out of her. 'I reckon something's really going wrong from the brain injury he had in the war,' she went on. 'Mum's always said the doctors warned her to expect personality changes. That he'd be difficult for a while. Only it's gone on all these years, and lately it seems to be getting worse. Something makes him fly off the handle and then he hits the bottle and all hell breaks loose.'

'That's why 'e lost 'is job at the dockyard back along, wa'n it?'

'Yes. He was only passed fit to go back to work towards the end of the war, but they had to give him the sack. And now he's lucky to hold down a job for more than a few hours. Huh!' She gave an ironic snort. 'It was a good job for us that the whole of Plymouth needed rebuilding or there wouldn't have been enough building sites for him to work at. Same place wouldn't have him back twice. But it's a vicious circle. He gets a job which puts money in his pocket, and once he's paid off the back rent and any other bills we owe, he starts spending money on drink and loses the job because of it. The thing is...'

She stopped. They had reached the corner of their street and she couldn't summon up the courage to go home.

'The thing is,' she repeated, her voice a hoarse whisper, 'I really believe he was a good man once. I remember little things about him. From before it all happened and Mum had me evacuated. And they're good memories. Even after the war when your mum got us this house to live in, there were happy times. I mean, I think my parents felt it was a come-down for them, but they were really grateful. Oh, Lord!' Her hand went over her mouth. 'I'm sorry, Ethel. I shouldn't have said that.'

She felt herself flush with shame, but in the dim glow from the street lamp, she saw Ethel shrug.

'Oh, you always was a bit more posh, like. Look at the way you speaks for a start.' And then Ethel shivered, clasping her arms across her chest. 'But

I's not standing on the corner bloody freezing all night. An' I doesn't want to be late for the pictures. You coming or what? Strikes me it'd do you good.'

Anna had to chuckle. Ethel was so down to earth and talking to her had provided some feeling of release.

'Yes, I think I will!' she answered with growing certainty. 'Don't know what's on, do you?'

'Not a clue. Don't matter when you'm in the back row, do it?' And seeing Anna's look of horror, she grinned back. 'Only kidding!'

Anna laughed aloud this time, but as they hurried down the narrow street, anxiety thudded in her heart again. 'You won't say a word to anyone, will you? You know, about—'

'My lips is sealed. An' don't you be late. Want to find that Bert afore we goes in! Really nice, 'e is!' she called back gaily as she left Anna at her front door and waltzed off to the little terraced house on the opposite side.

Anna took off her glove to rummage in her handbag, but that wasn't why her hand froze as she put her key in the lock. That was her father she could hear, wasn't it, ranting away inside? And her mother's raised voice as she tried to defend herself.

Anna's heart clenched with fear. God knew what she'd find inside. The 'B' film had been a light comedy and the main feature a John Wayne western with a love story thrown in. She could never understand how anyone was supposed to fall in love with John Wayne, but the evening had diverted her mind for some hours, and now she had returned to *this*. In desperation, she glanced back across the street, but the sliver of light from the hallway narrowed and was extinguished as Ethel closed the door behind her, and the pavements were silent and deserted once more.

Anna mentally braced herself as she let herself in. She slunk against the wall in a vain attempt to make herself invisible. If she closed her eyes, perhaps she would wake up to find it was all just a dream.

It wasn't.

'Why the hell didn't you tell me?'

Anna glanced up at her father's roar from the top of the stairs. He was on the landing, dragging her mother's head up by the hair as she tried to escape from him.

'I didn't want to upset you–'

'Upset me!' Her father's cry exploded like a crack of thunder. 'Don't you think I have a right to know that you've lost another one of our children?'

'But–'

'I thought your curse were going on a long time, and now you tell me it's 'cause it were a miscarriage, and I didn't even know you were pregnant! How could you? Or was it because it weren't mine and you'd got rid of it?'

'Vince, no!' Freda Millington's voice was a horrified. 'How could you think–?'

Anna had been cowering on the bottom step, stunned with horror. But at the sounds of her parents grappling at the top the stairs, well, she wasn't going to just stand by and–

'Stop it!' she yelled, and went to fling herself up

37

the staircase.

She didn't see quite what happened next. She heard another blow find its target and then a series of rapid bumps as her mother tumbled down the steps, knocking Anna off her feet. The wallpaper, the banisters, turned cartwheels before her eyes and the pair of them landed with a dull thud in a tangled heap at the bottom.

For a moment, Anna couldn't move. But the sound of her father clumping down the stairs made her claw her way through the fog and painfully she lifted her head. A dark silhouette was grabbing her father's coat and cap from the hallstand, and an instant later, the house shook as the front door crashed shut.

And then silence.

Anna dropped her head back on the floor, waiting for the grey dizziness to pass. A whimper fluttered from her lungs and slowly, very slowly, she began to drag herself upwards. Her mother was lying across her legs, pinning them down, and somehow she managed to twist round and pull herself out from underneath.

'Mum?'

Anna's own head was still spinning. It would take a few moments before either of them would be able to pick herself up. But her mum still hadn't moved, and Anna shook her gently. Several minutes ticked by, and as the muzziness cleared and her mother still hadn't stirred, a kernel of panic began to uncurl deep inside.

Anna shifted into a sitting position and shook her mother again. No response. Pulse racing, pounding in her ears. Trembling. A tiny, strangled sound in her throat.

'Mu ... um?'

She leant over, and realised how her mother's neck was lying at an unnatural angle. And then she looked into her eyes – that were staring unseeing at the wall.

Chapter Three

How long did she sit there, the blood draining down her limbs? Light-headed. Her hand had shot out to her mother's jaw. She knew she wouldn't find a pulse. But she had hoped.

Her own pulse drummed at her temples. Her stomach contracted. Rigid. Oh, dear God.

At long last, her body started to move. She hadn't told it to. It just did. Unfolding itself from its uncomfortable position on the cold linoleum. The lino that her mum polished twice a week. Religiously. Without fail.

She was standing. Her mother crumpled at her feet. What should she do? Her brain wouldn't answer. Instinct took over. And as she stumbled across the darkened, silent street, the cold made her shiver.

She knocked on the familiar door. Fred Shallaford opened it. Singlet and pyjama bottoms. Perplexed at the late visitor.

'Anna?'

She opened her mouth to speak, but the only sounds that came out were mumbled gibberish.

So she snapped her jaw shut and stared up at Fred's craggy face.

'What's up, little maid?' he frowned. 'Yere, you'd best come in.'

Fred stood back, scratching his balding head, and Anna groped her way past him and into the kitchen. Mabel was sitting at the table in an old dressing gown, hair still in curlers – Anna wondered vaguely if they had been there all day – and sure enough, puffing on a cigarette. Ethel was chatting away, and in the course of ten seconds, Anna caught the name of Bertie at least twice.

Then Mabel looked up, the welcoming smile sliding from face, and Ethel's eyes widened as she stared at her friend. 'Anna! You'm as white as a sheet. What's 'appened? Come on, sit yoursel' down.'

Ethel was on her feet, guiding Anna to the seat she had vacated. Anna obeyed. Meekly. Dissolving onto the hard, wooden chair with its chipped, scarlet paint.

'Drink this.'

Fred's swarthy hand with its oil-stained finger-nails slapped a small glass in front of her, and through the veil of her shock, Anna was ready to do anything she was told. She took a sip and the amber spirit scorched the back of her throat. She spluttered, pushing the glass away.

'Knock it back, maid.'

The trust Anna held in this kind family overtook her numbed brain and she dutifully swallowed the liquid in one gulp. Almost at once, she began to feel its warmth seeping into her body. She felt oddly weak, but soothed and comforted. Safe.

40

'Now tell us what's up,' Fred prompted gently.

'It's ... Mum,' Anna managed to stutter, for her teeth began to chatter as soon as she tried to speak. 'She's ... fallen down the stairs. And I ... I think she's dead.'

'What!'

There were audible gasps around the table and for once, Mabel's cigarette fell from her lips. She hastily retrieved it between yellow-stained fingers, stubbing it out on the ashtray only half smoked.

'You'm sure?' The horrified question catapulted from her mouth in a stream of grey smoke.

Anna nodded, and waited to see what would happen next as her own brain didn't seem capable of deciding anything for itself. It was Fred who came to her rescue.

'Give us your key, maid,' he said, 'or is the door open?'

Had she shut the door? Anna couldn't remember. But as he felt in her pocket, the key was there. Silently she placed it on the table, and with a dark glance at his wife, Fred picked it up.

'Where's your dad?' he asked grimly.

Her father? Oh, God. A barb of terror speared somewhere beneath her ribs.

'I-I don't know,' she stammered truthfully. 'Out somewhere. At the pub.'

'Hmm.' Fred pursed his lips. 'It's closing time. I'd best be there when 'e gets back. Ah, that sounds like Davy coming in. I'll take 'en with us.'

He went out into the hallway and Anna heard him talking with his son. It was a relief to know there would be two of them if her dad came back. Davy was only seventeen, a year younger than

Ethel, but he was as tall and broad-shouldered as his father and did a bit of boxing in his spare time.

'You'm shivering.' Mabel's unusually lowered voice drew Anna back to the Shallafords' warm kitchen. 'Us was just going to bed, but I reckons us could all do with a nice cup o' tea.'

It was all a bit of a blur from then on. Ethel placed an arm around her shoulders, 'loving her up', as she put it. The tea Mabel placed in front of her was strong enough to stand a spoon in with only a dribble of milk and heaps of sugar. Anna tried to sip at it but her stomach rebelled. And her lips could feel the dirty film on the rim of the cup.

Five minutes later, Davy was back, breathless and seemingly enjoying the crisis – until his mum clipped him round the ear. But it didn't stop him reporting how he'd run to the telephone box on the corner of the next street and dialled 999. An ambulance was on its way, but his dad was sure that, well...

So ... that was it, was it? Anna sat. Staring at nothing. Feeling nothing. Some time later, a plain-clothes policeman appeared. An inspector of some sort. Had she seen her fall? Yes, she had. She had just got in, and her mum had come out of the bedroom and onto the landing to greet her and then the next second she was tumbling head over heels down the stairs. Where was her father? Out at the pub. Which one? She didn't know.

'Leave the little maid alone, cas'n you?' Mabel pouted her lips in accusation.

'Sorry, madam. It's only routine, but I have to ask. Seems to be pretty straightforward, mind. They'll be taking the, er...'

Anna noted his light cough. Did he think she was an idiot? They'd be taking the body away, he was about to say, wasn't he? And then she saw Mabel's forehead crease.

'Does you want to go with your mum in the ambulance?' she said quietly.

Anna met her compassionate gaze. What was the point? She imagined the hospital. Cold, sterile corridors, still as death. Echoing footsteps.

She shook her head. 'D-Dad?' she croaked.

'My constable will wait for him with Mr Shallaford. Perhaps you could stay here until your father gets back, if that's all right?'

'Course it is, the poor lamb. Is that all now? The cheel's in shock, cas'n you see?'

Anna noticed him raise an eyebrow, but he turned and left the room, although she heard him mumble something about the possibility of further questions later.

It wasn't until she was tucked up in Ethel's bed in the room she shared with Primrose that it dawned on Anna what she had done. She had given the impression that her father hadn't been there, hadn't she? Somewhere deep inside, some defence mechanism had unaccountably taken over. In effect, she had lied. To everyone. Her mum had fallen down the stairs, she had said. Well, it was true, but she hadn't explained *why*. That her parents had been having a vicious row on the landing and her dad had become violent. He hadn't deliberately pushed her mum down the stairs, she was sure of that. In the struggle, her mum had lost her balance. But what if...?

She sat bolt upright in bed. Fred hadn't returned yet. What was going on at her own house across the street? Had her father come home yet? Was he being questioned by the police? Oh, God.

But then, there was nothing to arouse suspicion, was there? The bruises around her mum's throat from the recent throttling her dad had given her had faded. And her dad would arrive home from wherever he had gone to have the tragic news broken to him that his wife had fallen down the stairs and broken her neck. Anna was convinced he hadn't realised what had happened when he had stormed out, and God alone knew what his reaction would be when he was told.

The image of her mum lying there, so still, so twisted, seared into Anna's brain again. What the hell did anything matter? Her dear, frail, faithful mum was dead. Killed by devotion to the man her husband had once been.

Thinking, thinking, a million thoughts were turning somersaults in Anna's head. There was something she couldn't identify trying to push its way into her mind. Something she knew instinctively her mind was trying to blank out.

'Ethel?' she whispered into the darkness. 'Ethel, are you awake?'

But she knew she wasn't. She could hear her friend's steady breathing from the other bed where Ethel had squeezed in next to her little sister. Anna's eyes opened, staring at nothing. A narrow column of moonlight peeped in between the skimpy curtains, and her eyes gradually adjusted to the gloom. Familiar objects. The battered chest of drawers. The box of Ethel's toys which had now been passed down to Primrose. The rag rug where

Anna and Ethel had played together as children. All so reassuring. Comforting.

Too comforting. Allowing tears to well up inside her at last. She tried to hold them back, but they rose up in a deluge and began to stream down her cheeks in a torrent of big, fat pearls. She turned her face into the pillow, weeping until she had no more tears to shed. And some time in the small hours, when she still had not heard Fred return, she drifted into a restless, exhausted sleep.

'I always said your father was no good for our Freda.' Iris Catchpole folded her arms across her chest and hitched up her bosom. 'Married beneath her, and now look. Didn't look after her properly so she gets that weak that she faints at the top of the stairs. I could see it coming.'

Anna had been huddled on the settee in the little sitting room at the front of the house, staring at the glowing coals in the grate. The funeral had been a pathetically small affair with just a handful of neighbours coming to show their respects. Only Ethel and her parents had come back to the house – and Freda's sister, Iris, and her husband, Clarence. Anna had watched her father pick up the empty coal scuttle, presumably to refill it from the bunker out in the backyard, and the moment he was out of earshot, Aunt Iris had delivered her damning condemnation.

'Iris, dear, I don't think–' Uncle Clarence tried to mutter ineffectually, but was at once silenced by Mabel's indignant riposte.

'Saw it coming? 'Ow could you when you 'adn't bin to visit your poor sister in years? Us was

45

friends, Freda an' me, an' she told us what a proper cow you was, an' never lifted a finger when Vince were injured. Could've bin left a cabbage, an' what would *you* 'ave cared, eh?'

Anna blinked as Aunt Iris rose to her full four foot ten, her face suffused to a violent puce. 'Who on earth do you think you are? No better than a fishwife, and you're trying to tell me–'

But Mabel was standing firm, hands planted determinedly on her hips, and Fred stood up, towering protectively over his wife. Anna had been observing them, locked in her own fathomless grief, and not a word had sunk into her brain. And yet some small part of her must have been listening. Anger foamed up inside her, snapping the fragile hold she had maintained on her broken emotions.

'Oh, shut up, all of you! Mum's dead and all you can do argue!'

She sprang to her feet, glaring at them all in turn, and saw Aunt Iris's round, pink face puff up even further. It almost made her want to laugh.

'Well, I'm not going to stand here and be insulted,' her aunt was announcing. 'Come along, Clarence, we're going. We'd best leave the girl to her *dear friends,*'she added, casting a haughty sneer at Fred and Mabel. 'But I still blame Vince for my dear Freda's death.'

She snatched up her coat and marched the two steps to sitting-room door which miraculously opened from the other side and she collided with Vince who was coming in with the refilled coal scuttle. Anna saw her shrink back for a second before instantly lifting her head in defiance.

'Hurry up, Clarence, we're leaving.'

She swept past Vince out into the hallway and let herself out of the front door. Uncle Clarence gave an apologetic glance around the room, mumbled to her dad what Anna thought was, 'Sorry, old chap,' and shambled after his wife. Anna almost felt sorry for *him*.

But everything was suddenly forgotten as her eyes caught the expression on her dad's face. A look like thunder darkened his features, accentuating the deep dent in his forehead. Anna's heart flipped over. She needed to grieve, to let the emptiness inside her fill up with tears and wash away the pain, but instead every nerve in her body was stretched with tension. Her father had been like a closed book ever since he had returned on that terrible night to find that, when he had stormed out, his wife had not been lying stunned at the bottom of the stairs as he had thought, but dead. He had hardly uttered a word since. Was he bereft, imprisoned in sadness, or racked with guilt? Anna had no way of knowing, and the strain of it was destroying her.

'What you all looking at?' Vince barked now.

Without the habitual cigarette for support, Mabel seemed momentarily flustered, but it only took her a matter of seconds to gather herself together. 'I were just wondering 'ow dear Freda 'ad a sister like that,' she declared.

'Sister? More like one of those, what were they, gorgon creatures you learnt about at school, Anna? Medusa, wasn't it, the one with snakes for hair?'

Anna nodded in reply. She could just see the

47

head of Medusa, chopped off by the Greek hero Perseus, with her aunt's face emblazoned upon it. She felt a hysterical laugh bubbling up from inside. Almost. Her father's grim expression smothered it, and her strung-out nerves tightened further. What now? Her dad wasn't an educated man, but he was intelligent and strong. He'd had to be, brought up in a children's home with no known family and then left to make his own way in the world. Her mum had been his life, and Anna was sure that, in his own strange way, he must feel as torn as she did. If only...

'Well, good riddance, I says,' Mabel pronounced. 'But us must leave you good people. An' we'm really sorry about Freda. Real lady, she were. An' if there's ort us can do, you've only to shout. Bain't that right, Fred?'

The big man's head jiggled up and down. 'Thanks for the tea. An' Mabel's right. If us can do ort... Well, you knows where us is. You coming, Eth, or you staying with Anna for a bit?'

'I'll just 'elp Anna wash up. Pass us the tray, Annie, an' us can stack the dirties on it. Lovely sponge, by the way. Bake it yoursel', did you?'

Anna nodded. It had been good to have something practical to concentrate on as it had kept her mind from the tearing void her mum's death had gouged out of her heart. Now, as they did the washing-up and the crockery clinked echoingly in the damp scullery, the numbness swamped her yet again. Dear Ethel was chatting away, and though Anna was grateful for her attempts to cheer her up, she didn't hear a word.

'Well, I musts be off,' she suddenly realised

Ethel was saying. 'Meeting Bert tonight, I is.' But then the expectant grin that she had tried unsuccessfully to contain faded from her face. 'That's if you wouldn't rather I stayed yere with you,' she added apologetically.

Anna's heart plummeted to her feet. Oh, yes, she *had* hoped to have her dear friend's company that evening, but Ethel had been a tower of strength and it would be selfish of her to ask her to give up her precious hours with Bert. A nice chap was Bert, and Anna could see why Ethel was so smitten. Davy had met him at work, Bert taking the newcomer under his wing, and they had become friends. But being a station porter meant shift work, so it wasn't always easy to find time when he and Ethel could see each other.

'No, of course not.' Anna forced a smile, hoping her voice hadn't betrayed her disappointment. 'I suddenly feel exhausted.' Which, at least, was utterly true. 'Dad and I'll just have a quiet night in. I'll read a book. Something nice and gentle. *Little Women*, perhaps. Go on, now. Better make yourself look beautiful for Bert.'

'Huh, that'd be a fine thing!' Ethel grinned. 'Lucky 'e likes us as I is! Ta-ta, then, Annie.' And she suddenly crushed Anna in a huge bear hug before dancing away across the street.

Anna watched her for a moment, shaking her head. Oh, what would she do without Ethel? She closed the front door, leaving her hand resting on the latch as the cloud settled on her once again. That was that, then. Her mum was dead and buried. Despatched. As if she had never been. So what now?

She turned back into the hallway and a squeal lodged in her throat. She hadn't heard her father come up behind her, and now he grasped her wrist in a lock of iron, forcing her against the wall. His face was maddened, eyes bulging menacingly from their sockets.

'What the hell have you been saying?'

'What?'

Anna's heart had bucked in her chest, but as Vince poked his head forward so that their noses were almost touching, raging contempt swept her fear aside. This was her own father, for God's sake. She wasn't going to be afraid of him, and now that her mum was gone, she wasn't going to let him turn his temper on her instead.

'What do you mean?' she said levelly, her eyes scorching into his.

'Iris!' he spat back. 'I heard her! She said it were my fault!'

'Well, she was right, wasn't she?' All Anna's pent-up emotions suddenly exploded in unleashed fury. 'Only for the wrong reasons. She said you hadn't been looking after Mum properly and that was why she fainted. But you and I know different, don't we? You hit her and she lost her balance. You killed her, Dad, you killed her!'

In that moment, the hatred froze solid somewhere inside her driving away the last vestiges of affection she had ever felt for her father. The figure who pressed her hard up against wall was a stranger. More than that, he had become someone to be despised.

'If you *ever* breathe a word to anyone about what happened,' his grating whisper hissed into

50

her ear now, 'so help me God, I'll kill you, too!'

'Oh, don't worry,' she sneered back. 'If I was going to tell the police, I'd have done so in the first place. The miscarriage left her anaemic and she fainted, that's what they believe. So you're off the hook.'

'And it had better stay that way!'

'Oh, it will! But only for Mum's sake. Now, if you'd kindly let me go, I've got things to do.'

She glared back at him, her lips compressed in caustic disdain. She felt his grip on her slowly release and then suddenly jerk tightly again in one last, threatening gesture before he spun on his heel, and grabbing his coat and cap, thundered out of the door and slammed it behind him.

A shattering silence echoed in his wake. Anna's knees went weak and she slithered down the wall, her heart hammering inside her chest.

Dear Lord above, what was she to do?

Chapter Four

'Oh, Lordy love!'

'Sssh!'

Anna's heart had been beating nervously ever since the day of the funeral and she had hardly slept, tossing and turning or staring into the darkness of the night. And now, at last, she had the chance to confide in her friend, for if she didn't tell *someone,* she thought she might break under the strain.

Ethel clamped her hand over her mouth. 'Sorry,' she gulped in an urgent whisper. 'But … oh, Lord, Annie! What you'm going to do?'

'I don't know,' Anna moaned. 'I was rather hoping you might have some idea.'

Ethel's brow squeezed in a deep frown. 'Oh, come yere,' she sighed, and sitting together on Ethel's bed, they hugged each other tightly. 'Well, I knew things was bad with your dad, but not *that* bad. But … you sure you shouldn't tell someone?'

Anna vigorously shook her head. 'No. Definitely not. And who should I tell anyway?'

'The police?'

'Do you think I haven't thought of that?' Anna drew in a deep breath and let it out in a long, ponderous stream. 'Can you imagine what would happen if I did? They'd want to know why I hadn't told them in the first place. And they might not believe me.'

'Your word against your dad's, you means?'

'Exactly. Nothing could be proved, could it? Dad wouldn't end up in prison for manslaughter or anything. All it would do would make him furious, and then God knows what he'd do to me.'

'Oh. I sees your point. But … 'e could 'urt you anyway. So … oughtn't you to tell someone that 'e can be violent an' that you'm scared of 'en? You doesn't 'ave to mention ort about 'ow your mum… They could protect you from 'en.'

Anna worked her mouth into a knot. 'How? I'm eighteen. Too old to be put in a children's home or anything, and I'd hate that anyway. Besides, Dad's never actually hurt me, and I expect he has to before they'd do anything.'

52

Her heart began to pound again. She had only revealed her father's part in her mum's death, not his threat after the funeral. Despite the calm contempt she had displayed at the time, she had been terrified. But deep down inside, she recognised why she wouldn't tell anyone the entire truth. It was because it would be a betrayal of her mum's belief and loyalty, and Anna simply couldn't bring herself to do it.

But Ethel was glaring at her, one hand on her hip in a gesture of irritation. 'So you'm going to wait until 'e really 'urts you?'

Anna wrung her hands in her lap. 'In some ways I can't believe he ever would. But ... I don't intend staying around long enough to find out.' There. She had said it.

Ethel was staring back at her slack-jawed. 'You means ... you'm leaving? Running away? But you cas'n. I cas'n do without you. You'm like my sister. An' where would you go, tell me that?' she nodded triumphantly. 'An' what about your A levels an' all they fine ideas about becoming a secretary or teacher?'

'I know. And I'll miss you terribly. But I've got to get away. Surely you can see that?' Her determination strengthened as she spoke and she took Ethel's hands. 'It's the last thing I want, but I don't see that I have any choice. I was supposed to be going back to school on Monday, but I'll have to tell them I've got to keep house for my dad now.'

'They'll try an' persuade you otherwise.'

'I expect they will. But I'll say if things settle down, I'll go back next year if the authorities will allow it.'

She watched as Ethel sucked in her cheeks. 'That still don't solve the problem of where you'll go. Pity you 'asn't got a fiancé or ort. Could've got married an' got away from your dad like that. Only you'm always so busy with your head in your books, you 'asn't even got a boyfriend. An' you proper pretty an' all, like.'

Anna chuckled, and somehow she suddenly felt better. 'Trust you to think of boys. One-track mind you've got, Ethel Shallaford. But I have to admit I don't know where I'll go.'

'You got some money, then, to tide you over?'

Anna's smile faded. 'No. Not much.'

'Nor've I. I'd let you 'ave it if I did, mind.'

'Yes, I know you would.'

'What about your auntie?' Ethel suggested with a flash of inspiration.

'Auntie Iris? You must be joking!'

Ethel's face was still. 'Yes, I reckon I were.'

Suddenly the idea seemed so ludicrous that the tension snapped and they fell about with laughter, urging each other and holding their splitting sides.

'Summat'll turn up,' Ethel spluttered, trying to curb her mirth.

And Anna burst into tears.

'Yere, Anna. Someone left this on the next table. Let's 'ave a shifty. Might find summat in there for you.'

It had seemed an age before Saturday arrived. Having missed work the previous week, Anna had been anxious to get back. She needed every penny for her plan to run away, and she knew that Mrs Woodhead would be more than kind to

54

her, and she craved every ounce of comfort that was on offer.

'Oh, today's *Western Morning News?*'

'Yes. Look in the Situations Vacant. Might be summat suitable. Summat well paid so as you can afford your own place, or summat live-in.'

Anna's eyes opened wide with a touch of amusement. 'Like a live-in servant? You don't get those sorts of jobs nowadays, do you?'

'Well, there must still be posh 'ouses around that need people. Be very different now, though, I imagines.'

'Well, we mustn't spend too long looking. We've only got an hour for lunch, remember.'

'Yere we go, then.' Ethel began demolishing the newspaper and handed a page to Anna. 'You looks there an' I'll look in this bit. So...' She only hesitated for a moment. ''Ow 'ave things been with your dad?'

Anna's face fell. 'Oh, he went out and got drunk the night of the funeral. I guessed he'd gone to the pub so I made sure I was in bed early and, well, I moved the bed against the door. I didn't want him coming into my room half sloshed.'

'Oh, Anna.' Ethel was aghast. 'You'm right. You cas'n live like that.'

'As it happened, he didn't even try. I heard him come home, but he went straight to bed. He went back to work the next morning and he was all right for a couple of days, though you could've cut the air with a knife in the evenings. Thank God we had the television to watch. But last night...'

Her voice ended in a trail of desolation and Ethel's brow eased with concern. 'Yes?' she said.

'Well...' Anna turned her attention to the sheet of newspaper, her fingers toying with the corner. 'He went to the pub again, only it wasn't long before he was back. He'd bought a bottle of whisky, but he'd obviously had a few pints at the pub first. I could smell it from him and he was already tipsy. And, well, let's say he was a bit rough with me.'

She could feel the heat prickling around the collar of her blouse. From the look on her face, she could tell that Ethel realised she was being economical with the truth. But Ethel didn't press her and instead murmured, 'We'd best find you a way out, then.'

Anna's heart sagged with relief that she hadn't needed to go into detail, and turned her concentration on the newspaper. A moment later, she was startled by Ethel's exclamation.

'Oh, look! This could be interesting. *Wanted. Young lady of good character to join household staff at remote residence on Dartmoor. Equivalent six days a week. Full board and lodging, plus £3 per week wages.* Hmm. What d'you thinks of that, then, Annie?'

Anna tipped her head to one side. 'I didn't expect to find anything like that. But I don't just want to be a cleaner.'

'It don't say exactly what the work is. Wouldn't 'urt to ring up an' ask, would it? Might be just what you'm looking for. I wonder *where* on Dartmoor? You used to love going up the moor, didn't you, when us was evacuees in Tavistock? Not so keen mysel', but you was in seventh heaven as I remembers.'

A warm tide teased Anna's memory. She hadn't been back to Dartmoor since the war had ended and suddenly she was flooded with the need for those wild, endless miles of rugged landscape and majestic crags. Escape...

'What's the telephone number?' she said at once.

'Cheap day return to Princetown, please.'

'Three bob, please, miss.'

Anna took out her purse. At least that wasn't too expensive. But if she didn't get the job, it would be three shillings out of her savings. She would need to earn a lot more to put into action her other plan, which was to go to Exeter or possibly to Bristol, find herself some digs and then look for a job to support herself. You could hide in a big city that, and hopefully her father would never find her. But she would need time to save enough to get away, time when anything could happen with her dad.

Her stomach churned as she sat in the carriage, her emotions muddled and confused. Grief over her mum, anxiety about the interview, fear of her father and tearing sadness that things just shouldn't be that way. Whatever happened, she was going to have to leave behind everyone who should be helping her through her bereavement – and go to live among strangers instead.

But as the train puffed away from the suburbs of Plymouth and began to skirt the south-western edge of Dartmoor, Anna felt the tension easing away and a quiet excitement took its place. Glimpses of those far-reaching, empty uplands flashed past until the track broke out onto the moor itself. She was glad that she had a seat by the window. It had been another cold, frosty night, but now the sun was well up in a clear, ice-blue sky and the hills were crisply defined.

Anna remembered how, as a summer treat, Mabel would sometimes take her, Ethel and Davy on the train from Tavistock, change at Yelverton onto the Princetown line – as Anna was about to do – and then get off at Burrator Halt. Not that Mabel was a country girl at all. Far from it. But she clashed frequently with Mrs Ward at whose house they were all billeted. It gave her a break from *the old sow* – who incidentally was happy to take baby Billy off her hands for the day.

From Burrator Halt, they could go in many different directions onto the moor for their picnic of sandwiches and Tizer. Anna found herself smiling. All those fond memories. Before she knew what the war had done to her dad. Her mum came to visit her once a fortnight at the big house in Granville Road. She must have been quite posh, Mrs Ward, so it was no wonder she and Mabel never hit it off. But Mabel had found herself pregnant from Fred's recent leave and Mrs Ward had been very helpful when Billy was born. They had remained at her house for well over three years until Mr Hitler was being driven back and there was no more fear of air raids over Plymouth. Anna wondered vaguely if Mrs Ward still lived in Tavistock.

She sat on the station platform at Yelverton waiting for a little train to take her up to Princetown. The air was still and clean, already smelling differently from the way it did in Plymouth. A gentle contentment swelled up in Anna's breast. Perhaps she *could* find some peace after her mum's violent end. Nothing could bring her back, but Anna's life had to go on.

Her heart took courage as the engine and its one carriage began the long, slow climb. After the little station at Dousland, came the old familiar halt high above the reservoir. The surface of the water was a smooth, slate grey, but shortly the railway line turned its back on the man-made lake and soon made its way out onto the open moor.

Anna's breath was taken away by the spectacular scenery. The harsh, unforgiving wilderness rolled away as far as the eye could see, rising to a high, dramatic outcrop of stark granite here, dropping down to a distant, wooded vale there. As the track coiled upwards, the landscape became even more remote, the train snaking past jagged cliffs of quarries blasted out of the rocky hillside. Finally, the engine chugged along a straight run with miles of folding, barren hills in the distance, into the station.

As Anna stepped down onto the platform, she realised her spirits had been revived by the journey and she felt ready to face the interview ahead. She had been surprised at being the only passenger to get on the train at Yelverton, although she had seen a woman with a young child climb up into another compartment at Dousland. Now she saw them scuttle away through the station exit and only as Anna followed them did her heart begin to beat faster.

'You the girl come for the interview?'

Anna recognised the friendless voice from her telephone call, when it had explained somewhat curtly what her duties would be. A local farmer's wife apparently came in each day to clean and see to the laundry, but Anna might have to help her on occasion. She would, however, be more of an assistant to the housekeeper who also did the cooking, so that her duties would be many and varied, from turning down the beds to preparing vegetables and washing up. If she proved a good worker, he had intimated condescendingly, she might be trusted with superior duties in time. He had proceeded to arrange the interview, and now Anna wondered exactly who he was. Beneath his smart black overcoat, she spied an immaculate, snow-white shirt with an equally perfect tie and the lapels of a black jacket.

Anna squared her shoulders. 'Yes. Anna Millington.'

'Get in the front of the car. Only Lady Ashcroft rides in the back. And I hope your shoes are clean.'

Who did he think he was, Anna thought, for she had decided he must be some sort of servant? Resentment brewed up inside her, but she supposed she would have to swallow her pride. She needed this job to get away from her dad, if only for a short while until she had saved enough to go further afield.

'Yes, they are,' she answered frostily.

'Good. Now get in and mind your tongue.'

Anna felt like telling him where to stuff the job, and the thought of the colourful language Ethel might have used to tell him so made her smile to herself. So she obediently climbed into the front seat of the car, a huge, black, elegant affair polished so that the sun dazzled on it. Anna had never been in a car before so, if nothing else, she would enjoy the experience – and in such a splendid one, too! It moved so smoothly, the engine purring as they left the exposed village Princetown behind.

Anna vowed not to utter another word unless spoken to, and gazed out of the window instead. As from the train, the views were stunning, although over to her left rose the bleak daunting buildings of Dartmoor Prison. All around, though, the moor stretched to the horizon, the rough ground dotted with sheep, cattle or ponies left to roam free. Well, Anna thought, even if she didn't get the job, she'd have had a lovely day out!

They turned off the road into a wide, tree-lined avenue. Anna hardly had time to notice Ashcroft Hall, the large, imposing house at the end, as the car was driven round to the side and she was ushered in through a small side door along a dark, narrow, low-ceilinged corridor. A maze of small rooms led off to either side and she tried to peer in to those whose doors were ajar, but she couldn't if she was to keep up with the taciturn devil who led the way! Up a short flight of steps and they emerged into a kitchen – oh, it was enormous and–

But the man tutted irritably and so she trotted after him and soon found herself in a vast entrance hall with a grand, sweeping staircase. And it was beside this that the fellow stopped so abruptly that Anna nearly collided into his back.

'You wait here and I'll see if Lady Ashcroft is ready for you.'

Oh, help. Anna's courage shrank as he knocked on the door and waited for an imperious 'Come' before entering the room. Anna heard a few muted words above her hammering pulse, and then the man reappeared.

'Lady Ashcroft will see you now. And make sure you stand up straight.'

Anna flashed him a glance, wondering why she felt grateful for his advice. Clutching at straws, she supposed. But why would she be nervous? Lady Ashcroft could only be flesh and blood the same as she was, and she bet she had never witnessed the violence that Anna had. Seen her mother tumble to her death before her eyes. What could be worse than that? Not an interview. So she stepped purposefully into the room.

Lady Ashcroft was seated behind a small but very fine desk. She held herself erect and proud, her greying hair swept up and held in place with pins. A handsome woman, Anna considered, and she noticed the tailored, fine-checked jacket and cashmere jumper beneath. Beside her stood a tall, gaunt woman dressed in black whose icy gaze tried to freeze Anna to the core.

But she wouldn't let it. 'Your Ladyship,' she said clearly, and dipped her knee slightly. She noticed the shadow of a smile flit over Lady Ashcroft's face, but the other woman's expression remained inscrutable.

'Miss Millington,' Prudence Ashcroft spoke at last. 'You had a satisfactory journey?'

The tone was expressionless and Anna wasn't sure how to judge her. The least said, the better, perhaps. 'Thank you, Your Ladyship.'

'Good. Now I understand that you have no previous experience of being in service.'

'That is so, Your Ladyship. I've just left school.'

'A strange time of year to leave. I hope you weren't expelled?'

'Oh, no, Your Ladyship. It was because my ... my mother died recently.'

Anna saw Lady Ashcroft raise an eyebrow. 'I'm truly sorry to hear that. And what of your father?'

Anna felt the sweat break out down her back. 'My father says it's time that I made my own way in the world.'

'And you thought that entering service would provide you with a roof over your head as well as a job?'

Oh dear, this wasn't going well, was it? Lady Ashcroft was too astute for her. 'Partly,' she admitted, since she had nothing to lose. 'But I should welcome the opportunity to work for aristocracy. And I'm a hard worker and quick to learn.'

She noticed that twitch of Her Ladyship's mouth again. 'Well, you're well-spoken and seem intelligent. What were studying at school?'

'English, French and Geography, Your Ladyship.'

'Hmm. Useful subjects.' Prudence Ashcroft paused to consider. 'Well, Miss Millington, I like the way you conduct yourself. This is a small, intimate residence, so the quality of a member of staff is of extreme importance here, which is why I wanted to interview you myself. But I believe we can offer you a month's trial, would you not agree, Mrs Davenport?'

Anna lifted her eyes to the austere woman in black who pursed her lips in disdain.

'Yes, Lady Ashcroft,' was all she said.

'Well.' Prudence's face finally slid into a half

smile as she rose to her feet. 'I will leave you with Mrs Davenport who will explain your duties in more detail.'

'Thank you, Your Ladyship.'

Anna dipped her knee again as her new employer crossed the room. Oh, goodness, should she open the door for her? She leapt forward and did so anyway, her heart bouncing in her chest like a rubber ball.

'Thank you, Miss Millington. We have the makings of a good one here, I believe, Mrs Davenport.'

Anna felt the other woman's eyes boring into her back as she softly closed the door. Oh, Lord. She gritted her teeth and turned back into the room.

Chapter Five

Anna caught her breath at the timid knock on the front door. She had been hastily packing her little square case, though she had precious little to take with her. Underwear, socks, two nighties and her slippers. She had dressed in her working outfit, the same as she had for her interview – serge blue skirt, white blouse and navy cardigan. She would have no further need of her school gymslip, but the Aertex gym shirt, white shirts and grey pullover could be useful. Add to that two summer dresses, a twin set, a pair of slacks and a pair of white sandals, and it amounted to the sum total of her wardrobe.

She had just been about to put in her few

books, when the noise downstairs had startled her. Oh, no. Her dad hadn't come back from work, had he? Forgotten his flask and sandwiches or something? If he were to find her packing, it would be unthinkable. But then Anna melted with relief. Even if he had come back and had forgotten his key, he would rap on the door like a bull in a china shop. So, it wouldn't be him. But Anna had a good idea who it was.

She was right.

'I waited till your dad were safely out o' the way. I just 'ad to say goodbye again. Didn't seem right, saying it last night. Only I've got to dash or I'll be late for work.'

'Oh, I'm so glad you called!' Anna's nerves were on edge, but while seeing Ethel, if only for a few moments, boosted her courage, it also filled her with sadness. 'I feel awful, just sliding away and not telling anyone except you.'

'Needs must.' Ethel nodded in that matter of fact way she had. 'An' I promise I'll not tell a soul where you'm gone. Not even my mum an' dad. Or Maud an' Pam, cuz they'm bound to come asking for you some time. I'll just tell 'em I doesn't know where you'm gone.'

'They might not believe you. Everyone knows we're best friends.'

'I'll just say that you wanted a new start an' that you promised to write when you was settled. P'r'aps they'll forget about you in time. After all, you was never best friends with 'em like you is wi' me. But, oh dear, Anna, I got to go.' Her young face wrinkled with desperation. 'I 'ates to say goodbye, Anna. You take care now.'

Anna bit on her lip as a horrible emptiness welled up inside her. 'You look after yourself, too, Eth. And I hope everything goes on all right with you and Bert.'

The mention of her beloved Bert brought a smile to Ethel's distraught face. 'We certainly seems to be getting along proper fine. But... Oh, Anna! I'm going to miss you so much.'

'Me, too.'

They found themselves clasped in each other's tight embrace, holding on, wishing... But time was getting on.

'I just hope it's worth it,' Anna murmured. 'That where I'm going is far enough away for Dad not to find me.'

Ethel pulled away, and while the lump in Anna's throat was choking her, she saw the tears swimming in her friend's eyes.

'Oh, there'll be no reason for 'en to suspect you'm gone to live on Dartmoor. Now, I really musts go. Good luck,' she added, beginning to walk backwards down the street. 'An' don't forget to write!'

'I won't, I promise!'

Anna watched, her vision misted with unshed tears, as Ethel hurried along the pavement, turned at the corner to give one final wave, and was gone. Anna stood for a moment on the threshold, her heart in tatters. Her mum was dead, and now she didn't know when she would see her dear friend again. And her dad ... well. He had changed for ever, she was sure. She really mustn't allow any feelings of regret to get in the way of her decision. Her mum had clung to the past, hadn't she, and look where it had got her. Anna set her mouth in fierce determination and went back upstairs to finish packing.

She mustn't be long. Just the few family photos she'd taken from the drawer downstairs and one or two knicknacks her mum had given her. That was it. Nothing else to remind her of her previous life.

She had made her bed. The room was unchanged apart from her missing teddy bear that she had squashed into the case. And the note she had decided at the last minute to leave on the bed.

I'm sorry, Dad. I just had to get away. Look after yourself. And please don't drink too much.

Love

Anna.

She took her gaberdine raincoat from the hallstand. Put her head round the kitchen door. So many memories. Scarf wound about her neck, wriggling her fingers into her gloves. As she bent to pick up the case, her eyes stopped on the lino where her mum had died. No, she mustn't think like that.

She picked up the case and her umbrella as it looked like rain, and let herself out of the front door. A new life. She mustn't look back.

'You must not *ever* use the main stairs,' Mrs Davenport instructed as she showed Anna up to her room. 'Not unless you have had express permission for some specific purpose. The main stairs are only for the family and their visitors.'

Anna had been hurrying along behind the housekeeper in the narrow confines of the underground corridor she had been ushered along on

67

the day of her interview, and up the steps at the far end. But instead of going through the door into the impressive entrance hall, the austere woman led her directly into a small, rear hallway with a door and windows giving out onto the back of the house.

Anna had no time to dwell on the uncertainty that still gnawed at her as she followed Mrs Davenport up the endless flights of stairs that hugged the narrow stairwell right up to the attic rooms of the house. You could see right the way up, she realised with a shudder. It was a bit scary, that, because you could fall right from top to bottom as well. It reminded her … and she angrily thrust the horrific memory aside.

'This is your room,' Mrs Davenport announced with all the feeling of a block of Dartmoor granite. 'Now, what clothes have you got?'

How flipping rude! Anna thought at once. But then she supposed that the witch … oh, yes, Anna decided that's how she would think of her, dressed all in black. All she needed was a pointed hat and a broomstick! But concentrating her thoughts, she decided the witch was referring to her *working* clothes.

'What I'm wearing. And I have two spare white shirts and a grey school jumper.'

'Hurrump' was the best way Anna could describe the deprecating sneer. 'They'll do for now. I suppose they are school shirts designed to be worn with a tie? Well, you cannot sport an open neck with a button-up collar. Do you have a brooch you could wear at the neck instead of a tie? Nothing fancy, mind.'

'Yes, I think so—'

'Good. But on your first free afternoon, you will walk into Princetown and order some more attire from Bolt's. I shall tell you what to buy. Your shoes are sensible, I see, but you will polish them every night in the boot room. And you will need a pair of wellingtons to slip on if you are required to go outside. We cannot have wet footprints indoors. And you will need to be measured for a uniform for formal occasions, the cost of which will be deducted from your wages. Aprons are the only item you will be supplied with. Now, unpack your things and I will expect you downstairs in ten minutes. I trust you can find your own way below stairs?'

'Yes, Mrs Davenport,' Anna replied automatically, wondering if she shouldn't salute! But the battleaxe seemed pleased with her own monologue, jabbed her head in what seemed to Anna to be self-approval and marched out of the room. Anna heard her footsteps along the corridor and then fading down the bare wooden stairs.

It was only then that she realised she had been holding her breath, and now she let it out through puffed cheeks as she plonked herself down on the bed. Dear Lord, what had she let herself in for? And all the clothes she would have to fork out for! Her wages were only three pounds a week, and her plan was to save all she could until she could afford to move and find something more suitable. All those purchases would really set her back.

Oh well, there was nothing she could do about it – not unless she wanted to throw it all in and go straight back home to her dad. And she didn't want that, did she? She had made the break and she was going to stick by her decision. And maybe things might not seem so bad in time.

Ten minutes. Oh, dear. Probably only nine by now. She took in the tiny room at a glance. The ceiling sloped steeply so she must be right under the eaves of the house. A small window was built into the roof, and Anna went to look out. She imagined there must be wonderful views but today everything was hidden behind an opaque veil of mist.

Anna turned back to the room and quickly stowed her possessions in the chest of drawers, the only item of furniture apart from the bed and a small bedside table. On it stood an old oil lamp and a box of matches. Anna's heartbeat accelerated as she searched the ceiling and the wall by the door, the obvious places. But, oh glory! There was no electric light in the room, let alone a mains socket! She had seen that there was electricity downstairs but it evidently didn't reach the servants' quarters! And there was no fireplace, either. No wonder it struck so cold up there. She was used to an unheated bedroom but would she be allowed a hot-water bottle at bedtime? She sincerely hoped so! There wasn't an ounce of comsfort in the room, not even a rug on the bare floorboards.

She hurried back down the servants' stairs, passing what she guessed was the door to the first floor of the house. She could hardly believe this all still went on today. It was 1954, and yet this household belonged in the Victorian era. It was like stepping back in time, but she supposed that aristocratic houses still kept up these sorts of traditions. At least she didn't have to wear a uniform – except on special occasions. She wondered what that meant!

She found herself back in the gloomy corridor down in the bowels of the house, and followed the clink of crockery into the kitchen that she had glimpsed on her previous visit. What struck her first was that the room was so much brighter than the corridor, due to windows all along the outside wall, but Anna realised they looked out on a level with the ground outside. So, this hub of the household was half underground. Was lit also by two stark electric bulbs suspended over a giant table that dominated the room – and where Mrs Davenport was busily preparing some food.

'I said ten minutes, girl,' she said, glaring up accusingly. But before Anna could open her mouth in protest – her watch told her that she'd been less than that! – Mrs Davenport commanded, 'Get yourself an apron and give your hands a good wash and then come and help me. Lady Ashcroft will be requiring her lunch shortly and I've wasted enough time over you already.'

Indignation threatened to burst out from Anna's lips, but she somehow managed to swallow it down. She was fuming, but she'd show the old crow by proving what a good worker she was! She dutifully tied on a crisp white apron, scrubbed her hands at the deep, stone sink and presented herself at the table.

'Lady Ashcroft takes a light lunch,' she was told. 'Today I have prepared vegetable soup and a cold selection. Ah, Mr Jackson,' the housekeeper smiled as the said chauffeur – who Anna realised

71

was also the butler – entered the room. 'Would you carve some ham, please? And you, girl, display those wedges of cheese *nicely* on the small cheeseboard, and then cut two slices of bread, very thinly if you're capable, and butter them, making sure it goes right to the crust.'

Anna obeyed while Mrs Davenport arranged everything *just so* on a huge tray covered by a pristine cloth. The slivers of bread were almost like wafers and Anna spread the butter evenly. Yes, she supposed it *looked* very neat and uniform, though what difference it made to the taste, she couldn't possibly imagine!

'You call that thin?' Anna shrank back at the irate exclamation. 'They're like doorsteps! Get out of the way, and let me do it. Oh, I can see I'll have my hands full teaching *you!*'

Anna stood back from the table. Oh, you mean old woman! And she watched Mrs Davenport crossly saw two slices that, if anything, were thicker than the ones she had cut! Her lips were pursed almost as tightly as the older woman's were, ready to explode, but at that moment, one of several highly polished brass bells on the wall clanged tunelessly.

'There's Lady Ashcroft waiting,' the witch cackled, 'and her lunch isn't ready. Well, don't just stand there, girl! Fetch the cutlery and make sure you hold it by the handles.'

Anna jumped to it, doing this, that and the other as she was bid until the tray was perfected. It was then placed on a wide platform through a hatch, and pulling on some ropes, Mr Jackson hauled it upwards on a kind of lift. Well, I never,

Anna thought, but had no more time to marvel as she was instructed to go upstairs with Mr Jackson and open the doors for him.

The butler himself did not utter a word as Anna followed him up those few steps – she was going to dream of them for nights on end, she was sure – into the main hall and across to what was obviously a grand dining room. Lo and behold, the laden tray was waiting behind a pair of small doors in the hall.

'Lady Ashcroft takes her lunch in the breakfast room,' Mr Jackson deigned to speak at last. 'If you see her, you make yourself invisible. Understand?'

Anna gulped down her resentment and nodded. Yes, she understood, all right! It had been made abundantly clear to her that she was the lowest of the low. Dear Lord, how was she going to stand it?

'*Yes, Mr Jackson* is what you must say,' he told her icily. 'Now, I'll carry the tray and you knock on the breakfast room door, that one over there,' he indicated with a jab of his head as they went back out into the hall. 'Just one firm knock but not too loud, and wait until you hear Lady Ashcroft's reply before you open the door. And then stand back into the hall. She doesn't want to see any more of you than she has to.'

'Of course, Mr Jackson,' Anna answered, lifting her chin. Her cool tone must have brought him up short as she saw him blink in what passed as surprise. Good! She wanted him to know that while she was happy to show respect, she wasn't going to be treated like a doormat, and that seemed the first step!

She carried out her instructions perfectly, but as Mr Jackson advanced into the room with the massive tray, she heard Prudence Ashcroft's cut-crystal voice.

'Ah, is that young Miss Millington I see behind the door? Come here, child.'

Oh. What should she do? But she hesitated only a moment before crossing the threshold into the room. She saw Mr Jackson frown and direct his eyes sharply downwards. Did he mean she should curtsey? She bobbed her knees briefly, keeping her gaze on the luxurious carpet.

'I expect Mrs Davenport has thrown you in at the deep end,' she heard Lady Ashcroft's autocratic tone, 'but you're an intelligent girl and I'm sure you can cope. Now, we can't keep on referring to you as Miss Millington, so I want everyone to call you Anna. Is that understood, Mr Jackson?'

'Yes, Lady Ashcroft.'

'Very well. You may both go.'

'Yes, Lady Ashcroft,' they replied in unison, and dipping her knee once again, Anna backed out of the room following Jackson's example. Would he praise her for managing the unexpected moment so well? Not on your Nellie! But Anna was pleased with herself as they returned to the kitchen. So, she was to be called by her given name – somewhat better than *girl!* At least it was a step in the right direction.

'Shall I show Anna below stairs now, Mrs Davenport?' Mr Jackson suggested. 'Or do you need her urgently for something? And Lady Ashcroft wishes the girl to be called by her Christian name.'

'Does she now? Encouraging the girl to put on

74

airs and graces, if you ask me. But if Lady Ashcroft wishes it–'

'Oh, I won't! Put on airs and graces, I mean.'

'How dare you speak before you are spoken to!' Mrs Davenport took a step forward, brandishing the bread knife, and for a fleeting moment, Anna thought she might be attacked! Good God, she had come there to get away from such things! But then she realised that the knife had just happened to be in the housekeeper's hand as she was cutting more slices of bread. It seemed that the witch managed to contain her anger, though her next words were laced with contempt. 'You had better teach the girl some manners while you're at it, Mr Jackson.'

'This way,' he barked in reply, and Anna was relieved to scamper after him.

Mr Jackson gave her a swift tour of the maze of small rooms that led off from the corridor, and in his habitually gruff manner, explained each one's function. There was a boot room, a locked wine cellar to which only he himself held a key, the butler's pantry, and the housekeeper's room where Mrs Davenport saw to all the below-stairs accounts but also had a cosy chair by the fire. As far as Anna could tell, it was the only room below stairs to have a fireplace. The dairy had been made obsolete by the refrigerator, but the laundry was still in use, the washing being done once a week by the daily, Mrs Smudge, who was at this moment cleaning 'upstairs'. Mr Jackson hoped Anna could iron!

Back in the kitchen, Anna was shown the separate scullery where the washing-up was done, the sinks in the kitchen itself being strictly for food preparation. The house had been built in a bygone age and nothing, it seemed to Anna, had changed since. She would have been fascinated – if she hadn't gained the distinct impression that she was going to slave in it like a skivvy. And, apart from the kitchen, all the rooms were so dark that she was convinced she would turn into a mole! It was no wonder that the butler and housekeeper were short-tempered.

'Well, that's me done for the day. Alfie'll be yere in a mo to pick me up. Couldn't come on me bike in this yere fog.'

Oh, what a relief to hear a cheerful voice! What Anna saw first was a fat, be-aproned behind as Mrs Smudge came backwards, using her bottom to open the door since her hands were full of her cleaning materials.

''Ello, cheel! You'm the new maid?' she beamed as she turned round. 'I 'opes you last longer than the last one,' she whispered with a wink as she struggled past Anna with her dusters, brushes and brooms. 'See you tomorrow,' she called as, having stowed her equipment somewhere in the scullery, she came back through the kitchen and disappeared out of door again.

Well, at least she would look forward to working with Mrs Smudge, Anna mused, but just then the breakfast room bell clanged once more.

'That's Lady Ashcroft finished, so up we go. Anna,' Mr Jackson added as if he resented using her name.

Anna was appalled. The tray had been set out like a banquet for Lady Ashcroft to choose from,

76

and yet she had hardly eaten anything. And when Anna thought of how her dear mum had struggled through all the years of rationing to put a decent meal on the table, well, it was criminal. She sincerely hoped all that food wouldn't go to waste. And all the time and effort of preparing the tray for nothing. No wonder Her Ladyship required so many people to look after her!

Once Lady Ashcroft had been served her coffee, the servants were able to sit at one end of the enormous kitchen table to have their own lunch. The one pleasant surprise of the day was that they helped themselves from the ham and cheese that had been returned on the tray – Anna being made to wait until last, of course – and Mrs Davenport reheated the soup on the range so that it was piping hot. And Anna had to admit that it was delicious.

'Please may I ask when His Lordship will be back?' she plucked up the courage to ask, most politely, of course.

She saw them exchange glances, and Mrs Davenport rolled her eyes to the ceiling. Oh, Lord, Anna wondered in dismay, what on earth had she said now?

'Explain to the girl, would you?' Mrs Davenport sighed in exasperation.

Mr Jackson coughed lightly. 'There is no His Lordship. Sir Hugh was a baronet, not a lord of any sort. And sadly he died some years ago, so Her Ladyship is officially the Dowager Lady Ashcroft. Since Sir Hugh's death, she has preferred to live here rather than in London.'

'Oh dear, how sad,' Anna ventured. 'But I'm

sure Mrs Davenport mentioned family?'

'She may have done. A baronetcy is not part of the peerage, but unlike a knighthood, it can be hereditary. The son may claim the title upon the death of his father. Sir Gilbert comes to stay with his mother quite frequently. No doubt you will meet him soon enough. And Lady Ashcroft also has some distant cousins. But stop asking about things that don't concern you, and hurry up and finish your lunch. We all have work to do, especially you.'

He wasn't kidding! It seemed that Anna was to do all the washing-up, scouring and polishing the copper pans until they gleamed. She had to wash and prepare all the vegetables ready for Mrs Davenport to cook, and weigh out all ingredients on some cast iron scales. The housekeeper instructed her in the exact method of making tea – what a blooming waste of time that was, in Anna's opinion. Tea was tea, for heaven's sake. Although apparently not.

She seemed to be kept on her feet – running around like a blue-arse fly as Ethel would have said – for ridiculous reasons. The highlight of the afternoon was being taken to Lady Ashcroft's opulent bedroom to help Mrs Davenport change the sheets, which was done twice a week. Crikey. Surely once a week was enough? When Anna finally fell into her own bed, which she had been obliged to make up herself as well, it was with strict instructions to present herself in the kitchen at six o'clock in the morning without fail.

She lay in bed in the pitch dark. It was so silent, like nothing she had experienced before, no

78

traffic or people's voices from outside. She hoped she would sleep all right in strange room, but she was so exhausted that she didn't even say her nightly prayer for her mum before she fell fast asleep, clutching her threadbare little teddy.

Chapter Six

'You'm going out with Bert tonight, all dolled up like a dog's dinner?'

'I am that!'

Ethel set her face in a grin, hoping it appeared genuine. Thank goodness Bert was on earlies and was free, 'cause she really needed cheering up this evening. The first night for thirteen years, wasn't it, when Anna wasn't in hailing distance? Crikey, she were missing her already, and her only gone since that morning. How were she getting on? Ethel didn't like the sound of the place, even though she were the one who'd encouraged Anna to go for an interview. She didn't half feel guilty now, as if Anna had been swallowed up into a great big black hole and it were all her fault.

'Say goodnight to your sister now, Primrose,' Mabel ordered kindly, stubbing out her cigarette on the cracked plate from which Primrose had just been eating her tea of baked beans on toast.

'Nightie-night,' Ethel smiled a little ruefully as her mum heaved little Primrose into her arms. 'Don't let they fleas bite.'

'No fleas in our beds!' Mabel nodded emphatically, and Ethel grimaced. There had been once upon a time. Well, bed bugs, anyway. She remembered the legs of their beds standing in saucers of something that smelt disgusting to stop the little blighters crawling up at night. It had been when they had returned to the house after the war. Her dad hadn't exactly kept the place clean. Managed to break his leg, he had, leaving it slightly shorter than the other one, so he'd been discharged from the army. He'd gone back to working longer hours than ever on the railway. Important war work, he often declared proudly – which indeed it was, especially with Plymouth being a major naval port – and often dangerous, with Hitler aiming at the railway routes as well as the city and the dockyards in his air raids. And when Fred wasn't at work, he'd been a member of the home defences, patrolling the streets, so he'd hardly had time to eat and sleep, let alone keep the house clean. Not that it was spick and span now, but at least you didn't wake up covered in little red bites. And it was home. Unlike where Anna had gone.

'Night-night, Daddy,' Primrose beamed, leaning out from Mabel's arms to receive a noisy kiss from her dad who was also on earlies that week.

'Oh, I swears you gets 'eavier every day!' Mabel grumbled good-heartedly as she shambled out of the door in her worn slippers.

'Huh, all right for you!' Billy growled at once at his big sister. 'Going out enjoying yersel' when some on us 'as got flaming 'omework to do!'

'An' I didn't 'ave 'omework when I were at school?' Ethel retorted sharply. 'An' one day you'll be out at work, too, like Davy an' Dad, an' wishing you was back at school!'

'I likes 'omework,' little Sammy piped up, wide-eyed with earnest.

'Yes, us knows you does!' Ethel saw her dad grin, and ruffled his youngest son's mousy hair. 'P'r'aps us 'as *one* scholar in the family!'

'You calls that 'omework, reading a page of *Janet and John* an' doing a few sums, like?'

''E's only eight, Billy–'

Oh, thank the Lord for that, Ethel sighed as she heard a loud knock from the hallway. That was as near to an argument as her family ever got, but she could do without it tonight. That would be Bert at the door, though he was a bit early and she wasn't quite ready. Hadn't got her lipstick on yet, but the knock had sounded impatient for Bertie and she didn't want to keep him waiting on such a dank evening. So she hurried along the hallway, she pinched her lips to put some colour in them that way instead.

She pulled the door wide, vibrant with expectation, and her fingers turned rigid as they gripped the latch. It wasn't Bert, and a little gasp escaped her throat as she stared up into Vince Millington's maddened face.

'Where's my daughter?' he raged. 'Gone and left me, she has, but I'll wager you know where she's gone! And I bet it were you as put her up to it, as well!'

Ethel could smell beer on his breath and stepped backwards, pressing her back up against the open door. Bloody hell, she hadn't foreseen this, and for once, her brain couldn't think of an answer.

'I-I...' she stuttered, but her shock was so deep

that no words came out of her mouth.

'Who the 'ell does you think you'm be!' she heard her dad's voice storm from behind her, and her knees went weak with relief. 'I's bin a friend to you, Vince, but I'll not 'ave you coming into my 'ouse, shouting at my family like this! Now what's this all about?'

Ethel stared up at Vince, quite petrified. It were no wonder Anna were afraid of him if this were how he could be! But then she saw him take a deep breath after which he seemed calmer, though his lips were still clenched in an angry knot.

'My Anna's run off,' he grated. 'Packed her bags and gone. And I reckon *she* knows where to!' he spat, poking Ethel in chest.

'Keep your 'ands off my darter!' Fred at once barked back, and drew himself up to his full height. Although Vince was tall and strong, he couldn't match Fred, and he knew it. Ethel could see he was backing down, thank God. 'Now, does you know ort about this?' she heard her dad's reasoning voice as he turned to her.

Ethel tried to speak, but still no sound would come from her lips so she shook her head instead. She noticed her dad frown questioningly, but he spoke to Vince without hesitation.

'If Ethel says she knows nort about it, then she don't. So don't you come yere again bothering 'er, like, or you'll 'ave me to answer to.'

'Huh!' Vince snorted back. 'I'll go to the police, then. *They*'ll likely get *her* to tell the truth!'

'You'd be wasting your time. Anna be eighteen, same as Ethel yere. Not a child. From what you says, she's gone of her own accord. An' there be nort you can do about it. So I suggests you pushes off 'ome an' sobers up a bit. Now goodnight.' And he slammed the door in Vince's face.

Ethel thought she was about to faint. May God bless her soul, it was over! But it wasn't, was it?

'What's this all about, cheel?' her dad asked sternly.

'What's 'appening?' Mabel thumped down the stairs as if Beelzebub himself were after her.

'Seems Anna's done a runner,' Fred answered over his shoulder, 'an' 'er dad thinks our Ethel were in on it. I thinks us'd better 'ave a chat. In the front room.'

Ethel obeyed, moving like a machine. She was going to have to face the music now! The air in the unheated room made her shiver. It was only used for high days and holidays in the summer, or at Christmas if they could afford to burn some coal in the grate. But her dad's features had softened, and her mum, well, she sat down next to her on the lumpy sofa and put her arm around her shaking shoulders.

'Well, cheel?'

Ethel lifted her gaze to her dad's face, and sniffed. She hadn't realised she was crying. From sheer terror, she supposed.

'I knew she were going,' she admitted, her voice croaky and unrecognisable. 'Er dad 'as a bit of a drink problem–'

'So I sees...'

'An' she were frightened. But I doesn't know where she's gone, I swear!' she concluded with conviction. Well, it were only a half lie, weren't it? Somewhere up on the moor was all she knew. She didn't know the exact location or the address. 'Anna said she'd write when she were settled, like,' she added truthfully.

Her dad's lips had tightened fiercely. 'You'm going to 'ave be careful o' that Vince. If 'e lays so much as a finger on you, I swears I'll break 'is bloody neck!'

Ethel stared at her father and shuddered. Jesus, what she had got them all in to?

My dearest Ethel...

Every morning, Ethel scooted to the front door the instant she heard the postman in case there was something from Anna. She prayed that nothing would ever arrive in the second delivery when she was at work, but today her patience had been rewarded by a letter in the early post, two weeks after her friend had left and the horrible incident with her father. They hadn't seen hide nor hair of him since, except glimpses of him going to and from work. But thankfully he hadn't shown his face at Number Sixteen again.

Ethel had stuffed the letter into her pocket. She didn't like deceiving her parents one little bit, but it was best they didn't know that she had heard from Anna at all. Now she was on the bus, she eagerly tore open the envelope, glad that she had managed to conceal it from everyone else.

Sorry I've not written before, but there's no time during my normal working day. This is my afternoon off. I was supposed to walk into Princetown, which is about three miles away, because they want me to buy some more suitable clothes for my work here. I've got to pay for them myself, but I suppose they'll always come

84

in handy.

Blooming cheek, Ethel considered, feeling the anger rising inside her. Anna always looked nice, neat and tidy and with her light-brown hair tied up in a ponytail. Ethel liked it best, though, when she let it down. It had a lovely wave to it, and never seemed out of place, whereas her own hair always looked a mess, which was why she kept it short. But she wanted to have the letter read before she got to work.

But today the rain's coming down in stair rods and driving across the moor in a howling gale. You've probably got the same, but up here, it's so exposed that, well, it's hard to describe. Even Mrs Davenport, the housekeeper – and a right old dragon, I tell you – she said it was too bad for me to go. Mind you, she said I'd probably catch a chill and be no use to her, so I think it was that rather than any concern for my welfare!

Oh, love a duck, they sounded awful people! And she, Ethel, were the one to blame. If only she hadn't seen that advert in the paper! But it were done now, and she supposed Anna didn't seem completely down in the mouth. But she must read on.

So I've ended up sitting in my little attic room writing to you instead. Which is good because I can tell you lots. But I won't be able to post it for another week when hopefully the weather will be OK and I'll get into Princetown then.

I do have to work very hard, starting at six in the morning, and I'm not dismissed until nine in the evening. But there's a proper bathroom and a flushing toilet up here in the servants' quarters, which I'm not used to! There are two huge generators that provide electricity, because we're miles from any mains. There's no electric in the attic rooms, though, and the cooking's done on an old range because there's no gas either. And hot water comes from a coal boiler. We get through loads of coal, and one of my jobs is to keep the scuttles full for all the fires.

Ethel's brow creased. That sounded like blooming hard work. Poor Anna, having to make such a move. Ethel wondered if she'd have been able to do it. Probably not. So thank the Lord she had such a wonderful family, and her dear Bert, and all.

Mr Jackson, the butler, he's quite a stickler but he's not as openly hostile as Mrs Davenport. I helped him polish the silver. You use some stuff that smells vile and you have to wear gloves because it stains your fingers black. But he said I made a good job of it. Not that he said it with a smile. In fact, I don't think his face has smile muscles! Mrs Davenport's the one, though! She seems cross all the time and tries to make me feel two inches tall. I'm learning a lot about cooking from her, though. They use really expensive ingredients and we eat the same as Lady A and it really is delicious.

Give me fish and chips any day, or a fry up, Ethel scoffed. But then she thought of the lumpy porridge she'd just eaten. She wondered if *cornflakes* might taste better, but they sorts of cereals was dearer. And anyway, her dad said hot porridge stuck to your ribs better.

Some mornings I help Mrs Smudge with the cleaning, and she makes it quite fun. The house is so big that we hardly see the others. She doesn't go much on them, but she says she loves the house and making it look nice and she says Lady A's all right. And they need the money. It's hard being a farmer, she says. And she's right about Lady A. She demands respect and she can be quite formidable, but she doesn't treat me like dirt the way Mrs D does.

Anyway, I'm sure you've heard quite enough about me. I want to know how everything is with you. Are you still going with Bert? I do hope so, but I don't want to know all the details! Please give my love to all your family and tell them how I really appreciate all they did for me when Mum died. At least that's one thing. They keep me so busy here, it stops me thinking about her so much.

So, now you have my full address, you can write back to me. I'm really looking forward to it!

Take care of yourself

All my love

Anna

Ethel lifted her head and glanced out of the window. A lump had suddenly come to her throat at the picture of Anna in her lonely room at the top of the big, isolated house. Anna were *trying* to be happy, weren't she? But that were Anna for you. She got on with things. In her own quiet and determined way. It weren't fair, everything she'd had to put up with. Not that it had stopped the pair of them having a lot of fun together all the years they'd known each other, had it?

Oh, how Ethel missed her! She weren't a great letter writer herself, but she'd spend her lunch hour writing back. She'd tell Anna... No. She wouldn't tell her everything. She wouldn't tell her how Vince had come over to their house in a foul temper and making threats. Ethel was still a bit frightened. And of course, she hadn't told her parents how Freda had really come to fall down the stairs. Her dad would've gone spare if he'd known!

Life could be proper complicated sometimes, couldn't it? But there was nothing she could do about it except write a cheerful letter back to Anna. There weren't any trains on Sundays, but maybe they could work it so that when Anna had some time off, she could take the day's paid leave she had left and they could meet in Princetown. Yes, that'd be great, and she shoved the letter back in its envelope with a happy smile.

'Girl, you can take ten minutes' break,' Mrs Davenport said resentfully as she poured out cups of hot, steaming liquid for their *morning coffee*. 'We don't say *elevenses*,' she had corrected Anna on her second day. 'Such a common expression,' she had added with a sneer.

Anna had already been getting used to the witch's belittling attitude, so that by now she would have been shocked if the woman *hadn't* spoken to her like that. Stupid old biddy, Anna thought to herself. What good did it do her, making herself and everyone around her feel miserable? It was true that Lady A expected a lot of her and she had to be ultra efficient, but surely she'd achieve just as much in a more genial atmosphere?

'Don't you let that she-devil upset you,' Mrs Smudge had whispered one morning when Mrs Davenport had been particularly nasty to her. 'Like it to everyone, she is. Reckons she's jealous, I does, an' afeared someone can do the job better'n she can.'

'Wouldn't catch her blackleading the range, mind,' Anna had scoffed grimly, for that was the worst job she'd been put to. And Mrs Davenport refused to call her anything but *girl,* despite Lady Ashcroft's instructions. But this morning, Anna didn't care. A reply from Ethel had arrived in the post, and her heart had soared. And so she ran up the servants' stairs to her little room to read it.

She sat up, cross-legged, on the bed and glanced at her watch. Ten minutes. But she needn't have worried. Ethel's note was brief with no real news. Disappointment swamped Anna's expectant mood, and the black grief that hovered instantly in the wings clawed at her soul once more.

Oh, Mum. She got up and went over to the little window. It was one of those dull days on Dartmoor when the weather seemed to be asleep, with no rushing wind or lashing rain, penetrating fog or crisp sunshine. Just overcast, still and not particularly cold for the end of November. But visibility was good, and from so high up, Anna could see the barren folds of southern Dartmoor stretching away to infinity – or so it seemed. That part of the moor was especially bleak with no signs of habitation or, as far as Anna was aware, any of the dramatic tors that added power and excitement to the landscape elsewhere. Here it was as if the moor lay sleeping beneath the blanket of the sky, as if at eternal rest. Just like her mum.

She felt the now familiar tightness in her throat but she mustn't cry, although when she looked at her watch, she couldn't see its tiny hands through her blurred vision. Ten minutes? At that particular moment, she didn't care if she was late.

Mrs Davenport's scathing reprimand would be nothing to the pain in her heart.

She dashed the back of her hand over her eyes, stowed away Ethel's letter, and ran down the stairs.

Chapter Seven

'Let's see what a mess you can make of that, then,' Mrs Davenport gloated, hands on hips, as she nodded at the flower stand in the main entrance hall. 'And remember, some of those flowers cost a lot of money and Lady Ashcroft doesn't want them spoilt.'

Anna watched darkly as the housekeeper made her way through the servants' door with a smirk on her face. I'll show her, Anna seethed. Ever since Lady Ashcroft had told her that she had passed her month's trial with flying colours, she was convinced that Mrs Davenport had been looking for a reason to have her dismissed. But Anna was equally determined not to give her a chance, and this was *not* going to provide her with it!

She stood back and studied the stand. She had seen it so often before, of course, bedecked in Mrs Davenport's rigid arrangement, adequate in itself but looking more like a bird's nest stuck on a pole. The stand was elegant and deserved better, Anna considered. Perhaps... Could she possibly create an S-shape rather than the housekeeper's halo, with the tall lilies on one side, sweeping down through the chrysanths, and then with a swirl of the variegated ivy trailing down below? Now, then...

A massive stone fireplace dominated the hall, but Anna had never seen it lit. November had been chased out by an arctic wind rampaging across the moor from the north-east, and Anna was glad of the old liberty bodice she had on that morning under her blouse, and the thick black stockings she was obliged to wear. It was calm and peaceful in the echoing hall, away from the bustle of the kitchen and Mrs Davenport's constant haranguing. Anna found herself humming as she worked, standing back to study the effect and decide what to put in next.

She had been so absorbed in her creation that when the heavy oak front door suddenly opened and was nearly blown off its hinges, Anna was so startled that she literally jumped and nearly knocked the flower stand right over. Her heart thumped hard for a few beats as she stared in shock at the figure standing on the threshold. Clad in a thick greatcoat flapping around its knees, a scarf swathed a dozen times about its neck, and its head adorned with a leather flying helmet and goggles like saucers, the creature looked like something from outer space or maybe from a horror film.

Don't be so ridiculous, Anna chided herself. But she watched in bemused fascination as the apparition peeled first its gauntlets and then its headgear and goggles. Oh, goodness, it was real. A young man, and a handsome one at that. But what did he think he was doing, bursting in like

91

this as if he owned the place? Anna glanced past him, and just before he heaved the door shut against the wind, she glimpsed some glamorous-looking, open-topped sports car parked regally on the driveway.

'Excuse me,' she began indignantly, for who was he to interrupt her daydream like that? 'You can't just walk in–'

'Oh, for heaven's sake, girl, are you going to take all day?' Mrs Davenport's tirade cut across the hall as she emerged through the below-stairs door. 'You've other things to do than fiddle about–' She broke off abruptly, and Anna could have laughed with bitter contempt as the expression on the woman's face changed in a flash from rage to simpering humility. 'Oh, Sir Gilbert! How lovely to see you! But we had absolutely no idea you were coming.'

'It was meant to be a surprise!' the young man grinned affably. 'Oh, Mrs D, be a dear and make some tea, would you? And if you have some crumpets or scones or something? The pub where I stopped for lunch only did sandwiches and I'm positively famished.'

'Of course, Sir Gilbert. And apologies for the girl, here,' the witch added more sternly. 'She's spent ages arranging those flowers. Hurry up and clear away the trimmings, girl. You have other duties to attend to.'

'Well, I think she's made a jolly good job of them!' He winked at Anna, and her heart gave a little jump before he turned away and strode towards the drawing room. 'Mother!' he called loudly, but before he reached the door, it opened on the other side and Lady Ashcroft came out into the hall.

'No need to shout, Gilbert, dear.'

Sir Gilbert stepped forward and placed a respectful peck on his mother's cheek. 'Sorry, Mother. But you are pleased to see me, aren't you?' he cajoled.

'Of course, dear–'

'Don't you think this young lady has arranged these flowers absolutely beautifully? Quite the artist and very professional!'

He was smiling broadly, and Anna felt the crimson flood into her cheeks. He had evidently forgiven her mistake, and was now complimenting her handiwork. She didn't know which way to look.

'Why, Anna, I had no idea you were so talented.' Prudence Ashcroft's eyebrows shot up in surprise. 'Did you take the idea from a book – *Mrs Beeton's Household Management*, for instance?'

'I ... made it up, Lady Ashcroft,' Anna stuttered, politely dipping her knee.

'Well, I think you should always arrange the flowers from now on, is that understood, Mrs Davenport?'

Anna saw from the corner of her eye that the housekeeper was making for the kitchen to prepare the tea Sir Gilbert had requested.

'Yes, Lady Ashcroft,' she answered, tight-lipped. 'Indeed.'

And as she flounced through the below-stairs door, she threw Anna a look that could kill.

'If you've finished playing about with those

flowers now, young lady,' Mrs Davenport smiled with scathing sarcasm five minutes later, 'could I possibly trust you to prepare Gilbert's room while I get the tea he ordered? You can remember the way I showed you, I assume?'

'Yes, Mrs Davenport.'

'And be as quick as you can. We'll be really busy in the kitchen tonight with Sir Gilbert here.'

Anna couldn't really see what difference just one extra mouth should make, but the old crow would doubtless have her running round like a headless chicken, so she had better get on with the allotted task. She actually felt quite proud that the housekeeper had entrusted her with it, although she had a sneaking suspicion the crusty woman would be hoping she would botch it so that she could relish in chastising her! Anna vowed to do everything perfectly so that the she-devil couldn't possibly find anything to criticise.

The huge range had a water boiler at one end and Anna quickly filled four hot-water bottles from the *upstairs* drawer, topped up the boiler with fresh water from the cold tap, and ran up the servants' staircase. Sir Gilbert's room was opposite his mother's, with heavy oak furniture rather than the more elegant regency style in Lady Ashcroft's 'boudoir' – as Mrs Smudge called it with a wink as she polished away like a demon.

Anna quickly set to, turning down the bed and laying the hot-water bottles on the mattress. The air smelt a touch musty, so she opened both sash windows just an inch or two at the very top, and then as she started laying the fire, Mr Jackson came in with Sir Gilbert's luggage.

She was still on her knees by the hearth, carefully adding pieces of coal to the now blazing kindling, when she heard Mr Jackson return. Goodness, Sir Gilbert must have a lot of luggage, she reflected, but she didn't turn her head. This stage of the fire was critical and she was determined that nothing would go wrong with her preparation of the room.

'Ridiculous, isn't it?'

Anna was so startled that she dropped the lump of coal from the tongs. Fortunately it fell back into the scuttle and not onto the stone hearth where it would have made a black smudge that would be difficult to remove. Oh, no! It wasn't the butler this time, but Sir Gilbert himself! Anna leapt to her feet and bobbed a curtsey, keeping her eyes on the hearth rug while the blood raced about her body.

'Oh, I'm sorry if I startled you,' the voice came again. I was going to say it's ridiculous still having open fires to heat this mausoleum of a house. It's nice to have one blazing away in the drawing room, but we ought to have central heating installed. Mother won't hear of it, though. All that disruption, she says.'

Anna was rooted to the spot. Here was Sir Gilbert Ashcroft, *baronet,* talking to her like a normal human being. It was bewildering, and she didn't know what to think, let alone say, as she heard the young man walking about the room.

'Is there something particularly fascinating about that rug?' he enquired. 'You've been staring at it solidly for the past minute. You can look up at me, you know, or has Mrs D instilled the fear of God into you about speaking to us? Bit of a harridan, she is. But we have to forgive her. I'll let you into a secret,' he said, lowering his voice to a conspiratorial whisper. 'She was born on Mars.'

A frown pleated Anna's forehead. What on earth was he going on about? And then it dawned on her that Sir Gilbert was teasing her. It was so unexpected that moments passed before her lips twitched with a hesitant smile and she dared raise her eyes.

'Well, it's nice to see a pretty face about the place,' he was saying now with an amiable smile.

Hmm, not so bad yersel, Anna suddenly heard Ethel's voice in her head, and she had to resist the desire to burst into laughter. Sir Gilbert really was good-looking, with merry brown eyes that danced with good humour.

'Anna, isn't it?' he prompted.

This time Anna didn't hesitate with her reply. 'Yes, sir,' she nodded.

'Well, then, Anna, I mustn't detain you from your duties, you'll get into trouble with Mrs D.'

'Thank you, sir.'

She turned her attention back to the fire, feeling confused but more light-hearted than at any time since she had come to work at the Hall. Sir Gilbert was evidently arranging some of his belongings in the room, and Anna didn't feel afraid now to glance back once or twice as she waited for the first layer of coal to catch properly.

'Do you serve at dinner, Anna?' Sir Gilbert asked casually as he moved about the room.

'Oh, no, sir. I'm not considered, well, I'm sure you know what I mean.'

96

'Mmm, pity. Well, I must get down to the tea I asked for, or Mrs D will be after me! And I'm ravenous after the long drive from London.'

'And ... and I'm sorry for mistaking you for ... well, I don't really know who when you came in,' Anna ventured, feeling herself come out in a hot sweat again.

Sir Gilbert tossed a laugh into the air as he made for the door. 'You are entirely forgiven, my dear Anna,' he pronounced, and left Anna floundering in a deep but pleasant quandary.

Anna stood on the platform in a froth of excitement as the little train glided into the station with a gentle hiss of steam and a grinding of brakes. The exertion of the long walk into Princetown had kept her warm, but as she waited on the platform, the biting wind seemed to cut right through her. She could have sought shelter in the waiting room, but she simply couldn't contain herself by sitting still, and scoured the moor instead. The moment she saw the first puff of white smoke in the distance, she began hopping up and down in anticipation. And now as three doors in the single carriage opened and Ethel climbed down from the last compartment, Anna sprang forward like a jack-in-the-box.

'Ethel!'

'Annie!'

They clung onto each other, dancing around in a circle and grinning like Cheshire cats.

'Oh, you'm just the same!'

'It's only been a few weeks!' Anna laughed aloud. 'I'm not going to change in that time!'

'Nearly six weeks,' Ethel corrected her. 'And 'aven't I missed you! But what we'm going to do?'

'Bowden's Café.' Anna bobbed her head in reply, linking her arm through Ethel's. 'I'll have to start walking back about quarter to two, so we've got four whole hours together. I thought we'll have a cup of tea and then a wander, and then a bite of lunch. Either back at the café or in one of the pubs. Or there's a fish and chip shop if you fancy that.'

'Fish an' chips sounds proper lovely! So long as we can eat it out o' newspaper. Makes 'em taste so much better! But I didn't realise how big Princetown is,' Ethel marvelled as they walked briskly into the centre. 'I imagined a tiny little place, a few 'ouses, maybe.'

'Oh, no. It's quite a community,' Anna told her knowledgeably. 'All the prison staff and their families have to live here, and there's a lot of people employed by the Duchy of Cornwall. The Duchy owns most of Dartmoor, you see. Well, there is some private property, and then something called the Maristow Estate owns vast areas of the moor as well. So almost everywhere is either rented or what they call leasehold.'

'You've got me there!' Ethel grinned. 'But there's loads o' shops an' all! An' look! They little wild ponies running loose in the streets! Aren't they cute?'

'There's nothing to stop them wandering in off the moor, you see,' Anna explained, smiling herself at the endearing animals. 'Oh, that's Bolt's on the corner where I bought my new clothes. They sell *everything*, and they'll order in anything you

98

like. And back there, there's a town hall where they hold dances and show the latest films. No good to me, though,' she grimaced, pulling a long face. 'Ashcroft Hall's much too far, and I have to be in by nine, even when I've got the afternoon and evening off.'

'What does you do then? Oh, in yere?' Ethel asked as Anna opened the door to the café and a bell rang, summoning a pleasantly plump woman in a striped apron.

'My first customers of the day,' she beamed. 'So what can I do for you?'

'Pot of tea and two mince pies, please, as it's nearly Cristmas.'

'Won't be a jiffy, my dears.'

They took a table by the window and Ethel unbuttoned her coat in the warm atmosphere. 'Seems very friendly, like.'

'Mmm, she is. I've been into Princetown two or three times, but it's a long walk. I thought I might invest in a bicycle, like Mrs Smudge, our cleaner, has. Then I could go long rides on the moor instead of walking everywhere.'

'Doesn't you feel a bit scared, all alone out on the moor?'

'No, not really. I've got a map and I keep to the footpaths. And you can see for miles, so you can see anybody coming and avoid them if you don't like the look of them. But I'm more frightened if there are cows across the path! Huge, they are, when you get up close! But I want to hear all *your* news, not mine.'

'Not much to tell.' Ethel paused for a minute while the woman brought the tray of steaming tea and hot mince pies. 'Nort's 'appened really. Bert an' me is still going strong. I really thinks I loves 'en,' she admitted coyly. 'An 'e says 'e loves me, too. I knows it's a bit early to say, an' we've no money to set up 'ome as yet, but I feels certain there be a future for us.'

'Oh, that's wonderful!' Anna cried, thrusting aside a little prick of envy. 'Will you be able to be together over Christmas?'

'We've agreed to 'ave Christmas dinner with our own families, but see each other after that. You knows Bert only lives a few minutes away, so there's no problem.' Ethel bit lustily into her mince pie and noisily savoured the taste. 'What about you?'

'Oh, all time off is cancelled over Christmas,' Anna scoffed. 'Sir Gilbert, Lady Ashcroft's son, that is, arrived about a week ago and he'll be staying until well into the new year. Lady Ashcroft has invited some friends of hers. And also some distant cousin with his wife and entire family. There'll be nine adult guests and a toddler. So we're going to have our work cut out. I'm dreading it, to be honest.'

'Oh dear, Annie, that don't sound like much fun.'

Anna gave a rueful sigh. 'I don't suppose it will be. Mrs Davenport'll be in a dreadful temper, bossing me about and expecting me to do a dozen things at once. I'll be run ragged. Still...' she paused, her face brightening, 'at least Sir Gilbert's very nice. He talks to me sometimes. I told him the other day how I'd been doing my A levels but had to leave school when Mum ... when Mum...'

Whether it was chatting to Ethel again, Anna wasn't sure, but sorrow suddenly gripped her throat again and, for a split second, she thought she might start to cry. But she really mustn't when Ethel had been good enough to come all that way and make such an early start. So she managed to swallow down the feeling and smile wanly at Ethel's concerned face.

'Anyway,' she went on, shaking her head, 'Sir Gilbert said I could borrow any books I wanted from the library. Yes, the Hall has its own library! Mind you, I overheard Lady Ashcroft telling him afterwards not to fraternise with the staff.'

'Golly, she sounds a right old whatnot!'

'No, she's not that bad, really. I feel sorry for her in a way. She seems very lonely to me.'

'Not surprising if she won't even let her son talk to you.'

'Well, there you are.' Anna sighed, pushing aside her empty cup. 'Pity, though.'

Ethel raised a teasing eyebrow. 'Likes 'en, does you, this Sir Gilbert? An' mortal handsome, I suppose?'

'Oh, well, he is rather nice,' Anna stammered, feeling herself flush. 'I just enjoy having a few moments of proper conversation instead of being ordered about all the time. Still, never mind. It won't be for long. Even if I buy a bicycle, I reckon in about six months I'll have saved enough to be able to move on. Rent somewhere of my own and get a more suitable job. In an office or something. I could learn shorthand and typing at evening classes and still become a proper secretary. Which ... reminds me.' She hesitated as the fears came crashing down around her again. 'Do you ... do you see my dad at all?'

She noticed a shuttered look come over Ethel's face.

'Oh, we sees 'en going to an' from work sometimes,' she muttered evasively.

'He's still in work, then?'

'Seems so. Maybe you leaving brought 'en to 'is senses, like.'

'Nothing ... happened, then, when he found I'd gone?'

Ethel pushed forward her bottom lip and shrugged. 'No,' she lied convincingly, feeling as if she was back at school and talking her way out of some mischief she'd been up to. 'But mum saw your last letter arrive, so Mum and Dad knows I knows where you'm be. An' they wanted to know where I was going today.'

Anna drew in a breath. 'I suppose they'd have had to find out sometime.'

'Yes. But no matter.' Ethel suddenly pushed back her chair and got to her feet. 'You can show me around this yere Princetown an' tell me all about this Sir Gilbert fellow. Unattached, is 'e?'

'Oh!' Anna looked up in surprise from taking some coins of her purse. 'Do you know, I've no idea.'

'Maybe you'm in with a chance, then,' Ethel winked.

Anna blinked at her in amazement. The idea was preposterous. And as she realised Ethel was teasing her, the pair of them fell about with laughter as they left the café.

Chapter Eight

'My goodness, these have kept well,' Sir Gilbert observed appreciatively.

As Anna had entered the drawing room entrusted with the task of delivering the tray set with afternoon tea, Sir Gilbert had caught her eye as he lounged in an armchair by the blazing fire. One leg was crossed casually over the opposite knee, and without bothering to move the rest of his body, he had reached out and deftly swiped a scone from the passing plate.

'Mmm, they taste freshly baked,' he continued, evidently relishing the next mouthful.

Anna gave a little shiver of pleasure. She had been rushed off her feet over Christmas and the New Year, with never a word of thanks from anyone, and nothing but scolding from Mrs Davenport. And the house guests had treated her as invisible – except when they had wanted her to run some errand, of course! For two pins she would have walked out if she'd had anywhere to go. Which she didn't, of course. Only the odd kind word or secret, knowing wink from Sir Gilbert had kept her going.

It was the thought of those treasured, fleeting moments that filled her with courage now. 'Oh, but they are, sir,' she dared to reply even in Lady Ashcroft's presence. 'I made them myself this afternoon.'

'Really?' Sir Gilbert's eyebrows lifted. 'When you've so much to do with Mrs D in bed with flu? Well, I reckon you're up to Mrs D's standards, wouldn't you agree, Mother? You've done so well, Anna, and worked so hard with all our guests that I think you should have some time off, even if we are a man down on the staff, so to speak.'

'Really, Gilbert, that is just the time—'

'Oh, come, Mother!' he interrupted persuasively. 'Poor girl looks quite exhausted. Tomorrow afternoon, instead of preparing some ridiculous evening meal we can easily do without, Anna must have a few hours to herself.'

Oh, good Lord. Anna could feel her cheeks turn pink. 'Oh, but, sir...' she stuttered, hot with embarrassment.

'No, I insist. Surely we can survive on a cold evening meal for once? There must be enough cheese and cold meats and pickles left to feed us for weeks, if I know Mrs D. Isn't that so, Anna?'

'Oh, well, yes, I suppose there is,' she mumbled, averting her eyes.

'That's settled, then,' she heard Sir Gilbert declare since she dared not look at him again.

'Will ... will that be all for now, Lady Ashcroft?' she asked the carpet.

'Yes, child. We'll ring when we wish you to clear. And I must say that you do seem to be coping very well without Mrs Davenport. Well done, Anna.'

Well, that was praise indeed! Anna bobbed a half curtsey and scuttled out of the room. She closed the door quietly behind her and then stood for a moment to gather herself together. She felt all hot and flustered, and waited for the sensation to

104

drain away. But in its place rose a warm contentment as her thoughts settled on Sir Gilbert and the attention he appeared to be paying her.

Three hours she was to have to herself.

After two weeks of working almost non-stop from the minute she rose at the crack of dawn to the moment she fell exhausted into bed at night, three hours seemed to stretch ahead like blissful eternity. Escape. It was the fourth of January and bitterly cold, but there was no question in her mind. Wrap up warm and go for a nice long walk on the moor.

The sky was heavy with iron-grey, slightly jaundiced clouds that raced overhead. The raw, angry wind bit into Anna's face and she pulled her scarf up over her mouth and nose as she set off down the driveway. She must walk briskly, she decided, or she would surely freeze to a lump of ice. And she must also be careful. To walk alone on a remote part of the moor when the weather looked as if it could be closing in would be foolhardy. Already tiny pinpoints of white dust were being blown about in the air, scurrying in little swirling eddies where the wind caught them up against the stone walls that lined the roadside on that part of the moor. If it came on to snow properly, she might get lost, and so, reluctantly, she decided to keep to the road.

The one direction she hadn't been in as yet was up towards Postbridge. She had heard it was quite a beauty spot, with the road crossing the East Dart on an old stone bridge, while just a few yards downstream, the river was also spanned by an ancient clapper bridge made of three granite slabs resting on stone pillars. It was known as a favourite spot for tourists to explore, enjoying their summer picnics on the grassy bank. It might not be quite so inviting today, but it was a suitable place for Anna to aim for, although she wasn't at all sure she would get that far.

The road towards Princetown was now so familiar that she could walk along it blindfold. She dutifully kept to the right-hand verge facing the traffic, not that there was much on such a rotten day as this! The moor appeared at its bleakest, almost in monochrome, the bare twigs of hawthorn bushes and even the pine plantations black against the pewter sky. Even the hardy sheep and ponies seemed to have disappeared. Sheltering from the wind in hidden pockets or crouching against the stone walls if they had any sense!

Anna wondered if she wasn't being a trifle silly to go out in such weather, but despite the blustering wind, she was enjoying her walk. Release, freedom, the sense of peace that always invaded her heart when she was on the moor, even, to her surprise, on such a wintry afternoon as this. The sense of being close to her mum, even though when she had been evacuated and her mum had come to visit her, there had never been enough time to go up on the moor together. And Anna felt so close to her there, as if her mum was floating in that great open sky above her, and was listening to every thought that passed through her head.

She was approaching the isolated hotel nestling beside the river at Two Bridges, but instead of dropping down to the bridge, Anna turned sharp right onto the Moretonhampstead Road. The moor on her left swept up to stark tors or rocky outcrops, while to her right, it rolled far away into the distance. Anna found herself imagining what it must have been like to live up there in the days before cars and lorries, and when there were no telephone wires strung out across the open wastes to connect you to civilisation. You must have felt cut off from the rest of the world, Anna mused, and yet those stalwart people would have known nothing else. She even remembered seeing on her map the ruins of an old gunpowder factory not far from the road, with buildings and chimneys scattered along the Cherry Brook and across the hillside beyond.

Ashcroft Hall would probably have been different then, too, with far more servants at the beck and call of whoever had lived there. And without electricity, life as a servant would have been even more difficult with candles and lamps to light and keep clean. Would the servants have been completely downtrodden, or would there have been a kind master like Sir Gilbert?

Her heart began to dance a little waltz in her chest at the thought of those bright, teasing eyes and slow, languid smile. He was quite the most handsome young man she had ever seen, she was sure, and the most gentlemanly. He didn't treat her as a servant to be bossed around like some sort of inferior thing, but appreciated her hard work and wasn't afraid to say so. In fact, if it hadn't been for Sir Gilbert, Anna would have been thoroughly fed up and miserable!

He worked hard, too. Although he emerged from

the study for morning coffee and afternoon tea, he was constantly on the telephone or typing business letters. With two fingers, she chuckled to herself, from the slow, deliberate ping she sometimes heard as she passed the door. If only she had already done her secretarial course, she could have offered to do it for him and then, who knew what might come of their relationship? But, oh dear, what a ridiculous thought. And yet...

She had been so absorbed in her ponderings, her head down against the gale, that she hadn't realised that the snow was falling hard and fast now in large flakes rather than as powder, and was quickly settling on the ground. She looked and a little gasp caught in her throat. She was engulfed in a driving curtain of white that raced past her in vicious shafts and stung her upturned face. And the vast, wild expanse of the moor was rapidly being obliterated from sight by a savage, blinding veil.

Anna stopped dead, and slowly turned around. What an idiot not to have noticed! She could see but ten yards ahead of her, and it was suddenly getting dark. And other than the howl of the wind, there was not another sound, no sign of life. She was all alone out on the moor in what was becoming a blizzard.

Oh, crikey. Her heart gripped in panic and began to beat painfully. Thank goodness she had kept to the road and could follow it back without too much trouble. But as she trudged along, the wind was whipping about her, determined to knock her over, it seemed. She was getting cold with a nervous sweat down her back and her face

108

turning numb. Perhaps if she thought of Ethel it might help. Her dear friend would be at work, of course, serving customers in the kitchenware department; china, glass and cutlery shining in the bright lights of Dingles store. Later, Ethel, too, would have to find her way home, probably catching a bus through the dark streets. Anna imagined her opening her front door to a fug of smoke. Mabel'd be standing in the kitchen in her curlers and slippers, cigarette drooping from her mouth as she stirred some greasy stew on the stove.

Anna's own home would hardly be as welcoming. Her dad would return to an empty house, and Anna felt a pang of guilt. A need of those familiar surroundings. But she couldn't go back. Not now. It would never be the same again. Her mum was dead, and her dad, well, who knew?

Oh, what were those four dazzling lights coming towards her through the gloom? She had better step up onto the grass verge if she didn't want to be run over. Any driver out this weather would be concentrating on peering through the lashing snow and wouldn't be expecting to come across a pedestrian!

The vehicle crawled towards her. At each sweep of the wipers, the windscreen cleared but was at once splattered with snowflakes again. Anna stopped to wait for the car to pass, but all of a sudden, she recognised the long, sleek bonnet. Somehow she wasn't surprised when the car drew to a halt beside her and the passenger door opened.

'There you are!' Sir Gilbert's voice called as he leant over from the driver's seat. 'Thank goodness I found you! Hop in.'

Anna was overcome with relief. She jumped into the car without hesitation, her pulse racing now not with apprehension but with excitement! 'Oh, thank you, sir! I didn't realise I'd gone so far, and the snow started so suddenly. You didn't come looking for me especially, did you?'

'Of course I did,' he smiled, putting the car into gear and smoothly moving forward. 'When I heard you'd gone out in this, I had to, didn't I?'

'Oh, that's terribly kind of you!'

'Not at all. I felt responsible,' he answered without turning head as he concentrated on the road. 'After all, I was the one who insisted you took the afternoon off.'

'But I didn't have to come out in this, did I? I'm sorry, sir.'

'Don't be,' he replied lightly. 'I'm grateful for any excuse for a spin. Now, let's find somewhere to turn round.'

With the soft roof of the car in place, it felt really cosy. It was beautifully fitted out inside, and Anna could understand why Sir Gilbert was so proud of it.

'It's a lovely car,' she said appreciatively as they headed back in the opposite direction. She knew absolutely nothing about cars, but it would please Sir Gilbert to show some interest. And how her heart ached for him to like her even more than he evidently did already!

'Yes, she is,' he agreed heartily, his voice brimming with pride. 'A Jaguar XK120. So called because she can do a hundred and twenty miles per hour. Best money can buy in my opinion. It's a privilege to own her.'

'Well, then, I'm most privileged to be riding in her! I suppose it's a bit like being rescued by a knight in shining armour on a big white horse, except it's a gleaming sports car instead!' Anna grinned back.

There was a second's pause when Anna thought miserably that she had offended him, but then Sir Gilbert burst out laughing.

'I'm flattered,' he chuckled, slowing even further as they reached the junction. 'Do you drive?'

'Good Lord, no. Even my father doesn't. People can't afford cars where I come from. Oh! Shouldn't we have gone the other way?'

'To go home, yes. But if we go back, you'll start working again and we can't have that. So I thought I'd take you for afternoon tea at the Two Bridges Hotel.'

'Oh.' Anna was so stunned that for a moment or two she couldn't think of anything else to say. Sir Gilbert Ashcroft taking her for tea at a hotel! 'Oh, but ... dressed like this? And I'm wearing my wellies–'

'I've got your shoes in the boot.'

'What?' Anna gasped in bewilderment, not knowing what to think.

'Well, once I realised what had happened, I thought it would be a shame to waste your afternoon off.'

Anna shook her head with a smile. He was a one, Sir Gilbert. Happiness, elation began to bubble up inside her as he parked the car in front of the hotel. She quickly changed to her shoes and then, as they struggled the few yards to the main entrance, Sir Gilbert protectively took her arm. As if

111

she was his ... his... Anna almost felt giddy as the exquisite thought sizzled through her mind.

Five minutes later, they were served tea on a silver tray. Anna couldn't believe it. She was being treated as if *she* were the lady, the waitress nodding deferentially as she left them to it.

'I bet those scones aren't as good as yours,' Sir Gilbert said in a low voice, and one of his merry eyes winked at her.

'Oh, sir,' she mumbled, flushing with embarrassment.

'No, it's true. You seem to be so good at everything, Anna. Far too good to be working as a servant in my mother's household. So why did you leave school to come and work here when you're so intelligent? And do drop the "sir", at least when we're alone together.'

Anna was sure she blushed, but *Gilbert* was so relaxed and casual that she felt her confidence growing. She found herself telling him everything. Well, not quite *everything*. She didn't relate her father's part in her mum's death, or his violent threats towards herself. She simply told him that her father had said it was time she went out to work, and that after the shock of her mum's tragic death, she had felt the need to get away for a while, and this was the only way she could afford to do so.

'Poor little Anna,' Gilbert commented quietly when she had finished. 'Well, I will have to make your time at Ashcroft Hall a happier one, won't I? We must get to know each other better, and then who knows what the future might hold?'

Anna paused as she lifted the delicate teacup and saucer, and had a job to stop her hand from shaking. Whatever did he mean by that? It was clear that he liked her, but surely he wasn't suggesting that their relationship might develop into something more? Oh, goodness. But he was a baronet and she was a servant. And yet, this was 1955. Two world wars had levelled out society to a great extent, and she considered herself as good as anyone else.

'But I know so little about you,' she answered cautiously. 'I've told you all about me, but all I know is that you're a baronet and you live in a house in London and sometimes come to visit your mother at Ashcroft Hall.'

'Ha, ha!' Gilbert threw up his head with a soft laugh. 'Don't let the baronet thing fool you! We're not aristocracy, though my mother would have you think we are. No. Our family roots were never so grand. My great-grandfather was awarded his baronetcy in Queen Victoria's time for services in engineering. Marine engineering, in fact. In the time when steam-driven ships were developing apace. Anyway, if your father's a baronet, you can *claim* his title when he dies. It's a costly business and I wasn't fussed to be honest, but Mother insisted.'

'Is that still the family business, then, marine engineering?' Anna asked, becoming intrigued. 'So all those letters and phone calls, you're still running the business even when you're down here?'

'To a large extent, yes. But I do have some old and trusted managers who helped me a lot in the first place, especially when Father died. The business side of things, at least. I studied engineering at university so I was already fully qualified on the production and design front. We make parts for ships' engines, you see. For the Royal Navy as well as merchantmen, so we really played our part in the war.'

'You have your own factories, then?'

'Several. We supply all the main shipbuilders in Britain, and we export, too, of course.'

'You ... you must be very rich, then,' Anna considered, quite crestfallen. It accentuated the difference between them too much.

'Yes, very. But I still had to do my National Service. I did it just after the war, between school and university. But because of our connections with the Royal Navy, my father wangled me an admin job with the Admiralty, so I never even went abroad, thank God.'

'That was lucky. My best friend back in Plymouth has a young man. But he's eighteen, so he could be called up any time and he could be sent anywhere. Ethel will be brokenhearted.'

'Well, at least you know when it's going to end. Not like during the war. And then there was a strong chance that you wouldn't be coming home at all.'

His tone was suddenly so different from his usual roguish banter. Anna felt herself swell with emotion. Gilbert was everything she could want in a man: intelligent, a hard worker, kind, thoughtful, and yet with a strong sense of honour. That he was handsome and well off were bonuses. And the fact that he was showing such interest in her was a gentle balm mending her sorely tried spirit. Every cloud had a silver lining, the old saying went. Well, she would only ever see the loss of her dear mum as a tragedy that had shredded her heart. But coming to Ashcroft Hall, and the humiliation and unhappiness she had suffered there, would all have been worthwhile if something came of her relationship with Gilbert!

As they sat there, sipping tea in the hotel, it seemed to hit her between the eyes. She was falling in love, a new and exciting experience that tingled out to her fingertips. Suddenly she could have shouted with the joy of it.

'Well, I think we'd better get back while we still can,' Gilbert announced. 'It's coming down thick and fast. I hope we can still get up the hill.'

Oh, Lord. Anna kept her fingers crossed as she sat quietly in the passenger seat while Gilbert concentrated hard on driving up the steep hill with the perfect amount of acceleration for the tyres to grip without spinning fruitlessly in the deepening snow. Gilbert was obviously a skilled driver, though he puffed out his cheeks in relief when they reached the relatively flat road that would take them back to Ashcroft Hall.

It was pitch-black outside now, with not another soul on the road. The streaming snowflakes glittered eerily in the powerful beam from the Jaguar's headlamps. It really was a blizzard now, and unused as she was to travelling by car, Anna was aware when the tyres slid slightly on the treacherous surface. The road ahead was inches deep in snow and had merged into the grass.

All of a sudden, the inky sky was ripped in two by a jagged dagger of brilliance that for an instant revealed the pearly wilderness that surrounded them. A split second later, a great boom exploded overhead, and Anna let out an audible gasp.

'Good God.' Gilbert's voice beside her was flat with astonishment. 'You don't get that very often. Thunder and lightning *and* a blizzard.'

It was certainly something. But with Gilbert beside her, Anna didn't feel afraid. The storm flashed and raged around them, but before too long, they were safely back at the Hall.

As she went to get out of the car, Anna felt Gilbert's hand on her arm, and the sensation fizzed through her body.

'Better not say anything about having tea,' he said quietly. 'Mother might not quite approve.'

A little cloud passed over Anna's euphoria, but she quickly thrust it aside. No, he was right. If anything was to develop between them, they would have to break it gradually to Lady Ashcroft. And anyway, it was quite romantic, having a secret relationship. 'All right,' she agreed at once.

'And, Anna, I'm going back to London in the morning.'

'Oh.' Her elation deflated like a pricked balloon. But she knew he would have to go back soon, didn't she? 'Thank you again for rescuing me,' she said with a forced smile as she scrambled out of the car.

The blizzard continued all night. Anna awoke the following morning to a magical, twinkling ivory ocean as far as the eye could see. And she rejoiced. They were snowed in and it would be some time before Gilbert could return to London after all!

Chapter Nine

'You'm proper keen on that Sir Gilbert fellow, bain't you?'

Anna looked up sharply from stirring her cup of tea. It was late March, and the first time Ethel had managed to come up and see her since before Christmas. It had been a hard winter, the snow from the January blizzard lying thick and deep for weeks on end, only to be followed by more snowstorms earlier in March.

Anna shrugged, trying to appear casual and noticing the condensation streaming down the windows of the café. 'Well, he's the only one in the place who treats me like a human being,' she said somewhat guardedly since Ethel's suspicions had obviously been aroused. 'Actually, that's not quite true,' she admitted, though as much to put Ethel off the scent. 'Lady Ashcroft's quite nice to me nowadays, especially if we're alone for any reason. But when we were snowed in, it would have been *awful* if Sir Gilbert hadn't been snowed in with us. There was no escape, you see. You couldn't even get into the garden.'

'Really?' Ethel bit into her slice of Victoria sponge. 'Mmm, this is good. Mum's cooking's so bad I likes to make the most of it when I goes out.'

Anna couldn't help but smile as Ethel smacked her lips, but then she went on excitedly, 'It was quite an adventure, all that snow. Mr Jackson and

Sir Gilbert gradually dug us out, leaving me in sole charge of the entire house.'

'Oh, how come?'

'Mrs Davenport was in bed with flu. I quite enjoyed being housekeeper, actually. And I helped Sir Gilbert clearing the drive as well. Mr Jackson had to give up. Did his back in. So it was just Sir Gilbert and me. It was jolly hard work, but I did enjoy it. And we had lots of fun. We made a snowman and had snowball fights and...'

She paused, realising she was letting her tongue run away with her while Ethel observed her dubiously. 'It took over a week to clear a way to the road,' she concluded more sombrely, 'and another before the roads were clear enough for Sir Gilbert to get his sports car out and drive back to London.'

She waited as Ethel nodded and swallowed the delicious morsel in her mouth. And then she met Anna's eyes steadily. 'You fancies 'en, doesn't you?'

Ethel's gaze was so fixed that Anna had to take a grip on herself. 'Like I said, he makes my life at Ashcroft Hall more bearable. Without his visits, I think I'd have left by now.'

'Yes, I bets you would. You cas'n fool me, Anna. Us've known each other most of our lives. You lights up like a beacon when you talks about 'en.'

'No, I don't.'

'Oh, yes, you does.' Ethel's face had taken on that obstinate look Anna knew so well. 'You be careful, my maid. I knows you'm from a better class than me, on your mum's side leastways, an' far cleverer an' everything, like. But folk like us doesn't mix with folk like 'en. Seemed funny at first when it were just a joke, but if you'm getting serious, like, well, you'm playing with fire, you knows.'

A little voice at the back of Anna's mind told her that Ethel was right to be cautious, but then she hadn't met Gilbert, had she? If she had, she'd have known differently. 'Oh, Sir Gilbert's not like that,' she assured her friend. 'But, honestly, there's nothing between us, I promise.'

Even as she spoke, she was mentally crossing her fingers. There was, in fact, very definitely something between her and Gilbert. It felt very much like an electric charge whenever they were in the same room together. They had to hide it in front of everyone else, of course, but when they were alone, they were like friends. More than friends.

The best time had been when they had been clearing the drive and had stopped to play in the snow. At one point, she had slipped over, twisting her ankle slightly so that she hadn't been able to pick herself up straight away. Gilbert had shot over to her, kneeling in the snow beside her. He had helped her to her feet, his arm tightly around her. She had relished his closeness, holding on to him while she hopped on one leg until the pain had subsided. It was only a mild sprain, but seemed to have furthered their relationship, and she was pleased it had happened, despite the discomfort. And when Gilbert had finally been able to set out for London, he had given her a peck on the cheek when no one else was around. She had gazed into his smiling eyes, and her heart had turned a cartwheel of joy that was only dampened by her sadness at his departure.

He had returned for a long weekend near the end of February, and Anna had dreamily prepared his room, lovingly smoothing the sheets as she made his bed. When he had burst into the entrance hall with his usual hearty call, she'd had job to stop herself running from the kitchen and into his arms. Instead, she had waited until he had gone upstairs, and then scooted up to his room with the excuse that she had forgotten to put out the towels.

Anna saw his face light up as she came in.

'Anna, how jolly good to see you again! Here, let me take those.' He duly removed the towels from her arms and dumped them on the bed. 'Let me see you properly. Well, you're certainly looking well. I've missed your chirpy little face!'

Anna couldn't believe her ears and blinked at him in delicious amazement. 'I've missed you, too,' she ventured coyly, and the next moment found herself crushed in a tight hug while her heart tripped along in delight.

'You're just as beautiful as I remember,' he whispered, his voice suddenly ragged. 'That little snub nose, that lovely mouth, and those eyes.' He tipped his head to one side and frowned. 'You know, I can never work out quite what colour they are, blue or brown. I'm sure they change with the light. So, I shall call them smoky. My Little Smoky Eyes!'

He tossed his head with a light laugh, and Anna had smiled back. She could see it all so clearly again as she nodded reassuringly at Ethel across the table.

'Anyway, tell me about you and Bert,' she

120

neatly changed the subject. 'Have you heard from him since he was called up?'

'Yes. 'E's being sent out to Germany, like, an' 'e won't get 'ome leave for, I doesn't know, six months or more.'

'Oh, dear.' Anna's voice rang with sympathy, and she sought a way to cheer Ethel up. 'But I'd have thought Germany would be a relatively safe posting, so it's not all bad. And you can write in to Jean Metcalfe and get him a mention on *Two-Way Family Favourites*.'

'Yes, I suppose so,' Ethel grunted, obviously unimpressed.

'It'll probably go quicker than you think,' Anna tried to encourage her. 'And if you both save hard, you can get married as soon as he comes home, if that's what you both want. And he's bound to get his job back on the railways, so there'll be nothing to stop you, will there?'

And by then, Anna herself would have been able to prove her worth to Lady Ashcroft and perhaps she and Gilbert would be married, too, as it looked as if things were going that way. And she hugged to her heart the memory of the soft kiss he had placed on her lips just before he had left for London again.

'It's your afternoon off today, isn't it?' Gilbert asked as they met by chance in the upstairs corridor by the door to the servants' staircase. Or perhaps it wasn't quite by chance, Anna suspected gleefully. 'And what is my Little Smoky Eyes going to do with herself?'

Anna's brow puckered with curiosity. 'Go for a

walk, I expect. It's such a lovely day.'

'Indeed it is. I wouldn't mind a walk myself.' Gilbert glanced furtively about him and then brought his gaze back to Anna's. 'Wait for me at the end of the drive,' he instructed in a low voice. 'Now get along before you're missed.'

Anna's mouth spread into a broad smile. Oh, that would be super! She'd had to contain her jubilation at Gilbert's visit, which hadn't been easy under everyone's nose. He would be saying for a whole week and she would relish every minute!

She duly waited, skulking behind the last tree of the drive and admiring the drifts of daffodils beginning to open their heads in the spring sunshine. If anyone came along, she would pretend she had stopped to see to something in one of her wellingtons. Her heart had taken wing at Gilbert's invitation. A walk on the moor would be so romantic! She had never been in love before, and the sensation was exquisite, overwhelming. To think that the tragedy of her mum's death had brought her to the man of her dreams was ... well, she wasn't quite sure what. She only knew that her mum would have been so happy for her.

The thought cast a shadow over her present pleasure and set her mind on what Ethel had told her when they had met me some weeks previously. There had never been any trouble from her dad, Ethel had said. He appeared a reformed man, going to work each day and evidently holding down his job. A pang of guilt pierced Anna's side. Perhaps she should try get a whole day off and at least go to visit him. But then he might try to follow her back here and she didn't want anything to spoil her happiness. So perhaps she should wait until her future with Gilbert was secure before contacting her dad again.

The sound of a car coming along the drive banished all thoughts of her dad from her mind. She peeped out from behind the tree to see Gilbert in his beautiful sports car. She stepped across the verge and he stopped to let her in.

'Oh, I am looking forward to this,' she grinned as she settled herself in the passenger seat, and nearly squealed with joy when he leant over to kiss her briefly on the mouth. Her lips tingled and she had to look out of the windscreen to hide her flush of elation as Gilbert turned out onto the road. 'Just a pity we have to keep things secret for now,' she flustered in attempt to conceal her feelings, 'but I suppose there'll be time enough to tell your mother about us.'

Gilbert didn't reply as he concentrated on negotiating the right turn onto the Moretonhampstead road. You went back on yourself as well as going sharply uphill which, although Anna didn't drive, looked quite tricky so she shouldn't expect Gilbert to talk at the same time. But once they were bowling along again, she asked brightly, 'Where are we going?'

'Ah, ha, wait and see!' he teased. 'Just enjoy the view. Not that the moor's at its best just now. Still yellow from the winter, but it'll soon green up if this nice weather continues.'

Anna nodded in agreement and swivelled her gaze out of window again. A short way from the road on her left, she noticed a row of tumbledown buildings, a couple of old chimneys, and

strung out across the opposite hillside three sub-
stantial-looking ruins, remains of the gunpowder
mills she had seen on her map, she supposed.

'We must be nearly at Postbridge and the clapper bridge,' she observed as they left the ruins
behind. 'That's where I was aiming for the day the
blizzard set in. I've not tried going back since.'

'I thought as much, so we'll have a quick stop
there so you can see it, but then I thought I'd take
you somewhere else even more fascinating a bit
further on.'

'I can't wait!' Anna sang back.

They spent ten minutes at the pretty spot on the
river, standing side by side on the ancient bridge
and absorbing the peace and quiet. Anna suddenly
felt Gilbert cup her chin and turn her face towards
his. Her knees turned weak and she closed her
eyes as he brushed his lips against hers, sending
ripples down to her stomach. Oh, there was a need
in her, something she didn't understand, but she
was ready to let it swamp her like a tidal wave.

Back in the car, they zoomed along the gently
undulating road, only slowing to avoid a flock of
sheep wandering across the tarmac. The scenery
was stark and magnificent, but to Anna it was
one joyous blur.

'Look over there,' Gilbert's voice cut through
her reverie just as they passed the Warren House
Inn on the left. 'See that giant ring on the
hillside? That's where we're going. Grimspound.
It was an ancient village, Bronze Age, I think.'

'Really?' Anna strained her neck to look out of
the driver's window. 'How interesting! And there
are lots of even older things on the moor as well,

aren't there? Stone rows and circles and things.'

'Certainly are. 'Tis a mysterious place indeed,' Gilbert said, mimicking a Devonshire accent.

Anna chuckled, feeling she would burst with rejoicing. She shared so much with Gilbert, and this love of the moor which enchanted and sparked the imagination was the crowning glory.

Grimspound was amazing, a vast stone wall that would have protected the ancient village's livestock as well as its little round houses. They sat inside one of them, or at least the stone foundations that survived, imagining they were cooking over an open fire.

'Here, woman, eat,' Gilbert barked, passing some imaginary item of food to her. 'We eat, then children eat.'

Anna grinned back. 'How many do we have?'

'Twelve at the last count.'

Anna roared with laughter as they sat and enjoyed the fresh air on that mild spring day, happy and relaxed. Later they strolled back to the car, holding hands. Anna was sure she was in heaven, basking in blissful paradise. And this was just the beginning.

'Oh, good Lord! Your mother's had a stroke?' Anna looked from her bowl of creamy porridge the next morning with a cry of sympathy. 'Where does she live? You must go to her straight away.'

'How can I?' Mrs Davenport snapped back, her drained face regaining its colour. 'I can't leave Lady Ashcroft, especially when Sir Gilbert's here!'

'Yes, of course you can,' Anna insisted. 'And you must. Lady Ashcroft will understand, and I know

Sir Gilbert won't mind. Mr Jackson and I can manage, and Mrs Smudge, of course. We might have to cut corners and things might not be done to your high standards,' she put in persuasively, 'but I'm sure we can muddle through. Your mother is far more important.'

She spoke the words with conviction. Oh, yes. It might be Mrs Davenport's last chance to be with her mother. Anna felt she had to persuade her to go. She herself would have given the earth to have had the chance to say a proper goodbye to her mum.

In the event, Lady Ashcroft insisted that Mrs Davenport should leave immediately, and even instructed Mr Jackson to drive her right to Plymouth's main North Road Station to catch the train for London where her family lived. Anna felt deeply sorry for her, but she had to admit that the tensions below stairs were much relieved the moment the housekeeper had left. And what Anna had said to Ethel was indeed true. She really had enjoyed being in charge the week when Mrs Davenport had been in bed with flu. She recognised, though, that she would never have been able to run the kitchen without all that she had learnt from the older woman since she had come to Ashcroft Hall nearly five months ago now.

Taking her other half day off that week would be impossible with all the extra work, but she did manage to sneak a short walk with Gilbert one morning, her heart spilling over with the new and blithe sensation of being in love. And on the Thursday afternoon when Mr Jackson was driving Lady Ashcroft to her dressmakers somewhere in

126

Exeter, Anna sang to herself as she made preparations for the evening meal. Gilbert was at work in the study and Anna would not disturb him. But when all was ready, the boeuf bourguignon simmering slowly in the range oven, all vegetables prepared and the ingredients for the lemon meringue set out in separate bowls, Anna went up to Lady Ashcroft's room to make the bed which she hadn't had time to do earlier.

The room smelt wonderfully of subtle, expensive perfume which Anna breathed in deeply as she smoothed the soft, cotton sheets, taking pride in making the bed look perfect. And then, just for a few moments, she went to look out of the window and over the moor which was fresh and inviting in the continuing spring sunshine.

'Lovely view, isn't it?' Gilbert's voice behind her made her jump.

Anna felt a sudden sparkle of pleasure as she turned to face him. 'Certainly is.' She smiled back, drowning in the intensity of his shining brown eyes. They were standing very close and it didn't surprise her when he dipped his head to kiss her, his mouth warm and moist against hers. An entrancing thrill shot down her spine as he held her against him, his hand entwining in her hair as his kiss became more urgent and passionate.

'You're so beautiful, my Little Smoky Eyes,' he mumbled, tracing his lips down to the well of her throat. 'You deserve much more than this.'

His voice was thick, his words, so full of promise, swirling in Anna's head. She closed her eyes, and when she felt his fingers unbuttoning first her cardigan and then her blouse, she barely flinched as an enraptured desire, an enchantment plunged down to her loins and she allowed Gilbert to lead her to the bed she had just finished making. He lay down beside her, stroking the tops of her breasts and then slipping his fingers underneath her bra.

The sudden, unfamiliar sensation made her sit up abruptly with a sharp gasp. 'Please, Gilbert,' she managed to croak in a tiny voice. 'I've ... I've not done this before. I'm not sure–'

'Sh.' He placed a gentle finger against her lips. 'You do trust me, don't you?'

'Well ... yes ... but...'

'Then don't worry, my love. I'll look after you.'

He gave that caring, handsome smile, and Anna lay down again, still uncertain. But as he tenderly caressed her, the hesitation was forgotten as she became lost in her love for this good, kind man who had given meaning back to her shattered life. The breath quivered at the back of her throat as his hand moved up beneath her skirt. Should she stop him? But that might show she didn't have implicit faith in him. And as some instinct against which she seemed powerless overtook her, the doubt was driven away. She became captivated, bewitched, trusting as Gilbert slowly made love to her, drawing her on to the dizzy heights of some halcyon world she had never dreamt existed. Her body responded in glorious ecstasy, and when it was over, she lay curled up in his arms, safe and secure.

'Oh, my lovely Anna,' Gilbert murmured into her hair.

She lifted her head and smiled up at him. 'I do love you,' she whispered back.

'Yes, I know you do,' he answered languidly, dropping a kiss on her forehead. 'But we'd better get this room straight before my mother gets back.'

'Oh, God, yes!' She jumped up, straightening her clothes. But Gilbert caught her by the arm and pulled her back to him.

'Just one last kiss,' he smiled, and she melted against him once more.

*

Chapter Ten

Vince Millington's eyes swept about the clean and tidy room. Freda would have been proud of the way he kept the house. He owed it to her. Not a day went by when he didn't curse himself for what had happened. He couldn't believe he was responsible for her death. It was all a bit of a haze, but it had definitely been an accident. She had fallen because of him, yes, but he hadn't deliberately pushed her down the stairs. He had *loved* her, for God's sake, and his guilt was ripping him apart.

He blamed those damned headaches. They had been getting worse and worse, unbearable, driving him out of his mind. Turning to drink, getting paralytic, was the only way to blot out the pain, but once he had slept it off, his head thumped even worse. And then he had frightened his Anna, the only thing left in his life, so much that she had run away. But he was terrified that he would be convicted of manslaughter, banged up in some horrible prison cell whose walls would lean in on him, crushing his head even further, just as they had in the collapsed building.

Finding Anna's note was like being doused in icy water. He'd been to the pub on his way back from work and was already in a foul mood when he'd come home to the empty house. Staggering across to Number Sixteen in a maddened rage, well, he'd done it without thinking. But Fred Shallaford's words had cut through his drunken stupor.

He hadn't touched a drop since. Instead, he had stocked up on aspirin tablets. They didn't have quite the same effect and he couldn't lose himself in blissful oblivion, but he found if he took a double dose and went to bed, after a good sleep, he usually felt better. If only he could have Anna back, show her the person he truly was. But he had driven her away, and the feeling of blame was as bad as his crucifying remorse over his Freda.

Time for work now. Each time he went in or out of the front door, he saw her lying there. Oh, damn it! Damn the world, damn fate or whatever it was had brought him to this! There was no bloody way out. He was cursed whichever way looked at it.

He yanked open the front door and collided with the postman who was just about to put some envelopes through the letter box. Flaming bills, no doubt. But he had accidentally knocked other letters out of the fellow's hands as well, and they had scattered about on the pavement.

'Sorry,' he apologised gruffly.

'Not to worry, sir,' the postman replied jovially as they both bent to retrieve the post.

And then shock sliced into Vince's soul as he

went to pick up an envelope that was very different from the others. He recognised it – and the
handwriting – at once. It was pink with a flower
printed in the bottom left-hand corner. A little
writing set Freda had given Anna on her last
birthday. And it was addressed to Ethel.

Vince handed the envelope back to the postman and, taking his own post inside, shut the
door again and staggered across to the stairs
where he all but collapsed onto the bottom step.
Good God. He knew it! He had been right all
along. That young vixen had always known where
his Anna was staying. A red surge of anger sprang
up from deep inside and began to throttle him,
and he tore at his collar, ripping the buttons. He
was choking, gasping for breath, shaking his head
in disbelief. Anna had been deceiving him all this
time with the help of that trollop across the road!

For nearly six months now, he had kept house,
stayed off bottle, been as sober as a judge in the
hopes that one day his girl would return. And
now ... well, he'd find her, and he knew how. And
hang that bloody job he'd had to swallow his
pride to keep some days. He could do without it
today. What he needed was a drink.

Anna made Lady Ashcroft's bed as quickly as she
possibly could. Ever since Gilbert had made love
to her there that afternoon back in April, she felt
guilty whenever she went to the room. If he had
taken her to his own bedroom, it might have been
different, but as it was, the whole affair now
seemed tainted. She wasn't exactly sorry. She
loved Gilbert too much for that. But she wished

131

they had waited until they were married.

If only Gilbert felt ready to reveal their relationship to his mother. Anna yearned for his next visit, her heart empty and aching. Lady Ashcroft was quite kind to her nowadays, exchanging pleasantries and talking to her in an open and friendly way. Anna felt encouraged and was sure Gilbert had waited long enough. Although Lady Ashcroft might not overenamoured of the situation, Anna was convinced she would soon grow used to the idea. But so far there had been no mention of Gilbert's next visit.

'Lady Ashcroft wishes to speak with you,' Mrs Davenport announced with a disapproving wrinkling of her nostrils one afternoon. 'About her trip to London, I believe.'

A trip to London? It was the first Anna had heard of it. But, ah, yes! That was why Gilbert wasn't coming down! Well, that made sense. She supposed Lady Ashcroft was entitled to go and stay at the family home in London, but it meant that Anna probably wouldn't see Gilbert for another month, and her heart dropped like a stone.

'You wanted to speak to me, I believe, Lady Ashcroft,' she said politely a few minutes later.

'Yes, Anna, dear.' The older woman's tone was so exceptionally amiable that it took Anna by surprise. 'Now do sit down while I explain.'

Anna obeyed, perching on the edge of the chair Lady Ashcroft had indicated. Perhaps... Had Gilbert spoken to her about them at last? If he had, his mother's friendly attitude is certainly encouraging! Anna could have shouted with delight.

'You have shown yourself a good worker,' her

employer went on. 'But you have also proved your intelligence and your integrity in many ways. I may not say very much, but I observe. And I know that my son holds you in high esteem also.'

Her son. Gilbert. Oh. Anna's heart began to beat a nervous tattoo in her breast. Was Lady Ashcroft about to say that she approved of their relationship? Oh, please God, may it be so!

'You may have heard that I am, of course, going to London. And I should like you to accompany me. I had asked Mrs Davenport first because of her seniority, but I am happy to say she declined as she still feels bereft after the loss her mother. And to be honest, I believe you would make far better company for me.'

Anna was tongue-tied with happiness. London! As Lady Ashcroft's companion, personal maid, whatever! And she would see Gilbert again, too! She could scarcely contain the pure joy that rushed through her veins.

'You will even attend the wedding. There will be others in a similar position to yourself, but I will explain all to you, and I am sure I can rely upon you to conduct yourself accordingly.'

A society wedding. Oh, that would be wonderful! 'Of course, Lady Ashcroft. May I ask who's getting married?'

'Why, Sir Gilbert, of course. Did you not know?'

Every muscle in Anna's being froze rigid, the happy smile remaining fixed on her face while her dreams crumbled under her. Gilbert? Getting married to someone else? It couldn't be true! A shard of ice had speared her heart and Anna felt as if she was about to faint. But she mustn't. Lady

Ashcroft mustn't see the sudden agony that had sliced her in two.

'No. No, I didn't,' she somehow managed to drag the words from her suddenly dry throat.

'Well, Mr Jackson and Mrs Davenport know better than to gossip about the private matters of our family,' Lady Ashcroft smiled back. 'And it *has* all been arranged rather hurriedly. The reason being that Lady Francesca's poor father has just been diagnosed with cancer and is not expected to live many more months. He wants to see his only daughter settled before he dies, and this marriage, well, we've been discussing it for years, really. Before Francesca's dear mother died. She's a lovely girl and will soon be all alone in the world, so the sooner the marriage settlement is finalised, the better.'

Anna had sat, numbed with disbelief, as Lady Ashcroft's explanation filtered through to her brain. In one fell swoop, her hopes of a glittering future with the man she loved lay in tatters. She just couldn't comprehend it.

'I ... I don't understand,' she murmured, her lips feeling like rubber. 'You make it sound more like a business arrangement.'

She saw the woman's eyebrows arch in mild surprise but then a wistful smile shadowed Lady Ashcroft's face.

'Gilbert and Francesca have known each other all their lives,' she said with infinite calm. 'It has always been assumed that they would marry. It will be good for both our families. I think Gilbert has dragged his feet slightly, but, well, under the circumstances, he has accepted his duty. You know...'

She broke off, her voice wreathed in sadness, and even through her own tearing anguish, Anna felt compelled to look at her again. Lady Ashcroft's head was held high as she was determined to remain dignified, her expression totally controlled.

'In our world, we are brought up to accept certain things, no matter what our own feelings. My own marriage was more or less arranged, you know. I...' She hesitated, lowering her eyes, but seemed resolved to continue. 'There was someone else, but I did what was expected of me. And I did come to love Sir Hugh. We had a very happy marriage. Which I am sure Gilbert and Francesca will, too. One cannot always follow one's heart's desire. Gilbert understands that. And I believe you are sensible enough to understand it, too.'

Anna blinked at her, still reeling with shock. Had Lady Ashcroft guessed how she felt about Gilbert? How he felt about her? But why torture her by making her go to the wedding? Surely she would not be so cruel? But perhaps it was her way of making Anna accept the situation, just as she herself had evidently once bowed to family pressure.

Somewhere at the back of her mind, Anna felt some sympathy with the woman who sat so regally in the other chair. She might always seem so detached and in control, but had hidden regrets, too. Had spent her entire adult years living a lie. And now, recognising, perhaps, that Anna shared the same pain, she had finally revealed her misery when it was a lifetime too late.

But that was then and this was now. As a young woman, Lady Ashcroft might have given in, but

Anna jolly well wouldn't have done! She'd have fought for the man she loved, but now ... but now... A horrible coldness broke over her. There was nothing she could do, was there? It was all arranged. Why, oh why, had fate been so cruel? Was there any point in trying to speak to Gilbert on the telephone? In trying to talk him out of it? Her heart rose on the crest of some reckless hope, but was instantly dashed to smithereens. If Gilbert was going to rebel, he would have done so long ago.

'Yes, Lady Ashcroft,' she heard herself say. 'Will that be all?'

'Yes, thank you, Anna. And, Anna, I shall expect all I have told you to remain secret between us. I should not have told you had I not felt able to rely upon your complete integrity.'

Their eyes met across the room, sharing some deep compassion. Anna nodded briefly and then walked slowly out the room. She felt oddly calm, her heart numbing as the pain became too deep to bear. Gilbert was lost to her for ever.

He'd had all day for the anger to fester inside him. He'd needed a drink, even though it wasn't yet eight o'clock in the morning. But he hadn't touched a bloody drop since the day Anna had walked out, and there was none in the house. At least, he didn't think there was. He stumbled into the kitchen, flinging open cupboard doors, rifling along the shelves, not caring when he knocked over crockery or sent jars crashing to the floor, smashing open and spilling the contents over the lino. But nothing. Not even a thimbleful of cooking sherry at the bottom of a bottle.

He staggered back, falling against the table, and stared at the scene of destruction. The room looked as if a bomb had hit it. He threw up his head with a bitter, ironic laugh. That was how it had all started, wasn't it, with a bomb? God, his head was beginning to ache already. He felt stifled, suffocating. He must get out. And he groped his way to the front door.

He couldn't catch the bus to work. All those people crowding in on him, happy in their own little lives. Not knowing how he suffered because he had risked his life to save some strangers. And *how* he suffered! It was a bloody living hell. And now his daughter blamed him for his wife's death, and the girl had turned against him. Oh, he *must* find her, talk to her, *explain* to her. She must understand. She was all he had left.

He had wandered the streets, panic, sorrow, hatred and guilt washing over him each in its turn. As soon as the pubs opened at lunchtime, he ordered himself a pint and a chaser, downing them like a man who'd been lost in the desert for days. And he *was* lost. Lost in a desert of emptiness. Loneliness. He *had* to have Anna back.

'No, sir,' the barman's lips loomed in his face. 'You've had enough. You've been drinking ever since I opened, and I'm about to ring the bell for last orders.'

'An' I wan' ... another ... bloody drink!' Vince slurred back.

'Sorry, sir, but I'll have to ask you to leave.'

'I said ... I wan' ... another ... drink!' And he slammed his fist on the bar to emphasise the point.

'Want us to take 'en outside for you, eh, Barry?'

'Get your flaming hands off me! I can find the door myself, thanks very much!'

He lurched outside, knocking over a chair in the process. What could he do now? Go home? No, he couldn't bear it. The empty house. No Freda. No Anna. Silence ringing in his ears. His head was pounding. Torturing. And that young bitch across the road knew how he could get his life back. Get Anna back home where she belonged!

Where was he? Must have fallen asleep. Peered through sore, red-rimmed eyes. If he wasn't mistaken, he was in the park behind their home. Huh! Hardly a home. Not anymore. Just a horrible, mean little dwelling with not even a proper bathroom. If that Fred Shallaford hadn't found them the place, they might've got one of those brand-new council houses with all mod cons!

Those bloody Shallafords! He looked at his watch, blinking his eyes into focus. Nearly half past five. Ethel would be on her way home from work soon. And she knew where Anna was!

He was waiting, alert as a fox, and sprang out in front of her and had her pinned up against the wall before you could say 'knife'. She was staring up at him, eyes wide and bolting with terror. Well, let her suffer. She'd made him suffer enough!

'Where is she?' he spat. 'Where's my Anna?'

Ethel gazed up at him, her face white. 'I-I doesn't know,' she finally stammered.

'Oh, yes, you do! She writes to you! I saw a letter this morning!'

He banged Ethel's head back against the wall and watched her wince and suck the breath through her teeth before she looked back at him.

'The post don't arrive till after I leaves for work,' she retorted, bunching her lips in defiance. 'I really doesn't know–'

'Liar! You've known all along where she is. Now tell me!'

His fist drove into her stomach, for by Christ he'd get it from her. She doubled up, leaning over his arm, and he forced her shoulders up against the wall again. Her face was twisted in pain, eyes screwed shut.

'I doesn't ... know,' she groaned. 'She writes, but she don't give no address, I swears it.'

'Tell that to the marines! Joined at the hip, you two!'

This time, his fist smashed across her face, and there was an ominous crack. Through the black fog of his fury, Vince heard her scream. The force of the blow had bent her over to one side, and when he dragged her back up, blood streaming down from her nose. Vince took her by the shoulders and shook her like a rag doll.

'Now, where is she?' he bellowed in her ear.

He waited, breathing hard, giving her a chance to recover. He could feel her shaking, tears of desperation escaping from beneath her closed eyes.

'I doesn't know,' she moaned, spluttering through the blood that was dripping into her mouth. 'An' if I did, I damned well wouldn't tell *you!*'

That was it! Vince stood back, letting her slide down to pavement. She knew! Of course she knew! In a red flash rage, his boot flew out. He couldn't stop it. Fury overtook him, rampaging

139

through his deranged mind. He had to teach her a lesson! For everything that had happened.

'Hey, what the hell...?'

A man's cry in the evening calm, footsteps pounding towards him, shook Vince from his explosion of anger. He stood back, breathless, gazing in disbelief at Ethel curled up into a ball at his feet as she tried to protect herself. Dear God, what *was* he doing?

He took flight, running down the street. Paused at the corner to glance over his shoulder. The man had stopped, was bending over Ethel. Then another figure joined him and the first man took up the pursuit. Fast on his feet, speeding, catching him up.

Vince catapulted forward, drenched in a sweat of fear. Run, run, get away. Leap onto a passing bus. Out of the maze of backstreets to the main road. Nothing must stop him. If he was caught, he would be done for. Ethel, I'm so sorry. I didn't mean it. I was just so *angry*.

The main road. At last. There was a bus. On the other side, just pulling away from the stop. Salvation. He could easily dodge the traffic. The way was clear, and he blundered out into the road.

The lorry driver saw the man run straight out in front of him, and slammed on the brakes. But he knew it was too late and shuddered at the loud thud.

Mr Jackson looked up in irritation at the repeated ringing of front doorbell, and scowled. 'Who the devil can it be at this hour?'

'Impatient, whoever it is,' Mrs Davenport said.

140

Anna glanced across the kitchen as she put away the last the china dinner service, and watched as Mr Jackson made for the door. Well, it would be nothing to do with her, and she didn't really care. All she could think about was her conversation with Lady Ashcroft earlier that afternoon. She was still dazed, carrying out her duties mechanically. And the truth was slowly filtering into her brain. Gilbert was marrying some other girl. Some stuck-up flibbertigibbet who had stolen Anna's true love because she came from a privileged family. And Anna's life had been shredded into tortured ribbons. What was she to do? How could she get out of going to London with Lady Ashcroft? She couldn't go to the wedding. It would break her.

She didn't lift her head as Mr Jackson came back in. He or Mrs Davenport might see the tears she could feel welling in her eyes.

'Anna,' the butler said brusquely. 'Look sharp. There two policemen to see you. One's an inspector. They're waiting for you in the hall.'

Chapter Eleven

'Come on in, Anna, love. Ethel be still abed, but she's proper fine.'

Mabel's expression was a mixture of warm welcoming and deep compassion, and Anna was so grateful. After all, Mabel could have turned against her after what had happened, but instead

141

her friend's mum had taken her under her fiercely protective wing for the second time in her young life.

'Thanks, Mrs Shallaford. Is it OK if I go up?'

'Of course it is, maid. You'm welcome any time, you knows that.'

Anna nodded and hurried up the narrow, uncarpeted stairs, to Ethel's bedroom. Ethel had only been out of hospital a few days and was propped up on a mound of pillows, noisily working her way through the box of Quality Street Anna had brought her the previous evening. The bruising that had spread from her nose to both her eyes had faded from dark purple to green, and even to yellow on the edges. But when Ethel shifted in the bed, Anna noticed her wince from her cracked ribs and all but cowered with remorse.

'I feel so awful about this,' she muttered, 'and yet you've been so kind.'

'Well, it weren't your fault, Annie. An' there weren't no serious damage to me insides, an' to tell the truth, I doesn't think my mum's fussed over us so much since I were a tacker, so it's quite nice really. I's just sorry I weren't able to go to the funeral.'

'The funeral?' Anna started with surprise. 'My father did this to you, and you wanted to go to his funeral?'

'I wanted to support *you*, Annie.' Ethel's eyes were steady with earnest. ''E *were* your dad, after all. An' you knows what the doctors said arterwards. About the way 'e were. Could've just been severe depression, or summat to do with 'is brain from the war. We'll never know, I s'ppose. But

142

come on. Park your bum on there,' she smiled perkily, patting the bed.

Anna returned her smile somewhat ruefully as she sat down. Ethel hadn't changed, despite the attack. There wasn't an ounce of bitterness in her.

'I'm still so sorry. Especially about your nose.'

Ethel gave a wry chuckle. 'I never were an oil painting, so a slightly crooked conk won't make much difference! An' Bert's mum wrote to 'en to tell 'en what 'appened, an' Bert says 'e'll still love me, an' that's all I cares about. Told 'is CO that I's 'is fiancée so as 'e can 'ave some compassionate leave. Should arrive tomorrow some time.'

Her eyes were brilliant for the first time, Anna reflected, since the assault. Anna smiled back. 'That's great! How long's he got?'

'Just a few days, but it's better than nothing. Won't be able to get up to any hanky-panky, mind. Not that we would anyway,' Ethel added hastily as she turned a shade of pink. 'I means, a kiss an' a cuddle's OK, like in the back row at the pictures. But nort more. Don't believe in proper relations before marriage, us doesn't, neither on us. Shows a lack o' respect for each other, Bert says, an' I agrees. Only wayward strumpets does that kind o' thing.'

The words were spoken with conviction, making Anna's heart buck in her chest. Ethel was nodding adamantly, and Anna prayed that her friend wouldn't be aware of the strangling regret that clawed at her own throat. Ethel must never know her terrible, shameful secret. Ethel was all she had left, and she couldn't lose her now. And yet she felt she had betrayed her on two counts, her father and her affair with Gilbert.

Ethel was nodding, her eyes still bright, and then the happy expression slid from her face. 'What about you, now, Annie? What you'm going to do? You knows we doesn't like you being all alone at your 'ouse. Right welcome you are to come an' live yere with us. You knows Mum and Dad 'ave said so.'

Anna's guilt deepened. This, when she was to blame for everything. 'Yes, I know they have. And I'm very grateful. But I can't possibly accept. I'll ... I'll have to go back. For a little while, anyway.'

'What? Go back to Ashcroft Hall, you means, when they've treated you so bad, like?'

Anna looked down at her hands, playing with them on her lap. 'It's the only thing I can do for the moment. Even if I got a job in Plymouth straight away, I couldn't afford the rent on the house, and Dad left arrears as well. I can settle up with the landlord out of my savings, but I'd rather build them again before I branch out on my own. And life's not *so* bad at the Hall,' she went on with growing assurance. 'Lady Ashcroft's been really good over all this. She said I was to be as long as I needed. Some people in her position mightn't have wanted me back with all the scandal about Dad attacking you all over the papers, but she said none of it was my fault and I'm to go back when I'm ready.'

'She'd 'ave a job to replace someone as good as you, I reckons she meant,' Ethel scoffed. 'An' I bets that Sir Gilbert got summat to do with your decision, too.'

'Sir Gilbert?' Anna's heart fragmented at the

mention of name, but she mustn't let Ethel know of the agony that still tore her apart. 'Oh, he was married last weekend,' she managed to shrug casually. 'In London. You see, I told you there was nothing between us.'

'Oh. Oh, all right, then.' To her relief, Ethel looked quite satisfied. 'But are you sure you won't come an' live with us? I'd love you to.'

With the tension eased, Anna was able to smile broadly. 'Where would I sleep? In the bath – if you had one? And I couldn't stand your mum's cooking.'

She saw Ethel laugh, and then grimace as she held her painful ribs. Oh, dear. Another reminder, and Anna felt ashamed. She had lied to her dear friend again. At least, all she had said was true, but her main reason for returning to Ashcroft Hall was to prove to Ethel – and to herself – that Gilbert meant nothing to her at all anymore.

'You must be Anna,' the clear young voice stated with apparent delight. 'I've heard so much about you.'

I bet you have. The acid words sparked through Anna's brain in a flash of bitterness as she came through the servants' door and nearly bumped into the strange girl who was entering along the upstairs corridor. Anna had deliberately been avoiding the newly-weds who had returned from their honeymoon that afternoon. But she had to see Gilbert's wife sometime, and might as well have a visual image to heap her scorn upon. And so she lifted her head.

Mrs Francesca Ashcroft was a tiny wisp of a

thing, even more petite than Anna herself and certainly not much older. She had the air of someone who appeared lost in this great house, more like a timid maid on her first day of service, and Anna felt her disdain unexpectedly retreating. For a few moments, she was quite deflated and unsure of herself.

'Yes, I'm Anna, Lady Ashcroft.' And then she found herself saying, 'I hope you'll be very happy at Ashcroft Hall.'

'Oh, I'm sure I will be. I haven't been here since I was a child, and it isn't really how I remember it at all! It used to frighten me a bit, but now I can see it's just, well, dowdy and depressing. It could be really lovely, though, if it was updated a bit, don't you think?'

Anna was quite taken aback. 'I – well, I'd never really thought about it,' she stammered. 'I was just about to put these flowers in your room, if that's all right?'

'Oh, aren't they lovely! From the garden, are they?'

'Yes. Mr Smudge–'

'Does he still do the gardening? I remember how kind he was when I was little. Oh, let me open the door for you.'

'Thank you, Lady Ashcroft.'

Anna was overwhelmed. And a touch annoyed. She had wanted to hate this vixen who had taken Gilbert from her. Had wanted her to be haughty and aloof so that she could despise her even more. But Francesca was warm and engaging, and on first impressions, Anna rather liked her. It was so confusing, and Anna felt somewhat ashamed.

146

'Shall I put the flowers on this side table, Lady Ashcroft?' she asked amiably. 'If I put them by the window, they won't last so long.'

'Yes, thank you. Oh, they look perfect there. And so beautifully arranged. Did you do them?'

'Yes, I did, actually, Lady Ashcroft,' Anna answered with a touch of pride.

'I thought so. Gilbert said you were good at flower arranging. In fact, he said you're good at most things and that he reckons Mrs Davenport's a bit jealous because you'd probably do her job better than she does. I've only been here a couple of hours and already I can see she's a right old dragon.'

Her eyes had stretched with innocence, like two sunflower saucers of fine porcelain, Anna thought. As the lady dowager had said, her daughter-in-law was a lovely girl, like a fresh spring breeze, and was totally oblivious to Anna's tortured feelings over Gilbert. Anna vowed at once to make up for any rancour she might have shown towards her.

'She is a bit,' she smiled back. 'But she is very efficient and I've learnt a lot from her.'

'Well, I think you're very generous about her. She said she'd come and unpack for me shortly, but I'd much prefer you to do it. We could do it together. It'd be much more fun. In fact, I'm so glad you're here. It'll be so nice to have someone of my own age to talk to, especially when Gilbert's locked away in the study working. Lady Prue's all right, but I'd like to have you as my friend as well.'

She had taken Anna's hands, her eyes dancing happily, Anna gazed back almost mesmerised. The girl had a magnetic charm, and Anna had a vision of a whirlwind of twinkling stars swooping about the room with her, like in a Walt Disney film. Anna broke into a smile, both at hearing her mistress referred to as 'Lady Prue', and at Francesca's open and endearing manner.

'Of course, Lady Ashcroft. I'd be delighted.'

'Well, in that case, you must drop the "Lady Ashcroft" bit,' she grinned back. 'I much prefer to be called plain "Frankie".'

'How could you, Gilbert?' Anna hissed between clenched teeth. 'You led me on, made me believe there was a future for us. *Seduced* me, for God's sake, when all along, you knew you were about to marry someone else.'

She had found herself unexpectedly alone with Gilbert, and all her tamped-down emotions suddenly erupted in a fountain of anger. She hadn't been feeling too good the last few days, either, and right now she was powerless to hold back the festering rage that boiled up inside her.

'Hang on there, old girl.' Gilbert turned mildly surprised eyes on her. 'When did I ever say I'd marry you?'

Anna stared at him, and gulped, his words striking her beneath the ribs. 'You didn't,' she retorted. 'But you implied that you would. You talked about us having a future together. About telling your mother about us.'

'And I suppose I might have done,' Gilbert shrugged carelessly as he stirred his coffee. 'I *was* very fond of you, and under other circumstances, I might have considered you as a wife. But then there was this thing with Frankie's father. I didn't know that was going to happen, did I? Mother would have been frightfully upset if I'd backed out. She'd never have forgiven me. What was a chap to do? It was always understood that I'd marry Frankie, and I couldn't let her down just when she needed me, could I?'

'Needed you?' Anna shook her head in an agony of frustration. 'That poor girl needs you like a hole in the head!'

'Oh, come now, Anna. She'd have been devastated if I'd turned her down.'

Anna's eyes narrowed to frosty slits. 'For five minutes, maybe. Until she realised what a weak, spineless cad you are. If you'd had any guts, you'd have stood up to your mother long ago. I *was* jealous, you know. Broken-hearted and angry. But now I'm *glad* that you married Francesca because it saved me from it. I'm not jealous anymore. And I feel really sorry for Francesca for being tied to such a treacherous bastard for the rest of her life!'

She watched as his jaw dropped a mile. But she didn't wait for a reply. Instead, she spun on her heel and marched out of room. It would have been satisfying to slam the door, but she mustn't. It would show she had lost control. And for the sake of the gentle, trusting girl who was taking her breakfast in bed that morning, Anna must keep her sordid affair with Gilbert a secret.

That's what it seemed to her now, sordid and dirty. What a fool she had been! But telling Gilbert what she thought of him had been a release. The tension had emptied out of her, but with it, she felt even sicker than before. She couldn't go on like this, her stomach cramped with nerves all the time. She felt so awful, she had just been picking at her food recently. But confronting Gilbert – and realising she was well and truly over him – had set her much more at ease. As if the twisted threads of her life had miraculously begun to unravel.

She squared her slim shoulders resolutely. It was now mid June. She calculated that, in a month's time, she should have saved enough and could hand in her notice. By the end of July, she could be free of Ashcroft Hall and its unhappy memories for ever. Perhaps she would go and stay with Ethel for a week or so until she could find suitable digs, and then take her time looking for a new, better-paid job. Enrol in evening classes when the new term started in September. She didn't have to worry any more about her dad finding her, did she? So she could pick up her life again where she had left off, in Plymouth, among her friends.

The thought filled her with pleasure.

'I shall miss you so much when we go back to London,' Francesca declared in her trusting, childlike way. 'But you'll be here whenever we come to visit, so I'll look forward to it even more. I've rediscovered my childhood love of Dartmoor, but, of course, I want to be near Daddy for ... for as long as I can.'

Her bright, girlish voice trailed off in a sigh of sadness, and Anna saw her lower her eyes. Anna felt a twinge of guilt, for she couldn't tell Frankie that next time she came to stay with her mother-in-law, her new friend would be gone.

'It was like that for me when I came to work here,' Anna said instead, ignoring Francesca's last remark. 'I was evacuated to Tavistock during the war, you know. We used to come up on the moor sometimes. Get the train up to Burrator and have a picnic. Or sometimes there was a special bus excursion up to Princetown and we'd get off somewhere on the way because it was cheaper. Not with my mum, though. She'd had to stay in Plymouth because of my dad. He'd been badly hurt rescuing some people from a bombed building, you see.'

'Yes. Gilbert told me about it. And how your mother died in a tragic accident only last year, and your father … well, just recently. I'm so sorry.'

Anna gave a rueful smile. 'It wasn't quite how you might imagine. Not with my dad, anyway. It was an odd situation.'

'Really? Do you want to talk about it?'

Anna blinked at her and considered. She had to admit that having no one to talk to since coming back to Ashcroft Hall hadn't been easy, especially with the added problem of her torn emotions over Gilbert. No wonder she'd been feeling rough. Unburdening herself to Frankie might help, though she'd have to be careful what she said.

'All right. But I mustn't be long.'

Frankie had already sat down on the edge of the bed, one leg curled up beneath the other, and Anna went to join her. It crossed her mind that it was a bit like being with Ethel. Not that anyone could ever take Ethel's place.

'I was very close to my mum,' she began, pouting her lips to fight the grief that instantly tried to close her throat whenever she thought of her mother. 'I don't suppose I'll ever get over it properly. And I was there when it happened. She

151

was only thirty-nine.' Anna paused, lost for moment in her own thoughts. But then she looked up sharply, brimming over with remorse. 'But you lost your mum, too.'

'When I was little. I've no memory of her whatsoever, so it wasn't the same. But I'm dreading it when ... when... Going through what you are over your mother. And your father, too.'

Anna raised her eyebrows. Despite her juvenile manner, there was a depth in Francesca Ashcroft that reminded Anna in some way of Ethel. It struck her that she was going to miss Frankie, too.

'It was different with him,' she told her, almost apologetically. 'I still don't know how I feel about it. He'd been difficult ever since his injury in the war. His brain was affected, you see. He was a bit of a Jekyll and Hyde afterwards. So we weren't really that close anymore.'

'But he was still your father,' Frankie whispered. And Anna saw tears welling in her lovely eyes. She was thinking of her own dad, wasn't she, and what was to come? Anna instinctively squeezed her hand.

'It won't be easy for you either, but you've got your friends and your new family around you.'

Frankie nodded and sniffed, and Anna saw a light shining in her glistening eyes. 'Yes. And more than anything, I've got Gilbert. He's a wonderful husband, you know. So supportive. I know we've known each other all our lives, but I couldn't have married a better man.'

Anna arranged her face into a smile. A better man! Just now, Anna couldn't think of a more perfidious monster on earth! All her feelings of contempt and disgust rose up again, and she was gripped in another spasm of nausea. Only this time it was overwhelming and she knew she was going to be sick. She sprang up and dashed into the adjoining bathroom before vomiting into the lavatory.

'Oh, Anna, are you all right?' Frankie's concerned tones reached her from the doorway.

Anna straightened up and pulled the chain. Dear Lord, she felt awful, the tears the retching had brought to her eyes running down her cheeks. 'Oh, I'm sorry. Using your bathroom like that.'

'Don't mention it.'

'I think I must have picked up a bug or something,' Anna murmured miserably.

'You should go and lie down for a while. I'll tell them downstairs you're not well. We're all entitled to be ill sometimes, you know.'

'I don't know about that. Mrs Davenport won't be very pleased.'

'Don't worry about it. I'll deal with her.'

Her suddenly firm attitude took Anna by surprise. She was learning that Frankie was a much stronger character than she initially appeared.

'Go on, go up to your room,' Frankie was insisting now. 'Or would you like me to come up with you?'

'No. No thank you,' Anna replied, overwhelmed by her kindness.

'Up you go, then.'

Anna dragged herself up the stairs. Her little room, so cold in winter, was like an oven in the summer heat, despite the open window. She kicked off her shoes and lay down on the bed. Oh, that was better, the nausea passing now that she'd been sick. It must have been something she'd eaten, although no one else had been ill. If she had a little rest, she'd be all right. Just ten minutes and she'd go back downstairs.

She tried to get comfortable, but her chest was so sore and had been for a week or more. She got that sometimes when her period was late. It must be due soon. Trouble was, she was so irregular, she was inclined to lose track. And especially with everything that had happened – Gilbert's marriage, her dad attacking Ethel and then being knocked down and killed by the lorry – it had been the last thing on her mind.

So, when had she last been on? It was ... was ... ages ago. Shortly before she'd made the mistake of her life with Gilbert. Back in April. And it was nearly the end of June.

A cold numbness began to creep through her veins like a slithering evil and she sat bolt upright on the bed. Oh, God. No. Surely it couldn't be? After just that once? A desolate fist tightened in her chest. She was, wasn't she? She was pregnant.

Chapter Twelve

The shock had sent her reeling. It felt unreal, as if this wasn't happening. One of those moments when you feel detached, watching someone else's life and not your own. A sudden emptiness, a shell, devoid of all feeling. And then slowly, her

154

senses had trickled back. Oh, no. *Oh, no.* The words weighed down on her like a black fog from which there was no escape.

Dear God. She shook her head, wanting to throw out the terrible truth, but she couldn't, could she? Fate had played her a dirty trick and now she would have to face the consequences. Just as she thought her life was getting back on track, she had been dealt this devastating blow and now her world lay in splinters at her feet.

What was she to do? Her first thought was to turn to Ethel, but she couldn't. Her parents had been so good to her, but what would they think of her now with – she hardly dared say it – an illegitimate baby on the way? And she knew Ethel's views. What was it she had said? Only wayward strumpets get up to that sort of thing? Oh, Lord, she was all alone now. She would have to face the future on her own. With Gilbert's child.

So, she wasn't entirely alone, was she? Gilbert would simply have to take responsibility for his actions. A new life was growing inside her, and for its sake alone, she must fight. So when she finally found herself alone with Gilbert, she didn't hesitate. He was working in the study one afternoon and when he ordered some tea, Anna made sure she was the one to take it to him.

Her throat dried like desert sand at the sudden opportunity, but it was now or never. She could feel herself shaking as she walked along the below-stairs corridor, darker than ever because of the slab-grey sky that had given nothing but rain all day. But she had to be strong. There was nothing else for it.

Gilbert glanced up, and Anna saw him lean back in the chair and stretch. He had evidently been smoking as he worked. Now he reached out to retrieve a recently lit cigarette that was smouldering in the ashtray and drew on it deeply. Then stretching his hand away, he nonchalantly blew a ribbon of grey smoke towards the ceiling and shot Anna a languid half smile, almost smirking as if ... as if now he'd had what he wanted from her, she meant nothing more to him. The agony of her despair was at once swept aside. He had dishonoured and humiliated her. And now she was going to make him pay.

'Gilbert, we have to talk,' she said as she set down the tray. Her voice was controlled, perfectly polite but dry, and she marvelled at how calm she felt.

'Oh, yes?'

He cocked a casual eyebrow at her, and she wanted to curl her lip.. He wouldn't be so smug when he heard what she had to say!

'Gilbert, I'm pregnant.'

She watched him, waiting for his reaction. His face stilled, then the muscles around his mouth twitched and he suddenly leant forward to stub out his cigarette in the ashtray before lounging back in the chair.

'So? What's it got to do with me?'

His expression was superb, just like a little boy who had been caught red-handed and yet insisted on denying his offence. It made Anna want to laugh with withering contempt, but this was no laughing matter.

'What's it got to do with you?' she repeated

scathingly. 'You're the father, that's what.'

He shrugged, spurring Anna's disdain to a squall of rage, but she must remain in command.

'How do I know that's true?' he scoffed, though she could hear the caution in his voice. 'It could be anyone's.'

'So you admit you slept with me, even though you had no intention of marrying me? And who else am I supposed to have befriended living out here and working all hours? And I'm sure there'd be witnesses to our secret outings, the girl at the Two Bridges Hotel, for instance. But don't worry. I'm not out to make trouble.' She paused, noting the look of relief on his face. What a coward he was. It strengthened her resolve. 'There won't be any scandal. I'll go away. But I'll need an allowance.'

'What?'

'You don't expect me to live on thin air, do you? Or your child?' she retorted. 'Nothing extravagant. Just a moderate allowance so that I can live without worrying where the next meal will come from or how to pay the bills And you can come and see the child whenever you want.'

She stopped then, studying his face. He seemed to be considering her request, even though his expression was somewhat guarded. Her heart took courage.

'I'm sorry this has happened, Gilbert,' she said, her tone softer this time. 'But just set up the allowance and no one will ever know. I swear I'll never tell a living soul who the father is. For Frankie's sake. In the few weeks we've known each other, we've become good friends. She idolises you, and I wouldn't want her to know what a lying cheat you really are.'

She couldn't help the bitter scorn she had lent to her final words but she regretted them instantly. As Gilbert came round to her side of the desk, the eyes she remembered as light and teasing were now livid with anger. She gulped and stepped backwards, but she must stand her ground. She stared up at him, her jaw set.

'Frankie must never, *ever* know!' he growled at her. 'Do you understand?'

She blinked at him, too frightened by his attitude to answer. He must have taken her silence as a refusal, as the next moment he grasped her about the throat. She drew in a squealing gasp, and the image of her parents grappling at the top of the stairs flashed across her mind.

'Do you understand?' he repeated, caution flung to the winds as, in his maddened rage, he raised his voice to a shout. 'If Frankie ever finds out, I swear to God I'll kill you! Got it?'

He shook her until her head spun, his fingers pressing deep into her neck. She tried to nod but it was impossible with his hand choking her. He released her with such a forceful jerk that she staggered backwards with a cry of fear, toppling over a chair that crashed noisily to the floor. She let out a short scream as she fell, landing awkwardly on her back over the piece of furniture. Then, as she began to pick herself up, she saw Gilbert's eyes swivel fearfully towards the door. There were footsteps, and the next instant, the door opened and there was Lady Ashcroft, her face stretched in horror.

'What on earth's going on?' she demanded.

Anna glanced from her mistress to Gilbert, who was standing there dithering and looking so miserable that Anna's contempt spiralled. It was his own fault this had happened. If he had done as she had suggested, no one would have been any the wiser. But now...

Anna dragged herself from the floor. 'He's got me pregnant, that's what,' she spat accusingly. 'Made me believe we'd be married.'

'What?'

'It's a total lie, Mother,' Gilbert babbled evasively.

'No, it's not, and you know it,' Anna sneered back. 'I'm so sorry, Lady Ashcroft. You've been good to me, but your son tricked me. I wanted to go away without anyone knowing. All I wanted was an allowance for the child, and then he attacked me.'

She stood, rubbing her throat and wondering what would happen next. Lady Ashcroft's face was like stone, as if she was trying to absorb the shock of the scene before her, and it was Gilbert who spoke first. He gave a mocking snigger.

'Can you believe it, Mother? The girl's trying to get money out of me. Blackmailing me for something I didn't do.'

Anna caught her breath, feeling as if she had been hit by a sledgehammer. 'But ... but you didn't deny it a few minutes ago,' she stammered.

'Oh, Mother, surely you won't believe–?'

'How dare you!' Lady Ashcroft stepped forward as if she had suddenly come alive. But it wasn't her son she was condemning. Anna shrank back.

She had thought the woman might have accepted the truth. After all, she seemed to have guessed that there had been something between Anna and her son. But, oh, glory! How wrong Anna was.

'How dare you accuse my son of such a despicable act.'

'Oh, yes, it was despicable, all right! Leading me on–'

'Don't you *dare* speak to me like that. Gilbert would never do such a thing!'

Her words were like cruel barbs and she stood up to her full height. Like an indomitable battleship. And Gilbert came to stand at her shoulder. Smirking.

Anna gazed at their united front, and knew she was beaten. Her courage crumbled, but she must make one final attempt.

'No matter how saintly you think Gilbert to be,' she said steadily, 'it really is true. You can believe it or not, but he seduced me, I assure you.'

Lady Ashcroft knotted her lips. 'Get out of my house, you lying little minx. Pack your bags and leave. And don't expect a reference. And if you ever try to extort money from us again, I'll have the police onto you.'

'And perhaps they'd discover the truth.' Anna glowered back. There was nothing more she could do. She raised her chin in the air, her face a picture of composure. She must remain dignified in this, the most dreadful moment of her life, as she made to walk calmly out of the room. But as she stepped around the impenetrable wall formed by Gilbert and his mother, she stopped dead. For Frankie was standing in the doorway, her face as white as

160

a sheet. Dear Lord. Frankie had heard everything.

Anna's heart sickened. 'I'm so sorry, Frankie.' she mumbled wretchedly. 'It happened before I knew he was to marry you. Before I knew you existed. I loved him, and I believed he loved me. Honestly, I did.'

Frankie just stared at her, eyes huge in her pinched face, and automatically stood back to let Anna past. Anna raced up the stairs to her room, blinded by the tears that suddenly spilt down her cheeks. She grabbed all her possessions, stuffing them into her little suitcase, but with the extra garments Mrs Davenport had insisted she acquired, it wouldn't shut. So she threw out all the new clothes even if they had cost her hard-earned cash. At that moment, she really didn't care about the money. And she wasn't going to be needing the clothes again. What she'd need soon was a maternity smock.

She threw one last look about the heartless little room. They had hardly been happy times she had spent there, except when Gilbert... Oh, Mr Teddy! She had nearly left him behind, and now she squashed him into the case. Then she shrugged into her old gaberdine, took a deep breath, and gathering her pride about her, walked regally down the main staircase with her shoulders boldly braced.

They appeared to be waiting for her in the hall, as if they had expected her to make this last show of bravado. Well, she wouldn't disappoint them. She marched up to Lady Ashcroft and dropped her case almost on the woman's feet.

'You owe me a week's wages and a week in lieu

of notice,' she announced coldly.

She heard Gilbert snort and she shot him a despising glance, holding his gaze insolently until she heard Lady Ashcroft's stiff voice behind her.

'Pay her, Gilbert,' she commanded, and Anna wondered if, after all, she knew of her son's weakness but simply would not admit it.

'Oh, er...' But he obediently took out his wallet and withdrew a five-pound note.

'Six,' Anna said levelly. 'It should be six.'

'Oh.'

She waited while he drew out another note, and then snapped it out of his fingers. 'Thank you. It's precious little after what you've done, but it'll have to do.' And then she turned to Francesca who was still quavering by the study door. 'I really am sorry, Frankie, that you had to find out what sort of man Gilbert really is. And I wish you luck.'

She let herself out of the front door, deliberately leaving it wide open. It was strange that no one tried to make her use the servants' door, as if they all secretly acknowledged that she was indeed carrying the Ashcroft heir in her belly. She marched down the steps and out into the pouring rain.

'Anna!'

She had vowed not to look back, but at Frankie's desperate cry, she turned round. The other girl had run out after her, her pretty face creased with emotion.

'Francesca, come back at once! Leave the little trollop to her own devices!'

It was Lady Ashcroft's shouted command that halted her in her tracks. Well, it wouldn't be

Gilbert, would it, Anna scoffed? Gutless creature. Poor Frankie. Her face was distraught as she hesitated, dancing on the spot and glancing back over her shoulder towards the house.

'Take care, Anna!' she called from where she stood.

'And you! Good luck!' And then she muttered under her breath, 'I think you're going to need it as much as me.'

She turned away and began to walk purposefully down the long driveway. The rain was falling vertically as it had all day, with no wind to clear away the heavy clouds that sat over the moor in an immense slate-coloured dome. Anna trudged along, water already dripping from her nose and chin. Dear God, she was angry. Seething. Her fury driving away her despair. If she was to survive – and survive she would if only to show Lady Ashcroft and her precious son – she would have to make plans.

What were her options? Right now, she had little choice but to go to Ethel and call upon her family's generosity yet again. Would they turn her away when they knew the truth? But she needn't tell them. Not until she had sorted out her future. Hers and the child's. Somehow, she would find a way to support them both. She had no idea how, but the first step was to go back to Number Sixteen. To the untidy, disordered house with its world of welcome and Mabel's dreadful cooking. Anna's dishonesty would cut into her conscience, but needs must when the devil drives.

Her shoulders ached from carrying the case, and she dragged herself up the steep hill on the far side

163

of the Two Bridges Hotel. The sheeting rain had cut visibility to a couple of hundred yards, blotting out the view over the glittering thread of the West Dart. Only a handful of vehicles passed by on the road, their sidelights dull pinpricks in the gloom, and Anna jumped back to avoid the inevitable spray. Water was streaming down the road, the tarmac awash, and she bitterly regretted not thinking to collect her wellingtons from the servants' rear hallway. The rain had soaked right through her strong, serviceable shoes, and her feet were cold and squelching inside her sodden stockings. She was beginning to feel so dispirited, and only the thought of seeing Ethel before the day was out kept her going.

The forbidding buildings of Dartmoor Prison loomed out of the murk over to her right as she approached Princetown, making her feel even more depressed. The rain had penetrated right through her gaberdine and she was drenched and shivering. The few minutes she spent in the Post Office drawing out her savings gave her little respite, and then she crossed over the road and made her way towards the station. A group of ponies huddled forlornly against the wall, their coats striped with dark, wet streaks. Poor things. Well, at least *she* would soon be in the waiting room. Would she be glad to get there!

The little station looked so inviting, and Anna gratefully went to open the door. And then she noticed the blackboard propped against the wall, chalk half washed off in the rain.

NO TRAINS TODAY. RAIL STRIKE.

Anna stared at the sign in disbelief and her

164

shoulders slumped. Oh, sod it. She'd read about the strikes in the *Tavistock Gazette* but hadn't taken much notice. Oh well, she'd just have to take the bus down to Tavistock instead, and catch a bus from there to Plymouth if the mainline trains weren't running either.

She went to pick up her case again. And then stopped. The Princetown bus ran on Tuesdays, Fridays and Saturdays. And today ... was Wednesday. A tearing sigh fluttered at the back of her throat. It really wasn't her day.

Come on. Pull yourself together. There was nothing else for it. She would have to walk to Tavistock. It was what, ten miles maybe? Not impossible, and she thought probably nearer than Yelverton, which was the alternative.

She could have wept as she retraced her steps from the station and began to traipse along the road past the prison and out the other side of Princetown. It anything, it was raining even more heavily now. Her coat hung in a sodden curtain around her knees, water trickling from the hood and down inside her blouse.

Her spirits died inside her as she stumbled forward, one foot placing itself instinctively in front of the other, her vision blurred by the tears that had finally come, running down her cheeks and mingling with the rain. If only her mother hadn't fallen down the stairs. If only her father hadn't been changed from the man he once was. If only Hitler hadn't dropped that bomb.

She didn't see the pothole. Her ankle corkscrewed beneath her, and the next second, she was lying in the road, pain searing up her leg. It took her a moment to gather her wits. If she didn't get up, she could be run over, and so she scrambled painfully to her feet. It really hurt to put her weight on her ankle. Oh, God, this was all she needed.

Her chin quivered and a desperate sob broke from her lungs. She tried to brush away the tears from her face, but it was useless. Everything was so wet. She hobbled on, her soul shattered into a million pieces. She'd never make it.

She reached the junction at last and set off down the main Tavistock road. But it was just the beginning. Her ankle throbbed, her little case now weighed a ton, every inch of her cried out in agony. She couldn't go on. It was hopeless. She let herself sink down on the long, wet grass at the side of the road, put her head in her hands, and wept.

'Oh, you poor girl. I sees you from my window, comin' along the road, limpin' an' cryin'. You come on in to Queenie's cott, cheel, afore you catches your death.'

Chapter Thirteen

Anna raised her head and peered through her wet eyelashes. With the rain battering all around her, she hadn't heard the approach of footsteps and she was startled by the vision that had so suddenly appeared before her. She saw the muddy gumboots first, then the drab, shapeless skirt hanging over them, and finally the gnarled, wizened face that was looming over her, an old sack over the grey hair for protection. But what Anna noticed most were a pair of blue eyes so faded they were almost opal in colour, and yet as clear and bright as crystal.

The wrinkled face creased into a compassionate smile and the stranger picked up Anna's little case, holding our her other hand to help Anna to her feet. Anna felt she couldn't resist, as if she was under a spell. She stood up, and with the stranger's help, hopped across the road. She was led through a gateway and along a stony lane between a bungalow and a stone wall. At the end, not that far from the road, stood a small, single-storey cottage. Just then, the humble dwelling appeared to Anna like a palace.

The old lady paused in the tiny porchway to pull off her wellingtons and push her feet into some worn slippers. Anna bent to take off her own shoes, but the woman stopped her.

'No, cheel. Let's get you off your feet first.' And with a beaming smile, she took Anna inside.

The front door had opened directly into what was obviously the kitchen-cum-living room. Anna had grown used to the absence of mains gas at Ashcroft Hall and cooking on the massive range instead, and here in this tiny cottage, the arrangements were much the same, but with a far smaller blackleaded stove. The heat it threw out on this cold and miserable summer's day was, to Anna, like heaven.

'Take your shoes off now, little maid, an' get the wet clothes off an' all. You'm soaked to the skin. I assumes you 'as a change of clothes in that

167

there case? Dry yersel' on this.' She went to a hook on the wall, unwound a rope from it and let down a drying rack from the ceiling. The woman then took a towel from the rack and hoisted the thing back up. 'I'll leave you a few minutes to get changed,' she went on, 'an' then us'll 'ave a nice cup o' tea to warm us up.'

Anna mumbled her thanks, still too overwhelmed to think clearly. But she was engulfed in relief to be out of the rain, and obediently did as the elderly woman had instructed. She peeled off her sodden garments, aware of the rain clattering on the roof, and she took in the rough plaster on the inside of the stone walls, and the window sill that must be two foot deep. It was truly a delightful little cottage, and already its happy atmosphere was soothing Anna's wounded spirits.

'Right, then.'

By the time the woman returned, Anna was clad in a complete set of dry clothes since the rain had gone right through to her bra and even her knickers. She watched her saviour lift one of the plate covers on the range and set an old brown kettle to boil. Then she turned to Anna with that lovely twinkling smile again.

'You sit down an' let Queenie look at your ankle. Just done it, 'ave we?'

'Yes, in a pothole down the road. I didn't notice it.'

'Hmm.'

Queenie bent down with what seemed to Anna considerable ease for her age, and gently moved her foot this way and that. It was uncomfortable but bearable, and Anna waited for Queenie to

168

straighten up.

'Cold compress is what you needs on that. I'll get you one while that old kettle boils.'

She disappeared once more through a door at the back, and Anna heard the swishing of water before she reappeared with a wet flannel which she arranged on Anna's ankle and then kept in place by winding around it a bandage made of roughly torn-up sheeting. Within minutes, the pain began to ease.

'Now put your foot up on this yere stool, an' Queenie'll make the tea. Milk and sugar?'

'Just milk, no sugar, thank you.'

Anna was coming to her senses as the warmth of the room penetrated her goose-pimply flesh. What an odd situation, but what a stroke of luck that this Queenie had noticed her. Otherwise she didn't know what she would have done.

'This is all terribly kind of you,' she said sincerely.

'Well, couldn't leave a little thing like you out in the rain like that, could I now? Besides, there be nort Queenie likes more than a visitor. Scone? Made them this morning, but there'll be no customers in the tea room, not in this, so us might as well eat them ourselves.'

'Tea room?' Anna was astonished. How many other surprises did the old lady have up her sleeve?

'I'd just brought in my sign when I looks out o' my window an' sees you. Cream teas I does. Only in the summer, mind. Queenie's scones is quite famous wi' folk coming up on the moor in their motor cars. There's some as doesn't 'old wi' the likes o' fureiners, but I says why shouldn't everyone enjoy the moor?'

Anna was growing more intrigued, and her curiosity began to take her mind off her own problems. 'Have you lived here all your life, then?'

'I certainly 'as.' Queenie's eyes lit up with pride. 'Born in that there bedroom,' she said, nodding towards the door to one side of the range. 'Youngest o' ten chiller, me.'

'Ten children? All brought up in this little cottage?'

Queenie bobbed her head. 'I can mind a time when there were six on us sharing the other room. Three to a bed us was. But they'm all dead an' gone now. Two died as babbies. Three brothers was killed in the war, an' then two went to Canada. Broke my mother's 'eart. Then my other sister marries an' moves away up north somewheres, so it were just me an' my brother Albert that stayed at 'ome. Vowed never to leave my parents, I did. An' when they dies back along, it were just me an' Albert. Stone mason 'e were. Never married. An' when 'e dies, it were just Queenie left. Got nephews an' nieces. Somewheres in the world, I s'ppose. But I never 'ears from them.' A sad shadow passed over her face to be replaced a second later by a jolly smile. 'So this little place be my life. An' all the visitors God sends to my door, so you'm more than welcome.'

Anna had been listening intently to Queenie's tale. Evidently liked to talk, did Queenie, Anna could tell already! How tragic to lose one brother, never mind three, in the war. The First World War Anna realised she must mean. All that sadness, and yet to come through it all to such a sprightly

170

old age, well, Queenie must be quite remarkable.

'And I'm more than grateful. But,' Anna hesitated, wondering if it was polite to ask, 'you have a very unusual name, if you don't mind my saying so.'

Queenie threw up her head with a merry chuckle. ''As you never come across it afore, cheel? Oh, my! Tidd'n my real name. I's Victoria, really. After the queen.'

She raised an enquiring, impish eyebrow, and as the penny dropped, Anna joined in her laughter – when earlier that afternoon she had thought she might never laugh again. 'Oh, I see!'

'1893 I were born,' Queenie nodded emphatically, 'when old Victoria were still on the throne. Good times, they was. Afore the world went mad. So let's 'ope things stay settled down again now.'

'Yes. My friend's boyfriend's doing his National Service with the peacekeeping forces in Germany.'

'An' long may peace last. Now, then.' Queenie put down her empty cup with a purposeful flourish. 'What we'm going to do about you? Where was you going that were so urgent you needed to be dragging yersel' through this weather an' carrying a suitcase?'

Anna jolted upright in the chair. She had been so enjoying the conversation with this fascinating woman who seemed to exist in a different world that she had almost forgotten her own dire situation. To be reminded of it so bluntly was an unwanted shock.

'I was trying to get to Plymouth,' she answered evasively, 'but I'd forgotten about the rail strike and didn't realise there weren't any trains

171

running. And, of course, there aren't any buses until Friday.'

'You'd 'ave missed the last one even if there was. It's gone five. So why couldn't you stay where you was till Friday?'

Her bright, piercing eyes held Anna's gaze with such intensity that Anna had to look away. And yet some instinct compelled her to reply. 'I couldn't,' she mumbled, almost hoping Queenie wouldn't hear. 'Stay where I was, I mean.'

There was a short silence, and Anna felt all the misery bearing down on her again. But then she heard Queenie sigh softly. 'Ah.' There was another pause before she spoke again. 'I cas'n imagine a nice, polite young girl like you 'aving to leave somewheres wi'out good reason. If you asks me, there's a fellow involved. An'… oh, my, there's not a babby on the way an' all?'

Anna blinked at her, horrified. How on earth had she guessed her terrible secret? All the pain and guilt of the last few weeks tumbled down around her. She had no strength to resist and broke down in tears, covering her face to hide her shame.

'There, there, my lover. You 'ave a good cry.'

Suddenly Queenie was beside her, holding her, rocking her, and she buried her agony in the well-padded shoulder of this eccentric woman she didn't know from Adam, and yet she felt she had known all her life. She wept with wrenching sobs, washing away her despair until all that seemed left of her shattered dreams was an empty shell.

'Now, then,' she heard Queenie's voice as her tears began to subside. 'You can tell me all about

172

it or not, as you wants. But one thing's certain. You'm not going nowheres today on that ankle. Besides, your clothes'll take some time to dry, an' you needs to keep that foot up. So, for tonight at least, you stays yere wi' Queenie. You can 'ave Albert's old room. I'll air some sheets by the stove, so you'll be quite comfy.'

Anna sat up, wiping her cheeks with the back of her hand and sniffing. 'Oh, I couldn't possibly. You've already been so kind.'

'Strikes me there be no alternative. Anyways, I'll be glad o' the company. Now I keeps an 'ot-pot always going. Best thing when you 'as to keep a range alight all the time. An' mortal useful on a day like this. Can be killing on an 'ot summer's day, mind. But I'll need to add some carrots an' teddies. So if I goes an' digs a few up, p'r'aps you'll sit there an' peel them for us.'

'Yes, of course.'

Anna felt herself once again swept up in the whirlwind that was Queenie – Queenie what, she wondered? She felt dazed, but infinitely calm as all her emotion was spent and all that remained were the bare facts. As she sat, alone again for a few minutes, it all seemed quite simple. She was pregnant. And the father wasn't going to help her, so she would have to help herself.

'There now.'

Queenie was back with the carrots and potatoes, and while Anna peeled them on her lap, the old woman busied herself with hanging Anna's clothes to dry on the rack. And she wasn't so old at all, Anna calculated as Queenie chatted away. If she was born in 1893, that only made her sixty-two. No wonder she was so agile. It was her wrinkled skin that made her look so much older. Result of living an outdoor life in such an exposed location, Anna supposed.

'Do you grow all your own produce?' she asked as the woman stoked up the range firebox and added more coal.

Queenie shut the cast iron door and turned round with a proud grin. 'I certainly does. An' there's a couple of apple trees and a plum out the back an' all. An' I grows lettuces an' other salad stuff in the cold frames. Larnt it all from my dad. Used the manure from the peg an' the cow, us did. Only got 'ens an' the goats now, so makes my own compost from peelings an' things these days. Only got mesel' to feed now, though, you sees.'

'You keep goats and hens?'

'I does. That were goats' milk in your tea. An' I makes goats' cheese. Only dairy stuff I buys is butter an' cream. For the tea room mainly. Makes a little bit from that, I does, to top up my little pension. An' a small income from my savings, I 'as. In'erited everything from my parents an' Albert, see. So Queenie 'as everything she wants. Peppercorn rent I pays on this, 'cuz no one else'd want it. Not nowadays.'

'Oh, I think it's perfect,' Anna protested. 'It's so peaceful.'

'What? With the rain beating on that old tin roof? Drives you mad, oft times. But I'd never 'ave it any other way.'

She spoke with a passionate contentment that somehow filtered through to Anna's spirits like a healing balm. At that moment, she was so envious

174

of Queenie's peace of mind, even if her lot was a simple one. She was about to find out how simple!

'Excuse me, Queenie, but please may I use the lavatory?'

She saw the happy smile slip from Queenie's face. 'Ah, well,' she faltered, 'that won't be what you'm used to, I'll be bound. An earth closet in the shed is what I 'as. But us cas'n 'ave you going back out in the rain. So if you just pops in the bedroom, you'll find a po under the bed. Use that, an' us can empty it later. An' you'll be wanting to wash your 'ands arter. You can do that in the scullery. There be water already in the bowl.'

'Thank you,' Anna smiled back, although she wasn't at all sure about these arrangements! She limped into the room that was going to be her home for the night, on the opposite side of the kitchen from Queenie's. It was painted white with a little cast iron fireplace, blue gingham curtains at the window and what Anna recognised as a rag rug on the flagstone floor. Anna found the chamber pot under the iron bedstead and was grateful to use it, although pushing it back under the bed went against the grain.

Back in the kitchen, Queenie looked up with a smile as Anna hobbled out to the scullery. As Queenie had said, there was already some water in an enamel bowl in an old stone sink. In fact, it was more like a trough, and instead of a plughole, there seemed to be a little hole going straight out through the wall on a sort of stone spout. And there was something else missing, as well!

'All right, cheel?'

Anna returned Queenie's smile as she came

back into the kitchen and sat down again in the old chair. 'Yes, thank you. But,' she began curiously, 'I couldn't see a tap in the scullery.'

'That's 'cuz there bain't one. It's outside. Mod con, that. Used to draw water from the well, back along. But then they puts in a pipe an' now us just turns on the tap.'

Anna nodded dubiously. Mod con? Hardly. But she could hardly say so to Queenie. An earth closet – whatever that was – no gas, no electricity that she could see and the only running water from an outside tap. It was unbelievable, and yet Queenie's blithe serenity shone from her in a golden aura.

The simple stew was delicious and Anna found herself hungry for the first time in weeks. By the time Queenie had washed and put away the dishes, refusing to let Anna help her and renewing the cold compress as well, the incessant rain and leaden skies were drawing in a dismal evening, even though it wasn't yet eight o'clock. Queenie lit both the oil lamps that sat on the window sill and placed them on the table instead. The restful glow sent amber shadows dancing on the walls, and as Anna cupped her fingers around the mug of cocoa Queenie put in her hands, she felt herself fill up with warm pleasure.

'Is there no one we should call to let them know you'm safe?' Queenie suddenly asked as she sipped her own drink. 'Your mother an' father, for instance? Should've thought of it afore, but I could pop along to the phone box afore it gets fully dark.'

Anna felt cradled in blissful security and glanced up without the usual stab of hurt at the thought of her parents. 'No, there's no one,' she answered steadily. 'My mum was ... was ill, and she died last year. And my dad died in a road accident a few weeks ago.'

'What? Oh, my poor cheel. You should've said, an' there's Queenie putting 'er girt foot in it.'

'Oh, no. You couldn't have been kinder. I've sort of got used to being without Mum. And I wasn't really that close to my dad. So there's no one to call, thank you. I've got an aunt, but I haven't seen her since Mum's funeral. Wouldn't want to, either. Can't stand her.'

'So where was you going this arternoon, then?'

'Back to Devonport, where I come from. Ford to be exact. To my best friend there. She and her family have been so good to me. But they weren't expecting me, so they won't be worried. And, well, I don't know what they'll think about ... about me and the baby.'

'Well.' Queenie got to her feet. 'I musts put the 'ens away for the night afore old foxy gets them, an' see to the goats. An' then I's off to bed. Early start for Queenie in the morning. I've made up the bed for you, an' put in an 'otwater bottle. So you get a good night's sleep an' us can talk things over in the morning. You can tell me so much or so little as you wants, but there's always an answer somewheres, you knows. An' you can stay yere as long as you wants. It'll be nice to see Albert's room used again.'

'Thank you so much, Queenie.'

'Don't think nort on it. I 'opes you 'as a good night's sleep, cheel.'

Alone again, Anna sat a minute or two longer, listening to the rain just pattering now on the roof.

It must be easing off at long last. If it hadn't been pouring all day, she would have reached Tavistock by now, and been well on the way to Plymouth on the bus, wondering nervously if she could steel herself to lie to Ethel and her family. Now, though, she felt deathly tired and got herself into bed as quickly as she could. It was just about light enough to see without lighting the candle Queenie had given her.

She snuggled down between the warm sheets, cosy, safe, cocooned. Queenie was right. After all the trauma of the last few weeks, tomorrow was another day.

Chapter Fourteen

Anna was floating in that sweet, peaceful stillness between sleeping and waking, and her eyelids slowly flickered open. Sunlight was streaming in through the flimsy curtains, filling the room with happy optimism. Where was she? And then the strange happenings of the previous day percolated back into her mind. The dreadful scene at Ashcroft Hall and her own predicament blurred into a haze. What seemed important now was her future. She felt far more relaxed and confident about it, and all down to her new-found friend, Queenie.

Anna consulted her watch. Good heavens! It was a quarter to eight, and they had gone to bed about half past nine, it was the best night's sleep she'd had in weeks, ever since the day she had learnt of Gilbert's impending marriage and her father's death. And for the first time in ages she felt truly refreshed and ready to face life full on.

She sat up, and throwing aside the bed clothes, swung her legs over the side of the high bed. Would she be able to walk today? She tested her ankle very gingerly. It was still painful, but far less so than the previous evening. She dressed hurriedly, eager to see Queenie again and prove to herself that this lovely little cottage, this haven, hadn't all been a figment of her imagination.

She half hopped into the kitchen. The room was just as she remembered it, only now it was flooded with early morning sunshine. She stood for a minute or two, allowing its serenity to wash over her as she wondered what she should do next. But just then, Queenie came in through the scullery, happily humming to herself.

'Ah there now! Did you sleep well, cheel?'

'Yes, I did, thank you. Very well.'

'Good. Well, now you'll be wanting some breakfast. Or p'r'aps not if you'm suffering from morning sickness.'

Queenie's allusion to her pregnancy was so open that Anna didn't feel the least embarrassed or shamed. To Queenie, it was just a fact. Anna blinked her eyes wide. It was odd, but it was the first morning for ages that she hadn't woken up feeling nauseous.

'I feel all right this morning, actually,' she answered quite surprised.

'That's what a good night's sleep does for you,' Queenie nodded wisely. 'Nearly brought you a cuppa an' a ginger biscuit in bed. Best thing to stop the sickness coming on of a morning. But I thought it best to let you sleep on. But now you'm up an' dressed. Didn't wash in that there cold water, I 'opes.'

'No, I didn't—'

'Well, draw yersel' some 'ot water from the range boiler. Or p'r'aps you'd like to use the closet first? Queenie'll show you what to do. Don't s'ppose you've used an earth closet afore. Pop your shoes on. They'm dry now but us'll give them a bit of a polish later on.'

Anna nodded her head gratefully and was soon following Queenie out of the front door. The sun was dazzling on the puddles from yesterday's deluge, and Anna picked her way carefully through the mud, eyeing Queenie's gumboots enviously and wishing once again that she hadn't left her wellies at Ashcroft Hall.

Queenie opened the door to a small shed. At the end was what resembled a brick-built box, topped by a wooden plinth with a large hole in the middle. The lavatory seat, Anna imagined. Oh, dear. She didn't know whether to laugh or cry.

'When you've done,' Queenie was explaining in all seriousness, 'you simply takes a shovelful of earth from yere an' sprinkles it over. Trick is to 'ave the earth bone dry, then it absorbs everything, smells an' all. An' then once a week, I opens the trap door yere, takes out the tray an' empties it onto the compost heap. Both the lodges an' the 'ouse 'ad flushing lavatories put in, oh, when were it? Way afore the last war. I cas'n mind exactly when. But what would us do wi' one o' they new-fangled things, my dad said, when the Duchy wanted to build us one, an' all? An' I needs it for my vegetables. So you use it, an' while you'm 'aving a wash, Queenie'll get some breakfast. Porridge, an' then I've just collected this morning's eggs.'

Queenie turned back to the cottage, and Anna shut the shed door and put the hook across. Her old home in Ford had an outside privy in the brick-built wash house, but at least it flushed and was far more substantial than this wooden shed! Anna didn't fancy sharing her ablutions with spiders or any other creepy crawlies, not that there appeared to be any, a wary glance told her. Nonetheless, she didn't hang about!

Outside again, Anna hobbled back to the front door. In the blinding rain yesterday, she had scarcely noticed the pretty little garden in front of the house, and in front of that, a small field. Half of it was given over to neat rows of vegetables, and cold frames set against the enclosing stone walls. Beyond the cultivated area, the grass had been left to grow wild and was separated by a strong post-and-wire-netting fence. On such a beautiful morning, it all appeared idyllic. As Anna came back in through the porch, she noticed the rustic sign above her head. Holly Cottage. Surely it couldn't have a more romantic name!

Queenie was busy at the stove but smiled broadly as she gave Anna a jug for the hot water. Back in the bedroom, Anna stripped off her clothes, ready for her wash. And then she froze rigid.

She had caught sight of herself in the little mottled mirror on the wall above the chest of drawers. Around her throat, the shadows were just beginning to form. The necklace of purple roses from where Gilbert had half strangled her. Just like her mum and dad.

She sat down with a thump on the edge of the bed. Dear God. No. *Thank* God that Gilbert was out of her life, even if he had left her high and dry with his baby. She could see it more clearly than ever now. Little things she had chosen to ignore. He had always been weak, a bit like a spoilt child, but with his charms, he had led her by the nose. She was well rid of him. She may be feeling sorry for herself, but what about poor Francesca? Sweet, trusting Frankie.

'Three minutes!'

Queenie's jolly call from the next room made Anna swiftly wash the 'important' bits of her before throwing her clothes back on. Fortunately she was wearing a blouse with a turndown collar that always sat high and should hide the bruises coming out around her neck. Nevertheless, she sat down warily at the table.

'Take the top off your egg so it won't spoil while you eats your porridge,' Queenie instructed with the smile that seemed imprinted on her lined face. 'I bets you've never 'ad an egg that fresh afore.'

'No, I'm sure I haven't.'

'Arterwards I'll show you the 'ens what laid them, an' introduce you to Dolly an' Wilma.'

'The goats?'

'Indeed. Daft as brushes, an' they'll eat *anything*, so mind yersel'.'

Anna chuckled. This place was magical. 'And then I must be on my way,' she sighed with reluctance. 'I can't tell you how grateful I am.'

Queenie looked up sharply. 'An' where does you think you'm going? You needs to rest that ankle, an' remember there be no bus till tomorrow. Queenie cas'n stop you, but you'm an idjit if you doesn't stay at least another day. An' longer if you wants. Give yersel' thinking time.'

Anna took all of thirty seconds to consider. 'Well, I'd love to, if you don't mind. I can't think of anywhere I'd rather be just now. Thank you so much.'

'But whilst you'm yere, you needs to sort yersel' out. This lad duped you, I've no doubt. Now, I doesn't need to know ort, but if you wants to talk, I've good ears an' a still tongue – when it needs to be. Right, then.' She stood up decisively. 'If you've finished, come an' say 'ello to Dolly an' Wilma. Drive them into the field I does in good weather, but got to get them past they flowers an' the vegetables wi'out them eating the lot!'

Queenie hadn't been joking. The two goats were the naughtiest things on four legs Anna had ever come across. She did her best to help Queenie, but hopping on one leg wasn't very useful, and when Dolly gently headbutted her out of the way, she sat down hard on her bottom in a heap of helpless laughter. It really was just what she needed to lift her from her depression – and her fears for the future.

'Oo-ee!'

The bright voice behind her made Anna turn round. By the gate, a middle-aged woman was smiling at her, clearly surprised at seeing a strange face.

'Morning, Olive!' Anna heard Queenie's cheery voice reply.

'Lovely morning after yesterday, isn't it? I was just going into Princetown and wondered if you needed anything?'

'That's proper kind o' you. I could do wi' some plain flour an' some Golden Raising Powder if you can carry them.'

'Oh, yes. Only want a few bits myself. So, you going to introduce me to this young lady?'

'Of course. This be Anna. Staying wi' us a few days, she is.'

'Pleased to meet you. Anna,' the woman nodded her head. 'I'm Olive, Queenie's neighbour in the lodge here. Well, I'll leave you to it. See you later.'

'Thanks, Olive. I'll 'ave the kettle on for when you gets back.'

'I'll hold you to that!'

Anna watched Olive set off down the lane with a basket on her arm. 'She seems nice,' she said to Queenie.

'She is that. Been neighbours thirty year or more, us as. 'Er 'usband's called Clifford. An' next door on that side, that be Crow 'Ouse,' she went on, indicating the substantial, two-storey building on the opposite side of the cottage from the lodge. 'Daisy, Gladys an' Betty lives there. Three sisters. All very nice. You'll meet them by an' by. An' that old farm'ouse up the lane behind us, they'm proper nice, too. But I cas'n stand yere gossiping. I've work to do.'

She winked jovially and Anna smiled to herself as she followed her inside. Queenie was a right old chatterbox and she knew it, but a happier person Anna had never known.

Anna could hardly remember a day she had enjoyed so much. She had helped Queenie as best she could to bake fresh scones and a sponge. There were indeed customers in the tea room which was a wooden extension on the far end of the cottage, and they were kept busy all afternoon making pots of tea and pouring out glasses of Queenie's delicious home-made lemonade. Anna found the time flew by and it all helped her to forget her own problems. By the time Queenie shut up shop for the day, Anna felt as if she had been helping her in the café and cottage all her life.

'That were a good day's work,' Queenie declared as they finally sat down to a cup of tea themselves. 'There. That's your 'alf o' the takings. Reckons you deserves it.'

'What?' Anna stared at the pile of coins Queenie had pushed towards her across the table. 'Oh, no. I can't take that money. I did so little, and you *have* fed me for two days as well.'

'Think nort o' that. But you was a great 'elp to me. Could do wi' someone like you all the time. Not as young as I were, an' a little 'elp about the place wouldn't come amiss.'

Anna smiled with a wistful sigh as she leant back in the chair. 'It has been a nice day. It's so peaceful here, and you've made me feel so at home.'

'Then,' Queenie began tentatively, 'maybe you'd like to consider it your 'ome. For as long as you likes. Think about it, at least.'

Anna's eyes stretched wide. Was Queenie really offering her a home? 'Well, yes, I will. If you

185

really don't mind having me around for a while.'

'Wouldn't 'ave asked you if I didn't mean it. But you stays on one condition. That you sees the doctor in Princetown. Visits twice a week from Tavvy. At Top Bolt's, next to the town 'all. Youth club it be now, but it'll always be Top Bolt's to me. 'Ad a lovely china shop on one side, an' on the other, it were mainly 'ardware. An' afore that, when I were a cheel, it were the Co-op.'

A happy glaze had veiled Queenie's opal eyes, and Anna watched her with a contented smile. If only she could stay with Queenie for a little while, she felt it might give her the strength to face the future. For when the baby came.

The man at the desk looked up at her with a welcoming smile. His thinning hair was grey at the temples and there were deep laughter lines around his mouth. Altogether, he had a reassuring air about him which gave Anna confidence.

He picked up the card Anna had filled in for the lady in the other room, and read it before glancing up at her over his spectacles.

'Anna Millington?'

'Yes,' she answered nervously.

'Do take a seat. I'm Dr Franfield. Dr Brodie's on holiday so I'm standing in for him. But I see you're a new patient, so you wouldn't have been expecting him anyway. Now, what can I do for you?'

Anna shuddered with shame. She lowered her gaze and the first time she tried to speak, nothing came out. So she took a mental hold on herself and began again.

'I think I'm pregnant,' she mumbled. 'No, I

186

know I'm pregnant.'

'Well, let's just make sure, shall we? When was your last period? You could just be late. It happens sometimes, particularly if you've been under stress at all.'

He proceeded to ask her various questions in such a calm and friendly way. A lovely, considerate man, Anna thought vaguely. She bet *he* would never have treated anyone in the callous way Gilbert had treated her.

'Now, just hop up on the couch and I'll have a little feel of your tummy, if I may. Just relax, that's it. Right, all done. Come and sit down again when you're ready.'

Anna rearranged her skirt, grateful that the examination had been so swift. She sat down again and looked at the doctor, a tiny flicker of hope that she might be wrong struggling to keep aflame. It was soon snuffed out.

'Well, from what you tell me, I would say that yes, you are pregnant,' Dr Franfield informed her gently. 'I can just about feel the uterus which fits with your dates.'

Anna felt the grey depression pressing down on her again. His confirmation made it all so final, when she had been desperately hoping... Her despair must have shown on her face as she saw the doctor remove his glasses, sit back in his chair and consider her over steepled fingers.

'I gather from your expression that congratulations are not in order. And I see that you wear no wedding ring, so I assume it's Miss and not Mrs Millington?'

His tone was sympathetic, but Anna could only

187

nod in reply.

'Does the father know?'

This time her bitterness towards Gilbert galvanised her tongue into action. 'Yes, he does. But he doesn't want to know. And besides, I don't think I want him in my life now that I know what he's really like. But–'

She broke off, sick at heart. But the doctor was shrewd.

'But you don't know what to do. Which way to turn. Parents?'

'Both dead.'

'I'm so sorry.' He gave a compassionate smile. 'So, there's no one?'

'Only my best friend. In Devonport. But I'm not sure how she'll take the news and I wouldn't want to put on her. So there's really only Queenie.'

'Queenie?'

'An elderly lady. She lives in an old cottage at Rundlestone, just down the road. She took me in. I've been with her for the last two weeks. She's been marvellous.'

'But you're worried what will happen when the baby comes? And whether or not you should give it up for adoption?'

'The thought has crossed my mind, yes,' she almost whispered, and was grateful when Dr Franfield continued the conversation for her in what seemed his usual confidential tone.

'Well, only you can make that decision. But let me give you a word of advice. Be very cautious about going into a home for unmarried mothers. Many of them *are* very good. But some will try and force you to give up your baby. So be warned.

Don't let anyone pressurise you into signing over the baby just like that. If you do decide on adoption, there are many legal processes which must be gone through properly. And you can change your mind right up to the moment when the adoption is finalised.'

'I see. Yes. Thank you for that. But,' Anna sighed again and shook her head, 'I don't know how I could afford to keep the baby.'

'You'll be entitled to allowances, you know.'

'Really?' Anna sat up straight, and a sudden light shone its way into the uncertainty of her future.

'Oh, yes. I'm not sure of the exact figure, as it goes up periodically. But it must be nearly three pounds a week, you and the baby together.'

'Oh,' was all Anna could say in her surprise.

'So there's a lot for you to consider. But in the meantime, as I said, I'm only acting as locum while Dr Brodie's on holiday. But you can register with me if you prefer, and I'd be happy to talk things through with you any time. You'll find us in Plymouth Road in Tavistock. That's my son and myself,' he added with glowing pride. 'He's just joining me in practice. It would mean you'd have to come into Tavistock for your check-ups, or the local midwife could come to you. She'd soon let me know if there was anything she wasn't happy with. Now,' he smiled genially, 'I just need to check your blood pressure and a few other things. After all, your health and the baby's are the most important things.'

Ten minutes later, having thanked Dr Franfield profusely, Anna was walking along the road past the prison and back towards Holly Cottage. Ever

189

since the day Queenie had taken her in, there hadn't been a drop of rain and July was turning into a heatwave. The rolling hills and sharp contours of Dartmoor's rocky tors were starkly defined in the clear, scorching sunlight, the sky overhead a deep, azure blue with not a cloud to be seen. The moor was spinning its mysterious web, catching Anna in the thread of a thousand thoughts triggered by what kind Dr Franfleld had told her.

Perhaps things weren't as had as they seemed, after all.

Chapter Fifteen

Anna picked up Queenie's little blackboard with its CREAM TEAS AND REFRESHMENTS sign, and sauntered back along the lane. It had been another lovely day with a fair number of customers. Anna wondered how long the good weather would last. It was already the end of August and the main tourist season would soon be over once the children returned to school. Anna didn't want the idyllic summer to end and just wished everything could go on as it was.

'Been busy, haven't you?' Olive called from the garden of the lodge.

'Certainly have. I've got to clear up, but would you like to pop in for a cuppa with Queenie?'

'Thanks, Anna, but I've got to get Clifford's tea. You know what a stickler he is for having his

190

food ready on the dot.'

'Never mind. Pop in tomorrow morning, instead.'

'I may well do just that.'

'See you later, then.'

Anna carried on up to the cottage. A bit grumpy was Olive's husband, but he was in charge of the water-pumping station just down the road. It was a responsible job and that was probably what made him so serious.

Anna herself couldn't have been more contented. As well as baking for the tea shop and preparing their own meals, over the last few weeks they had made jams and pies from the whortleberries they had gathered on the moor. Any surplus from Queenie's kitchen garden that could be pickled or preserved was now stored in bottles and jars in the huge kitchen cupboard. Soon it would be the turn of the apples and plums from the trees at the back of the cottage. It was all so satisfying, and Anna gave a slow, mellow sigh.

'Oh, cheel, what would I 'ave done wi'out you these last days?' she heard Queenie declare from the armchair. 'You'm a godsend, Anna, really you are.'

Anna knew she flushed with embarrassment. 'How about a cuppa and some cake?' she suggested, neatly changing the subject. 'There's some Dundee left. Your favourite. I'll just see to the goats–'

'They goats can wait ten minutes. You make us a nice cuppa an' put your feet up. Anyways, us needs a little chat, you and me.'

Anna gulped, feeling as if she'd swallowed a golf

ball. She knew what Queenie was about to say. The summer had been fun, but with leaner times on the way, Anna would have to move on. She was dreading it, putting off the moment of departure as long as possible.

'Yes,' she answered in a small voice as she turned away. The kettle was still on the range from the last pot of tea for the shop, and was hissing with steam. It would only take a minute to top up the pot and cut two wedges of the cake.

'You knows you'm showing,' Queenie said without preamble. 'Needing proper maternity dresses any time, you'll be. An' I wants to know what you'm going to do.'

Anna paused as she stepped across the kitchen, a cup and saucer in each hand. This was it. She put the teas on the little table between the chairs.

'You've been so good to me,' she answered, her voice quavering. 'But I know it's time for me to sort myself out. Find somewhere for the baby and me to live.'

'You'm not thinking o' leaving me?'

'Oh, Queenie, I can't stay here. It wouldn't be fair on you. People would talk. Give you the cold shoulder.'

'An' what would I care if they did?' Queenie answered fiercely, her old face gleaming with determination. 'You knows I've told people you'm my niece, an' what could be more natural? You'm 'aving a babby, but your poor 'usband were killed in a road accident. Just like your daddy if you thinks about it. An' you wanted to make a new start wi' your auntie. Now then, I kept my dear old mum's wedding ring. You wears that, an' nobody'll

192

be any the wiser.'

'You're so kind, Queenie, really you are,' Anna murmured, her heart aching. 'But some people in Princetown already know me. They'd know it was a lie. And what about Olive?'

'Olive can keep a secret. An' anyone else can go take a running jump. An' what else you'm going to do? Find yersel' some pokey little room somewheres? 'Ave the child cooped up in some town backstreet when it could 'ave the whole o' Dartmoor to run wild in? Or p'r'aps you'm thinking o' giving it away?' she concluded with uncharacteristic sharpness.

Her tone stung into Anna's heart and she lowered her gaze in brutal agony. 'I don't know,' she choked. 'I've been trying not to think about it.'

'Then it's time you did. You an' me, us gets on so well. We'm a team. An' this old cottage, 'e 'asn't seen a little one since I were a tacker. 'E cas'n wait to 'ear a babby's cry again. Don't give the babby away,' she pleaded. 'Give it a chance.'

Anna lifted her head. Queenie's words had exploded with such passion that it shook her to the core.

'Is it ... is that really what you want?'

'You, me an' the babby? Of course. No one could give it more love or a better 'ome than you an' me. Think on it, cheel, an' in the meantime, let's see if that ring fits your little 'and.'

The railway strike had long been settled, and Anna gazed out of the carriage window with a blank stare, hardly noticing the lovely countryside as the train chugged south across the pretty

Bere Peninsula. She had taken the early morning bus down to Tavistock and had gone to register with Dr Franfield.

'Are you sure you want to be on my list?' the kindly man asked. 'It means you'll always have to come all that way, and with the baby in tow? Dr Brodie's very nice. I'm sure you'd like him.'

'But he's only in Princetown twice a week, isn't he? So it wouldn't make much difference, really.'

'Just so long as you've thought about it.' To Anna's relief, Dr Franfield gave his friendly smile. 'So, let's see how you're progressing, and on your way out, fill in a form for my wife. She's the receptionist. And she'll arrange for the midwife to visit you for the next couple of months, and I'll take over nearer your time.'

'Thank you, Doctor.'

It had all gone so smoothly, Mrs Franfield being bright and welcoming and with no hint of disdain at her being an unmarried mother. Would Ethel be the same? Anna's stomach was taut and filled with butterflies. She had told Ethel she had met Queenie in Princetown and they had become good friends. And that when Queenie had learnt that Anna wanted to leave Ashcroft Hall but didn't want to leave her beloved moor, she had invited her to go and live with her. But now it was time for Anna to face the music and reveal her shameful secret to Ethel.

Anna had taken the alternative railway route from Tavistock North Station, as after running down the Bere Peninsula and the eastern bank of the Tamar, the train stopped at Ford Station, not so far from Anna's old home. She got off the train

194

and began to walk through the familiar narrow streets. Ethel had taken a week's holiday, but with nowhere to go and Bert in Germany, she had been delighted to know that Anna wanted to come and visit her. But as Anna trod the uneven pavements, she felt as if the rows of little houses were pressing in on her. Had she really spent most of her life in these crowded backstreets? Her mum had died here, and her dad... It no longer felt anything like home. It seemed hostile and unfriendly, and now she was about to confess to Ethel – and possibly lose her friendship for ever.

She hesitated with her hand on the knocker of Number Sixteen. But she had delayed long enough, and girding up her courage, rapped loudly on the door. She heard footsteps running down the hallway, and the next instant, she was locked in Ethel's tight hug. Thank goodness. Ethel hadn't noticed. Yet.

'Oh, it's proper grand to see you, Annie! Come on in! Mu ... um! She's here!'

Ethel bustled her down the hallway in a flurry of excitement and into the kitchen. Mabel was sitting at the table, sipping tea from a cracked mug, and somehow managing to hold a cigarette in the same hand. Anna felt detached from the familiar scene, as if she was watching a film. Oh, she wanted so much to be part of it, like she always used to be, stale cigarette smoke and all. But she couldn't be. Gilbert and the child he had given her were about to ruin everything.

She waited, mentally holding her breath, while Mabel looked up at her with a welcoming grin. She put down the mug and, unusually, the cigarette, and stood up.

'Annie, love!' she beamed as she came round the table. 'Fred were really upset to know 'e'd miss you. You'm looking very well! Putting on ... weight...' She paused, and Anna saw the colour drain from her face as her jaw dropped. 'Oh, my God,' she muttered under her breath.

Anna felt her shame ooze from every pore. Her throat closed up and she couldn't speak. Couldn't move. Just stood there.

'What's up, Mum?' Ethel's suddenly bewildered voice came from behind her.

Anna saw Mabel swallow. 'If I's not mistook,' she croaked in disbelief. 'Anna's 'aving a babby.'

Shocked silence. For what? Thirty seconds? Ethel came round in front of her, her face a mask of incredulity. 'Annie?' she breathed.

Anna looked at her, and hot tears welled up in her eyes. She watched as Ethel's gaze moved down to her swelling belly, then back to her face. No one spoke. Or moved. For an interminable time.

Then Ethel's lips screwed mutinously. 'It were that Gilbert chap, weren't it? Blooming gentry folk! Sweet-talked you, I bets. Led you on wi' promises o' marriage an' what 'ave you. An' now there's a babby on the way, the bastard's dumped you. Oh, Anna, 'ow could you 'ave fallen for it? Oldest trick in the world!'

'I know,' Anna choked. 'You were right, Eth. I should've listened to you.'

'Well!' Mabel huffed up her sagging bosoms. 'Just you wait till I tells Fred. Cas'n let the devil get away wi' it! Specially not wi' our Annie. Go an' see the shyster – wi' our Davy an' all, 'e will –

an' *make* the bugger marry you!'

Oh. O-oh, Anna wanted to moan. Why was it there were horrible, deceitful people like Gilbert in the world, when there were others like the Shalla-fords who'd hearts of gold and would share their last farthing with you? To them, it was a straight-forward problem with a straightforward answer. Life wasn't always like that, though, was it?

'I – it's not that simple,' she stammered. 'He was engaged. I didn't know. And now he's married.'

'Oh, Lordy love!'

'And I wouldn't want to marry him now even if I could. Not now I know what he's really like.' Anna lifted her head, the rancour she felt for Gilbert giving her confidence. 'I only wanted a small allowance. And I think he'd have given it to me. But then he got angry and ... and went for me. And Lady Ashcroft heard, and then he denied everything and she threw me out.'

'What? But I thought as you got on well with 'er?'

'I did. Eth. But when it came to it, I suppose her pride and her classy upbringing were just too much. She called me a trollop. And I deserved it.'

'Oh, no, you didn't, little maid!' Mabel cried. 'Too innocent an' trusting, an' maybes pretty stu-pid, but a trollop? Never! Believed you was in love, I be certain, an' after all what 'appened to you, you was grabbing at 'appiness. Never should've gone off on yer own like that. Daft idea it were that you two buggers dreamt up atween you. Would've stopped you, us would, if us'd knawed.'

'But I was frightened of my dad–'

'Well, enough said, maid. You sit down yere, an'

Eth, you make a fresh pot o' tea,' Mabel ordered, taking charge in the way only she knew how. 'No good moaning over spilt milk. Got to decide what's to do. We'm good as family to you, Annie, you knows that.'

She was pushing Anna down into a chair and Anna nodded tearfully. Oh, Mabel. You're so kind, but ... 'Eth?'

'Bloody bugger, I'd strangle the bastard if I could get 'ands on 'en!' And to emphasise the point, Ethel slammed the mug of tea on the table in front of Anna with such anger that the tea slopped over onto the tablecloth. Not that it mattered very much. It was so stained anyway, and had more than one cigarette burn in it. Anna wondered when it'd last seen the inside of the washtub. It was all so typical that her mouth curved into a smile.

'That's better!' Ethel grinned. 'Now, what we'm going to do wi' this little tacker when it comes?'

'Queenie and me are going to fetch it up,' Anna answered. It suddenly all seemed so simple.

'Sounds a lovely soul does this Queenie.'

'Oh, she is. She ... she reminds me of you, Mrs Shallaford.'

'Hurrump,' Mabel snorted with embarrassment. 'Well, so long as us sees summat o' you, an' all.'

'Of course you will.'

'An' I wants to be godmother,' Ethel put in adamantly.

'Oh, Eth, do you? I was so worried you wouldn't want to be friends anymore.'

''Ow could I not? Like sisters, you an' me.'

'That's right! An' when you two've finished 'ugging each other, you can 'elp me wi' the dinner.

198

Bangers an' mash us is 'aving in your honour, young Annie.' Mabel nodded her head as she retrieved the cigarette that had nearly burnt through on its own, and proceeded to light another one from its smouldering tip. 'You sure you wants to live up on that there moor? I'd offer you an 'ome here, but I doesn't know where us'd put you. Not likely any o' these are going to move out soon.'

'It's very kind of you even to think about it,' Anna replied, feeling more relaxed as she sipped her tea and hardly noticed the unpleasant film on the mug. 'And how are things going with you and Bert?' she asked Ethel eagerly.

Ethel pulled a long face. 'Well, 'e's got another eighteen months nearly of his service to do. Thinks they'll likely keep 'en in Germany. But we'm both saving 'ard, an' when 'e comes 'ome...'

She plunged into the animated details of all their plans, chatting on merrily, almost without taking a breath. Anna was happy to sit back and listen, while opposite her, Mabel nodded approvingly as she took a few drags on her new cigarette before popping it into the usual place at the corner of her mouth so that she could get on with the dinner. Anna felt a warm gladness seep into the very core of her. All this time she had been petrified of telling them about the baby, her stomach turning somersaults whenever she thought about it. How silly of her. She should have known how these good people would have taken the news. Mabel was right. They *were* her family. She had Queenie as well now, so she was very lucky if she thought about it. Now she could face the future with strength in her heart.

Chapter Sixteen

Anna was walking back from Princetown, looking forward to Queenie's cheery welcome at Holly Cottage and mulling over the ugly scene in Bolt's Store. She had been ordering some dress material and maternity patterns and the woman behind her at the counter had evidently noticed what she was buying.

'Huh! I doesn't know how you can bring yersel' to serve her,' she had sneered at the shopkeeper. 'That ring don't fool me. Seen her in yere afore, I has, an' she weren't wearing no ring then. Got hersel' into trouble, an' thinks she can still mix with good, honest folk like us. Unmarried mother, it's disgraceful. Should be locked up.'

Anna had gulped, wanting to disappear into thin air. It had been a horrible incident, but the shopkeeper had been so understanding. As for the customer, well, it was the first open hostility Anna had come across, and there would be plenty more where that came from, she was sure. She would just have to harden herself against it. For so many years, she had held her head high over the situation with her father, and with the support of Ethel and Queenie, she could do so again over the baby.

Oh, damn Gilbert Ashcroft! Damn him to hell! And as for this child he had lumbered her with, well, she wasn't sure what she felt about it. Queenie seemed passionate for her to keep it, but what did she truly want herself? She really couldn't answer her own question. She felt all topsy-turvy, she reflected grimly. The child would be her own flesh and blood, and she should love it. But it would also be Gilbert's. Would it grow up to be like him? If she had it adopted, she would be free. Free of Gilbert and his artful lies and deceit for ever.

She sighed with dejection. Oh, what a chain of events. It was like a row of dominoes all falling on each other, and she was the end one taking all the strain. But she did have a choice. Unlike poor Francesca, who was tied to Gilbert and all his falsehood for life.

Frankie. Anna wondered what had happened to her, caught up in the hoity-toity society it had been her lot to be born into. Had her father died yet? She had all that grief to go through. And in the meantime, she would have to suffer the humiliation of knowing her husband was a cad and a liar.

Poor Frankie. Anna still thought of her as a friend. A friend she yearned to support, despite the harrowing circumstances of their relationship. But she couldn't just walk up to Ashcroft Hall and ask to see her now, could she?

But maybe there was a way.

My dearest Frankie

No, that wasn't right. She had only known the girl a few weeks, and although they had grown very close, their relationship wasn't as deep as her friendship with Ethel was. And if she worded the letter in too friendly a way after all that had happened, Frankie might consider she had no right to address her with such familiarity. It could put her off reading the letter altogether, and Anna didn't want that.

Dear Francesca

That was better. Not Lady Francesca, that'd be too formal. Yes, *Dear Francesca* was perfect.

I can't tell you how sorry I am about the way we parted. It must have been a terrible shock to you. I really value the friendship that grew up between us, and I had planned that you would never know what had happened between Gilbert and me. If I had known he was engaged, I would never have let it happen, but I truly believed he loved me and that one day we would be man and wife.

How can you ever forgive me? I really don't know. But I hope and pray that you and Gilbert get over it. I do worry about you so much, and if there is anything I can do to help, I will always be here as a friend. I have been living not so far away with a lovely, elderly lady, called Queenie. She's become like a second mother to me and she wants me to go on living with her when the baby's born. At the moment, that's what I plan to do. I will fully understand if you never want to see or hear from me again, but if you ever want to contact me, the address is Holly Cottage, Rundlestone, near Princetown.

Your friend as ever
Anna

Mrs Smudge looked up from the table in the farmhouse kitchen, her face stilled with astonishment, and then her mouth widened into a hesitant smile. 'Anna, what a surprise! I wondered what–'

She broke off as her gaze was inevitably drawn to Anna's clearly thickened middle beneath her gaberdine raincoat. 'It were true, then,' she faltered. 'You left the 'All cuz you was pregnant.'

'Yes,' Anna answered, ready to defend herself, but she was sure this down-to-earth, jovial woman she had always liked would understand – once she knew the truth. 'I don't know what the gossip was, and I'm sure Mrs Davenport made me out to be a slut, but it wasn't like that. And before you ask, Gilbert *is* the father.'

'Sir Gilbert?'

Anna snorted and shook her head. 'I suppose they kept that hidden, did they? I'm supposed to have gone behind the bicycle shed with any Tom, Dick or Harry I could pick up in Princetown, am I?'

'B-but ... Sir Gilbert? 'E'm the only one o' them up at the 'All us 'as any time for. Known 'en since 'e were a tacker. Always such a nice lad.'

'Yes. Exactly. Just what I thought.' Anna paused before releasing a wistful sigh. 'Oh, I suppose he's not a *bad* person. He's just weak under all that show of self-assurance. I think he did have genuine feelings for me, but when it came to the crunch, he didn't have the guts to stand up to his mother over it.'

'Not even when he knawed you was pregnant?'

Anna sucked in her cheeks. 'I didn't realise until it was too late. I'd never had any experience of ... of that sort of thing before. I was just a complete and utter naive fool from the start.'

Mrs Smudge nodded in agreement. 'Good to see you, anyways. 'Ow did you get yere?'

'I walked. I'm living just the other side of Princetown now.'

'You walked all that way, an' in your condition? Well, take the weight off your feet now. Should've asked you afore, but it were a bit of a shock to see you there. So, sit yersel' down an' 'ave a cup o' tea.'

'Thank you. Some tea would be lovely.'

Anna sat down at the table and waited while Mrs Smudge went to fetch another cup and saucer from an old wooden dresser. The cluttered room was almost as much of a mess as Number Sixteen, and just as homely and reassuring.

'I 'as to say, us couldn't imagine you gettin' yersel' into trouble,' Mrs Smudge admitted as she handed Anna the cup of tea.

Anna lowered her eyes. 'No, nor could I. It only happened once, and I regretted it straight away. It's no excuse, I know, but I loved him and I really thought we were going to be married. I had no idea Francesca even existed, and now I've ruined her life as well.'

'Lady Francesca?' Mrs Smudge was horrified. 'She knaws all about it? That it were Sir Gilbert?'

'Yes. It was the last thing I wanted. Only, because of Gilbert's appalling behaviour, she found out. And that's why I've come.'

'To me? I doesn't understand.'

'Would you ... please could you give her this?' Anna reached into her pocket for the envelope. 'It's the only way I can be sure she'll get it. I didn't get the chance to explain properly. Or to apologise. I can't tell you how dreadful I feel about it all. Francesca and I had become friends, you see. This can never put things right, but I would like her to read it. Would you … would you mind?' she asked, seeing the misgiving on Mrs Smudge's face.

'No. I doesn't mind. I'll take it, but I doesn't know when I'll be able ter give it to 'er. Just arter you left, I over'eard 'Er Ladyship tellin' Sir Gilbert ter get 'is wife back to London afore ort else 'appened. I wondered what she meant, but now I reckons she were referrin' to you. Left the very next day, they did, an' I 'aven't seen either on them since.'

'Oh.' Anna felt her heart weigh down with sadness. 'Poor Francesca. Can you imagine how she must feel? And with her father dying as well. He … has he…?'

'Still alive as far as I knaws, but very poorly. The doctors was right that 'e be not long fer this world.'

'And now I've ruined the one thing Frankie had to hold on to.'

Mrs Smudge inclined her head, lips pursed. 'It takes two to tango, cheel. An' Sir Gilbert ought to 'ave knawed better than to lead an innocent young thing like you on. But there'll be plenty fer blame you alone.'

'Oh, yes,' Anna scoffed bitterly, remembering the customer in Bolt's. 'I've found that already. Our next-door neighbours, even. Well, Olive's all right, but her husband won't speak to me now. Or the people across the road. But there are three elderly sisters who live in a house just by us, and they've been quite understanding.'

'An 'oo's *us,* then?'

'Queenie.' Anna smiled at the thought. 'Lovely lady. Took me in on the day Lady Ashcroft threw me out. She has very little and the cottage is pretty primitive, but Queenie has a heart of gold. I think she was quite lonely before, and she wants me and the baby to live with her.'

'An' you wants fer bring this babby up in this cottage on the moor? An' what future will it 'ave when it grows up?' Mrs Smudge frowned dubiously.

'Well, it'll have plenty of fresh air and good food!' Anna enthused. 'Queenie grows all her own vegetables and things. And she keeps goats and hens. Said she might even get a piglet in the spring, like in the old days, she says. I'm going to have the baby in the maternity home in Tavistock, though. The midwife said the cottage isn't really suitable.'

'Got it all worked out, then.'

'With Queenie's help, yes.'

But as Anna walked home across the moor, Mrs Smudge's words echoed in her brain. But what else could she do? For the moment, all she could think of was to bring the child safely into the world, and to provide for its earliest needs. After that, the future would have to take care of itself.

Chapter Seventeen

'Oh, Queenie, it's been a super Christmas Day,' Anna commented, stretching lazily. 'So much better than last year at the Hall.'

It was eight o'clock in the evening and they were

both lounging in the old, lumpy armchairs that they had pushed up to the little range. They must have sat there for a couple of hours, chatting, knitting, Queenie reminiscing about life at the cottage when she was a child. Things hadn't really changed much, except that she'd had all her family around her, and she related amusing tales of various larger-than-life characters, all long gone. Now Queenie had opened the firebox door and they were toasting their toes in the heat.

Anna took a deep breath, watching the mound beneath her dress lift even higher and then fall as she sighed ponderously. 'Queenie,' she faltered, and had to whip up her courage to continue, 'I know we've been preparing for the baby, but ... do you really think it's the best thing for us to keep it? I mean, we'll give it a good home, but is it right for it to grow up without a father? And things will always be a struggle. We'll never be able to afford decent clothes and shoes and things for it. Don't you think,' she hesitated, watching the expression on Queenie's face, 'don't you think it would have a better chance if it was adopted into a proper family? And if we keep it, one day it'll have to know the truth about its father.'

She chewed on her lip, wishing she hadn't spoken as Queenie put down her knitting.

'An' what about you, Anna? Does you wants to keep it or gie it away?'

Anna had never seen those opal eyes so intense, and she couldn't hold their steady stare. She bowed her head.

'I don't know,' she murmured. 'Sometimes I do and sometimes I don't. I think it's knowing who the father is. I know I loved Gilbert when … when it happened, but now I despise him, and that's what's making me doubt myself. I mean, if I really *was* widowed, it would be so much different.'

She dared to look up now, and saw Queenie's lips had firmed to a fine line.

'Your feelings is all over the place,' she said pensively. 'Near your time, you'm be, an' that's 'ard enough for any woman. You knows my opinion, but it's not my decision to make. Just don't you go doing ort you might regret later. Give it time. The babby won't know no different till it's much older. Now, I cas'n see to knit no more in this light, so I suggests us 'as a nice cup o' tea afore us goes to bed.' And so saying, she heaved herself out of the chair.

Oh, dear. The conversation hadn't solved anything. But Queenie was right in one thing. Anna shouldn't make a hasty decision. But she'd been thinking about it ever since she had realised she was pregnant.

She hauled herself to her feet and felt her stomach tighten with ferocious force. Dr Franfield had warned her about these practice contractions. Braxton Hicks he had called them. They got very strong towards the end, but he promised she'd know the difference when the real thing came. She couldn't wait to be rid of the physical burden, but what next when the bump inside her had become a proper little human being?

If only her mum was still alive for her to talk to, but if she was, none of this would have happened, would it?

Anna's eyes flew open and she caught her breath, gritting her teeth. Oh, that was really painful. It was the third time it had woken her up, and though she couldn't see her watch in the dark, she was sure it wasn't that long since the last one. This was it. Oh, Lord. She had prayed it would happen during the day. Now she would have to wake Queenie.

She blinked her eyes wide, clearing her thoughts as the pain subsided. She gave herself a moment's respite, then threw the blankets aside and sat up on the edge of the bed, snuggling her feet into her slippers and pulling on her dressing gown. The January night struck cold, despite the glowing coals in the little fireplace, and Anna started shaking, her teeth chattering uncontrollably.

She lit the candle, just about able to make out its shape, and the hesitant flame flickered eerily through the shadows. The room that had become her haven. The drawer she and Queenie had turned into a warm and comfortable crib for the baby. What would they do when it got bigger, she had wondered. But perhaps...

Ooo. Just as she reached the bottom of the bed, it came again, making her bend double, and she clung onto the iron bedstead with her free hand, praying she wouldn't drop the candlestick. Oh, heck. And she took deep, controlled breaths, just as the midwife had shown her.

At last it was over. Five minutes at most since the previous one. Call by the time the contractions are half an hour between, Dr Franfield had instructed. So what was happening?

'Queenie!' she called in panic, but through the

thick stone walls of the cottage, Queenie couldn't hear her. She made it into the kitchen, shouting again, and as she reached the centre of the room, she felt something snap inside her. The next minute, something warm was trickling down her legs and into a puddle on the floor. She stood, too frightened to move and trembling like a leaf.

'What is it, cheel?'

Queenie appeared in the doorway leading from her room on the far side, looking like some guardian angel in her voluminous white nightgown, her grey hair falling over her shoulder in a long, thick plait.

'Oh, Queenie,' Anna squealed in a tiny voice. 'It's the baby. I think something awful's happened.'

'Oh, cheel, your waters 'ave broke, that's all.' Even in the candlelight, Anna saw the seamed face move into a smile. 'You just sit down. Yere, put this towel underneath you, an wrap yersel' in this yere blanket.'

She quickly opened up the vents to the range and then left Anna for a few minutes. By the time she returned fully dressed, the coals were coming to life again.

'Right,' she announced decisively, shoving her arms into her coat. 'I'll go an' ring Dr Franfield, an' by the time I gets back, that old kettle'll be singing away an' us can 'ave us a nice cup o' tea while we'rn waiting. Now then, torch, money. I'll be back as quick as I can. You just relax, cheel. Queenie'll take care of you.'

Yes, I know you will, Anna reflected gratefully. But it still seemed an eternity, waiting there alone in the near dark, the hem of her nightie cold and wet. Perhaps she should change into a clean one, but she didn't fancy stripping off. And then her stomach knotted up again, taking her breath away, and she was counting, breathing. Oh, God, did it have to hurt this much? Queenie, hurry up, please! What if the older woman had slipped over? It would be icy outside, and nobody would hear her if... Don't think like that. It would be all right...

'Dr Franfield's on 'is way,' Queenie blustered as she came back in. 'Going to take us to the 'ospital in 'is car. 'Ow's about that, then?' she chuckled. 'Queenie riding in a motor car! Now, your little case be all packed, so we'm all ready. So let's 'ave us this cuppa.'

'Oh, Queenie.' Anna grasped her gnarled hand as she passed the chair, and the worn face gazed down on her with a warm smile.

'This be it, cheel,' she soothed. 'This be it.'

'There we are. As handsome a little chap as I've ever seen.' Dr Franfield beamed as he placed the bundle into Anna's arms. 'And arrived just in time for us all to have breakfast. And I must get back home in time for morning surgery. Keep her down here for a couple of hours to get some rest, Sister, and then take her up on one of the wards.'

'Thank you so much, Doctor,' Anna said, wondering how her tongue managed to work when she felt so muzzy and light-headed. 'I'm sorry to have got you up in the middle of the night when you've got a full day's work ahead.'

'Occupational hazard,' he grinned back. 'I'll send Miss Witherspoon in if you feel up to it. I'm sure she'll want to see her great-nephew.'

Queenie's great-nephew. And her own son. Anna felt a fragile movement in her arms, and looked down.

A tiny, round, red face framed by the blue shawl the midwife had wrapped around the little head and body. The eyes were closed and screwed up, the nose like a little button. And then the rosebud mouth stretched into a gummy yawn and settled into working at the air. Anna's hand found its own way to stroke the soft cheek, cup the forehead. The shawl slipped off his head, revealing a cap of brown curls plastered to the skull.

A new little person, whose life – whose future – depended on her. So tiny. So helpless. So innocent, and not deserving of the label of bastard. But she could protect him. He was so ... perfect. She gazed down on the peaceful face, and her heart squeezed in awestruck fascination. She had never seen anything so small, so precious. She couldn't take her rapt eyes from him, and scarcely glanced up as the figure appeared at her side.

'Oh, Queenie, isn't he beautiful?' she breathed, her spellbound gaze at once drawn back to the little miracle in her arms. She sought out one of the hands, tiny as a doll's, the nails like little pink jewels. Counted each finger and thumb.

'Oooh.' Queenie gave a long wondrous sigh. 'Oh, yes. She's an absolute angel.'

Anna's eyes swivelled upwards. 'It's a boy, Queenie. A boy.'

Queenie shook her head as if bringing herself to her senses. 'Of course,' she murmured, 'just a slip o' the tongue. I be so overcome. Oh, you'm so

212

lucky, cheel.'

'Let me take him now,' the midwife smiled. 'You try and get some sleep, and then baby will be wanting his first feed.'

'Oh.' Anna's voice quavered with reluctance, but she allowed the kindly woman to remove the bundle from her arms.

'And Miss Witherspoon, I'll tell you all about visiting hours.'

'Queenie, you must be exhausted. Go home and get some sleep, and don't worry about visiting. It'll be so difficult for you.'

'Don't you go worrying none about me,' Queenie answered with a stern smile. 'You'm the one what needs rest now.'

'She's absolutely right. He may want a snooze now, but this little fellow will soon be demanding your attention. Try and nod off for a bit. If you need anything, just ring that bell.'

'Yes, thank you, Sister.'

Alone in the room, Anna snuggled down in the bed. Her undercarriage was so sore, she didn't think she'd ever recover. And as for 'making love' as they called it, well, she'd never be doing that again! Right off men for life, she was. Widowed. And happy to stay that way. She had that dear little bewitching wonder to care for now, and that was enough.

She was taken upstairs in the large, converted house – or two houses knocked into one, as she believed the maternity home had once been – in a wheelchair, with the infant clasped on her lap. When she had been gently woken with the ubiquitous cup of tea all waiting, she had been astounded to find that all she was interested in was holding her son again. And when she had been shown how to coax him into taking his first feed, it had filled her with enchantment to feel that she was providing life-giving sustenance for this little creature from her own body. Now she had managed some rest, she was overflowing with excitement.

There were just four beds in the ward, giving it a homely, relaxed atmosphere. Anna's only disappointment was that the baby was once again taken from her. It must have shown on her face.

'It's so we can rest,' a voice came from the next bed.

Anna looked across. A young woman was half lying on an arrangement of pillows, the starched white sheet tucked tightly across her. She looked a ghastly colour, and she had a drip going into her arm, but she managed a wan smile.

'Caroline Cresswell,' she introduced herself, 'but everyone calls me Carrie. Sorry I won't be much company today. Had a Caesarian yesterday, and I feel pretty bad.'

'Oh dear, I'm sorry to hear that.'

'I'm sure I'll feel better soon. I had a lovely little girl. What about you?'

'A boy,' Anna answered, amazed at the swell of pride in her breast. 'I'm Anna, by the way. Anna Millington.'

'Pleased to meet you, Anna. Oh, here comes lunch. Food in here's not at all bad.'

'Oh, good. D'you know, I'm suddenly hungry. They offered me something earlier, but I was still

214

feeling sick from some injection Dr Franfield had given me.'

'Oh, he's my doctor, too. Very nice man and very respected. We're very lucky. His son's a doctor, too.'

'So I believe. I've not met him, though.'

'I have. He's very nice, too. Specialises in joints and broken bones and things, apparently. Dr Franfield senior does babies and women's problems.'

'Lovely bedside manner he's got, hasn't he? I live up on the moor, which makes things a bit awkward. D'you know, he came out in his car in the middle of last night to bring me in here himself?'

'Doesn't surprise me,' Carrie commented, hauling herself into a sitting position as the bed trolley was brought up by a portly nurse. 'Live in Tavistock myself.'

'Come along, ladies, stop nattering and eat up,' the nurse reprimanded them. 'And lots to drink, remember. You'll have your little ones to feed again shortly.'

Behind the woman's well-padded back, Carrie caught Anna's eye and pulled a face. Anna had to stifle a giggle. She sensed that Carrie Cresswell was going to be a pleasant companion for the ten days or so she was supposed to stay in hospital, and it would be really good if they became friends. Anna had to admit that, much as she loved Queenie, she missed company of her own age. With it being so awkward to see Ethel, and with Frankie, well, she didn't know what was happening with her, it would be nice to have a good friend she could actually see once in a while, especially one who had a child of exactly the same age.

'How you'm doing, then, cheel?'

'Queenie! How on earth did you manage to get here?'

'I 'ad a word wi' Mrs Cribbett in Princetown, an' Mr Cribbett drove me yere in 'is lorry. An' one o' the other Mr Cribbetts will bring me another time.'

'Oh, how kind!'

'That's what living on the moor all your life does for you. Now, I wants to see this little tacker of ours again.'

The babies had been placed in their mothers' arms ready for visiting, and Anna loosened the infant's shawl so that Queenie could see him better. Queenie's pale eyes misted over, and Anna felt a pang of sadness. Queenie would have made a wonderful mother if she'd had the chance.

'Little angel,' she whispered. 'An' you looks proper ... serene yersel'.'

'I've fed him three times,' Anna announced proudly. 'Had to have help the first time, but I managed it on my own after that. There's a knack to it,' she said knowledgeably, 'but he's very eager. Three minutes on each side to start.'

'Oh, aren't we the expert?' Queenie laughed, her chin wobbling up and down. 'Decided on a name yet, 'as us?'

Anna tore her eyes away from the minuscule face. 'Well, no. Not really. I thought I'd wait. Until...' She couldn't finish the sentence. Until she'd decided whether or not to keep him?

'Deserves a name, anyway,' Queenie said softly.

216

'Can I make a suggestion? 'Ow's about Charlie?'

She pronounced the name with such tender compassion that Anna blinked her eyes wide in bewilderment. But – Charlie. It had a good ring to it. And Charles Millington sounded proper grand.

'Yes, I rather like that. Charlie. Yes, Queenie. I'll call him Charlie.'

And as she bent to kiss the little forehead, she noticed a tiny tear, like a pearl drop, trickle from Queenie's eye.

'Oh, look! He's opened his eyes!' she suddenly cried in delight. 'Hello, Charlie! I'm your mum!' she told him as he looked up at her with a puzzled frown.

Chapter Eighteen

'My, is it time to go already?' Queenie sighed almost in annoyance. 'I's only just got yere.'

'You've been here for the whole of visiting!' Anna chuckled. 'And you mustn't come every day. I know how awkward it must be for you.'

Queenie nodded. 'Depends on 'oo can give us a lift. Been so kind everyone 'as. Pity that there bus don't go at the right times, an' not every day at that. P'r'aps I–'

'Come along, ladies. Visiting's over.'

'Sorry, Nurse. You'd better go, Queenie.'

'Well, just one more kiss for little Charlie.' The older woman bent over to place her lips on the baby's forehead. 'I'll get in to see you again as soon as I can.'

'Yes, I know you will, Queenie. You just take care now.'

She watched as Queenie left the ward, the last visitor to go, but she still paused at the door to blow a final kiss before she disappeared. Anna sighed with contentment and relaxed back against the pillows, cradling Charlie in her arms.

'Is that your mum?' Carrie asked from the next bed.

Anna closed her eyes briefly. 'No. Queenie's a sort of adopted aunt. I live with her.'

'Really?' Anna could tell that Carrie's reply was tempered with caution. 'She seems a very homely sort. And ... what about your husband if you don't mind my asking?' she said guardedly.

Anna bit her lip, cross with herself for letting it slip that she lived with Queenie. But there were bound to be questions asked when no husband appeared. Anna mentally braced herself, ready to keep to the story that her husband had been killed in a road accident, but then she raised a nervous eyebrow in Carrie's direction and held her breath. The other young mother seemed the sort who would understand. She hoped she was right.

'I'm not married,' she dared to mutter.

Her heart put in an extra beat, and she saw Carrie lift a surprised eyebrow. 'Oh dear, I'm sorry,' the girl answered, but there was no malice in her tone. 'I shouldn't have asked. I didn't mean to pry.'

But Anna felt encouraged by her attitude. 'No, it's all right. I don't mind telling you. You see, I was deeply in love. At least I thought I was. And

I honestly believed we were going to be married. Only it turned out he was already engaged to someone else. It wasn't until after he was married that I found out I was pregnant.'

'Oh, Lord. You were led right up the garden path. I thought you didn't seem the type to, well, you know what I mean. So, living with Queenie, is that because your parents don't want to know?'

'Oh, no. My parents both died fairly recently,' Anna replied almost automatically, it seemed. She was getting used to explaining to people. She wondered how many times in her life she would have to do so.

'Oh, crikey, Anna, how awful!'

'My father was knocked down by a lorry. Last summer. And my mum died the previous autumn. She wasn't well and fainted at the top of the stairs. She fell down and broke her neck.'

'O-oh, Anna! And there's me upset because my parents live so far away, they can't come to see me and Poppy until next week.'

'Oh?' Anna eagerly latched on to the change of subject. 'I thought as you didn't have a local accent.'

Carrie gave a light, tinkling laugh. 'No, I'm from Surrey. I met Jeffery when we were here on holiday a few years ago. We'd rented a cottage and something went wrong with the electricity. The owners got in touch with Trembath's in Tavistock. In West Street. Do you know it?'

'No, I don't. I know Tavistock a bit, but not that well, I'm afraid.'

'Well, they sent out an electrician. It was Jeffery. We got chatting, and one thing led to another, and, well, here we are!' she grinned. 'Happily married and with our first baby. Oh, I'm sorry,' she said, the joy slipping from her face, 'That sounded terribly smug.'

'Oh, don't worry. I'm right off men at the moment,' Anna told her with such conviction it astounded even herself. 'In fact, I don't think I'll look at another man ever again.'

'Oh, I'm sure you will. One day.'

'No, I won't. Only little Charlie here. I shall devote myself to bringing him up and nothing else. In our little cottage up on the moor.'

'Gosh, that sounds idyllic.'

'Oh, it is. In many ways. But there's no electricity or anything, so it's quite hard work. It'll be a super way of life for a little one, mind.' And suddenly Anna found herself looking towards a happy future, bringing up Charlie with Queenie's animals, wandering on the moor, going to school in Princetown until he was eleven, and then hopefully to Tavistock Grammar. She would make sure Charlie had every opportunity for a fulfilling life. And she was really looking forward to it.

'Ah, Mrs Cresswell and Miss Millington?'

It was afternoon rest time, and Anna had been quietly dreaming of Holly Cottage, the green moorland fields baked in sunshine, the goats, Queenie's wrinkly smile, and a little boy running towards her on unsteady, chubby little legs. She sighed at the interruption and opened her eyes. For a moment, she thought she must still be caught up in the contented vision her mind had conjured up for her. Standing at the bottom of their beds was an extremely handsome young man. He was relatively tall, slim, and dressed in grey flannels, a subdued jumper over a shirt and tie, and a smart jacket. He somehow seemed familiar, and when he smiled at them, Anna felt something light up inside her.

'I'm so sorry to disturb your rest, ladies,' he said politely. 'My father asked me to pop in. He's been called away on an emergency and so can't get in to see you this afternoon as promised. So I'm afraid you've got me instead. Oh, sorry. I should have said. I'm Dr Franfield. Junior.'

'Yes, we've met before,' Carrie said chirpily. 'At the surgery in Plymouth Road.'

'Did we? I'm so sorry. I'm afraid I don't remember.'

'Oh, it was just in the hallway as I was going in to see your father for a check-up.'

'Ah. I'm sorry, I still don't remember. But anyway have either of you any worries?' He picked up the charts at the bottom of each bed and ran a professional eye over them. 'These look fine. And Sister's pleased with you both. So any problems?'

As he looked at them, Anna noticed his incredible blue-green eyes, the strong jaw and pleasantly curved mouth. Oh, yes. He was the image of his father who must have been very attractive in his youth.

'No, everything's fine, thank you,' she answered.

'Well, in that case, I'll leave you in peace. My father will be in tomorrow to give you both a full examination. And apologies once again for disturbing you.'

Anna found her eyes following him as he left

the room, and then she heard Carrie sigh from the adjacent bed.

'Gorgeous, isn't he?'

'Carrie! You're not supposed to say things like that! You're a married woman!' Anna teased.

'Ah, but *you're* not.' Carrie raised a speculative eyebrow. 'I wonder if he's married or footloose and fancy-free.'

'Really, Carrie! Now, shut up and go back to sleep or whatever you were doing!' Anna chuckled back.

'Spoilsport!'

Carrie pulled one of her cheeky faces, but snuggled down again, and Anna did the same. It wouldn't be long before Charlie would be brought in for his next feed and she would have the joy of holding him again, rubbing his little back to wind him against her shoulder, breathe in the fragrance of his downy head. But into her mind kept filtering the image of the man who had stood at the foot of the bed for all of three minutes. Dr Franfield junior was an unattainable world away from her, but something had moved inside her at the sight of the attractive male and his warm, pleasant manner. She pushed the thought aside. It would take all her efforts to provide a good home for Charlie, and from now on, that was all that mattered to her.

'Ethel! Mrs Shallaford!'

'Annie!'

'Little maid!'

'Oh, how lovely to see you!' Anna was overjoyed at her unexpected visitors. 'I never thought you'd come all this way!'

'Try keeping us away!' Ethel grinned. 'When us got Queenie's telegram... Oh, look at 'en, Mum! 'E's so tiny!'

Anna proudly drew back the shawl so that Ethel and Mabel could see Charlie properly. 'He's a little love, isn't he?' she breathed, still enchanted herself.

'Oh, you forgets 'ow little they be,' Mabel smiled, all gooey-eyed. 'An' that's from someone what's brought five little tackers into the world. Do 'e be'ave 'issel', Annie?'

'I think so. But they bring them to us strictly every four hours for feeding, so I don't really know what goes on in between. I bathed him myself today, and they let me out of bed to change him now, as well.'

'You'm feeling better, then?'

'Oh, yes. Raring to go. A bit sore, but I can't wait to get home. Would you like a hold, Eth? But not for too long, because I can't get enough of him myself.'

She carefully handed Charlie into Ethel's arms, but having dealt with so many younger siblings, Ethel was quite an expert. Anna relaxed back against the pillows and smiled up at Mabel as she rummaged in a large shopping bag.

'Just a few bits for you. Old babby clothes. Not expecting to need 'em again messel'. Leastways, I 'opes not!'

'Oh, how kind! Thank you so much.'

'You got a name for 'en yet?' Ethel glanced up, her expression besotted.

'Yes. Charlie. It was Queenie's suggestion. She's

223

been a brick. She's somehow managed to get in every other day. Mind you, I think she's bludgeoned people into giving her a lift!'

'Come on, Eth. 'And 'en over. My turn.'

Charlie protested mildly at being passed over to a new person, but he soon settled down in Mabel's practised arms. Anna smiled, totally content.

'Did you come on the train?'

'Us certainly did,' Ethel confirmed. 'Chose today 'cause it's my arternoon off and us could leave early. Mum arranged for Primrose an' Sammy to go 'ome with friends arter school.' She sat back with a sigh and tipped her head. 'You does look 'appy, Annie.' But then her face clouded. ''Is Nibbs 'asn't put 'is face in, at all?'

'No, thank God.' Anna screwed up her lips. 'And I hope he never does.'

'Good. You an' Queenie can look arter the little chap proper fine. An' us'll always be there, too.'

'And Carrie, here.' Anna directed her head towards the next bed where Carrie and Jeffery were deeply engrossed in adoration of their daughter. 'We've become good friends. She lives in Tavistock so we can use the bus to see each other.'

'That'll be nice for you.'

'Oh, do I detect a touch of jealousy?' Anna laughed.

'Probably.' Ethel admitted. 'I really does miss you. An' with Bert away...'

It wasn't like Ethel to be downcast, and Anna reached out and squeezed her hand. 'Never mind. You know he'll be back for good in just over a year. And when Charlie's bigger, it'll be easier for me to come down to you.'

'I's not certain it will be! 'E'll be bigger an' 'eavier then.'

'Oh, I'm going to keep my eyes open for a second-hand pushchair. You know, the sort where the handle and the footrest fold down. People put ads in the Post Office window in Princetown, so I'm hoping I might find one through that. It'd still be too cumbersome to take on a city double-decker, but I'm sure it'd be all right on our country bus. I know all the drivers and I'm sure they'd help me on and off with it.'

Ethel's fleeting morose moment seemed to have passed. 'You sounds just like me, planning everything.'

'Us never 'ears the end of it!' Mabel chipped in. 'Yere, does you want another 'old, Eth? I really needs a fag. But I doesn't suppose...?'

She glanced questioningly about the sterile, clean-smelling room, looking so forlorn that Anna had to chuckle. 'I'm sorry, Mrs Shallaford. I think you'll have to go outside.'

'Ah, well. Yere, take the babby, Eth. I'll wait for you down by the entrance. Us'll see you again soon, Anna, love.'

'Thank you so much for coming. Give my love to everyone And thank you for all the clothes.'

'Cas'n think of a better 'ome for 'em. TTFN, then,' Mabel called, already fumbling in her handbag for her cigarettes before she was even out of the room!

Ethel shook her head. 'Mum's a one, bain't she?'

'She's always been so kind–'

'Oh, 'ello, little man!' Ethel crooned in delight.

225

''E's opened 'is eyes. Oo, they'm ... I's not sure what colour they be. Bit like yourn, maybe. Sort of greyish. But 'e's a proper 'andsome little chap. Oh, dear.' She jiggled Charlie up and down as he suddenly wriggled, his face puckering up as he began to grizzle. 'Feeding time, is it?'

'Not supposed to be yet,' Anna frowned. 'But perhaps he's hungry anyway. After all, his stomach can't tell the time, can it? Oh, Eth, I've got such a lot to learn about babies!'

'Well, I's certain 'e'll let you know when 'e wants summat! Yere, take 'en back now. Mum'll be waiting, an' us've got a train to catch.'

Anna gratefully took Charlie back into her arms and smiled as Ethel bent to give them both a kiss on the cheek. It seemed such a grown-up thing to do. But Charlie had done that to them, hadn't he? Made them grow up. A lump suddenly swelled in Anna's throat.

'Oh, Eth, we'll always be best friends, won't we?' she croaked.

'Just you bets, kiddo!'

And Ethel left Anna smiling. She cradled Charlie against her, giving him her little finger to suck. His tiny lips closed around it, and he settled down contentedly. Oh, she couldn't wait to get him home and start their new life together!

'Good morning, mothers,' the smartly dressed gent greeted them as he entered the ward with Sister. 'I'm the registrar. Would you like to register the births of your children with me now? Save you a trip to my office in town later on.'

The other two beds had become occupied in the

last few days by pleasant enough women, one of whom had given birth to twins. But Anna and Carrie hadn't felt the same affinity with them as they had instantly done with each other. Now, though, there was a general consensus that attending to the official business while they could would be most convenient.

'You first, my dear?' the man suggested, looking towards Carrie.

'Yes, if you like,' she smiled back, and the registrar went over to her.

Anna tried not to listen as she aimlessly turned the pages of that week's *Womans Own* that Queenie had brought in for her. But she found her ears tuned to the conversation by the next bed, and her pulse began to race. It would be her turn next, a moment of decision. The moment when she could say, no, it will be better for Charlie to be adopted. But she knew she couldn't do it. She loved him too much. Selfish as it may be, now that she had cared for, cuddled, fed by her own breast the scrap of humanity who had somehow wormed his way into her heart, she could not give him up.

'Now, then, Mrs ... er?' the registrar said, turning to her.

She glared up at him, her chin jutting determinedly as if he were the enemy. 'Millington. Anna Millington.'

'I need the child's details first, please. Name and date of the birth.'

'Charles Millington. Twelfth of January.'

'Oka ... ay.. Cha ... arles, and the twelfth,' the fellow repeated as he filled in his ledger with perfect handwriting. 'Now, the father's full name

227

and rank or profession, please?'

Anna's mouth filled up with bile. Rank? Baronet. What a fiasco! If Gilbert had meant to marry her as she had believed, Charlie would have been in line for the baronetcy. Now the only title he would ever bear was 'bastard'.

'Can you put "father unknown", please?'

The fellow raised an eyebrow. 'Ah. Am I to take it that you are *Miss* Millington and that the child is illegitimate?'

Anna gulped. It was such a horrible word. She was grateful when the registrar lowered his voice when he spoke again.

'In that case, the father's details will be left blank. I can only insert them if the father is present and you both agree to it.'

Anna sighed with relief. At least she hadn't been forced to acknowledge Gilbert as Charlie's father. She just wished – oh, how she wished – that she had a loving husband to help bring Charlie up. But she and Queenie were determined to make a wonderful life for him, and what better place to grow up than Dartmoor?

Chapter Nineteen

'You'm up early, cheel.' Queenie's face was a picture of concerned surprise as she waddled into the kitchen in her dressing gown. 'Don't say as the babby kept you up all night?'

'No, just the opposite,' Anna beamed. 'He

didn't wake up for his night feed until five o'clock. He's gone back to sleep now, so I thought I might as well get up.'

'It's only just gone six, mind,' Queenie frowned. 'You'll be mortal tired later on.'

'Probably,' Anna grimaced. 'But it means he might start going through the night soon. Oh, at last! But they say most babies start going through the night about six weeks, so Charlie's bang on target.'

'Yes, the little lover. Cold last night, weren't it? Let's 'ave a nice 'ot cup o' tea as soon as the kettle boils.'

Five minutes later they were sipping their tea in easy silence by the amber glow from the oil lamps, the quiet before the busy activities of the day. On top of all the usual chores and caring for the goats and the hens, there was Charlie to look after. He filled their lives with joy, and Queenie was only too happy to sit with him on her lap and cuddle away his whimperings. Not that he cried a great deal at all. He was a contented little soul, and when he was awake, his intelligent eyes followed them around the room.

Today Anna would be washing Charlie's nappies, the one job he created that she hated. They had been soaking overnight in two buckets in the outhouse in a weak solution of disinfectant. Later she would have to scrub them and then boil them up with Omo in a huge old saucepan on the range, then rinse them in several lots of water. Fortunately, Queenie had an old mangle in the yard which helped enormously, but it had been bitterly cold outside, and Anna's hands were becoming sore and chapped.

Light was beginning to peep through the gap in the curtains and she got up to open them fully. 'I think it's going to be a nice day,' she spoke over her shoulder. 'It's a bit frosty, but there's a lovely sunrise.'

'Well, end o' February. Spring'll be just around the corner if we'm lucky. I tells you what, mind. Proper maudlin I be about them closing the railway. Been there all my life, it 'as. I cas'n get my old brain to think it won't be there arter next week.'

'I know. It's such a shame. I've always thought what an amazing sight it is, the old train chugging across the moor. They're going to run the buses every day instead, though, aren't they? And at extra times as well.'

She paused, her fine brow puckered. Queenie was staring ahead of her, eyes glazed and a vacant expression on her face. A dart of horror shot down Anna's spine.

'Queenie?' she prompted, her heart heating nervously. 'Are you all right?'

To her relief, Queenie blinked her eyes wide and looked up at her. 'Sorry, cheel? Oh, yes. I were just thinking about the train. Always got through, it did. Roads blocked wi' snow, but the train got through. Leastways, all but a couple o' times. 1927 as I do mind. And 1947. Worst snow since the Great Blizzard of 1891, they said.'

'1947? Oh, yes, I remember that!' Anna was so happy that Queenie had only been daydreaming that she felt quite animated. 'Funny, really. To think of you living up here in the snow, when I was walking to school in it down in Plymouth. Not so

230

far away, and yet not knowing the other existed. And yet, here we are now... Funny thing, fate.'

'Oh. I wouldn't know about that. All I know is that I'll miss that there train. Ah, well.' Queenie gave a heartfelt sigh, making Anna frown again. She must find a way to cheer her dear friend up again.

'Let's have breakfast in peace while Charlie's still asleep,' she said brightly

'That'll be a first!' Queenie chuckled, and Anna felt satisfied as she began to set on the table the bread, butter, their own home-made jam, milk from the goats, cornflakes and the packet of Sugar Puffs she had treated herself to. Feeding Charlie, she felt constantly hungry and yet she had very quickly regained her figure.

'Oh, there's the postman,' she said as she happened to look out of the window.

'Oo, 'ow exciting! I'll get it!'

'OK. I'll top up the pot.'

Anna busied herself with the tea and then sat down at the table to wait for Queenie who was chatting with the postman. They didn't get much post, so Anna glanced up expectantly as Queenie came back in, squinting at the envelope in her hand.

'It's for you, cheel, I think. Cas'n see proper like wi'out my glasses.'

'That's odd. It's postmarked London. I don't know anyone in London. Oh. Not unless...'

Her heart gave a little jump. Yes. It must be from Frankie. She had almost given up on expecting a reply to the letter she had entrusted to Mrs Smudge. She didn't even know if the farmer's wife had managed to pass it on, though evidently she had, or Frankie wouldn't have known where to send a letter to. Anna held her breath as she began to read the childish handwriting, for heaven knew what it contained.

Dear Anna

Mrs Smudge secretly gave me your letter when we came down to Ashcroft Hall a few weeks ago. I read it and burnt it straight away in case anyone found it. This is the first chance I've had to write back without anyone knowing.

Well, at least that didn't seem like the prelude to something nasty and accusing. But Frankie was clearly under pressure, and that was cause for concern. Anna pursed her lips as she read on.

Of course I don't blame you for what had already happened. Gilbert obviously isn't the person I always believed him to be, so we were both fooled by him. It's hard to think that he was unfaithful before we were even married, but much as we were childhood sweethearts, looking back, I think he was pressurised into the marriage. Lady Ashcroft can be a formidable force when she wants to he, but it's poor excuse for the mess it has made of all our lives.

She was absolutely livid, you know. Outwardly, mainly at you, but I think at bottom, really at Gilbert Although she denies it, I think she knows jolly well you were telling the truth. I overheard her telling him off, saying how disgusted she was with him and that he had sullied the name of Ashcroft. The next morning, we were bundled back to London. She could see how you and I had become friends and obviously wanted to put an end to it. So we'll have to be very careful.

Everything's strained between Gilbert and me as you

232

might imagine. And then my father passed away just before Christmas. We'd hidden everything from him, of course, so at least he died thinking he was leaving everything as he wanted. I miss him so much, I can't tell you.

Oh dear, poor Frankie. Anna chewed her bottom lip. She knew what it was to grieve for a beloved parent. She still wanted to believe that everything had been a bad dream. That she would snap her fingers and find herself back in Ford with her mum and dad. And now Frankie, too, was lost in that same emptiness.

Anna shook her head and forced herself to read on.

Christmas was horrible, but afterwards, Gilbert thought it would be good for me to go down to Ashcroft Hall for a break. So he does still consider my feelings. In fact in many ways, we're a normal married couple. It's just that our 'relations' don't feel right anymore, knowing that he'd been with you before.

Anna pulled herself up sharply. That made it sound so cold and sordid. And it hadn't been. Not on her side, anyway. But there was no malice in Frankie's words. She was only trying to express how she felt. If there was to be any chance of their friendship continuing, Anna would just have to accept it.

You must have had the baby by now, so I hope it all went well. I wonder if you had a boy or a girl? And I must say that I'm actually quite jealous. It would be wonderful to have a child to love unreservedly, but we haven't been blessed yet. But I'd love to see your child, and to see you again, too.

Please don't write to me again. It isn't fair on Mrs

233

Smudge, and it's too dangerous. If Gilbert or his mother found out we'd been in contact, they'd never let me come to Ashcroft Hall again. But next time we do, I'll try to get word to you and we can meet secretly somewhere. I'm learning to drive, so perhaps I can borrow Gilbert's precious car one day when he's occupied in the study. I'll really look forward to it, and in the meantime look after yourself and the little one.

Your friend always
Francesca

Anna lowered the sheet of paper onto her lap. She was so lucky. She might not have much money, but she had Charlie, she had Ethel and her family, Queenie, and now Carrie. Frankie was well off – no, more than that, rich – but she had nobody except a husband she could never trust again, and a domineering mother-in-law.

As if to echo her thoughts, an impatient wail had started to filter in from her bedroom. Charlie. More than ever, she couldn't wait to scoop him up in her arms.

'I'll get 'er!' Queenie dived in, already halfway to the door.

Anna shook her head with a smile. After his feed, she would give Charlie his bath and he would probably stay awake a little longer before she put him down again. And then she could get on with the nappies.

She glanced over her shoulder as Queenie came back into the room, crooning over Charlie's scowling cries. Queenie doted on him as much as she did, as if she were his real grandmother. In future years, Anna would have to be careful that Queenie didn't spoil him too much!

But what had Queenie said just now? I'll get *'er?* Anna knew that sometimes Queenie used the Devonshire "er' meaning 'he', but Devonshire for 'him' was "en'. So, Queenie had actually said, 'I'll get *her.*' Anna gave a cold shiver. It wasn't the first time she had noticed such a slip of the older woman's tongue. She prayed it would be the last.

Anna watched the bull-nosed bus rumble to a halt beside her. Her darting eyes eagerly scoured the windows. Ah, there they were! The door opened. There was Carrie with Polly in her arms and they hugged each other as tightly as they could without squashing the child between them.

'You're here at last!' Anna crowed jubilantly. 'It's so good to see you both!'

'Phew! I don't know how you manage coming down to Tavistock so often for the baby clinic.'

'It's not easy!' Anna laughed. 'You wouldn't believe that such little things need such a lot of paraphernalia just to come out for a few hours, would you?'

'Well, we're here now,' Carrie announced triumphantly, then paused to gaze around her. 'Gosh, is that Holly Cottage? How quaint!'

'Come along in. Queenie can't wait to see you again, either. She's planning on taking us for a picnic.'

'Lucky it's such a nice day, then.'

'Really warm for May, isn't it? Almost like summer.'

They ambled along the uneven lane to the cottage. Carrie was all eyes as she went inside. Queenie had jammed open the front door so that

235

a brilliant shaft of sunlight flooded over the flagstone floor.

'Not opening the tea room today,' she informed
her young friends importantly. 'You'm all right
wi' a little stroll on the moor?'

'Oh, yes. But I can't carry Polly very far, I'm
afraid.'

'Ah, ha, we thought of that!' Anna chortled.
'I've made a sort of carry-sling for Charlie that I
use quite a bit, so I've made one for you as well.'

'Did you? Oh, how kind! This is going to be
quite an adventure, I can see!'

A little while later, they set out across the moor.
The air was still and fragrant with the scent of
gorse, the rolling hills greening up in the warm
sunshine and the towering granite tors standing
out majestically in the distance. At last, they came
to the spot Queenie had been aiming for, a flat
grassy area next to a lively stream. Anna shook
out the rug and they settled the children on it
before opening their own picnic. Queenie
produced a small kettle which she filled from the
brook, then she gathered some dry heather and lit
a small fire on a large flat stone that she declared
she had used many times in her life so that there
was no risk of the flames spreading.

'We could have had a thermos,' Carrie whispered out of earshot.

'Yes, I know. But it wouldn't be the same. Not
for Queenie, anyway. I couldn't spoil it for her.'

'Oh, she's coming. Gosh, you are clever,
Queenie!' Carrie said, raising her voice. 'I've got
an electric kettle. Couldn't manage anything else!
And with Jeffery being an electrician–'

'How is he, by the way?'

'He's fine, thank you. Loving fatherhood! Worries about his mum, though. She's in a home, you see. A good one, but she's completely senile, so when Jeffery's dad died, there was really no alternative. We take Polly to see her sometimes, but she really doesn't know who we are.'

Carrie paused, a rueful expression on her lips. It seemed strange to see her normal buoyant self so deflated and Anna squeezed her hand. She always envied Carrie her happy marriage and loving home, but it seemed nobody's life was without its problems.

'Try not to let it spoil your day out,' she said limply.

Carrie at once broke out in a smile. 'You're absolutely right, of course. This is a real treat! Nothing like eating out of doors, is there? Those sandwiches look good. What's in them?'

'They'm Spam with mustard.' Queenie dipped her head proudly as she unfolded one packet of greaseproof paper. 'An' they'm egg an' cress. Our own eggs, an' us growed the cress on the window sill.'

'Oh, how splendid!'

'It is, isn't it? And just now, I want everything to stay just as it is. For ever and ever. Don't you, Carrie?'

Carrie grinned as she lounged back on the rug. 'Yes, absolutely. And I'm so glad we met in the hospital. With me being relatively new to the area, and Jeffery having no family to speak of and mine so far away, it's good to have a new friend.'

'Where does your family live, then, cheel?'

'Surrey. At least, my parents do. My brother's up north.'

'I didn't realise you had a brother,' Anna said in surprise as she bit into one of the egg sandwiches.

'Mmm, yes. Jack. Older than me. Did his National Service and then got an apprenticeship in gardening up in Yorkshire. Fully trained now, though, he is, but he stayed on at the same place. He's passionate about gardening. Out in all weathers. Not like me. I love my garden in the summer, but in bad weather, you can keep it! Oh, I think I'd better open Polly's jar of baby food. She's starting to grizzle.'

'Peace over!' Anna laughed as Charlie began to join in. But she felt she could never be happier than she was at that moment.

Chapter Twenty

The slight young girl who sidled into the Tavistock café glanced furtively over her shoulder up and down the street before swiftly shutting the door behind her. She was well dressed in a blue summer frock belted at her tiny waist, and a grey, short-sleeved bolero of fine angora. Her neck was adorned with a double row of real pearls and her appearance smacked of money, but it was all at odds with her dark-shadowed eyes and her lost, nervous manner.

Anna didn't recognise her at first. She'd had her hair cut, too, so that it sprang about her head in a halo of blond curls, and it was only as she spied Anna with baby Charlie and made a bee-line for her that Anna realised who it was.

'Frankie!'

Anna stood up, arranging her face into a broad smile, resolved not to show her dismay. Gone was the flushed young bride. Before her stood a timid, fearful mouse with grey smudges beneath her cornflower blue eyes.

'Anna!' Francesca leant forward and kissed her on the cheek. Constrained, and not like the bubbly girl she had known. 'Oh, this must be the baby!' Frankie gave what Anna thought might be a forced smile as she drew back and looked down at the pushchair parked beside the table.

'Yes, this is Charlie,' she replied warily.

But she needn't have worried. Frankie's face was suddenly radiant with admiration. 'A boy, then!' she grinned. 'Oh, he's lovely!'

'He might be now, fast asleep and looking as if butter wouldn't melt,' Anna laughed nervously. 'But he's a right little monkey when he's awake. Crawling now, he is, and in to everything!'

'How old is he, then?' Frankie asked, pulling out the other chair and sitting down at the table.

'Eight months. I can't believe how the time's flown.'

'No. I don't suppose you can.'

Anna detected a rueful sigh in Frankie's reply, as if for her, it had seemed an eternity. To cover up the awkward moment, she caught the waitress's eye across the room. Her brow corrugated into a frown while they waited for the woman to come over. Frankie's eyes had been scanning the other customers as if she was worried someone might recognise her. Anna's heart bled for her. Had she really been reduced to this?

'You got my note all right, then?' Frankie began when they had ordered. 'I was afraid you wouldn't. Or that you wouldn't come.'

'Yes of course And your letter. Back in February, wasn't it? I thought ... well...'

'I know.' Frankie lowered her beautiful eyes and Anna noticed her restless fingers repeatedly smoothing the check tablecloth. 'I wanted to write but I had to wait until it was safe. I thought it'd be better if Gilbert believed I'd forgotten all about you.'

'Are things really that bad?' Anna looked across the table and saw Frankie swallow.

'Yes. It's as if what happened with you and Gilbert must be swept under the carpet. Wiped out. Once or twice I tried to talk about it but he got so angry, I daren't mention it again.'

Her eyes flicked upwards at Anna as if she had said too much. But the difficult moment was diffused by the waitress arriving with their order. By the time everything was on the table, Frankie's mood seemed lighter.

'And you? Are you managing all right? I thought it was atrocious the way you were treated.'

'Oh, I couldn't be happier. I mean, things are tight money-wise, but we manage. It's hard work but it's fun living with Queenie. The cottage is pretty primitive. It's a bit like stepping back a hundred years.'

Anna bit her lip at the irony of her words. That was exactly how she'd felt when she had first gone to Ashcroft Hall and been treated like a scullery maid in Victorian times. She was well out of it. Unlike Frankie.

'This Queenie sounds a lovely lady.'

'She is. You must meet her sometime.'

'Oh, I don't think that would be wise.' Frankie glanced up from stirring her cup of tea. 'If I parked the car by the road there, someone might see it. It's pretty distinctive, and if it got back to Gilbert or Lady Prue, they'd want to know where I'd been. And they'd soon find out you were living there. There'd be hell to pay.'

'Hell?' Anna was appalled.

'Yes. But enough about me.' Frankie's face suddenly brightened. 'I want to hear about you and Charlie.'

'Well, he keeps me busy every minute of the day! We don't really see any other children up at Princetown, but I made a friend at the maternity home. She lives here in Tavistock and we see quite a lot of each other. And then there's my friend, Ethel. I told you about her if you remember. Back in Plymouth. So, overall, I'm quite content.'

'Good. I'm so pleased to hear it. But is there anything you need for Charlie? Money, for instance? That's one thing I've got plenty of,' she snorted, her voice for the first time tainted with bitterness.

'No, honestly. We manage fine. Oh dear, no peace for the wicked!' Anna grinned as Charlie stirred, blinked open his eyes and began to grizzle. She lifted him out of the pushchair and sat him on her lap, opening her bag and giving him a Farley's Rusk to suck on.

'He's teething,' she explained to Frankie.

'Poor little thing. I suppose they can't understand. Does he say anything yet?'

'Good Lord, no. He's only eight months.'

'Is that too early? I've no idea about babies, you see. Not having one of my own.' Frankie licked her lips wistfully but the next moment was smiling again. 'I've finished my sandwich. Let me hold him so you can have yours.'

'Would you mind? I've got a bottle of milk made up if he gets fed up with the rusk. You don't have to feed him, though. He can hold it himself.'

She settled Charlie on Frankie's lap and the other girl took him with a woman's natural instinct, Anna reflected, as she watched Frankie support Charlie with one hand while the other was ready to catch the rusk if he dropped it. Their meeting had fallen into place, the initial reserve over, and for ten minutes they chatted away like old friends. Then Charlie started fidgeting and holding out his arms towards his mother.

'I'd better take him back,' Anna said, 'before he starts yelling his head off and spoiling everyone's lunch.'

'Yes, I suppose you'd better.'

Frankie sounded reluctant, but she lifted Charlie up towards Anna who had stood up to take him across the table. As she did so, the short sleeves of the bolero rode up over her upper arms. Anna gasped in horror as she gripped Charlie against her chest. On both Frankie's arms were livid bruises as if someone had recently grabbed hold of her with brutal force and tried to shake the life out of her.

242

'God, Frankie,' Anna breathed in disbelief. 'Did ... did Gilbert do that?'

Frankie's cheeks at once flushed as if with guilt and she hastily pulled her sleeves back into place. Her eyes met Anna's almost defensively for a moment, but then her face dissolved as moisture collected in her eyes and she nodded slowly.

'He ... he wanted ... you know,' she whispered distraughtly. 'I was tired and wanted to go to sleep, but he ... he insisted. He said it was no wonder we weren't getting a child.'

She hung her lovely head and Anna stared at her in horror. She had seen a flash of that other vile, latent side of Gilbert's nature herself, hadn't she, the day she had told him she was pregnant? No longer the charming, persuasive young gentleman, there was a secret violence in him when he couldn't get his own way. But to have turned on his defenceless, wronged wife like that was despicable.

'Oh, Frankie,' Anna repeated, utterly horrified. 'Oh, if only there was something I could do–'

'You have. Meeting you here has been a real tonic to me. And Charlie's a little love. I'm so glad I've seen him. But now I must go.' She rose to her feet decisively. 'I do hope we can meet again like this.'

'Of course we can. I'll look forward to it.'

'I don't know when, though. It could be months. I'll get word to you in the same way.' She opened her handbag and took out her purse. 'There, that'll cover the bill. And take this for Charlie.'

She quickly placed two ten pound notes on the table, and Anna's mouth dropped open. It was a

243

fortune. 'Oh, I can't possibly–'

'It's Gilbert's money. Charlie's his child, and if he won't accept any responsibility for him, then I will. Take care, Anna.'

She spun on her heel and made for the door before Anna had a chance to say goodbye – or shove the notes back in Frankie's hand, although she had to admit that the money was more than welcome. She watched her friend leave the café, her heart weighing heavily in her breast. Frankie wasn't the sort to fight back, but what could she. Anna, possibly do to help? She hugged Charlie tightly and kissed his little forehead before sitting him back in the pushchair. How blessed she was!

'Thanks ever so for the lift, Jeffery.'

'All part of the service,' the young man grinned back. 'I'm proper glad you an' Carrie enjoyed the film. Does you both good to get out without the little ones once in a while.'

'Mmm, yes, it does. I'm so lucky to have Queenie to babysit. But I think I'd better go in before she starts wondering where I am.'

'OK, see you soon, then.'

'Thanks again.'

Anna got out of the little Austin Seven and turned up the lane beside the lodge. The dank mist of the November night made her shiver, and once Jeffery had turned the car round and disappeared into the murk, an eerie silence muffled the moor once again. Anna hurried along the short distance to the cottage, which was no more than a long, low shadow in the gloom, and crept silently inside. Despite what she had said to Jeffery, she expected

Queenie to be fast asleep in bed. Anna knew she herself would feel tired the next day but it was worth it to have a few hours to relax. Going to the pictures with Carrie and enjoying the heroism and excitement in a repeat showing of *The Dam Busters,* which she had missed when it had been shown in Tavistock the previous January, had been a welcome change – even if she would really have preferred something more romantic. It had been like being back with Ethel, making her feel young again – even if she was only just turned twenty!

The cottage felt instantly cosy and welcoming after the penetrating damp outside. Queenie had left one of the oil lamps on very low so that a diffused amber glow reflected on the whitewashed walls. Anna tiptoed towards the range, not wanting the heels of her shoes to click on the flagstones. It was only then that she heard the low, hushed crooning and realised that Queenie wasn't in bed but was sitting in one of the sagging armchairs. She must have been having trouble with Charlie and was rocking him to sleep on her lap. Anna could hear the muted snuffling he made when he was nodding off, so she didn't want to disturb him just at the wrong moment.

'There, there, Charlotte, my darling,' she heard Queenie's soft, lilting whisper. 'You go to sleep, my little one. Mammy's yere. She won't let you down again.'

Anna's heart froze. Dear God. Was Queenie losing her mind? But somehow she didn't think so, although there had been the occasional, odd moment – always with Charlie – when some deep-seated, emotional memory seemed to stir.

Queenie looked up, startled for a second as she evidently hadn't heard Anna come in. Then she inclined her head towards Charlie who must have only just drifted off, as his mouth was still working in the way babies do before they sink into their deep slumber.

Anna smiled down knowingly, attempting to conceal her concern. In the jaundiced shadows. Queenie's face looked even more seamed than usual, tinged with a wistful contentment that spoke of hidden, past regret. Anna was curious, but above all she wanted to heal the hurt that she read in Queenie's strange, opalescent eyes.

'Er's just gone off,' Queenie mouthed. They both knew they would have to wait a few minutes until Charlie was so heavily asleep that he wouldn't wake up again as he was slid into the cot Anna had bought second hand, together with the pushchair, from someone in Princetown.

Anna sank into the other chair, the enjoyment of the evening with Carrie dissipated by her worry over Queenie's murmured words. There was some buried but never-forgotten secret in the elderly woman's heart. Something that rose, unbidden, to the surface and was so strong that Queenie was powerless to resist it.

At last Charlie seemed well asleep and so Anna took Charlie from Queenie with a grateful smile. She felt uneasy and wanted a little cuddle with her son before putting him down for the night. She watched him for a second or two in the apricot shadows cast by the luminous coals in the grate. His face was peaceful and serene, and she felt she could watch him all night. She reluctantly dragged herself away. There was another matter to be resolved.

Back in the kitchen, Queenie was making some cocoa, shuffling about in her worn slippers and her old dressing gown.

'Oh dear, he hasn't had you up all evening, has he? I'm ever so sorry.'

'Oh, no, cheel. 'Er'd just woke up a bit grizzly, like. 'Er was soaking so I changed 'is nappy an' gave 'en just a little feed an' a cuddle. So don't you fret none. You deserves a night out yere an' there. Good film, were it?'

'Yes, it was. Takes me back, going to the flicks. Ethel and I used to go quite often. We had a television, but it wasn't the same as the pictures.' She answered almost without thought and sat down, cupping her hands around the hot drink Queenie handed her. She shivered with apprehension and felt as if she was taking her life in her hands, but she had to ask for both their sakes. 'Queenie, who was Charlotte?' she gulped.

She heard the old lady draw a breath and for some gruelling seconds there was total silence. Anna thought she had made a terrible mistake and was torn with remorse.

Queenie gave a huge, wrenching sigh and Anna glanced sideways at her. Queenie's eyes had become glazed as she stared into her cocoa, but her hands were strong as they held the mug quite firmly.

'I suppose you should know, cheel. No one else in the world does. No one what counts, that is. An' if I 'as to tell someone, I thanks the Lord it's you.'

247

Her head bobbed up and down as if she were accepting her own words, but as she sipped her cocoa, Anna thought she had changed her mind. Or perhaps she had become so lost in her own emotions that she had forgotten Anna was there, or so entangled that she couldn't find her way out. Anna swallowed her own drink, expecting that to be the end of it. But then Queenie put down her empty mug decisively on the table, and leant back in the chair again.

'I were deeply in love. Much like you was. Farmer's son, 'e were. Good, 'ard worker. 'Ad our lives all planned out, us did. Take over the farm eventually, that were the plan. Us was so 'appy. Still got the engagement ring, I 'as. Cheap, worthless thing, but it meant the world to me. An' then the war came along.'

Her dreamy, reminiscing tone suddenly hardened and her lips twisted with bitterness. Anna lifted her eyes to this dear woman who had become like a mother to her. Queenie was gazing ahead, her face set, and Anna judged it best not to interrupt.

'Lord Kitchener needs you,' Queenie's voice crackled with contempt. Didn't 'ave to go, Clive didn't, especially being a farmer. But 'e wanted to do 'is bit. No white feathers for 'en. Be an adventure, 'e says, 'is eyes shining. An' it'll be over by Christmas,' she scoffed acidly in a way Anna would never have believed of her. 'Well, it were for 'en. One o' the first to fall. An' by the time 'is parents got the telegram, I knew I was 'aving 'is babby.'

Anna audibly gasped. She hadn't meant to, but

it was the last thing she had expected. Not from Queenie, who always seemed so practical and in control.

'With 'er going away, us'd got carried away a few times,' Queenie went on. ''Oo could blame us, really, like? But back then, it were a terrible thing. Well, you knows yersel', cheel, 'ow things can be for you 'aving Charlie out of wedlock. But then, it were even worse, believe me. A sin. I couldn't bring that shame on my family. So I went away. Said I wanted to do my bit, an' all. An' I did. In a munitions factory. Only I stopped to 'ave the child. A little girl. I called 'er Charlotte, though I doesn't know if the couple what adopted 'er kept the name. I never knew where she went, but I expect it were to a good family. All I knows is that she be out there. Somewheres…'

She broke off in a trail of sadness, leaving only the dark, shadowy stillness of the night. Anna sat, not daring to move. Hardly daring to breathe. Only her heart tearing in two as she shared Queenie's crushing grief.

'And … that's why you wanted me to keep Charlie,' she croaked when a good minute had passed.

'Yes, cheel.' Queenie sounded more resolute now. 'I didn't want you to face the same regret as I always 'ave. It were the biggest mistake o' my life. Came back yere arter the war, I did, an' no one knew no different. But I knew that out there, somewhere, were a little girl… She'd be in 'er forties now, of course. P'r'aps wi' chiller of 'er own. So, when you turned up, cheel, it were like God 'ad given me a second chance.'

'Oh, Queenie.' Anna released her sigh through

gently pursed lips, her insides choked with emotion. 'I can't imagine... But, thank you. For everything.'

She got out of the chair now and went to give Queenie a huge hug, patting the elderly woman on the back. So much sorrow. But then she felt Queenie pushing her away.

'Give over, cheel. It's all in the past. What matters now is you an' little Charlie. An' if us doesn't get to bed soon, us'll be all yonderly tomorrow.'

'Yes, you're right. Goodnight, then, Queenie. And thanks again for babysitting.'

She left Queenie nodding and went off to her room, closing the door softly. Dear Queenie. But who'd have thought...? She changed and slid silently into bed, mulling over Queenie's story as she drifted asleep.

Chapter Twenty-One

'Spoke to Gladys, today, I did, while you was out. Finally off at the end o' next week. Miss those three old biddies, I will. Been Queenie's neighbours since ... well, I cas'n remember a time when they wasn't there. Three unmarried sisters, eh... Albert used to tease us that they was three witches, cuz they was old even then. But three nicer women you cas'n meet.'

Anna cocked an eyebrow in Queenie's direction. Charlie had been having his afternoon nap while she had battled her way to Princetown through the

January snow to do the shopping. Now Charlie was full of beans, sitting on the rag rug spread at their feet and playing with the few toys they could afford for him. Anna had bought him a wooden train for his first birthday the previous week, and he was crawling along the edge of the rug and pushing the little engine on the flagstones next to it.

'Yes, I'll miss them, too,' Anna agreed. The three elderly sisters who lived in the big old house almost next to Holly Cottage had always been kind to her. If they had been a touch sceptical over the story that she was Queenie's long-lost niece, widowed and left with a baby to bring up alone, their qualms had soon been dissipated. They had taken Anna on face value, always friendly, and doted on Charlie like old maiden aunts. Unlike Olive's husband, who always lifted his nose in the air and turned his back whenever he saw her.

'Still, you can't blame them for wanting to move somewhere more convenient. And that old house is so big and draughty, and the new one's got all mod cons. It'll be much easier for them, and they are getting on a bit.'

She threw Queenie a questioning glance. The Crow sisters were a lot older than she was, but it was obvious that Queenie was finding her hard-working life at Holly Cottage increasingly taxing. Anna sometimes wondered how Queenie would manage without her help. And at least Crow House had had running water inside the kitchen and a flushing indoor lavatory – luxury far beyond the primitive facilities that served Holly Cottage. But before Queenie could reply, Charlie

251

crawled over to his mother, hauled himself into a standing position using Anna's knees for support, and was now gleefully bobbing up and down as he bent and stretched his legs in this wonderful new game he had discovered for himself.

'Well, I reckons it takes all folk different, like,' Queenie pronounced from her chair. 'But I cas'n imagine living anywheres else. 'Ave to carry me out feet first in a box, they will, from yere. Born in 'Olly Cottage, Queenie were, an' she'll die in it, too.'

A sudden, dark cloud threatened Anna's buoyant mood. She loved Queenie almost as much as she had her own dear mother, but she could envisage a time when Queenie would find living at Holly Cottage beyond her. But Queenie could be as obstinate as the proverbial mule, and getting her to leave her beloved home and move into more suitable accommodation as the Crow sisters were doing might be nigh on impossible. But hopefully that would be way, way in the future.

'Oh!' Anna gasped, suddenly overwhelmed with emotion. 'Oh, Queenie, did you see that?'

Bouncing up and down in front of her, Charlie had relinquished the support of her knees, and tottered half a dozen steps across the rag rug, chubby hands held up before him, before sitting down hard on his bottom.

'I certainly did!' Queenie exclaimed, her cheeks creasing as she grinned proudly from ear to ear.

Charlie swivelled his head round to stare back at his mother in comic astonishment at his own actions, and then he broke into a beaming smile. Anna's stunned eyes went from his delighted little face to Queenie's joyful, wrinkled one, and back again. She felt her own heart ready to burst with elation, wiping out her misgivings of a moment earlier. For Charlie had taken his first steps.

Dear Annie
I cas'n tell you how happy I am. At long last Bert's finished his National Service and he's coming home for good. I feel I could burst, I'm so happy, like. Only one more week and he'll be here. I cas'n believe it.

Anna's lips curved into a smile as she paused to take another bite of the toast she had cooked by spearing it onto the toasting fork and holding it in front of the open firebox.

She didn't envy Carrie her brand-new electric toaster. Being in the trade, Jeffery was able to purchase electrical equipment at cost price, Mr Trembath being very generous to his electrician who could always be relied upon to do a good job. The Cresswell home possessed a radio, a television and even one of the new plug-in record players. Anna didn't mind not having any of these, though she always enjoyed listening to music when she took Charlie down to Tavistock on the bus to spend a day with Carrie and baby Polly. If it wasn't nice enough to sit in the garden in the summer, or to wrap up warm and go to feed the ducks along the old Tavistock Canal, they would enjoy themselves in the sitting room, hopping around to the beat of Tommy Steele's *Singing the Blues* or some such hit. The one thing Anna really envied was Carrie's Mark One washing machine. It was old by modern standards and still only had a hand-worked mangle, but it would be a lot easier than scrubbing Charlie's nappies on the wooden wash-board and scraping her knuckles raw!

Bert's going to buy us a proper engagement ring, he says. Imagine that, Annie! My mum never had no ring. Dad couldn't afford it, but Bert's been saving up. Seen a lovely one in the pawnshop window, I has. I hopes it's still there when Bert comes back, coz I really likes it. Dad reckons Bert'll get his job back on the rail-way, and then maybies us can get one of those mortgage things and start to buy our own place instead of rent-ing. Fancy that, eh! But us'll have to save a lot more for the deposit, so us'll have to wait longer afore us can tie the knot. But it'll just be great to have Bert back home.

'What she say then, young Ethel?' Queenie interrupted Anna's reading of the letter that had arrived in the post that morning.

Anna gave a knowing chuckle. 'Oh, she's full of Bert coming home as you might imagine.' She put down the sheet of paper and picked up the cloth to wipe Charlie's hand. He was sitting in his high chair, again bought second hand and transported to Holly Cottage balanced on the pushchair. The toddler was learning to feed himself with a spoon and was ladling mixed-up Farex into his mouth with dubious success.

'Lovely time o' year for an 'omecoming, mind, the spring,' Queenie nodded sagely. 'So what else does she say?'

'Oh.' Anna took up the letter again and scanned Ethel's scrawl. 'She says she'll drop me a line after Bert arrives and she knows what they're doing. She'll probably take some of her holiday, and either they'll come up here or we can go down there for a party, maybe. You'd come, too, wouldn't you, Queenie? Oh, Charlie! No!'

Anna sprang up, her arms thrust towards her son. But she was already too late. Charlie had lifted up his bowl and tipped its contents over his head, laughing uproariously as the gooey mixture oozed through his hair and began to dribble down his face.

'Oh, Charlie, you mustn't do that! You naughty boy!' Anna chided, but Charlie was beaming gleefully at her, his little cheeks pink with delight. Anna whisked away the bowl before he could create even more chaos with it, and glanced round in desperation for the cloth. And then amongst all the pandemonium, a sudden urgent hammering broke out as if somebody was about to break down the front door.

''Oo can that be?' Queenie pulled in her chin with an irritated frown. 'I'll go, maid.'

She covered the few steps to the front door while Anna attempted to clear up the mess. She didn't really care who their visitor might be. She was cross with Charlie, but she supposed in his own mind, he was just playing, he was too young to understand an explanation, so she must be firm but not too angry in showing him her displeasure.

Out of the corner of her eye, she saw that Queenie had come back into the room, her stance and the tilt of her head somehow indicating that something was amiss. Anna's thoughts at once turned to Ethel and her heart leapt into her throat. Surely nothing had happened to Bert at the very end of his stint? But, lingering indecisively in the doorway, was neither Ethel nor the telegram boy, but a small, waiflike figure with wild blond curls looking windswept and out of place above an immaculate scarlet coat with a silver-fur collar.

'Frankie! What on earth–?'

She got no further as Frankie's face crumpled and she hurtled across the room and flung herself into Anna's arms, sobbing uncontrollably. Anna was flabbergasted and tried to pat Frankie's back without soiling the smart coat with Farex. She was quite at a loss, and then Charlie started to protest at this invasion of his morning routine and was instantly howling loudly. To Anna's relief, Queenie came to the rescue, whisking the child out of his high chair and pacifying him on her lap.

Anna nodded her thanks and then turned her attention to Frankie. The other girl was crying wretchedly, clinging onto Anna as if her life depended on it. Over her head, Anna shrugged bewilderedly at Queenie's raised, questioning eyebrows.

'There, there,' she soothed just as she did with Charlie whenever he fell over and hurt himself. 'Whatever's the matter?' she asked for the third time in an effort to get some sense out of her.

She soon had her answer. Frankie finally drew away and stared at her, sniffing, from her tear-stained face. A great, livid mark stood out on her cheek in a clear handprint, bright crimson but already with a bluish tinge in the centre. And beneath the bobbing curls on her forehead was the purplish-yellow fading blossom of an earlier bruise.

'Oh, Anna, I'm sorry,' the poor girl gulped, her eyes still swimming with moisture. 'You were the only person I could turn to. I don't know how much longer...'

She looked in danger of bursting into tears again, and Anna nodded towards the table. 'You sit down there and have a cup of tea, and then you can tell me all about it.'

Frankie obeyed meekly, swallowing down her threatening tears. But she seemed a little calmer, and as Anna filled a mug from the pot and pushed it in her direction, she considered that introductions might help settle her friend down.

'Frankie, this is Queenie.'

The two strangers acknowledged each other with a bob of the head, and Frankie's inbred manners came to her aid. 'Yes, I gathered you must be,' she said, more steadily now. 'I'm pleased to meet you.'

'Likewise,' Queenie answered reservedly, not quite sure how to take this young girl who had landed on her doorstep from a different planet, or so it seemed to Queenie, from her posh clothes and the cultured way she spoke. And yet the cheel was in such distress. She was almost glad when Charlie started grizzling again and she had to jiggle him up and down on her knee once more.

'I know I said I'd never come here,' Frankie croaked, her voice strained as she battled with the last remnants of her tears. 'But I didn't know what else to do. I just had to get away.' For a moment, she seemed to be verging on the edge of hysteria again, but with a huge sigh, made an evident effort to retain a grip on herself. 'I didn't take the car, though, so no one should have any idea where I am. I just said I was going for a walk. It was all quite calm, really. It wasn't until I got to the end of the drive that it all burst out of me. I just started walking towards Two Bridges and then I thought of you, and I just kept walking. I didn't realise how far it is, though. I think I've got a blister.'

'I'll get you a plaster. An' summat for ... for...' Queenie waved vaguely at Frankie's face as she set Charlie down on the rag rug, where thankfully he began to play with his toys like his normal happy self.

'Gilbert, I assume?' Anna suggested quietly as Queenie rummaged in one of her cupboards.

'Who else?' Frankie answered, the sarcasm of her words not reflected in her flat, expressionless tone. 'He's still blaming me for not being pregnant after nearly two years of marriage. He seems obsessed by it, and sometimes I do feel guilty. Especially when he ... gets into one of his moods about it.'

'And hits you, you mean?'

Frankie glanced up darkly. 'Yes. But at least he's still gentle and loving when ... when we're in bed. He does still love me. I'm sure of that.'

'Well, 'e do 'ave a funny way o' showing it,' Queenie put in.

'Oh, no. You don't understand. It's just this overwhelming desire for a child that gets to him sometimes and makes him violent. And usually when he's had too much to drink.'

'But not at this hour of the morning, I take it?' This said contemplating the fresh mark on Frankie's cheek.

'A hangover,' Frankie replied wryly. 'That's why I was able to slip out.'

'And Lady Ashcroft? Does she know?'

'I'm sure she must do. But she turns a blind eye. And I've heard her having a go at Gilbert for not producing an heir. She seems driven by it, too. As if it's, I don't know, almost a sin that nothing's happened yet.'

'Huh! Queer folk, gentry like,' Queenie muttered as she handed Frankie a plaster and placed a bottle of witch hazel on the table.

'So, what are you going to do about it?'

Anna's voice was firm, for surely Frankie wasn't going to sit back and take it on the chin? But the girl turned to her, eyes wide with surprise.

'Do? What *can* I do?'

Anna almost felt like shaking Frankie herself! But then... Frankie was different. Gentle. Stoical. Accepting. Even if it meant she suffered as a result.

'You could stand up to them. *Both* of them. Tell Lady Ashcroft to mind her own flipping business. Well, not in so many words. But better still, tell her – really sort of confidentially – that you're upset yourself that you've not had a baby yet. But make sure *you* start the conversation, as if you really want to talk about it. And as for Gilbert, tell him if he doesn't stop knocking you about, you'll leave him.'

Frankie gasped and stared at her, totally aghast. 'Oh, I couldn't possibly do that! Think of the scandal! My father would turn in his grave!'

'Well, forgive me, Frankie, but your father's dead and you're the one suffering the abuse. And while you're at it, tell them both that you want to be seen by Lady Ashcroft's own doctor. I'm sure she must have one. Or some specialist in Harley Street, isn't

259

it? It'll really show her you're worried about not having had a child, and it'll stop Gilbert hurting you. He won't want some eminent physician asking questions about how you get your bruises.'

Frankie seemed to consider for a moment. 'Yes, I suppose that's a good idea. But Gilbert's always so sorry afterwards. When he's sobered up.'

'Frankie, a decent man wouldn't harm a woman no matter how drunk he is. In fact, a decent man wouldn't get that drunk in the first place. I know you love Gilbert. As I did myself once. And you can go on loving him if you want to. But he's *weak,* Frankie. And unless you want your life to be a complete wreck, you've got to do something about it!'

'Oh, Anna, I wish I was as strong as you,' Frankie breathed out on an enormous sigh. 'I will think about it, though, I promise. But can we change the subject now?' She suddenly sat up, her face brightening. 'Could I play with Charlie, do you think?'

'You're welcome!' Anna smiled back, deliberately putting Frankie's problems to the back of her mind, for surely they had been sufficiently discussed. 'He's a mucky little toerag just now! But I'll be bathing him shortly.'

'Oh, can I help?'

'Of course you can. If you don't mind getting soaked. He splashes around like nobody's business!'

She watched as Frankie took off her coat and, getting down on her knees on the rug, began building a tower with Charlie's bricks which he then joyfully knocked down, laughing in his little gurgling way while the strange woman happily

260

retrieved them for him and began again. Anna met Queenie's gaze over their heads. They both of them doubted that Frankie would take the slightest notice of Anna's impassioned advice.

Chapter Twenty-Two

'Well, I never! I's 'ad more post arrive yere since you'm been living wi' me than in my entire life.'

'Get away with you! Anna chortled back. 'For me, is it, then?'

'No, as it 'appens.' Queenie wagged her head proudly. 'For me. Looks official, like. Typed brown envelope. Probably from a solicitors telling me I's been left a fortune by some long-lost cousin in America, or summat.'

'Or that your pensions going up by a bob a week or some other vast amount.'

'Yes, more like,' Queenie grimaced as she sat down at the table.

'Nothing for me, then? Eth's not written since we went to Bert's homecoming party, and that was three months ago.'

'That were a grand day!'

'Certainly was. I've never seen Eth so happy. And she'll be spending every spare minute with Bert, so I shouldn't really expect a letter from her. No, it's Frankie I'd like to hear from.' Anna paused as she spread Marmite very thinly on a slice of toast and cut it into fingers for Charlie. 'Not heard a dicky bird from her since she came

261

here that day. I do hope she's all right.'

'So do I, cheel. A nicer maid you couldn't meet. Just goes to show, mind,' Queenie sighed ponderously. 'All the money in the world cas'n bring you 'appiness.'

'No. And you can't live other people's lives for them, either.'

'Well, worrying about it won't get us nowhere,' Queenie stated decisively. 'I'll just read about my fortune,' she winked, her pale eyes twinkling mischievously, 'an' then I'll get some scones in the oven afore I opens up the tea room. Got to make a living some'ows!'

Anna carried the dirty plates over to the sink. It seemed perfectly normal to her now to have a sink with no taps. It was the same granite affair that had been put in when the cottage had been built over a hundred years previously. Anna placed the enamel washing-up bowl in it and then went to fetch some hot water in a jug from the range boiler.

'Oh, my God.'

Queenie breathed in the words rather than speaking them, and Anna turned to grin over her shoulder and tease Queenie by suggesting that there really *was* a long-lost relative. But then she saw Queenie's ashen face and realised it had been no exclamation of joy.

She dropped the dishcloth back into the water and crossed the room, drying her hands as she came. Queenie was staring down at the letter in her lap, the paper shaking so that it rustled ominously. Anna's heart missed a beat, for surely something must be terribly wrong.

262

'Whatever is it, Queenie?' she dared to ask.

Queenie lifted her grey head. 'Read it yersel', cheel,' she said, her voice hollow. But Anna had barely taken the sheet of paper when the elderly woman went on, suddenly fired with indignation, 'Unin'abitable, my foot! What the 'eck does they think I been doing but living in the place these last sixty year or more, an' my parents afore that? No sanitation, indeed! They needs to come an' see it! Eat off my floor, you could, it's so clean!'

'Yes, I'm sure you could,' Anna murmured. Her eyes were travelling cursorily over the letter, concentrating on taking in at a glance what it contained. But now it was her turn to be shocked and she rocked on her feet. 'Oh, Queenie.'

''Ow dare they say it's been condemned!' came the heated reply. 'Perfectly adequate, it is! We'm warm an' cosy, bain't us? An' just cuz us 'as to fetch in the water, don't mean to say–'

'But it doesn't meet current health regulations, it says,' Anna broke in, shaking her head as the vile coldness of acceptance settled in her stomach. 'And they are right,' she said, talking even though she seemed to have no control over her speech. 'We don't have a flushing toilet, inside or out. There's no foul-drainage system whatsoever, and our water does come from an outside tap.'

'Well, they can change all that if they musts!' Queenie crossed her arms beneath her bosom in the stubborn gesture Anna had seen before. 'Queenie's not moving from yere an' that's a fact. They can come in an' modernise the place if they wants, but I's not budging!'

Anna contemplated Queenie's red, inflated face

263

and her own heart plummeted to her feet. 'It says here it'd be uneconomical to do that,' she said lamely.

'An' what do *that* mean when it's at 'ome?'

'It means ... it means it would cost too much. It means...' She caught her breath, sucking in her lips before she ventured in a tiny voice, 'We're going to have to move out.'

'Over my dead body–'

'They've offered you a two-bed house in Princetown. With...' She hesitated, dreading Queenie's reaction. 'With a little garden.'

'An' 'ow can I be doing with a *little* garden? 'Ow am I supposed to keep Dolly an' Wilma in a *little* garden, an' then there's the 'ens–'

'You'll have to ... get rid of them, I suppose,' Anna cringed. 'But there'll probably be enough room to grow some of your own veg.'

'Get rid on them?' Queenie was outraged, her cheeks puce with anger. 'Oh, no, I won't, cheel! They cas'n force me to move out–'

'Unfortunately, I believe they can.'

'An' 'ave you seen the rent they wants to charge me for that there *nice little 'ouse?* Ten times what I pays yere! I cas'n afford that, even if you 'elps out. An' you've got Charlie to feed an' clothe, an' there'll be bills for water an' electric light an' God knows what else. An' wi'out the garden to grow teddies an' the like, an' the café to bring in that little extra–'

'That's another thing,' Anna interrupted before her courage failed her. 'They say you shouldn't be running the tea room.'

'What!' Queenie fumed, and Anna could see the

pulse beating furiously beneath the wrinkled skin at her throat. 'Well! My mother ran it all through the Great War, an' she sold cigarettes to the troops training yereabouts, an' all. So 'ow come they suddenly objects to it? Well, I doesn't care what they says. I's staying put, an' I's opening up the café today, an' all!'

Anna watched, reeling herself and totally at a loss, as Queenie hurled herself to her feet and stomped towards the range. Anna closed her eyes with a sigh, returning little Charlie's grin with a rueful curve of her mouth. She was shaken to the core. Living at Holly Cottage had been her salvation, one of the happiest times of her life. She simply couldn't imagine leaving it.

'Oooo.'

Queenie gave a muted gasp and suddenly swayed precariously, her gnarled hands outstretched as if to catch her balance. Anna sprang up like a jack-in-the-box, grabbing hold of Queenie and staggering under her weight. Instinctively, she managed to reach out one hand, pull one of the kitchen chairs behind Queenie and help her lower herself onto it.

'Queenie, what's the matter?'

'Oh, I doesn't know, cheel.' Queenie took in a deep breath as if to calm herself. 'I ... I came over all funny, like. It sort of ... went dark for a minute. Could you ... could you fetch us some water?'

'Of course.' It was done in a trice and Queenie took the glass from her in a hand that still shook. 'Queenie, will you be all right for a few minutes? Charlie's strapped in his high chair so he'll be safe enough. I'm going to the phone box to call

Dr Franfield.'

'Oh, no, you'm not!' The old lady's voice was adamant. 'Queenie's fine now. It were just a funny turn. I doesn't want no doctor prodding us about.'

'But, Queenie–'

'No. Look, I's proper clever now. If you calls the doctor, I won't let 'en in.'

'Oh, I really think–'

'No! I be as right as rain now. I doesn't want no one interfering in my life. I be quite capable o' living in this yere *condemned 'ouse,* an' I'll not 'ave no one thinking otherwise!'

Her face was screwed up with such frightening ferocity that Anna caught her breath. She'd never seen Queenie look like that and it really scared her. She would have liked to defy her and fetch Dr Franfield anyway. But that might make matters worse, and she didn't want that.

'All right,' she said reluctantly. 'But if it happens again, I'm definitely calling the doctor. And we're not opening the tea room today. You're going to sit with your feet up and have a nice quiet day. Or as quiet as Charlie will let us,' she added as the child began to bang his spoon on the high chair tray.

For a few seconds, Queenie looked at her daggers, but then Anna could almost see reason overtake her.

'If you insists,' she conceded. 'One day won't matter, I suppose. But I'm opening up tomorrow.'

Anna was hardly swamped with relief. She was sure Queenie should see Dr Franfield, and then there was the matter of the cottage. It really was a bombshell, and Anna felt the sudden anxiety over their future knock her sideways. Presumably she could go with Queenie – if she could be persuaded to move – for where else could she and Charlie go? Dear Lord, she had thought their idyllic life would reach on for ever. But now, heaven alone knew what was in store for them!

Charlie was running towards her on his sturdy little legs, his beaming face vibrant and alive and his eyes dancing with glee. Behind him, the green sea of the moor rose up to a sharp, dramatic tor on the skyline, and all was bathed in a shimmering, golden light that drifted down benignly from the azure dome of the sky.

Charlie ran into her arms and she swung him into the air, twirling him round so that his legs kicked joyously and unrestrained. Suddenly a thunderous crash exploded behind them, shattering the peace of the summer afternoon and bringing their game to a juddering halt. They both turned, their laughter dying. Holly Cottage, the haven of their lives, was in ruins, the tin roof gone, the massive stones rent asunder. The walls crumbling and covered in encroaching ivy.

Anna jolted awake, hardly daring to breathe. All she could hear was the familiar, lingering silence of the dead of night, too early yet for the sonorous chorus of the awakening birds. Her heartbeat slowed again. She was snugly in bed in the cottage, Charlie fast asleep in his cot. They were safe. At least, for the time being.

The shock of the letter they had received that morning slunk back into her thoughts. What were they to do? She would have to plead for time. Time to persuade Queenie that there was no alternative but to leave the beloved place that had been her lifelong home apart from the time she had spent away during the Great War. It would break her, but it seemed to Anna there was nothing else to be done, and they wouldn't be far away. But to see the cottage fall into ruin as Anna had seen it in her dream, or perhaps even be demolished, might be more than the old lady could stand.

What was that? Yes, she had definitely heard a noise, like someone moving about the cottage. No, more like lumbering around. And then a dull clatter as something hard and solid fell onto the flagstone floor. Then a long, agonised moan.

Anna shot out of bed and, a second later, she was in the kitchen. There was just enough light from a pale half-moon outside to make out the shape of a figure dressed in a long white night-gown slumped over one of the kitchen chairs which lay on its side on the floor.

'Queenie!' Anna heard a voice she didn't recognise as her own scream into the night.

'Chee ... eel,' Queenie rasped as Anna dropped on her knees beside her. The breath scraped in her throat, her arm clutched across her chest. 'You ... an' Charlie ... everything ... to me.'

'Yes, I know,' Anna whispered quickly before a lump closed her throat. And then somehow, perhaps her mind grabbing at some concrete, practical action, she managed to say to Queenie, 'Let's get you more comfortable.'

She grasped her under the arms, every muscle straining as she dragged Queenie off the chair and across to one of the armchairs. But she simply wasn't strong enough to lift her into it, so instead she propped her against it, stuffing loose cushions behind her.

'Stay there. I'm going for the doctor.'

'Not ... going ... nowheres,' Queenie's voice, suddenly so old, gasped, and Anna caught her slow, muted cry of pain.

She sprang to the door. Oh, good Lord, did she have the right money for the phone box? But, oh, yes! Olive and Clifford had just had a telephone installed! That would be so much quicker than running along the road to the public call box.

She stumbled, barefoot, to the lodge, trying to hold onto reality as her mind reeled in panic. She rang, banged with all her might, on the door, her efforts echoing through the night. Oh, come on!

Suddenly the wood yielded and she pulled back. A bleary-eyed Clifford opened the door, and in the glimmer of moonlight, Anna saw his scowl deepen when he saw who it was.

'What the hell do *you* want at this hour?'

But Anna ignored his attitude. 'Queenie. I think she's having a heart attack. Can you ring the doctor?'

Clifford's expression at once changed. 'Of course. What's his number?'

Anna told him, and as he picked up the receiver in the hall behind him, she dashed back to the cottage, her heart knocking against her ribs. She fell on her knees, almost faint with fear as she realised Queenie's eyes were closed.

'Queenie?' she squealed.

'Yes, cheel. Queenie's yere.' But she didn't open

269

her eyes.

'Is it any better?'

'A little,' Queenie groaned, and Anna knew she was lying.

'I'll light the lamps. The doctor's on his way.'

She tore herself from Queenie's side, and yet it was a relief to have something to do. Her fingers trembled with the matches, and it took her twice the normal time to have the lamps alight, flooding the room with their familiar smell and casting a flickering, jaundiced glimmer on the walls. She shivered, suddenly aware that she was still only clad in her nightdress. She must have given Clifford quite a fright, she mused almost hysterically as she hurried into Queenie's room. She dragged the eiderdown from the bed and took it into the kitchen and tucked it around Queenie's tense form, as she must be cold as well as in such pain, even though the summer night was mild.

'Thank you, cheel.'

Her voice was barely a whisper, shaky, weaker than before. Anna's stomach was clamped in a vice, her teeth chattering, so cold herself. It must be the shock. She crept into her own bedroom, careful not to wake Charlie, and retrieved her dressing gown. Queenie? Yes, still there, answered her question with a muted grunt. Stoke up the range, get the room warm.

It was as she shovelled on more coal that she heard Queenie's gasp, a sort of low rattling as she drew air into her lungs. Anna dropped the shovel and flew to her side. Queenie clung to her, staring up at her, mouth and eyes wide open.

'Cheel,' she managed in an unearthly cackle,

270

and then she fell limp in Anna's arms.

Oh, dear God. Please, God, no. Anna wanted to shake life back into her. But Queenie had perhaps just lost consciousness. Yes, that was it. So she rocked her gently instead. Back and forth. Silently. Tears meandering down her cheeks and dropping like cobwebs onto Queenie's grey hair.

'Oh, good Lord.'

Anna lifted her head, and through her tear-blurred vision saw Olive's familiar shape in the doorway. She had evidently thrown on some clothes, as she was fully dressed, though her hair was all awry.

'Clifford told me as soon as he'd spoken to the doctor. He's on his way.' The other woman caught her breath as she came into the room. 'Oh, God. Queenie. She's not...?'

Anna stared up at her. Numbed. Her senses deadened to everything but fear and grief. And yet she was alive to every sound in the cottage, every flicker of the oil lamps.

Olive hadn't been able to say the ultimate word, and Anna shook her head fiercely. 'No. No, she's not. She'll be all right till the doctor comes,' she assured her, smoothing Queenie's grizzled head.

Olive sank down beside them and gently felt Queenie's wrist for a pulse. She said nothing, but after a moment or two, replaced Queenie's gnarled hand in her lap and patted it.

'He won't be long, Dr Franfield,' she murmured quietly.

Anna nodded and went on rocking Queenie's lifeless form, willing her to live, trying to pump her own life force into the woman she loved so dearly. And so they waited. In the crystal silence of the night.

They heard the rumble of an engine, the sound of running feet. The beam of a torch, the figure of a tall man in the doorway.

'Dr Franfield,' Anna gulped in relief.

He crossed the room and Anna relinquished Queenie from her arms, carefully laying her head back on a cushion. She watched, every nerve taut, as the doctor listened to Queenie's chest, his brow knitted in concentration. His practised fingers felt beneath the folds of her jaw, then he took a small torch from his bag, and lifting each of Queenie's closed lids, shone it into her eyes. Flicking it back and forth a couple of times. Then laid the flat of his hand on her forehead. And all the time, Anna held her breath, praying. Please, God...

Dr Franfield sat back on his heels, his cheeks drawn in. And the bud of hope withered and died in Anna's breast.

'I'm so sorry. Miss Millington. Anna,' he said gravely but with the deepest kindness. 'There's ... nothing. She's already beginning to turn cold. I should say she passed away about twenty minutes ago. Shortly after your neighbour called me.'

His words, heavy with sympathy though they were, were shards of glass in Anna's heart. 'Are you sure?' she demanded at once, her voice touching on hysteria. 'There must be something–'

The doctor slowly shook his head. 'It's too late. I'm afraid she really has gone.'

A terrible ache swelled up in Anna's throat, strangling her with sorrow. As tears filled her eyes and began to drip down from her chin, she gathered Queenie in her arms again and held her. So close. As if she could never let her go.

Dr Franfield put a comforting hand on her shoulder and then got to his feet. 'Could you make us all some tea, please, Mrs ... er...?'

'Olive.' The woman heaved with an oppressive sigh as she, too, stood up. 'A good friend was Queenie. For many a long year. A sort of institution, you might say. Born in this cottage she was. And always said she'd die in it, too. It's what she would have wanted.'

Their voices floated over Anna's head, as did the sounds of Olive making tea. Queenie. Oh, Queenie, you can't have gone. We had so much to look forward to. Charlie growing up, going to school. Queenie, don't leave me. Please.

Her words were in her head, reverberating in her skull. Or perhaps she moaned them as she continued to rock Queenie in her arms. No. No. This hadn't happened. Why, oh, why?

She angrily shrugged off the good doctor's hands when he tried to lift her. He waited a moment, then dropped down on his haunches beside her.

'You have to let her go, now, Anna,' he whispered gently. 'She was a lovely lady, but now she's gone. And you must think of Charlie. You'll have him to care for in the morning, and it's already growing light.'

His words were soothing, a soft balm. She raised her head that was buried in Queenie's shoulder, and with the greatest care, laid her back on the floor. She sniffed, her heart dragging in pain, and ran the back of her hand across her dripping nose. Yes. Charlie. Of course. He'd be awake soon. To

Queenie, Charlie had been her own lost baby Charlotte come back to her. So Anna must pull herself together for both their sakes.

Goodbye, Queenie. My dearest, dearest...

Dr Franfield helped her to her feet and Olive led her away. Over her shoulder, she saw the doctor lift the quilt over Queenie's still, lifeless face.

Chapter Twenty-Three

"Eenie?"

Charlie looked up expectantly, head cocked to one side, as he sat in his high chair. Anna gazed across at him, choking on the grief that raked her throat. She felt empty, her heart scoured of feeling. Nothing but the all-encompassing misery that held her imprisoned in a hostile grey shroud from which she felt she would never break free.

First her dear, innocent mother, then her poor father whose life should have been oh, so different, and now... Anna felt as if her heart would quite literally break. She was aware of it beating too fast, nervously, as if it would soon give out. She felt strange, shaky, wanting to lie down and yet she knew she wouldn't sleep. And although she tried to resist the agony of it, her eyes kept being drawn to the spot on the floor in front of the armchair where only hours earlier Queenie had died in her arms.

Dr Franfield had been wonderful. 'She was a great lady from what I knew of her,' he said kindly,

274

for he was a great believer in talking openly about the deceased. In not letting the pain of bereavement fester inside. 'Quite a character.'

Anna nodded, since speech seemed beyond her. But then, to her surprise, she found herself saying, 'But she was only sixty-four.'

William Franfield raised an eyebrow. 'Really? She looked so much older.'

'Yes, I know. I think it was the hard life she'd always led. Up here. Out in all weathers.'

It was William's turn to nod. 'And had she always been in good health?' he asked gently.

'She had seemed sort of tired to me recently,' Olive put in.

Anna looked up a little sheepishly. 'And she'd had a few funny turns. As if she'd lost herself. Just for a few seconds. I put it down to thinking about things in the past. Memories. But yesterday morning, she had a terrible shock. She got a letter. We've got to move out. The cottage has been condemned.'

'Good Lord!'

'You can imagine how Queenie felt about that. She was livid. And then she went all peculiar. Nearly fainted, and she said everything went dark. It was over in a matter of moments. I wanted to call you, but she wouldn't have it.' She met William's steady eyes, her already thrumming heartbeat accelerating painfully. 'If I'd *made* her see you yesterday, she wouldn't have died, would she?'

William frowned at her. 'Now, don't you go blaming yourself. From what you say, she might have had one or two very tiny strokes. I'd probably have found something not quite right and given her something for it. But this was a massive heart attack and nothing would have prevented it. So, no more of that sort of talk.' He leant across and squeezed her shaking hand. 'Now, is there anyone else you'd like me to call for you?'

Ethel. Of course, Ethel. And her mum. But the luxury of a telephone was beyond them or any of their neighbours in Ford, so it was out of the question. It would have to be a telegram later on in the morning when the rest of the world had woken up.

'No, not really,' she mumbled.

'I'll stay with her,' Olive said protectively.

'Well, if it's all right with you,' the doctor began, rising to his feet, 'I'll use your telephone again. To call the undertakers,' he added under his breath. 'I could give you a mild sedative, Anna, but you've got Charlie to look after. I'll call again later, after my rounds. And you might want to say your last goodbyes,' he suggested delicately.

And so daybreak had ticked on into morning. The July dawn sent shafts of sunlight spilling into the cottage. Anna drew back the curtains, folded back the quilt and let the rays fall on Queenie's peaceful face. Like an angel. The undertakers came, two mature men, solemn and respectful in dark suits. She kissed Queenie's cold, marble forehead one last, final time.

Olive had stayed a little longer, but then had popped back home to wash and dress properly and make Clifford his breakfast since nothing must break his routine. The world outside was turning again, birds singing. The occasional vehicle passing on the road. All so normal. And yet never again would it be the same.

Charlie had woken and Anna hugged him tightly as she lifted him from his cot. She must be jolly and bright for him. He was eighteen months old. He would forget.

'Queenie's ... asleep,' she answered him. And at that moment, Olive returned, eyes red-rimmed so Anna knew she had been crying. Odd that. Anna's own tears wouldn't come.

Things to do. Charlie's bath. The goats, the hens. Olive went into Princetown for her. Sent telegrams to Ethel and to Carrie. Called into Daisy, Gladys and Betty, the Crow sisters, in their new home. Various others who knew Queenie so well.

William Franfield returned as promised, accompanied by his wife, who Anna already knew, of course, as she was his receptionist. But now she introduced herself as Deborah.

'I'll help you arrange the funeral,' she smiled sympathetically. 'I assume there's little money, but we can fill in some forms. I'll do everything I can to help, and you can ring me any time. You might have to bear with me on occasion, mind. Our son gets married in two weeks' time, and our daughter will be arriving from America with her husband and baby the day after tomorrow. We've not met our grandson so we're very excited.'

Deborah Franfield failed to suppress her proud smile, and Anna realised the good lady was trying to encourage her with talk of happier events. She indeed felt pleased for them. Fleetingly.

'Is that Dr Franfield junior?' she asked, vaguely remembering the handsome young man who had once stood at the bottom of her and Carrie's beds in the maternity home.

'Yes. The sad part is that immediately after the honeymoon, they're going straight off to Germany for three years so that Edwin can do his National Service. He was able to defer it while he did his medical training, but they've caught up with him now. And it'll be three years instead of two because he'll go in as a medical officer on a short commission. But at least they'll be in married quarters together. We'll miss them both terribly, though.'

'I'm sure you will,' Anna answered mechanically. But not as much as I'll miss Queenie.

'And I've had to get a long-term locum,' William grimaced. 'Still, seems a good chap I've taken on.'

And so the day went on. So much to do. To arrange. As well as care for Charlie. Ethel appeared in the afternoon. Mabel had gone to Dingles as soon as she had read the telegram. Ethel had managed to get the afternoon off and the following day so that she could stay with Anna overnight. Other people came and went. Shaking their heads. Couldn't believe Queenie had gone. There was no word from Carrie, and William didn't return again in the evening as promised.

'Probably on an emergency,' Ethel decided, wisely nodding her head.

It wasn't until that night that Anna's frail hold on herself snapped. The glass bubble in which she had existed all day, watching everything going on around her as if this was all a dream and she wasn't part of it, suddenly shattered. And she wept and howled her grief in Ethel's arms until there were no more tears to shed, and her heart and soul lay empty and withered in her breast.

She moved through each day, trying to remember all the things she must do. Feed the hens. Bring in some water. Get dressed.

'Bickit, Mummy?'

'What? Oh, Charlie. I'm sorry. Here you are, darling.' Forgetting he had already had two biscuits that morning.

The undertaker came the next day and she thanked God Ethel was there. It was Ethel who arranged things with him while Anna sat in the chair, her face pale and her eyes like mud. Later, with gentle understanding, the vicar asked what he could say about Queenie during the service, but he could drag little from the girl who sat like a hollow shell in the chair, while her friend who had opened the door to him had to fill in what she knew of Queenie Witherspoon.

'So where are you going to live?' Olive asked her the day after Ethel had left.

Another night with scarcely any sleep, drifting into the shadows. Dark smudges beneath her eyes. Food sticking in her throat. Her limbs not wanting to move. Oh, she just wanted to sit in a chair and sink beneath the waves that washed over her.

Olive's insistent gaze drew her attention. What had she said? Oh, yes. She shook her head.

'I really don't know.'

'Well, you're obviously going to have to move from here. I'm afraid I can't offer you a home. Clifford, well, you know. I'm sure Gladys and her sisters would have had you if they'd still been

living next door, but their new house is so *small*,'
She paused, working her lips. 'What about the
place Queenie was offered? Perhaps you could
have that. We could go to the Duchy's offices–'

'I couldn't afford it. Not on my own.'

'Oh, dear. Well, you'll have to find *somewhere*'.'

'I've got a month. I'll start looking after ... after
the funeral.'

'All right.' Olive was satisfied, for now at least.
'And I'm happy to help you. But, Anna, you must
pull yourself together. For Charlie's sake.'

Charlie. Oh, God, where was he? Anna snatched
at her breath, then almost collapsed with relief. Of
course. Taking his afternoon nap. Safe in his cot.
Yes, Charlie must come first, no matter what.

The postman came the next day, offering his
condolences, since he had heard in Princetown
that Queenie had died. Who'd have thought it, eh?
Anna thanked him, though his sympathies
opened up the raw wound again. She took the
post, several envelopes, which was unusual. All
sympathy cards with such kind and well-meant
words that Anna wanted to cry again. But she
mustn't, though her throat ached with the need of
tears. Charlie. Every time he asked for Queenie,
she must smile and think of some way to distract
him. Even though it twisted the knife in her ribs.

Nothing from Carrie yet. But she expected she
would come to the funeral.

But what was this? A London postmark, and,
yes, it was Frankie's writing. Oh, how she had
longed to hear from her. To know that she was all
right after the way she had turned up on their
doorstep in such a state back in the spring. But

280

now Anna felt she couldn't stomach someone else's problems. She was in the black depths of despair, and only Charlie, with his winning smile and his new game of bending over like a length of rubber and grinning at her backwards and upside down as he pushed his head between his legs, could pluck her from her misery.

She left the washing-up that was piling up in the tapless sink. What did it matter now Queenie was dead? She herded the goats past the vegetables and into the front part of the garden. It was more like a field, really. It was no wonder Queenie had scoffed at the idea of a little patch of ground at the house she'd been offered. Was it that letter and the state Queenie had got herself into over it that had caused her heart attack? But what did it matter? Wouldn't bring her back, would it?

Anna somewhat absently played ball with Charlie in the field, and then he decided that Wilma and Dolly were more fun. They didn't seem to mind him too much. Anna used to be worried that they might hurt him, but not anymore. It was as if they appreciated that he was a baby. They weren't giving milk recently. Needed the services of a billy again. But what was the point now?

Anna sat down on the long grass. Frankie's letter was in her pocket, and *perhaps* she had the strength to read it. And when she thought of poor Frankie's face and the bruises she had seen before, she felt ashamed that she hadn't read the letter at once.

My dear Anna and you, too, Queenie.

Oh. Anna thumped the paper down on her lap. Out in the sunshine, watching Charlie's antics, she had felt more relaxed, as if she could imagine... She gritted her teeth, steeling herself to read on.

I'm so sorry I haven't written for so long, but it isn't always easy. And I'm sorry for descending on you like that as well. But you were both so kind and really helped me. And do you know what? You were right! I took your advice. I spoke to Lady Prue and she made arrangements for me to see a specialist in Harley Street. It wasn't very pleasant but he couldn't find anything wrong with me. He said specifically to Gilbert that it was just a matter of time and we both had to be patient. The only thing he found was that I'm a bit anaemic and he's given me some pills. Said it might make all the difference, so we're keeping our fingers crossed. And as for our marriage, it's made it so much better again. As if we've made a fresh start. Gilbert's never hit me again, and its all down to you, Anna, so thank you so much!

I still think we should keep our friendship a secret, though. I could see things going bad again if Gilbert found out. He'd be furious, and I do want to keep on seeing you. We're driving down on Monday. I'll try to make some excuse to go into Tavistock on my own on Thursday and meet you at the same place for lunch, if that's OK. And please bring dear little Charlie with you. But don't worry if I don't turn up. It'll only mean I couldn't get away. We'll be down for a couple of weeks and I'll try to get in contact in some other way.

So, hopefully, until next Thursday, and thank you again for everything,
All my love
Frankie

Anna sat back with a little breath of relief. She had fully expected a tale of woe, her mind conjuring up a sorry picture of Frankie, battered and bruised with purple marks all over her. But things seemed to be looking up. She was so pleased for her, and the thought cheered her up somewhat.

Monday. The funeral was Tuesday. And on Thursday, she and Charlie would catch the bus into Tavistock. She would have to break the news to Frankie, of course, that Queenie had died, but Frankie hardly knew her. She had only met her the once, so perhaps that would make it easier. Not just for Frankie, but for herself.

She looked up as Charlie ran towards her, his cheeks pink from chasing Wilma who had picked up his ball and made off with it. Charlie stood in front of her, his mouth in a cross pout, and pointed fiercely at the frolicking goat.

''Eenie!' he demanded. 'Ball!'

Anna shut her eyes. When it came to taking anything from Wilma, Queenie was the only one who could do so, and Charlie knew it. Anna bit on her lip, but couldn't stop herself from bursting into tears.

Chapter Twenty-Four

Ethel and Mabel were the last mourners to leave. Everyone else was long gone, but Anna's dear friend and her mum had stayed as late as they could. But they had to catch the bus down to Tavistock, clamber up the steep hill to Tavistock North Station and then take the train down across the Bere Peninsula and eventually to the station at Ford.

'I just wishes us 'ad room in our 'ouse for you an' Charlie,' Mabel declared for the second time as she collected her handbag. 'But we'm packed in like blooming sardines as it is.'

'Yes, I know. It's a very kind thought, though, thank you,' Anna answered, jiggling a tired Charlie in her arms. She'd been hiding behind a mask of politeness during the wake, a reaction against the agonising torment of the funeral service and the burial itself. She felt cross with herself that this sensation of detachment extended to Mabel as well, but she supposed it was her way of coping.

If she was honest, she was rather pleased that the chaotic little house in Ford was already bursting at the seams. It would save her the embarrassment of having to decline any offer of a home with the Shallafords. She loved them dearly, but she was used to the calm if humble surroundings of Holly Cottage, and the wild, savage beauty of the open moor. She couldn't imagine bringing up Charlie in the claustrophobic maze of backstreets, or the dingy, nicotine-stained rooms at Number Sixteen. And she was sure the choking fug of cigarette smoke would be bad for Charlie. She had noticed more than ever the sharp, stinging odour of cigarettes that radiated from Mabel. Even as she gave Anna a goodbye hug and began to walk down the short lane to the road, she was already fumbling in her bag for her packet of Player's Bachelor Tipped.

'An' I just wishes Bert an' me was married an' you could live wi' us,' Ethel chimed in as she and Anna went to stand together on the threshold.

284

'Yes, that'd be lovely,' Anna agreed, although in truth she wasn't sure about playing day and night gooseberry to a newly wed couple, either. 'But don't worry. I'm sure I'll find somewhere. We've got a few weeks yet. Olive's been asking around for me. And Deborah Franfield, the doctor's wife, she's keeping her eyes open in Tavistock for me, as well.'

'Well, you knows where us is. Bye-bye, Charlie. Be good for Mummy. See you soon, Anna. Take care.'

Ethel kissed Charlie on the cheek, and in trying to copy her, the little chap only succeeded in blowing a raspberry which made both girls laugh instead of saying what might have been a tearful farewell. Anna watched Ethel catch Mabel up and then they both waved as they turned the corner of the lodge and were gone.

'Just you and me now, Charlie,' Anna whispered, and as she closed the door, it really felt as if she was closing the door on her old, contented life. And she truly didn't know what would happen next.

Half an hour later, she had settled Charlie down for the night, and when she came back into the kitchen, the silence struck her like walking into a brick wall. After all the people who had crammed into the cottage, it suddenly seemed horribly quiet. The large church of St Michael and All Angels in Princetown had been almost full, for over her lifetime Queenie had been well known and loved by all. So many faces that Anna didn't recognise had come to pay their respects, but only those who had been particularly close to her came to the graveside and back to Holly Cottage. Olive, of course, the Crow sisters, the lady from Bolt's, four members of the extensive Cribbett family, the postman, the woman from the farm up the hill behind them, and even Clifford had all squeezed into the kitchen.

Now a deathly stillness hung in the cottage, and Anna flung open the door to let the warm, summer evening flow inside. There were still remnants of the wake to clear away, the odd used cup she had missed, crumbs on the floor. But when all was done, that vile emptiness enshrouded her again, setting her stomach churning, and for once, she wished vehemently that she had a radio or a record player like Carrie's. It was odd, that. She hadn't heard a word from Carrie. She had expected her to come to the funeral, but perhaps she had gone on holiday and received neither the telegram nor the short note Anna had sent her. It was the summer and the holiday season, after all. Perhaps Carrie, Jeffery and the baby had gone to stay with Carrie's parents in Surrey. Yes, that was probably it.

Anna shut away the goats and the hens for the night and then sat down outside the front door on the old bench she had so often shared with Queenie, watching the evening fade and listening to the world gradually silencing into night, a blackbird winging home to its nest. All so familiar. The world would go on, even if Queenie was no longer in it. A half-moon floated upwards into the deepening velvet of a clear sky, its silver glimmer reflecting the myriad stars that were scattered across its indigo eternity. Was Queenie's soul up there somewhere, smiling down benignly on her? She hoped so.

Anna shivered and pulled her cardigan more tightly around her. She realised she must have been sitting there for a couple of hours, not wanting to face the loneliness of the night. It must be nearing the witching hour, as Queenie always called it, and Anna reluctantly went inside. Still she didn't want to go to bed, and she read for half an hour in the dim lamplight. But the words were dancing up and down on the page, and she kept going over the same line again and again. She really should go to bed.

She slid between the cool sheets and closed her eyes, images of the day chasing each other round in her head, a little like a jumbled Pathé News at the pictures. The faces of those who had come to the funeral, the vicar's solemn words, the cheap wooden coffin, since, though Deborah Franfield had given it another name, this was a pauper's burial. Anna had insisted the undertakers drape over the ugly box the pretty patchwork quilt that Queenie herself had made. Anna couldn't afford flowers from the florist, but had made a posy from the garden, roses from Queenie's two bushes by the front door, sprigs of lavender, the last tall spray of deep-blue delphinium. It had been placed at the head of the coffin during the ceremony, and then had been put aside as Queenie was lowered into her eternal resting place. Anna had glanced up, and through her tear-blurred vision, caught Deborah's encouraging half smile. Despite the arrival of her daughter and new grandchild from America, and her son's imminent marriage, the good lady had found the time to catch the bus up to Princetown for the funeral, though she hadn't come back to the cottage. Queenie's cottage. And now Anna's. But not for much longer.

She turned over. Heard an owl hoot. Somewhere a fox barked eerily into the night. Oh, Queenie. She tried to conjure up other pictures in her mind. Charlie as a tiny baby. Or playing with the goats. But Queenie's face kept floating back, smiling, laughing. Cold and still. Anna's silent tears soaked into the pillow. Still awake. A pigeon cooed. At once, a blackbird answered, the loud shrill of tweeting sparrows. The window became a lighter square in the gloom. Dawn was breaking, and lulled by nature's chorus, Anna finally slept. But not for long.

'Mummy!'

Oh, dear. Anna dragged herself awake, her head thudding with a headache. She crawled out of bed in a daze to start the new day. Moving mechanically, her muscles aching. At least the sun was shining again, the sky a pale, duck-egg blue that would deepen as the hours passed. Things to do. Clinging to the daily routine. Household chores, the goats, the hens. Charlie. Thank God for Charlie.

She sat him on the potty, for this weather was ideal for potty-training. 'Oh, Charlie, what are we going to do?' she sighed, so tired that she couldn't think straight. And then she noticed that Charlie had indeed performed into the potty.

'Oh, good boy!' She stood him up, pulled up his new pants and hugged him. He was such a good little fellow, apt to be cheeky and, it had to be said, with his father's charm. It made Anna think of Frankie's letter. Gilbert seemed to be over his anger, and she was so pleased for them both.

'We're going to Tavistock tomorrow,' she told Charlie, who blinked at her uncomprehendingly. 'We can look for a new home.'

But what could she afford? A room in someone's house with a gas ring in the corner? Sharing a bathroom with strangers? Nowhere for Charlie to play when he was used to having the field to run in, or the entire moor when she took him for a walk? And would anyone take her in, an unmarried mother with a young child - even if she pretended she was a widow? Oh, Queenie. Why did it all have to end?

Chapter Twenty-Five

Thursday dawned bright and clear once more, promising another glorious day. After a week virtually without sleep, Anna had finally succumbed to exhaustion and slept well, feeling much better when she woke up. There was so much to do before they caught the bus down to Tavistock. The goats would have to remain locked in their pen while they were out, as would the hens, but the goat shed and the coop would both need their daily clean. Indoors, Anna had let the washing-up pile up, and she felt she must see to that, too.

By the time Anna got to the café in Tavistock, it was gone half past twelve and she only just managed to get a table. She even had to fold down the pushchair as much as it could go and stow it in the corner behind her, the place was so crowded. She sat Charlie on her lap, and hoped Frankie would indeed be able to get away.

'Anna!' Frankie's face wrinkled with anxiety as she came towards her. 'You look rough. Has something happened?'

Anna felt her soul cave in and crumble. 'Oh. Frankie, I'm so glad you managed to come. Yes, something awful *has* happened. Queenie's dead.' There, she had said it. Raw and blunt. But there it was.

Frankie's face tightened into taut hues. 'Oh, my God. I don't believe it. When?'

'Last week. The funeral was Tuesday. I feel ... oh, I don't know how I feel. And now I don't know which way to turn.' She stared up at Frankie, helplessly and yet expectant, as if she expected her friend to have an answer.

'Oh, I'm so sorry. Is there anything I can do? You helped me so much, and I hope I can help you back.' She glanced at Charlie as she sat down, and smiled. 'Hello, Charlie. How are you?' She reached across to tickle his tummy, and he laughed gleefully, drawing up his chubby knees. It was a happy moment, and eased away any tension before Frankie's expression became serious again. 'Poor Queenie. What on earth happened?'

Anna lowered her eyes wistfully at the stab of pain. 'It was a heart attack. So sudden.'

'Oh, gosh, how dreadful!'

'Yes, it was. In the middle of the night, too. It was just like a nightmare. I still can't believe it.

And to make matters worse, the cottage has been condemned and we've got to move out. Queenie was in such a state about it, I think that's what brought it on. And now I don't know where Charlie and I are going to live.'

It was just then that the waitress came over, interrupting their conversation to take their order, but as soon as she had done so, Frankie asked, 'So, what've they said about the cottage?'

'Hang on just a second. Charlie's getting fidgety. I've brought his favourite picture book. That'll keep him quiet.' Anna reached into her bag and brought out the gaily coloured cardboard book which Charlie opened at once.

'He's going to be intelligent,' Frankie observed with a smile.

'Yes, he's a bright little thing.' Her voice trailed off again in a thread of sadness, and Frankie bit on her lip.

'Tell me what they've said about the cottage,' she prompted.

Anna's lips twisted in bitter resignation. 'It's been condemned, not having mains *any*thing. And they won't pay out to modernise it, so we've got to move out. Only with the small allowance I get for Charlie and me, I can't afford much.'

''Ilma!' Charlie grinned, jabbing his finger at a picture of a goat in his book, and he swivelled his head to look up at Anna in expectation of praise.

'Yes, it looks just like Wilma, doesn't it?' she answered absently and then she added half under her breath. 'I suppose I'll have to get rid of the goats and the hens somewhere, as well.'

'Well, I can't help you with that, I'm afraid, but

I do have money of my own, now,' Frankie announced, her pointed chin jutting out firmly. 'My father's money is all being held in trust until I'm twenty-five, but I came of age since I saw you last, and now I get a very generous allowance from it. All my own. Nothing to do with Gilbert. So, I'll send you a cheque every month.'

Anna's jaw fell open. 'Frankie, you can't–'

'It's for Charlie, not you. Can't have him being brought up somewhere awful. Would there be anywhere up on the moor, do you think?'

'I can't find anywhere suitable,' Anna told her, trying to ignore the matter of Frankie's astounding offer. 'I did enquire about the place Queenie had been offered in Princetown, but as soon as they'd heard she'd died, they let it to someone else. Not that I could've afforded it.'

'Well, you could've done now. Here's twenty pounds. You may have to pay a month's rent in advance. Go on, take it, I insist.'

'It certainly would help.' Anna chewed on her lip as she fingered the two crisp notes. 'On one condition. That I pay you back one day. When Charlie starts school, I'll get a job.'

'If it'll make you feel better! Now, if I'm not mistaken, that's our lunch arriving.'

For the first time since Queenie's death Anna felt hunger pangs gnawing at her stomach. With a good night's sleep under her belt at last, a full meal inside her and Frankie's moral and financial support, she suddenly felt able to cope. Queenie had been dead little over a week and the raw pain still ate into Anna's heart, but she was starting to feel positive about the future.

After lunch, Anna made her way to the letting agency in Duke Street that the waitress had directed her to. She told the man at the desk what she was able to afford, upping it a little now that she had swallowed her pride and accepted Frankie's generous offer. The fellow balanced his horn-rimmed spectacles on the end of his bulbous nose and looked down at her disdainfully.

'There's not many places will take a young child with a ... hurrump ... mother on her own,' he said, clearing his throat.

'I'm a widow.' Anna lifted her chin, meeting his gaze steadily. 'And I believe the rent I can afford is quite adequate.'

He pushed his ugly lips forward. 'Hmm, well, let me see.'

In the end, he showed her three possibilities. One was a flat above a shop in Brook Street that Duke Street ran into. But although a good size, it could be noisy and there was no garden. A large room with a private bathroom in an even larger, detached house in Courtenay Road – with use of the garden *if the child can behave itself* – was also up for rent. But Anna wasn't sure she could live with the landlady! The only place that tempted her was a two-bedroom terraced cottage near the top of Bannawell Street, with its own little back garden that caught the afternoon sun. But it really would be pushing her finances, even with Frankie's help, and so she went away to think about it.

She was feeling exhausted again, her head reeling. It really was quite a task trying to find somewhere decent to live! Fortunately, Charlie had been as good as gold, and then he had nodded off

293

in the pushchair as she walked back down the steep hill into the town centre. Perhaps she should look in the local paper, but she mustn't leave the decision about Bannawell Street too long or it might be snapped up by someone else.

Her brain was whirling with conflicting thoughts. It was quite a responsibility, and one, if she considered it, she hadn't been faced with before. She needed time to think. And someone to talk it through with. Not Frankie, because she wasn't sure when they would meet again. She couldn't speak to Ethel as the Shallafords didn't have a phone, and Ethel didn't know Tavistock anyway. Carrie did, but...

Perhaps Carrie was back now from staying with her parents or wherever else she had been. It was worth a try. It wouldn't be much out of her way to cut through Bank Square and across to Carrie and Jeffery's house in Exeter Street.

The road was dusty, the air tainted with the smell of tarmac that had been baked in the sun for days on end. It was not unpleasant, and Anna pondered that, unusually, they hadn't had rain since before Queenie had died. Had the good weather helped, or had it seemed incongruous that the world was bathed in sunshine when Anna's soul was dark with grief? She wasn't sure, but then she didn't feel sure of anything anymore.

As she approached Carrie and Jeffery's house, she noticed a car parked by the kerb, and a middle-aged couple were unloading some shopping and other items from its boot. Anna didn't pay much attention until, as she drew nearer, she realised that the front gate to Carrie's house was open and the man seemed to be aiming for it. Then the woman, who had been leaning towards the back seat of the car, emerged with a little girl in her arms. At the same moment, Carrie appeared at the open front door, looking pale and drawn and so unlike her usual, merry self that Anna stopped in her tracks. Carrie came down the short garden path, and when she glanced along the road and saw Anna, her eyes widened with surprise.

'Anna!' She rushed through the open gate and out onto the pavement. 'Oh, am I glad to see you!' And then she burst into tears and flung herself into Anna's arms.

Anna was astonished and awkwardly patted her friend's back. 'What on earth's going on?'

'It's ... it's Jeffery,' Carrie gulped between sobs, and pulling back, she tried to wipe the rears from her cheeks with the back of her hand. 'Oh, Anna, I'm sorry.'

'Jeffery? What–?'

'He's in hospital.'

Anna's confused frown deepened. 'Oh, Lord, what's happened?'

'Oh, Anna, he's ... he's got TB.'

Anna gasped, and something like ice trickled through her, despite the afternoon heat. Dear Lord, hadn't she had enough shocks lately? 'TB?' she muttered. 'Oh, good God.'

'Yes, he–'

'Hello, dear. Are you Anna?' the woman with little Polly half asleep in her arms came up behind Carrie smiling, but with a tired look in her eyes. 'I'm Carrie's mum. Sorry I can't shake hands.'

'Oh, yes, hello, Mrs ... er...'

'Call me Rene, and this is Roger,' she nodded over her shoulder. 'The two R's.'

'Oh, yes,' Anna repeated, still bewildered.

'I think we'd all better go inside and we can explain everything.'

'Yes,' Anna said yet again.

They all trooped indoors and Anna negotiated the pushchair over the threshold. She left Charlie asleep in the cool hallway while Rene herded her and Carrie out into the garden.

'I'll put the kettle on,' she smiled kindly. 'Roger'll keep an eye on the little ones.'

'Thanks, Mum.'

The girls sat down in two deckchairs that were already out in the shade of the only tree in the garden. Anna noticed even more how awful Carrie looked, her eyes shadowed in a grey face. They must make a right pair, Anna thought glumly, as she'd glanced her own reflection in the mirror that morning and saw how drained she looked herself.

'So, tell me all about it,' she prompted, though she wasn't sure she really wanted to know what Carrie was going through. 'TB? I can't believe it. Not Jeffery. He's always so fit.'

'I know. I can't believe it, either.' Carrie shook her head, looking close to tears again. 'He'd not felt well and had this persistent cough for weeks. And then he started coughing up blood, so he went to see Dr Franfield. He ordered an X-ray and some tests, and there it was. He got Jeffery into the sanatorium straight away. And then among all the chaos, your telegram arrived. I'm so sorry about Queenie, really I am. But I just

296

haven't had a minute to contact you.'

'I don't suppose you have. I thought it was strange I didn't hear from you. I thought you must be on holiday. Oh, golly, what a time we've both had. But, I hardly dare ask it, how is Jeffery?'

Her heart strained as she saw the desperation on Carrie's face. 'Well, he's in the main building at the sanatorium which is where new patients start. Has his own room with huge doors opening to the outside, so it's like being outdoors all the time. They say he'll recover, but it'll take time. Oh, but, Anna,' she squealed as her eyes filled with tears again, 'what if they're wrong? What if–?'

'You mustn't think like that,' Anna heard herself say. God, that sounded such a cliché.

'If only he'd been immunised,' Carrie despaired, and Anna noticed her wringing her hands. 'You know we had it when we were at school? But Jeffery'd already left school when they started doing it. And then there's Polly. Dr Franfield gave her a little test injection like we had at school. He'll test her again in six weeks, and if it's still negative, he'll vaccinate her to be on the safe side. And then he'll have to test her again six weeks after that because it doesn't always take in young children.'

'Oh dear, it all sounds pretty complicated. But how on earth did Jeffery catch it? You think of TB and overcrowded slums in industrial cities, not living *here* and with a decent standard of living.'

'That's what I thought, but you can pick it up anywhere. Jeffery did a wiring job a while ago and the old man was coughing all over the place, so perhaps it was that.'

'But I'm sure Jeffery'll be all right,' Anna said

confidently. 'Dr Franfield is so good.'

'Yes, I know. He was absolutely wonderful. You know, it was the same day Queenie died.'

'Ah, that must be why Dr Franfield didn't come back in the evening when he said he would. Not that there was anything for him to do. It was just him being kind. I'm surprised Deborah – that's his wife – didn't tell me about Jeffery. She knows we're friends, and she came up to the funeral.'

'Not allowed to, I don't think,' Rene said as she came out carrying a tray. 'Patient confidentiality, I think it's called. Now, I thought you might actually prefer cold drinks rather than tea. Lemon squash with ice out of the fridge, but I can brew up some tea if you prefer.'

'Squash'll be fine for me, thank you,' Anna answered gratefully. 'I'm so hot traipsing around the town and an ice-cold drink'll be just the ticket. So where's the sanatorium, then?'

'Didworthy. It's a mile or so outside South Brent going up onto the moor.'

'Golly, that's a long way, and an awkward journey. How are you getting there to visit?'

'Dad's been driving me.'

'Oh, of course. How silly of me.'

'Well, we came as soon as we heard,' Rene said, declining Anna's offer to have her deckchair and sitting down on the dry grass instead. 'I'd just got in from work – I've got a little job in a dress shop, just part-time in the afternoons – when the phone rang. I was so shocked, as you might imagine. Roger was still at the bank, so I rang him there. He couldn't just drop everything and leave, especially if he was going to be away for some time. So he had to stay late to organise things. I packed a case while I was waiting, and we left as soon as Roger got home. Got here about two in the morning, I think.'

'Of course, your dad's a bank manager, isn't he, Carrie?'

'Yes, he is. But Mum and Dad simply have to go back this weekend.'

'How are you going to manage, then?' Anna asked, and her own problems seemed pretty minimal by comparison!

Carrie shook her head. 'I'll have to get there by public transport, I suppose. Train to Plymouth and then another train to South Brent. Or apparently there's a bus from Tavistock to South Brent twice a week. But you have to walk a mile from there up a winding country lane. The most awkward thing is that children aren't allowed.'

'Oh dear, it's not going to b easy for you.'

Carrie took a huge breath and released it through pursed lips. 'No, But Jack, bless him,' she went on, brightening somewhat, 'You know, my brother Jack I've mentioned before, he's giving up his job up north to come and be with me. But this time of year, he's really needed, so he's got to work out his month's notice, but then he's coming to live with me.'

'How wonderful to have a brother like that!' Anna agreed, deeply impressed. 'He's a gardener, isn't he?'

'That's right,' Rene confirmed, and Anna was aware of her proud nod. 'Really made something of himself despite... And I really admire him for taking this big step to help his little sister,' she smiled, nodding affectionately at Carrie. 'I didn't want to leave my employer in the lurch. She's nearly eighty, you see. I would've done, mind, but when Jack said it was time he made a change in his life, well, it seemed ideal. And it's always nice to have a man around the place.'

'He can't come until the beginning of September, though,' Carrie grimaced, 'so I'll be on my own until then. But, I think that's enough of my problems. It really is so good to see you, Anna. Just chatting with someone else helps. But what were you doing in Tavistock?'

Listening to Carrie's dreadful news, Anna had almost forgotten. 'Oh, we've got to leave the cottage so I've been looking for somewhere for Charlie and me to live,' she replied, trying not to appear too gloomy.

'And have you found anywhere?'

'No, not really. Only one place, but it's a bit expensive. I need to think about it. I'll get the paper tomorrow and see if there's anything in that. We've got a few weeks yet.'

'It must be really strange without Queenie. You must feel so lonely up there without her.'

'Yes, I do rather.'

They fell into silence for a few minutes as they sipped at their cool, refreshing drinks, each one locked in her own private thoughts. And when Rene suddenly spoke with startling enthusiasm, Anna jumped and spilt some squash down her front.

'Oh, we are stupid!' Rene cried. 'The answer's staring us in the face. Anna, why don't you and Charlie come to live here with Carrie? At least until Jack comes, anyway.'

'Oh,' the two girls chorused, and then Carrie went on, quite elated, 'Oh, Mum, you're a genius! Anna, you will, won't you?'

Anna stared at the happy relief on Carrie's drawn face. She took a second or two to take it in, and then grinned back.

'Yes, I'd be delighted!'

Chapter Twenty-Six

Roger dropped Anna and Charlie home in his car. Beside them on the back seat were a few empty cardboard boxes Carrie had found around the house. For that night, Anna was to start packing.

She had no idea what to do about the few pieces of furniture. Were they Queenie's, or had they come with the cottage? She would simply leave them behind, and take only what she wanted of the more personal items around the place. Now, Roger waited while she filled Queenie's two shopping bags with as many jars of home-made pickles and preserves as she could, as she was sure Carrie could make use of them.

She certainly didn't have long to get organised. Roger was to collect as much as he could the following morning before driving Carrie to the sanatorium in the afternoon. That only left the evening, as Rene and Roger were leaving for home on the Saturday morning.

Once Charlie was settled in his cot for the

night, Anna set to. She found some old wooden orange boxes in the outhouse and packed Queenie's best china and glasses that had mainly been used in the tea room. She wouldn't need them at Carrie's, but she would once she had a place of her own. Another box took pots, pans and other kitchen equipment, all of which could be stored in Carrie's loft. There was little ornamentation in the cottage, so that just left her own and Charlie's personal possessions.

Anna hesitated with her hand on the latch to Queenies room. It would feel criminal rifling through the dear woman's things, but it had to be done. Anna took a deep breath and walked in. At least she would be doing it with the greatest reverence and respect.

She checked the pockets of Queenie's few clothes, but found nothing of any importance, just a half-crown piece. There was nothing she wanted herself, just a few pieces of cheap costume jewellery. Anna already had the best, Queenie's mother's wedding ring, on her own finger.

A shoebox of papers. Something to do with Queenie's pension. Oh, yes. Anna would have to sort that out. A few age-stained letters dating back years. Nothing that made any sense. Only one had a legible address and appeared to be from one of Queenie's brothers who had gone to Canada. Anna would write just in case, even though the letter was over twenty years old.

The bottom of the box was lined with a piece of tissue. Anna was about to replace all the irrelevant papers when she noticed there was something beneath the thin, faded pink sheet. Drawn by curiosity, she lifted out a small, yellowing envelope. Her heart jolted, for written on it in faded ink were the words 'my darling little Charlotte's hair', and when Anna opened it, she found a tiny brown curl.

Oh, Queenie.

The wave of tears broke over her in a drowning crest. Queenie, who had made that supreme sacrifice that had dogged her all her days. Queenie, who had become to Anna like the dear mother she had so tragically lost. And now Queenie herself was gone.

I'll never let Charlie go, Queenie, I promise.

Anna shook her head, setting her jaw fiercely. This really wouldn't do.

The next morning, she rang Mrs Smudge early, before she would be leaving for Ashcroft Hall, since her only day off was Sunday. Please would she take two goats and some hens off Anna's hands? Yes, she would. Her Alfie would come and collect them that evening. And she also agreed to pass on Anna's new address to Frankie as soon as she got the opportunity.

And so, on Saturday morning, the cottage seemed empty. Before leaving for the long journey home, Roger kindly drove up, helped Anna dismantle the cot and took it, the high chair and a bundle of bedlinen and towels back to Carrie's house for her. There was no room for Anna and Charlie in the car, so they would follow on later by bus.

Anna knew she was putting off the moment of final departure. She kept finding things to do, like cleaning the empty cupboards, although heaven knew why. But Charlie was getting restless with just his train to play with since all his other toys were waiting for him down at Carrie's. So Anna took his hand and walked round to the back of the cottage to the empty goat shed and chicken run. She just had to say a last goodbye to every part of the place that had become the cornerstone of her life.

Anna crouched down in front of Charlie. Perhaps she shouldn't have brought him out here, but hopefully with Polly to play with all the time, he would soon forget all about the goats.

'Dolly and Wilma have gone to live on a proper farm,' she told him, not sure that he would fully understand but she felt she should tell him anyway. 'They'll be much happier there. And we're going to live with Polly.'

'Polly?' Charlie's doubtful expression brightened considerably.

'Yes. Come along now. We've got a bus to catch.'

As they crossed the yard, she noticed the door to the outhouse was slightly ajar. Through the gap, she glimpsed Queenie's old mangle. Now that Charlie was partially potty-trained, there weren't so many nappies, but at least now she could wash them in Carrie's machine! The thought cheered her and they hurried back inside the cottage to collect the pushchair and the bag with the very last of their possessions safely stowed in it.

'Mustn't forget your train, Charlie!' she grinned.

One last quick check that she wasn't leaving anything behind. Then she steeled herself to pop Charlie in the pushchair and, with one final glance around the kitchen, she pulled the door to behind her, closing another chapter of her life.

'Goodbye, Queenie,' she murmured under her breath. 'Thank you for everything. And God bless.'

She turned away. Come on. Carrie needs you.

'Bye-bye, Anna dear!' she heard Olive's voice from the front door of the lodge. 'Keep in touch, won't you?'

'Of course, Olive!' Anna called back. 'And thank you for your help.'

'Not at all. You take care of Charlie, now. And good luck!'

They waved at each other, and then Olive went back inside and Anna walked the short distance along the road to the bus stop.

Anna was feeling pretty pleased with herself. She and Charlie had been living with Carrie and Polly for scarcely a week, but though her heart dragged whenever she thought of Queenie and Holly Cottage, things were looking up. That morning, she had secured a job at the Bedford Hotel down in the town centre, and would be starting the following Monday. She would start at seven o'clock every morning to help serve the breakfasts, and would finish at midday after morning coffees had been cleared away. Carrie would look after both the toddlers, and then in the afternoons, they would swap over so that Carrie could go to visit Jeffery.

The long spell of fine weather had broken in a thunderstorm, but after a few days of welcome rain, the summer sunshine had returned. Anna

had taken the children down to play in the pleasant park known as The Meadows. They had fed
the ducks along the disused Tavistock Canal, one
of Charlie and Polly's favourite activities and
Anna had to drag them away. It would be slow
going back up to Exeter Street. The children had
to take turns in the pushchair while the other
literally toddled along at a snail's pace.

Once they reached home, the children went out
into the garden where they sat on a rug spread on
the lawn, playing with some gaily coloured
wooden bricks. Anna knew they would be quite
safe and went into Carrie's kitchen to get some
drinks. She was getting used to all the modern
appliances and had to admit it was a lot quicker
and easier to turn on the electric kettle than to
wait for water to boil on the range. It was nice,
too, to have light at the flick of a switch again,
and to watch television of an evening!

She was back out in the garden, sipping her
own glass of cold lemonade while the children
played at her feet, when she thought she heard a
noise at the front door. That was odd. Carrie
wasn't due back for hours. Apprehension gripped
at her stomach. Surely they weren't being burg-
led? She got up quietly, her heart pounding, and
tiptoed in through the kitchen. Yes, there was
definitely someone in the hallway.

Oh, crikey.

She was shaking with fear, but also with outrage.
How dare anyone break into her friend's house,
her friend who already had enough troubles? And,
oh dear God, the children! She would defend
them to her last breath!

Anna picked up Carrie's heavy frying pan which seemed to be the only weapon to hand, and stole to the door. She opened it a crack and her heart took a huge leap in her breast. A man was in the hall, bending down over something, but Anna was too incensed and terrified to care what.

She catapulted forward and went to thwack the frying pan with all her might over the intruder's head. But at the last instant, he looked up, his eyes wide with horror, and dodged away so that Anna's blow missed his head and landed instead with a resounding wallop on his shoulder. The fellow let out a yelp of pain and fell back against the door, putting up his hands to defend himself from further attack.

Anna stood over him, wielding the frying pan and ready to hit him again if need be. She wasn't sure what to do next and was utterly petrified, but she mustn't let him see.

'What the hell do you think you're doing?' she demanded, praying her voice wasn't trembling as much as the rest of her was!

'I might ask you the same question! What are you doing in my sister's house?'

'What?' Anna blinked at him, and wanted to die from guilt as realisation dawned. 'You're … you're not–?'

'Carrie's brother, Jack,' he confirmed, wincing painfully as he rubbed his shoulder.

'B-but you're not due here for another couple of weeks,' Anna stammered defensively.

'Well, as it happens, Miss Whoever You Are, they found someone to replace me who could start straight away, so I didn't have to work all of my notice, after all. Thought I'd get a warmer welcome than this, mind.'

'But ... how did you get in?' Anna wanted to know, still reluctant to believe him – or to admit to her mistake.

'With a key, of course. Carrie gave me one when I came to stay ages ago. So would you mind putting that frying pan down and letting me get up?'

Oh. Oh, Lord. What a dreadful thing to have done. Anna stood back and watched as Jack got up, sucking breath through his teeth as he put his opposite hand up to his injured shoulder. As he did so, Anna noticed the striking resemblance to Carrie, the same strong jawline and generous mouth. His eyes, though, were a startling blue just like his father's.

'Oh, I am *so* sorry,' she apologised, squirming with shame. 'I honestly thought you were a burglar.'

'Well, I'm glad you were prepared to defend yourself, whoever you are.'

'Oh, I'm sorry. Again,' she said awkwardly, although the tentative half smile that was creeping onto Jack's face was making her feel more at ease. 'I should have introduced myself. I'm Anna, Carrie's friend. I'm living here for the time being. Carrie wrote you a letter–'

'Yes, it came yesterday, but I didn't have time–'

He broke off sharply, but then gave a casual shrug that made him wince again, and Anna bit guiltily on her lower lip. 'Let me get you a drink. You must be gasping after that long drive.'

'I came by train. I do drive, but I've never

needed a car of my own. Erm, where shall I put my things?' he asked, indicating the large rucksack and a holdall on the floor. Anna realised shamefaced that it was his luggage he had been bending over and not some article he was intent on stealing!

'Oh, I don't really know.' Anna experienced a stab of shock as it dawned on her that Jack's unexpected arrival had set the cat among the pigeons in other ways, too. She had taken over the spare double bedroom that Rene and Roger had vacated. She had Charlie sleeping with her in his cot, but Polly had the third room to herself. Anna had fully intended to find a place of her own before Jack came, dropping Charlie off at Carrie's before work each morning, but now what was to happen?

'I'd leave them there for now. Go through to the garden while I get you a drink. On second thoughts, I'd better come with you first. The children might be frightened if a strange man suddenly walks in.'

'I'm not that strange, am I?' Jack questioned with a lift of his eyebrows, and Anna's mouth curved as she realised he was teasing.

'You know what I mean. So come on through. This is Polly,' she announced as they went into the garden. 'Polly, dear, this is your Uncle Jack.'

The little girl looked up and promptly plugged her thumb into her mouth.

'Golly, she's grown. But I haven't seen her since she was a few weeks old.'

'And this is my little boy, Charlie.'

Jack turned to the other child, solemnly holding

out his hand. 'Hello, I'm Jack.'

Charlie gazed back, his mouth hunched in a thoughtful pout while his eyes travelled critically over the newcomer bending patiently over him. At last, he put his little hand in Jack's as it seemed it was what was required of him, and his mummy was standing there, smiling, so it must be all right.

'Don't let me stop your game,' Jack went on, releasing Charlie's hand which the little boy snatched behind his back for a moment, then, deciding Jack was no threat, went back to playing.

As Jack straightened up, it clearly caught his shoulder again. 'You've got a right strong arm on you there,' he murmured. 'No bad thing, but I wish I hadn't been on the other end of it.'

'Oh dear, I can't apologise enough. I think Carrie's got some witch hazel in the medicine cabinet. I'll get you that drink and then I'll go and look. Would you like some lemonade?'

'I could murder a cup of tea, actually, if it isn't too much trouble. Milk, no sugar, please.'

'OK. Won't be a jiffy.'

She sprang inside, glad to escape Jack's arresting, deep-blue eyes – and her own guilt. Would she ever live it down? She left the tea to draw while she went upstairs to fetch the witch hazel and some cotton wool.

'There. I found the witch hazel, she announced, taking everything outside.

'Oh, good.'

Jack had arrived wearing a faded blue shirt, open at the neck and with the sleeves rolled up to his elbows. He must have begun the day with a

310

knitted jumper over the top, and this had been tied about his thin waist by the sleeves when he arrived and had now been discarded over the back of the deckchair he was lounging in. Now, without further ado, he proceeded to unbutton his shirt and pull it down over his shoulder.

Anna was glad she had already put the tray down or she might have dropped it. Jack appeared not the least embarrassed, but *she* was! The last time she had seen a man's bare torso had been – well, not even *then*, as Gilbert had had his wicked way without either of them removing any clothing other than the necessary. No, the only time Anna had seen half-dressed males had been at the Tinside Lido in Plymouth, or at Tavistock's open-air pool at the top of Bannawell Street when she and Carrie had taken the toddlers there for their first experience of swimming earlier that summer.

Anna gulped, but as she tried to conceal her embarrassment, was aware of a pleasant tingle of excitement curling within her. She had sworn she would never be drawn to another man, not after the way Gilbert had deceived her. And yet Dr Edwin Franfield, William and Deborah's son, had struck a chord in her heart just for one fleeting second. She had learnt that he was engaged – and now, of course, had been married just the previous weekend – and she had never thought any more about the question of the opposite sex ever entering her life again.

Now, though, inexplicably, her heart flipped over in her chest. Jack was of average height and, despite his almost overlean build, was broad of shoulder. Surprisingly, he wasn't at all bony, but his upper arms and shoulders – as much as she could see of them as he hadn't removed his shirt completely – were finely muscled. From his strenuous work as a gardener, she assumed. There was a tan mark around the back of his neck, below his slightly overlong hair, ending in a deep V on his chest which was covered in a scattering of fine hair.

She was jolted out of her astonishment at her own feelings by Jack leaning forward for the cotton wool and bottle of witch hazel.

'You'd better let me do that,' she said, amazing herself again. 'I'm so sorry, Jack, but I split the skin, right on your shoulder blade. You won't be able to see, and if you get witch hazel in it, it'll sting like crazy. In fact, it wouldn't surprise me if it doesn't need a stitch or two. Perhaps you'd better pop down to William's surgery. It'll be opening soon. That's Dr Franfield. We've seen so much of him lately, what with Jeffery and everything,' – meaning Queenie, but she would maybe tell him about that later – 'that were on Christian name terms now.'

'That's the most important thing. Jeffery, I mean. How is the poor devil?'

'Holding his own, thank God,' Anna replied, relieved to have something else to talk about as she dabbed the witch hazel over Jack's reddening skin. 'They say he'll make a full recovery, but it'll take months.'

'Well, that's why I'm here to help.'

'It's really good of you. Not many brothers would give up their job and their entire way of life to help out their sister.'

'You flatter me. But I was due for a change. I didn't really have any sort of life outside the estate. I even lived in a room over the stables. It was all quite old-fashioned, really. I had my meals provided, so what else did I need? I hardly ever went off the estate except maybe to visit local nurseries.'

'Really? Did you never have any social life of your own? A girlfriend?' *An attractive chap like you,* she added in her head.

Jack's face seemed to close down. 'No,' he answered brusquely, and Anna felt the ease that was coming between them disappear again. 'Well,' he said, swallowing down his cup of tea. 'If you tell me where I'll find this doctor, I'd better get down there.'

'Go down into the town centre,' Anna directed him, feeling oddly disappointed, 'over the other side of the square and turn right. Go down there and it's a hundred yards or so down on the right. There are some terraces of big Victorian villas opposite the park. It's one of those. You can't miss it. There's a sign saying "Surgery" by the gate.'

Jack glanced at her with a dark frown. 'Sssurgery,' he repeated, hanging onto the initial 's'. 'Right. I'll see you later.'

He unfolded himself from the deckchair and disappeared into the house. Anna felt all at odds with herself. She may have made a terrible mess of her first meeting with Carrie's brother, but she wasn't too sure about *him,* either!

Chapter Twenty-Seven

Carrie let herself in the front door, weary but relieved that at the sanatorium they were pleased with Jeffery's progress. The aroma of cooking greeted her. Having Anna there was a godsend. How on earth she would have managed to visit Jeffery if she hadn't been able to leave Polly with Anna, she really didn't know.

As she turned into the hallway, she nearly tripped over a large rucksack and a holdall on the floor. What the blazes...? But before she had time to ponder further, the figure of a man appeared in the kitchen doorway and her heart leapt as she realised who it was.

'Jack! I thought you couldn't get away for another few weeks?' She hugged him tightly and then frowned since, as they drew apart, she noticed him stifle a wince. 'What's the matter, Jack?'

'Oh, your friend and I had a minor contretemps when I arrived. She thought I was a burglar and hit me with a frying pan.'

'What!'

'I can't tell you how dreadful I feel about it,' Anna said as she poked her head around the kitchen door. 'I had to send him down to William to have a couple of stitches put in.'

'Oh, dear.' But when Carrie glanced back at Jack, he was smiling.

'I'm sure I'll live. More importantly, how's Jeffery?'

Carrie tipped her head optimistically. 'Well, he's already improving. But it's going to be a long job.'

'Well, I'm here to help. And I'll come with you to the sanatorium next time you go, if that's OK.'

'Oh, yes! It's such a tedious journey, I'd be really glad of the company. And I know Jeffery would love to see you.'

'Sorry to butt in,' Anna interrupted them, 'but I think we should get the children off to bed. I took them to the park this afternoon so they didn't get their nap and they're both exhausted. Then we can have our meal in peace.'

'Good idea. Oh, hello, Polly, love!' Carrie smiled as her little daughter came out into the hall and clamped herself around her mother's legs. 'Say night-night to everyone.'

'Come on, Charlie, bedtime for you, too, my lad.'

'Jack,' Charlie declared decisively, and grabbed hold of Jack's hand.

Anna felt her face redden. 'Oh, dear. Would you mind? Would you read him a story, otherwise he'll never settle down.'

Oddly, she saw Jack and Carrie exchange wary glances, but then Jack answered evasively, 'I'm not much good at reading stories, but I can make one up for him.'

'Even better!' Anna laughed as Charlie pulled Jack towards the stairs. 'But doesn't Mummy get a kiss, too?'

Twenty minutes later, the three adults were

sitting outside as it seemed a pity to waste such a pleasant evening indoors. Despite the occasional train that rumbled past on the embankment at the bottom of the garden, it was like relaxing in a tranquil oasis, since all three had had a long, tiring day in one way or another. But the garden was showing signs of neglect. The warm weather combined with the recent rain had encouraged everything to grow – including the weeds!

Jack had obviously been thinking the same thing. 'I'll mow the lawn in the morning,' he offered. 'And the beds need some attention. And those roses need deadheading. *Belles de Crécy*, aren't they? Very fragrant. I love purple roses. Such a subtle colour, don't you think?'

A flutter of breath caught at the back of Anna's throat. She had always thought of the bruises her father had inflicted on her mum as purple roses. But Jack was right. The blooms on the two rose bushes in Carrie's garden were very beautiful.

'Always the gardener!' Carrie chuckled. 'I remember when we were little, you used to take me round the garden, and would get quite cross when I couldn't remember all the names of the plants you kept telling me.'

'You should've written them down for her,' Anna suggested. 'I always find things like that easier to remember when I see them written down.'

'Ah.' Carrie's eyes darted across at Jack for a second, and then she dug her fork into her shepherd's pie again. 'So, what are you going to do now you're here, Jack? You'll need a job, won't you?'

'I've got one.' Jack surprised them both with his announcement. 'At least for one morning a week, so it's a start. But I've got quite a lot of savings to tide me over.'

'So ... what's this job, then?' Carrie asked, non-plussed. 'You've only been here for a few hours and you've got one already.'

'Ah, well, I have Anna to thank for that. When I went down to the doctor, I explained who I was. First thing he did was give me some sort of TB test if I'm going to be visiting the sanatorium. Then we got chatting as he saw to my shoulder. When he learnt I'm a gardener, he said he could do with somebody one morning a week. And he's going to ask around and see if he can find other customers for me as well.'

'Oh, that's super. Well done!'

'Well, if I can build up a reasonable clientele, it'll keep me going. I'll need to earn a bit of cash if I've got to find somewhere to live.'

'Somewhere to live?' Carrie echoed. 'But you're going to live *here*.'

'And where am I going to sleep? The couch is fine for a night or two, but I don't fancy it on a permanent basis.'

'Oh, I won't hear of that!' Carrie protested. 'No. I'll move Polly in with me. That chair in her room opens into a bed, so you won't have to sleep on the floor or anything. It's just that I wasn't expecting you for a few weeks yet. Anna was looking for somewhere to live, you see, and with Jeffery... But didn't you get my letter explaining that Anna and Charlie were here?'

'Well, yes, I did get a letter from you. But I didn't ... read it.'

'I should be the one to move out,' Anna broke

317

in, suddenly feeling uncomfortable. 'It isn't fair on–'

'No. I'm quite happy to have Polly in with me. I want you *both* here. But, Jack, you should have sent a telegram or something.'

'I did think of it, but I thought it would be a nice surprise for you if I just turned up.' And then, flashing his eyes across at Anna, he added wryly, 'I didn't realise I'd get such a hostile reception.'

Anna wanted to curl up and die. Did he have to rub it in? Surely she'd apologised enough!

'Well, it was your own fault for not getting someone to read my letter for you. Really, Jack–'

Carrie stopped in mid sentence and gave a short gasp. Anna blinked in astonishment, wondering if she had heard right, and glanced up to see Jack turn his head away. Then she saw Carrie swallow.

'I'm sorry, Jack. I didn't mean to let it slip. But Anna will need to know. Jack can't read or write, you see, Anna. He's what they call word blind.'

Anna's eyebrows arched. She was astounded and yet intrigued at the same time. And she must play this right. She didn't want to give Jack any more reason to deride her if they were going to be living in the same house! 'Good Lord,' she said guardedly. 'I've never heard of that.'

'It's not that he's stupid or anything. Far from it. It's a sort of medical condition. People are only just starting to recognise it.'

'So how...?' Anna questioned, becoming genuinely interested.

'They thought at school I was just lazy,' Jack explained, his eyes lowered towards his empty plate. 'No one could understand it. I could do anything orally, but when it came to anything on paper, it was useless. Mum and Dad were so good about it. And Mum tried so hard to help me, but... When I look at a page, I just see a great jumble of shapes, and try as I may, I just can't make any sense of it.'

'Gosh, that must make life so hard for you.'

'Unbelievably at times.' But then he looked up, his eyes narrowed almost as if he was judging her reaction. 'It wasn't until my National Service medical that it was diagnosed. It was a relief at long last to be told it wasn't my fault. But ... it still makes me feel such a fool.'

'Well, I have to say I'm amazed. But now that I know, well... And while we're making confessions, you know I'm not really widowed? I was never married in the first place.'

Jack's eyes didn't leave her face. 'Yes. Carrie told me when you were in the kitchen. Does that make us equal, then?'

'Equal? No, not at all. *You've* done nothing to be ashamed of, but I really was a complete and utter fool. And a real hussy in some people's view.'

'You don't strike me as anything of the sort.' Jack held her gaze in the most unnerving way. 'Vulnerable, maybe, Carrie said you were deceived by some upper-class rotter. But ... it's nice to have someone be so understanding about my problem. Thank you.'

His deep-blue eyes, almost indigo in the twilight, continued to bore into hers and his mouth stretched into a tentative smile. Anna felt an unexpected warmth wrap itself around her. They

319

had, most definitely, got off on the wrong foot but she couldn't deny that she felt a confusing attraction towards Carrie's handsome brother.

'Better take these plates in and do the washing-up,' Carrie announced, getting to her feet. And, despite her agonising worry over Jeffery, there was a secret smile on her lips as she went indoors.

'How did you get on, then?'

Anna glanced up as Jack came out into the garden. 'I was about to ask you that,' she smiled back. 'Here, have my chair. We had sandwiches for lunch. I'll bring yours out. Cup of tea?'

'Just some water would be fine, thanks.'

Anna went into Carrie's modern kitchen. She was feeling more relaxed in Jack's company, yet at the same rime, her heart thrilled with excitement whenever he smiled at her. It was a quiet, self-effacing smile, a little wary, perhaps. Endearing. Anna had to pull herself back. She had felt somewhat like this once before, and though Jack appeared a totally different character from Gilbert, she wasn't going to be fooled twice! Nevertheless, she stopped to put some ice in his glass before taking his lunch outside.

'William has some sort of nephew out on the moor somewhere near Princetown,' Jack was saying to Carrie as she handed him the tray. 'Oh, lovely, thank you. I'm starving. And ice, too. You're spoiling me. Anyway, as I was saying, this nephew – well, he's a very distant nephew, I believe – has recently opened his house as a hotel. It's quite a mansion, apparently. Deborah was explaining to me that it dates back to the time when some well-to-do chap, Sir Thomas something-or-other, founded Princetown back in the eighteenth century. He had some madcap scheme to cultivate the moor up there, but, of course, he failed. But not before he'd persuaded some friends to join him, and this house – Fencott Place it's called – was one of the results. Been in William's family – or rather this distant relative's – since the 1870s.'

'Well, that's all very interesting,' Carrie broke in, 'but what's that got to do with you?'

'Mmm, I was coming to that,' Jack mumbled as he chewed on a mouthful of sandwich. 'William thinks they may well need a gardener.'

'Really? Oh, that would be good.'

'Well, hopefully. They only opened at Easter but they're doing very well so far. The nephew and his wife run it between them, with just a friend of the wife's from Princetown helping them. William and Deborah are going to see them on Sunday and they've asked me to go with them.'

'Yes, they're so kind, aren't they, William and Deborah?'

'Certainly are. They asked if you two would like to come, too, with the little ones, of course.'

'Oh, that'll be lovely,' Carrie replied, her face brightening. 'It'll make a nice change.'

'I can't go, though. I'm working on Sunday until midday. What a pity. I'd have loved a trip out on the moor.'

Anna suppressed a rueful grimace. Her heart ached for the sense of peace the moor inspired in her, and she longed to feel part of its vast openness and dramatic landscape again. But she wasn't sure she wanted to be cooped up in the back seat of

William's car with Jack, even if it wouldn't be for very long. She felt bewildered and unnerved by Jack's presence, and perhaps a little breathing space wouldn't come amiss.

'That's all right,' Jack seemed to delight in telling her. 'William won't be picking us up until one. So that's settled, then.'

'Oh. Right.'

Muddled emotions seemed to spin Anna round in circles. She had only known Jack a few days and already he had put her through a mangle. Her heart still strained with grief over Queenie, and now she was being dragged in different directions by Carrie's brother, first the business over the frying pan, and now... He seemed a pleasant and amiable fellow but hadn't Gilbert? No! She wasn't going to let herself be fooled again. She was here to support Carrie and make as good a life for her son as she could.And any male she met along the way would remain firmly on the sideline!

Chapter Twenty-Eight

'I'd forgotten how stunning the moor is,' Jack declared, dipping his head to look out of the window of William's Rover. 'I've only seen it a couple of times, mind.'

'You had moors in Yorkshire, didn't you?' Anna replied a touch sharply. She had been caught up in a web of sorrow as the car had effortlessly taken the steep hill from Tavistock up onto the

322

open moor, all the memories swamping her in a tidal wave. Queenie, and the contented years she had spent with her. And now she was gone.

Jack nodded vigorously. 'Oh, yes. Hundreds of square miles of them. But they're different in character. Just as beautiful but in a different way.'

Inwardly Anna gave a petulant sigh. She wanted him to say something she could disagree with but so far there was nothing she could pick him up on. Oh dear, what was the matter with her?

'Keenie?'

Charlie suddenly bounced in her lap, pointing his chubby finger in exuberant expectation. He had evidently recognised where he was, and Anna's heart lurched as they passed between the lodges on either side of the road. Set a little further back was Holly Cottage looking so empty and forlorn. So lost without the homely woman who had spent her entire life there. Already the little front garden was becoming overgrown and neglected.

Anna had to gulp down the lump in her throat. 'Not today, Charlie,' she muttered, and then, forcing brightness into her voice, she went on perkily, 'We're going to meet some new friends instead.'

Charlie seemed satisfied, beaming as he clambered across onto Jack's lap. Anna caught the amused expression on Jack's face and felt obliged to say something.

'Do you mind?' she murmured with embarrassment. 'He seems to have taken a shine to you.'

'Not at all. I'm flattered.' And then Jack's eyes took on a compassionate intensity. 'Is that where you lived?' he asked softly. 'You looked so sad just now.'

The lump reappeared in Anna's gullet and she had to nod in reply. On her other side, Carrie squeezed her hand. Anna sniffed and gave a watery smile.

'Not long now,' William announced from the driver's seat and turned off towards Princetown. Anna was glad that they had left Holly Cottage behind, but she had brought some flowers to put on Queenie's grave, and William stopped the car outside the church gates.

'Would you like me to come with you?' Carrie asked gently.

'No, I'll be all right, thank you. I'd like a few moments alone if you don't mind.'

'Well, don't be too long, dear,' Deborah said kindly from the front of the car.

She wasn't. It was too unbearable to think that Queenie's remains were lying, cold and decaying, just a few feet below the ground. But, just in case there was some way her dear friend could hear, she whispered to her how she was now living with Carrie and that she and Charlie were happy. She didn't mention Jack.

The centre of Princetown was busy with parked cars and coaches. Ponies were following visitors in the hope of titbits, and people were taking snapshots of them.

'No wonder Daniel's hotel has taken off,' William commented as he negotiated all the obstacles.

'Dartmoor's becoming a real tourist attraction,' Deborah agreed. 'And there aren't many hotels slap in the middle of it. And I'm sure people will appreciate all the personal touches Daniel and Lily are giving their place. And of course, there are the guided walks Daniel's giving across the moor. Not every hotel offers that.'

They turned the corner by Bolt's. Anna glanced at it wistfully, remembering the day she had ordered maternity patterns there. It seemed a lifetime ago. Now Charlie held her world together, and she couldn't imagine having ever even contemplated giving him up for adoption. Her attention was distracted, though, by William driving the car up Tor Royal Lane. After they had passed the sharp bend by the entrance to Tor Royal itself, they continued out on one of the loneliest parts of the moor Anna had ever seen. She had never been out this way and was struck by the bleak, desolate beauty of it.

'This is Hound of the Baskerville country,' William informed them. 'So look out for any strange beasts.'

'Oh, you fool!' Deborah laughed merrily.

'Seriously, though, this road is a dead end. It stops at the old Whiteworks tin mine. And beyond that is Fox Tor Mire. It's what Conan Doyle called Grimpen Mire in the book. You wouldn't want to get stuck in one of the bogs, I can tell you.'

William gave a wry chuckle and then turned in at some large wrought iron gates. Anna suddenly felt the butterflies in her tummy. Although very different from Ashcroft Hall, the imposing building reminded her too much of the time she had spent working for Lady Prudence. But no sooner had William parked the car than a black-and-white collie bounded out of the front door to

325

greet then, followed by a young couple who Anna guessed must be the Daniel and Lily she had heard so much about.

'Deborah, William, how good to see you!' Lily kissed them both on the cheek. 'Pity Wendy and Ian are on holiday, and Celia's on duty, didn't you say?'

'Who are they?' Carrie whispered at Anna, but Deborah had evidently heard her.

'Wendy and Celia? They're our other daughters. You must meet them soon.'

'And you most be Jack,' Lily turned to them, 'and you must be, let me see, you must be Carrie because you look like Jack, so you must be Anna! Am I right?'

Lily turned on them such a lovely, open smile that Anna at once felt more relaxed. Lily was about the same age as herself, and exuded warmth and confidence. Perhaps it came from having a loving husband at her side. Certainly Daniel was tall, dark and quite the most handsome man Anna had ever clapped eyes on, and as they all trooped inside, Anna notice him drop a natural, affectionate kiss on his wife's red-gold hair. Envy pricked Anna's heart. One day perhaps...

'William, would you mind showing everyone round?' Lily asked genially. 'I've got some bits to finish off in the kitchen and Daniel will bring some drinks out onto the terrace.'

The tour didn't take long but Anna was entranced by the house. It was impressive enough as a hotel, let alone as a private residence! And yet the atmosphere was friendly and inviting, so unlike the stiff coldness of Ashcroft Hall. But

326

maybe that was down to the people living in it!

'So you can see why I could do with some help,' Anna heard Daniel say to Jack as they sipped drinks out on the terrace. It overlooked a huge well-tended garden – well, more like grounds, Anna considered – where the children were romping about on the lawn with Trojan, the dog. 'There's always so much to do, and if I had someone in to do the garden one day a week, say, it would really help. So what do you think?'

'Sounds excellent to me. I haven't got any tools of my own yet, though, or any transport.'

'I've got all the tools you could ever need,' Daniel grinned back. 'Through that gate is the old stable yard, and there's all sorts there. But what sort of transport are you looking for?'

'A small van of some sort, I suppose. But big enough to put a lawnmower in.'

'Tell you what. I saw in the paper the GPO are selling off some old vans at their depot Plymouth way. But come and have a look round. How long till dinner's ready, Lily love?'

'Half an hour, but don't be too long. I want you to carve,' Lily answered and then she turned a sympathetic smile on Carrie. 'I hear your husband's in the TB sanatorium at Didworthy. How awful for you.'

'Well, it certainly came as a shock,' Carrie replied. 'But he's made reasonable progress so I'm not quite so worried as I was.'

'Modern drugs,' William nodded wisely. 'It can be completely cured nowadays. I reckon you'll have Jeffery home by Christmas.'

Anna noticed Carrie release a heartfelt sigh.

'That'd be wonderful, but Christmas seems an awfully long way off. And it's such an awkward journey for visiting. Thank goodness Jack's going to take me when he's got transport of his own. That's why he gave up his job in Yorkshire to be with me.'

'What a nice brother to have! You're very lucky. He must be a lovely chap.'

'Yes, he is. Don't you agree, Anna?'

At that moment, Anna felt she could have throttled her friend for putting her on the spot like that. 'Oh well, yes. I mean, we've hardly had time to get to know each other that well, but, yes, he does seem very nice.' And she had to admit to herself that it was true.

'Who wants to come for a spin in the van? I want to make sure she can make the climb up onto the moor.'

Anna raised an eyebrow as Jack got to his feet, evidently burning with enthusiasm over his new mode of transport, however ancient. She supposed she could understand his excitement at this major step towards building his own little business, but cars – or ex GPO vans in this case – didn't do much for her. And somewhere at the back of her mind festered Gilbert's adoration of his flashy sports car. No. Anna had no desire whatsoever to travel in Jack's newly acquired jalopy.

'Oh, Jack, I really think I've had enough of gadding about for a while,' Carrie sighed. 'I'm really looking forward to you driving me to the sanatorium on Wednesday, but just now I'd rather put my feet up. Why don't you take Anna? I'm sure you'd like a trip up onto the moor, wouldn't you, Anna? You've been saying how you miss it.'

Oh. Anna withered under Carrie's strained smile. She really did look tired and Anna didn't have the heart to argue. And it would be churlish to take the wind out of Jack's sails with a refusal. She should be happy for him, and it wasn't his fault she felt inexplicably topsy-turvy whenever she found herself alone with him.

'That'd be lovely,' she murmured. 'This weather could turn any day so we might as well make the most of it.'

'Go on, then. I'll look after the kiddies.'

'Are you sure?' Anna asked doubtfully, hoping Carrie would change her mind.

'Yes, go on, the pair of you.'

'Just give me five minutes to change, would you, Jack? I don't want to go in my waitress uniform.'

'Yes, of course.' Jack gave his easy-going smile. 'We can go for a walk while we're there. You can show me some favourite spot of yours.'

Oh, dear. That was even worse. Alone, with Jack, on the lonely moor. It wasn't that she didn't trust him. It was just that she felt so *awkward*.

'She might be ten years old, but hopefully there's some life left in her yet,' Jack was saying proudly as he unlocked the van a little later. 'And she *is* the right colour. For me. As a gardener. Green,' he explained. 'They've painted out the GPO lettering but I don't think I'll have anything put on instead.'

'Why do men always refer to their cars as *she?*'

329

Anna said scathingly as she got into the passenger seat. The only cars she had ever travelled in were Lady Ashcroft's Rolls Royce, Gilbert's Jaguar and William's Rover. The Morris Z van seemed tinny and pretty basic by comparison – even to Jeffery's modest Austin that she had been in a couple of times.

She caught the hurt look on Jack's face and wished she hadn't said anything, but then he gave a light laugh.

'Do you know, I've absolutely no idea. Perhaps it's because you get attached to them. Like sailors and ships, I suppose. Right, come on, girl,' he encouraged the engine as he pulled out the starter button. 'Oh dear, I said it again, didn't I?'

But then he was concentrating and Anna felt able to sink into silence. Jack seemed to her a good driver, and as the van strained its way up onto the moor, Anna's heart was inevitably snapped up into contemplation of the wild, open spaces she knew and loved. Banks of heather were still in full bloom, swaying blissfully in the gentle breeze, but the overall impression remained the verdant hues of green stretching to the horizon in fold upon fold of distant hills. Peace. And Anna could feel close to Queenie again.

'So where would you like to walk?' Jack's unwelcome voice cut into her reverie.

'Oh well, if we stop soon after where they're building the new bridge,' Anna suggested unwillingly, 'there's a nice walk along the Walkham Valley. The scenery's quite varied. You can go as far as Ward Bridge and come back on the other side, but I've never gone all the way round. It was always too far with Charlie, and today it wouldn't be fair on Carrie, not when she's already had the children all morning as well.'

'OK, we'll just go so far and turn back,' Jack agreed quite amicably. 'The drive's let me see what the old lady's capable of, and that was the object of the exercise. You just show me where to stop.'

Anna could hardly believe she was doing this. She pointed out the small car park and then they walked back down the road and turned off through a farmyard, following the track out along the far side. The rising ground to their left was strewn with granite boulders, and on their right, the valley dropped down towards the river. Sheep scattered nervously as they passed, while a herd of black cows tore unperturbed at the rough grass, their teeth rasping as they chewed.

'You were very fond of this Queenie, I gather,' Jack broke the silence as they walked along. 'Tell me about her. That's if it's not too upsetting. Up here on the moor you seem, I don't know, distant. Sad and yet as if you've come home. I noticed it when we came up with William and Deborah. Tell me to mind my own business if you like, but sometimes it helps to talk.'

Anna felt like doing just that, telling him to mind his own business. But when she cast a scornful sideways glance at Jack, she caught him looking at her with a concerned expression in his deep, intense eyes.

'I'm not prying, really I'm not,' he assured her, his generous mouth twisting awkwardly. 'I'm genuinely interested.'

'Is there a difference?' she bristled.

331

'Yes, of course there is. We're living under the same roof and you're my sister's best friend. Besides which...'

He broke off, colouring slightly as he looked away. Anna felt herself flush with remorse. Jack was obviously sensitive to her tangled emotions and she shouldn't be so touchy.

'I'm sorry,' she apologised. 'It's just that I still feel raw about Queenie. I loved living up here on the moor. But now, well, I suppose it holds too many memories.'

'Yes, I can understand that. Carrie said you'd been through a lot. Lost both your parents tragically before all the business with the chap who left you with Charlie.'

Anna chewed on her lip and was glad that they had come to the point where the track ended at another farmyard. The footpath ahead went through a couple of gates and Jack held them open for her. Their initial meeting aside, he couldn't have been nicer to her. Surely it wouldn't hurt to tell him what had happened in her life? They paused as they crossed a bridge over a bubbling, cascading brook, and Anna took a hold on herself.

'I used to live in Ford,' she began. 'It's an area of Devonport where the naval dockyards are.'

They walked on, up through the wood and following the path as it wound between ancient trees and strange rock formations dripping with emerald moss. It was a place of mystery, and somehow it seemed unreal as Anna related her story to Jack. She even told him the truth about her mother's death. What did it matter who knew now that her dad was dead, too? They came to a standstill when she finished, the still, uncanny silence of the wood sighing around them.

'Fate's not been kind to you,' Jack said at length. 'I hope things turn to the better from now on. You deserve it.'

Anna smiled wanly. 'Thank you. I hope so, too. For Charlie's sake.'

'And for your own. Having to leave school when you could have had a proper career must have been awful for you. I mean, it wouldn't have been so bad for an idiot like me who was so useless at school–'

'You're hardly an idiot...'

'Well, I felt like one. Jeered at by the other kids half the time.' Jack faltered, glanced at her darkly and then lowered his eyes to his feet as he ground the toe of his shoe into the earth. 'I left on my fifteenth birthday. No point in staying a day longer. Dad managed to get me a job at a nursery growing seedlings for farmers. Didn't matter that I couldn't read and write. Or when I did my service. But it was through my CO that I got the horticultural apprenticeship afterwards. I loved every minute of it. I was able to bury myself doing exactly what I wanted with my life. No one to pass snide remarks behind my back.'

Anna felt her heart soften, and the weight that had been dragging her down seemed to lift and float away. Hadn't she done the same thing as Jack by hiding the secret of her father's behaviour from everyone except Ethel? 'You said once you never had any girlfriends or anything,' she ventured as her confidence strengthened.

Jack gave a wry snort. 'No, I didn't. Never

wanted to leave myself open to ridicule again. No. I kept myself to myself. So coming down here to start a new life was a big step for me. But I felt I had to for Carrie's sake. Dad could hardly leave his job in the same way I could leave mine. I sometimes wish, though, that I could have another go at reading and writing. I'm older now, and maybe without the pressure of others around me...'

The words were out of Anna's mouth before she had a chance to stop them. 'I could teach you,' she said, amazed by the force with which the idea had struck her.

Jack's eyes stretched wide. 'You? But–'

'I told you I wanted to be a teacher. I'll never be able to do my training now. Not with Charlie. But I'll give it a go with you if you like.'

Jack still seemed dumbfounded. 'Would you really?'

'Of course. No idea how good I'll be,' she found herself laughing.

'And I'll probably be a useless pupil.'

'Then we can be useless together! So that's settled, then. And now I think we should start heading home.'

'Yes, you're right. Thank you, Anna. And maybe I can help you.'

'Oh, yes?' Anna raised an enquiring eyebrow as they set off back through the wood.

'Yes, indeed. Wendy – that's William and Deborah's daughter, the one who's a secretary for a solicitors' – well, I heard her mention that they need a part-time clerk at her office. Maybe you'd be interested. It'd be better paid and far more interesting than waitressing. And better hours.

And you'd be with Wendy and she's quite a scream from what I've seen of her. She's best friends with Lily. It was through the Franfields that Lily and Daniel met, you know.'

'Oh. I didn't realise that. You've only been working at these places a few weeks, and you've got to know all about everyone, haven't you? But I would be really interested in the job.'

This time, Anna grinned back, her heart fired with optimism. She felt more pleased than she could ever have imagined having broken the ice with Jack. All her doubts about living at Carrie's house with him seemed to have dissolved into thin air.

Chapter Twenty-Nine

Francesca tripped lightly down the staircase of Ashcroft Hall, her heart fluttering at the prospect of escaping the lugubrious confines of the great house for a few hours. But her chest tightened in familiar anguish as Gilbert came out of the drawing room and sprang up the stairs to meet her.

She mentally gritted her teeth. 'Right, I'm off then,' she declared, not daring to meet Gilbert's scowling face.

'Why is it the minute we get down here, you fly off to Tavistock?' he growled irritably. 'We're supposed to be here to look after my mother.'

'We've been here nearly a week and Lady Prue's perfectly all right,' Frankie retorted, sweat oozing from every pore at her own defiance. 'The doctor said it was a mild stroke, just a warning. And I happen to love Tavistock and all its lovely little shops. I thought I'd start my Christmas shopping.'

'You can do your shopping somewhere decent like Harrods or Selfridges. If you were to spend less time gadding about and put your mind to giving me a son. I'm sure it would hasten my mother's recovery no end.'

Frankie caught her breath at the dart of sadness in her own heart. 'Oh, Gilbert, please don't keep bringing that up,' she begged. 'It hurts so much. You know I want a child as much as you do. And if there was—'

'Oh, you do, do you? Prove it then. Let's go back upstairs now.'

Frankie felt the thump inside her ribcage. 'What ... now? But it's the middle of the day.'

'So?'

'Gilbert. I really don't think—'

The hand that whipped through the air came at her with such speed that she didn't have a chance to dodge out of the way. Gilbert's palm slammed across her cheek so that she staggered sideways, almost losing her balance on the stairs, and pain shot through her scalp as he started to drag her back upstairs by the hair. She was too stunned even to scream, directing all her concentration on stumbling after Gilbert without falling down the stairs.

'Well?' he demanded, releasing her with a jerk once they were inside their bedroom.

Frankie swallowed. 'All right. If that's what you want.'

336

'It is,' he glowered, though the anger on his face slackened as she began, with bitter resignation, to unbutton her coat.

He wasn't rough. She had to give him that. His assumed dominance was enough to boost his ego, and though she was reluctant, she did her wifely duty and it wasn't unpleasant. When it was over, Gilbert seemed happy and relaxed, and made no objection when she dressed again and took the car keys from the table.

Gilbert lay back in the bed, hands clasped behind his head and his body purring with satisfaction. He loved Frankie, really he did, and if his temper got the better of him sometimes, well, he was truly sorry. But he was desperate for a son – if only to get his mother off his back.

It was odd, though, the way Frankie beetled off to Tavistock whenever they came down to his mother's. It was a quaint old market town, granted, but surely it wasn't *that* fascinating? So what was the attraction?

Gilbert suddenly felt as if he had been shot through with a bullet. Surely Frankie wasn't *seeing* someone? No, surely not! But his heart blackened with suspicion as the image of his meek little wife in bed with another man exploded in his head. He catapulted from the bed, every nerve stinging with jealousy. He threw on his clothes and, storming down the staircase, barged his way below stairs.

Mr Jackson sprang to attention at the unprecedented invasion. 'Can I help you, Sir Gilbert?' he asked, driving the amazement from his expression.

'Give me the keys to the Rolls,' Gilbert demanded gruffly. 'I want to go out and Lady Francesca has taken the Jag.'

'Would you like me to drive you, sir?'

'No, there's no need. Just give me the keys, man.'

An astonished Mr Jackson reached into his pocket and Gilbert fairly snatched the keys from his hand. Within a minute, he had wrenched open the car door and started her up, crashing the unfamiliar gearbox in his maddened haste. He skidded round the corner of the house, scattering gravel, and hurtled down the drive.

He turned left towards Tavistock, for surely Frankie wouldn't be stupid enough to be actually going in the opposite direction? Gilbert put his foot down, and damned any animal that might be on the road. The other side of Two Bridges he had to swerve around a black bullock that had wandered away from its herd grazing on the verge, and Gilbert swore under his breath. But as he breached the top of the hill, he could see the Jag in the distance. He slowed down. He didn't want Frankie to see him in her mirrors. After all, you didn't see Rolls Royces on the moor that often so she'd know it was him. But as the road descended into Tavistock, he accelerated. He had to take the chance if he didn't want to lose sight of her.

Another car got between him and Frankie as they came into the town, but he was able to follow at a distance across Bedford Square and up the steep hill opposite. But then she turned into a narrow street on the right, and as the road began to sweep uphill, the jaguar pulled in and stopped. Gilbert slammed on the brakes, terrified that Frankie might glance back down the road and see him. She didn't. As she got out of the car, she made a beeline for one of the houses and knocked on the door.

Gilbert's heart was pumping furiously, his muscles coiled and ready to spring out of the car and punch his wife's lover in the face. But astonishment felled him as the door was opened not by a man, but – dear God above – by his little Smoky Eyes. And in her arms was a child of about two years old. By its clothes, it was a boy. Gilbert froze as the penny dropped.

His son.

It had to be. She hadn't been lying about being pregnant. He had never doubted it, to be honest, and it was his. She wouldn't lie about something like that. Her innocence had been refreshing. That, together with her pretty face and slender figure, was what had attracted him to her. She wasn't unlike Frankie in that.

Frankie. How long had she been deceiving him? Visiting Anna when she claimed to have been going shopping? Gilbert was poleaxed and, for the first time in his life, sat drowning in indecision. Bloody little minxes, both of them. And as the shock subsided, rage swirled into its place and the need for revenge flared into his throat and throttled him.

Anna and Ethel linked arms, heads bent together as they walked up the hill to Tavistock North Station, their breath mingling in a halo as it collided with the sharp, frosty night air.

'This yere 'ill don't get no easier, do it?' Ethel grumbled good-heartedly.

'You're just unfit,' Anna chuckled back. 'You should get more exercise.'

'Don't 'ave much bloody time, does I, working all week at Dingles an' now serving in the pub of an evening?'

'Well, it was good of you to find the time to come and see Charlie and me,' Anna teased. 'I've really enjoyed it.'

'So 'ave I, my maid,' Ethel replied, sounding so much like her mum that Anna gave a secret smile. 'An' it's good to see you looking so 'appy after all you've bin through.'

Anna nodded with a rueful arching of her eyebrows. 'Yes. I'll always miss Queenie, just like I'll always miss Mum and Dad. But I can't bring any of them back, so I've got to look forward. And it's great that Carrie has said I can stay on when Jeffery comes home next week.'

'Just in time for Christmas, eh?'

'Yup! A double celebration! Carrie's mum and dad are coming down, and then after Christmas, Carrie and Jeffery want to put Polly back in her own room, which you can understand. So Jack's moving out next weekend. Only two doors down, mind. The lady there's a widow and she could do with the company as well as the rent.'

'Just as well. Jack still being so near, I means, when 'e's so mortal keen on you.'

'What?' Anna halted in her tracks. 'What d'you mean?'

'Oh, Anna! Poor chap's in love with you, and you's no idea? It's there in 'is eyes whenever 'e looks at you. An' 'is eyes follow you about the room. Hook, line an' sinker for you, 'e is!'

'Don't be so ridiculous,' Anna huffed as she started up the hill again. 'And come on, hurry up or you'll miss the train.'

'Now you listens to me,' Ethel puffed in her endeavour to keep up. 'Not all men is like that Gilbert. My Bert, for instance, an' my dad an' my brothers. An' Jeffery from what I knows of 'im. An' that Jack's a good sort, I sees that. Only 'e's too darned shy to say ort. You think on it, maid. Now.' She stopped decisively as they finally arrived at the station. 'Don't you wait for the train, not in this snipey weather. An' you've got your posh job in that there solicitors' office come morning. That's not summat you ever thought you'd be doing, is it, learning about the law?'

'No, it's not,' Anna agreed. 'I'm only a clerk but it can be really interesting. And Wendy's a great laugh. Takes her work utterly seriously, mind. Well!' She drew in a huge breath and released it in one go, relieved that the conversation had moved away from Jack. 'It's been a wonderful afternoon. Have a super Christmas, and give my love to Bert and your mum and dad and all the family, won't you?'

'Certainly will. 'Appy Christmas to all o' you, an' all. An' you remember what I said about Jack. Better get in some mistletoe.'

She skipped off into the station, turning to wave cheerily before she disappeared inside. Anna waved back, and then stood for a moment. Dear Eth. Despite her other fantastic friends, Eth would always be her soulmate. But ... was she right about Jack?

Anna turned back down the hill. Yes. Despite

their initial clash, she had to admit that she and Jack had got on extremely well in those months they had both been living in Carrie's house. That walk on the moor together had really cleared the air. But was the tension she had felt before that simply because she had indeed been attracted to him? She didn't *want* to be attracted to anyone ever again, so was it denial that had made her feel like that?

Jack was a lovely person, she had soon learnt that. He was kind and gentle, and the way he talked about his now full list of clients proved how thoughtful and considerate he was. He was passionate about his gardening, but as winter had come on and there was less work of that nature to do, he had begun helping his customers in other ways instead.

Up at Fencott Place, which seemed to be attracting business out of season as well, he helped Daniel with the maintenance of the house and outbuildings. Apparently Daniel had also written a novel based on his own experiences in Korea. The book had been snapped up by a London publisher and had just been released in time for Christmas. He had been obliged to go off on a promotional tour just at the wrong time as far as the hotel was concerned, so Jack's help had been invaluable to Lily. Indeed, the previous weekend, there had been a houseful of guests wanting the full Christmas works who had been booked in before Daniel knew he would have to be away. Jack and Anna had gone up to help. It had been great fun but it had been Carrie's idea that she should go and her friend had offered to look after Charlie for her. So

... had Carrie seen what Eth had, and was trying to push her brother and Anna together?

Anna turned pensively into Exeter Street. Almost every evening, she and Jack sat up at the table together. She had made teaching cards for him, using a thick, dark crayon to write large, bold letters that wouldn't run into each other in the way he had explained normal-sized print did. While Carrie was engrossed in *Dixon of Dock Green* or was dancing around to *The Billy Cotton Band Show,* Jack would pore over the cards and was beginning to master simple words. It seemed that large, well-spaced letters were the key. Whether or not Jack's brain could ever be retrained to read normal-sized print, only time would tell. But at least he would he able to read certain things he had never been able to before.

And he was certainly keen – or was there another reason for his enthusiasm? Later that evening, Anna studied him furtively as he slowly and carefully copied one of her cards in an exercise book. He wasn't strikingly handsome like Daniel was, but he was still good-looking enough to set any girl's heart beating. A tense muscle twitched at his strong jaw, his generous mouth set with concentration, and his sapphire-blue eyes were riveted on his work. Anna's heart made a frenzied leap in her breast. 'Yes, she *could* he drawn towards Jack. But could what Ethel had said about Jack's feelings towards her possibly be true?

'Hello, Anna. Have a good morning?'

'Oh, hello, Jack,' Anna smiled back as she came in to investigate all the chit-chat she could hear in the sitting room. Popped in for a lunch break?'

'I have indeed. But I mustn't be long. Mrs Baldicott expects me at two on the dot.'

'Mummy!'

Charlie ran over to her and she swung him into her arms. 'I hope you've been behaving yourself for Auntie Carrie,' she grinned. 'And Jeffery, how did you get on at William's?'

'He's proper pleased with me. Reckons I should be able to go back to work by March. Part-time to start, anyway.'

'Oh, that's excellent news! I'm so pleased!'

'Here, there was a letter for you this morning,' Carrie said, handing her an envelope.

Ah, good. Perhaps it was from Frankie. Anna hadn't heard from her since she called in a couple of weeks before Christmas. She had seemed almost over happy, as if her contentment was forced. At least, that was how it had appeared to Anna, and the worry of it had been niggling at the back of her mind all over the festive period. But the envelope was typed and Anna sat down disappointedly in one of the comfortable armchairs.

A few seconds later, a horrified cry escaped her lips. She vaulted to her feet, opening her fingers with a shudder and dropping the sheet of paper as if it were on fire. Her bolting eyes stared about her, the anxious faces of her friends blurred and distorted. And when the room began to spin and she swayed precariously, there were suddenly, miraculously it seemed, strong arms around her, and someone was holding her tightly against his chest. Someone who smelt of fresh air and good, solid earth.

'Anna, whatever is it?' Jack asked urgently, and now she seemed steadier on her feet, he leant back to frown into her ashen face.

She lifted her head, eyes wild with anguish. 'It's ... Gilbert,' she scraped the words from her stricken throat. 'He ... he wants to claim Charlie as his son. He wants to take him away from me!'

'What!'

She scarcely heard the shocked voices about her as she continued to stare into Jack's strong, familiar face. Her chin began to quiver and her head drooped with a wrenching sob, but Jack's hands moved onto her shoulders and he gave her one short, sharp shake.

'Look at me, Anna,' he said firmly, and when she turned her head away with a deep moan, he repeated the command so fiercely that she felt compelled to obey. His jaw was set and his eyes bore so intently into hers, it was as if he could see right inside her. 'We won't let him. *I* won't let him, I promise you!'

Anna gulped. Good, kind Jack. She thanked God he was there. He would, he *would* move heaven and earth, she knew. Charlie ... oh, the thought was unbearable, and she was ready to sink into the comfort Jack was offering her. Tears were trickling down her cheeks, and as she shook in his arms, she buried her head in his chest and wept against him.

Chapter Thirty

'Oh, that's preposterous!' Wendy declared dramatically. 'He can't do that, can he, Ian?'

After a lunch hour when her only attempted mouthful stuck in her throat, Anna found herself back in the office. She was still shaking and feeling sick with worry, her gaze fixed on Ian's face as he concentrated on the letter.

'He says I deliberately ran off with his child,' she groaned hysterically. 'He says he can give Charlie a much better home when all I have to offer is a life of struggle, and that's absolutely true.'

'No, it's not.'

Behind her, his hands resting on her shoulders in support, Jack's voice was steady. Blow Mrs Baldicott, he had said when he insisted on coming back to the solicitors' with her. She and Charlie were far more important than one cantankerous client. Now, as Anna studied Ian's beetling brow, she was glad to feel Jack standing steadfastly behind her.

It seemed an excruciating age before Ian lifted his head from the letter. 'This is just a bluff,' he said at length. 'He's probably expecting you to cow down because you don't know what else to do. But we know better.'

He smiled encouragingly, offering Anna a seat. It seemed so weird, unreal to her, in this familiar place where she worked every morning. She would never have expected to become one of the practice's clients.

'First of all,' Ian went on, 'is he named as the father on the birth certificate?'

Anna's eyes were wide in her pale face. 'No. He didn't want to know when I told him I was pregnant. Just watched as his mother threw me out.'

'And he's made no attempt to contact you since?'

'No, not until now.'

'Excellent!' Ian beamed back. 'Well, if he wants to assert his rights, he'll have to prove he's the father, and that might be pretty difficult for him. Now, present company excepted, who else believes Charlie to be Gilbert Ashcroft's son?'

Anna sucked in her cheeks. 'Frankie. His wife.'

'His wife?' Ian repeated in a more cautious tone, Anna realised with dismay.

'Yes,' she answered, her voice trembling as she spoke. 'We've remained friends – in secret – ever since I was dismissed from the Hall. Two and a half years ago now. They're both desperate for a family. Gilbert in particular wants an heir. It's a sort of heritage thing for him. He must have found Charlie and me through Frankie. But I know she would never have told him, not unless... Oh, Lord.'

'Unless what?'

'Unless ... well, I discovered afterwards that he's apt to be violent sometimes. When he can't have his own way.'

Ian gave a triumphant snort. 'And he expects to gain custody? Well, that's all good from our point of view.'

'But not from Frankie's. God, what a mess.'

Ian raised an eyebrow at the distress in her voice. 'But one I'm sure we can sort out. So, who else knows?'

'Well, his mother, I suppose,' Anna replied with a tearing sigh. 'The Dowager Lady Prudence Ashcroft. She walked in when I was asking Gilbert for an allowance. She refused to believe that her son would have done such a dishonourable thing and called me a liar. But I think, deep down, she knew it was true.'

She glanced, shamefaced, at Jack, pinching her bottom lip between her finger and thumb, but he rubbed her arm compassionately. 'We'll get through this, you'll see,' he assured her, but she could draw no comfort from his words, well meaning though these were.

'Anyone else?' Ian prompted.

'Mrs Smudge. The cleaner. But I don't think Gilbert has any idea that she knows. And as far as I know, the other two servants knew I was dismissed because I was pregnant, but Gilbert's part in it was all hushed up.'

'Right. Well, none of this provides absolute proof. And even if Charlie looks a bit like his father, well, I'm not sure what water that would hold in court. It strikes me he hasn't got a leg to stand on. But,' and here he fixed Anna's gaze, 'even if by some fluke, this Gilbert managed to persuade a judge that he is Charlie's father, no judge is going to give him custody after his track record. No. At worst, he might he allowed to see Charlie once in a while under strict supervision. But I don't believe it will ever even get to court. I

348

think he's just trying to put the frighteners on you so that you'll give Charlie up for adoption without any fuss.'

Anna had been listening as if through a fog, trying to concentrate but not sure she had taken in all of Ian's words. So she was glad when Jack asked, 'So what happens next?'

'Well. We'll write back to his solicitors. We won't say a great deal to start with. Try and nip it in the bud. Save any details for later on in the unlikely event that we need them. But I'll pass it on to Clarence.'

'Yes, it's more his speciality,' Wendy nodded vigorously. 'Only he's in court this afternoon. But of course, you know that, Anna.'

Yes, she did. But she wished vehemently that Clarence, one of the senior partners who specialised in family law, had been there to confirm Ian's opinion.

'Now, don't worry, Anna,' the younger solicitor was saying. 'It'll be all right.'

'I hope so,' Anna croaked, a lump the size of a golf ball in her throat.

'Well, I suggest I take you home,' Jack broke in. 'No point in going on discussing it any further at the moment. You'll be in tomorrow morning anyway.'

'You really mustn't worry... Oh dear, sorry, telephone!' Wendy rolled her eyes at the shrill ring. 'See you tomorrow,' she mouthed as she lifted the receiver.

'Come on.' Jack opened the door and ushered Anna through. Outside, the blustery January wind plucked at her coat as she stood on the pavement. It seemed incongruous that the town appeared just as normal, safe and familiar, and yet she had been threatened with losing her beloved child – no matter what anyone else could say to reassure her. She felt invisible, as if the passers-by could see neither her nor the anguish that stabbed at her heart.

She started when Jack took her by the elbow. 'You shouldn't go back yet,' he murmured. 'Let's go for a walk by the canal.'

He stepped up to the kerb, checking that the road was clear. Anna was happy to be led across, grateful for Jack's arm firmly about her as they turned into the park. Without her saying anything, he knew instinctively that she would feel stifled indoors, and that she needed some fresh air to clear her head and calm her nerves, even if it was so bitterly cold.

The park was almost deserted, just an old man slowly walking an equally old black Labrador with a grey muzzle and grey eyebrows. Further along, a woman in a red headscarf was playing with a young terrier haring about after a ball, but that was all. It was too cold to go out unless you had to.

'What about Mrs Baldicott?' Anna asked, suddenly coming to her senses.

'Oh, I'll explain to her, and tough if she doesn't like it. It's not as if there's any gardening to be done this time of year. I'll call round later to see if she needs anything urgent like changing a light bulb or anything. You're far more important.'

Anna felt herself well up with gratitude. 'That's good of you, Jack.'

'It's what friends are for. Pity the pubs are shut.

What you need is a stiff drink rather than a walk in this cold wind.'

'Oh, I don't know. It's giving me a chance to get my head straight with nothing else to think about.'

She gulped in a lungful of air and let it out in a heavy sigh as her eyes scanned the park in an attempt to calm herself. Jack must have heard her and shook his head as he walked along beside her.

'I'm sure Ian's right,' he said gravely. 'No matter what this Gilbert can or can't prove, no judge is going to take Charlie away from you. Not from such a loving and stable home as you've made for him.'

'But that's just it. We don't even have a home of our own!'

'Maybe not yet. But the situation you have is a darned sight better than most. Now!' He stopped and turned her towards him, looking down at her with infinite compassion in his eyes. 'I want you to stop worrying. Everything will be all right. And … and I'll always be here for you.'

His voice had become husky, his expression intense as he bent his head down towards hers. Their faces were so close, and Anna stared back up at him, trusting and ready to melt into the comfort he was offering her. And somehow her worry over Charlie dropped away and she wasn't at all surprised or flustered when she felt Jack's lips brush hers so softly that she wasn't quite sure it had actually happened. But it was as if that fleeting, delicate kiss had pumped strength into her, and her heart was beating, vital and alive, once more.

Jack jerked back from her, with his face creased remorse. 'God, I'm sorry. This is hardly the time.

351

But ... but I've wanted to do that for a long time.'

His steady, questioning eyes hadn't left her face and she felt the tight knot in her chest relax. Ethel, Carrie, they had both been right. And she...? She suddenly felt sheltered, warmed, and hope blossomed inside her.

A smile crept onto her lips, like dawn breaking through the shadows of night. She reached up on tiptoe and her lips tingled as she kissed Jack again. Swiftly, but on the mouth. And then she stood back, waiting to see what would happen next. The ground felt solid beneath her feet. Not like when Gilbert... Then she had floated away on some ridiculous fantasy, but now... This was for real.

Jack's face moved into that slow, hesitant smile and he stepped forward, enclosing her in his arms and tucking her head under his chin. 'We'll fight this together,' he muttered into her beret. 'Whatever happens, I'll always be here.'

Yes. Just like he had been for his sister. Dependable, like a rock. Oh, Jack. Her cheek rubbed against the old, rough jacket he wore for his work, and she was disappointed when he released his hold and took her hands instead.

'Perhaps we should go back before we freeze,' he suggested with a lift of his eyebrows.

She nodded, aware of the exquisite glow when Jack slipped his arm around her shoulders and she leant against him as they turned for home.

'What!' Gilbert barked down the phone. He had been waiting for weeks for a reply from his lawyers, and now it had come, it wasn't at all what he had wanted. 'What d'you mean, she's got a solicitor? She can't possibly afford one.'

'Well she's got one somehow, Sir Gilbert,' the reserved voice came down the line. 'I did warn you that it's a lost cause. The girl's denying that you're the father. And you're not named on the birth certificate.'

'But of course I'm its father!' Gilbert stormed into the receiver. 'What other chance did the bitch have to see anyone else?'

'On her day off perhaps? And I should learn to moderate your language if it ever goes to court, which I very much doubt. Unless you can find some way to prove the child is yours—'

'Isn't there a blood test or something?' Gilbert interrupted.

'Blood tests are inconclusive. They can sometimes prove that you're *not* the father, but never that you actually *are*. There's a new thing called DNA testing, but it's only in its infancy and it'll be donkey's years before it comes into the public domain.'

'Damn and blast—'

'As I say, I'd give it up if I were you. And anyway, even if he was persuaded the child is yours, I don't think any judge would look kindly on someone who seduced an innocent young girl when he was about to be married.'

'Innocent? Wouldn't surprise me if she *wanted* to get pregnant so that she could get money out of me!'

'Now, now, sir, you can't go about making accusations like that!'

'Oh, yes, I bloody well can, and I'll find myself another solicitor if you won't back me up!'

'I rather wish you would, Sir Gilbert. My bill for the work I have already done will be in the post. Good day to you, sir.'

The telephone clicked and the line went dead. Gilbert fumed and slammed the receiver back into its cradle. Dear God, he wanted that child! It wasn't far short of three years since he and Frankie had been married and there was no sign of anything happening despite what that old quack had said. When she'd had the stroke, his mother had declared with tears in her eyes that, before she died, she wanted to see a grandson to inherit the family fortune. She had recovered, of course, but she had mentioned it several times since.

Ah, his mother. He *must* do what she wanted.

And then a sly smirk curled his lip. So he needed proof that Anna Millington's child was his, did he? Well, then...

He flicked through his diary. It was chock-a-block with meetings for the next few weeks, but after that...

He lifted the receiver and dialled through to his secretary. 'Get me Ashcroft Hall, would you?' he purred in his usual, charming voice.

Chapter Thirty-One

'Oh, good, Mother. I've been waiting for the opportunity to speak with you.'

'Pardon, dear?' Lady Ashcroft turned from the drawing room window, using the stick she had taken to since her mild stroke, but more for effect, Gilbert suspected, than because she needed one. 'The daffodils are well in bud. Won't be long before they're out. The drive always looks so lovely in the spring. Frankie's gone into Tavistock. I was just thinking how she's blossomed from a timid little thing into a confident young woman. Just a pity she hasn't had any children yet. You know it's my dearest wish–'

'That's just what I want to talk to you about,' Gilbert interrupted, his voice quavering ever so slightly. 'Do come and sit down.'

'Oh, Frankie's not preg–?'

'Afraid not, Mother.'

'Oh.' Lady Ashcroft sighed, straightening her tweed skirt as she lowered herself into the lea-ther-upholstered chair she favoured. 'She hasn't had more tests? There's nothing wrong, is there?'

'No, Mother, nothing like that. It's just that...' He hesitated, for once in his life feeling hot under the collar, he swallowed hard. Knew he was sweat-ing. 'Well, you know it's been nearly three years. And quite honestly, I'm beginning to wonder if it will ever happen.'

'Oh, Gilbert, you mustn't give up. It's bound to happen. You *must* have an heir. Otherwise all your hard work – and your father's and grandfather's and his father's – will go to your distant cousins, and what have they ever done to deserve it?'

The disdain on her face was hardly encouraging. Gilbert wasn't sure how she might take what he was about to say, but it was a solution of sorts, though she might take some persuasion. His pulse accelerated nervously and he took a deep breath.

'You know that I have an heir.'

Prudence Ashcroft's face turned to granite, creasing into deep crevices. 'What do you mean?' she grated.

Gilbert felt his palms sweating as if he was a little boy being told off by his teacher. 'You … you must remember Anna Millington,' he faltered.

His mother's features hardened further. 'There's no need to bring that up again,' she barely articulated through clenched teeth.

Gilbert cleared his throat. 'Actually, I think there is. Under the circumstances. I discovered recently that she's living in Tavistock. And she has a son. *My* son. And I'm claiming custody.'

Lady Ashcroft's gasp echoed round the spacious room like a roll of thunder, sending Gilbert rocketing to his feet. 'It makes sense, don't you see? Frankie and I can adopt him. No one need ever know he's my … my–'

'Your illegitimate son,' she finished for him. 'Well, I'll not have any little bastard in our family! How dare you even suggest–'

'It'll all be done perfectly legally. Only, Anna's objecting–'

'I bet she is! At least she's having the guts to stand up to you! She was a good girl, Anna. I had plans for her, you know. Until you got your lecherous hands on her. Poor girl was in love with you, God help her. Never mentioned the fact that you were about to marry Frankie, did you? Conducted herself superbly when I told her. Only I hadn't realised things had gone so far.'

Gilbert had been staring at her, slack-jawed, but now he came back like a shot. 'So you acknowledge that the child was mine?'

'I never doubted it,' she spat back.

'Then swear it for me in court. She's denying the kid's mine. But if you say how she came to me, begging for an allowance–'

'I will do no such thing!' Each word was pronounced separately, heavy with loathing, and Gilbert jerked back at the hatred in his mother's expression. 'And I will not see our name dragged through the courts just to admit to your shameful behaviour. Your father would turn in his grave. And taking the child away from its mother, no, I will *not* be a part of it! It would break the poor girl. How could you even think of it? No, Gilbert. You are nothing, *nothing* compared to your father. You're weak and spineless, and I regret pushing you into marriage with poor Frankie. But I will not have you ruining her reputation and our family name. Now get out of my sight!'

For a moment, Gilbert stood transfixed, unable to move a muscle. He had always done whatever his mother wanted, had played the dutiful son. And now she had turned on him.

It was all Anna Millington's fault. Well, he'd bloody well find a way to get even with her. He would have the child if it was the last thing he did. And spinning on his heel, he stormed out of the room.

'Mmm, that was nice.' Jack smiled down at Anna, his eyes creasing at the corners as their lips pulled apart. 'I only came to ask if you'd like to go to the pictures tonight. I wasn't expecting such a lovely kiss in the middle of the day.'

357

Anna grinned back. 'Well, it was a lovely surprise to see you. What's on?'

'*A Tale of Two Cities* with Dirk Bogarde. I've never been able to read the book, of course, so I'd love to see it.'

'Yes, so would I! Carrie?' she called as Jack followed her into the kitchen where they had been having lunch.

'Uncle Jack!' Charlie shouted, jumping down from the table to run into Jack's arms.

'Would you and Jeffery mind babysitting tonight while Jack and I go to the flicks?'

'Course not. Jeffery still gets so tired when he's been at work, even if it is only part-time. All he wants to do is go to bed early, anyway.'

'Ta ever so! Now, cup of tea, Jack?'

She reached into the cupboard for an extra cup as Jack sat down at the table next to Polly, and Charlie at once clambered onto his lap. Anna smiled over her shoulder. She and Jack had been walking out ever since that dreadful day when she had received the letter from the London solicitors. Jack had always been the perfect gentleman as they walked in the park or up on the moor, or went for a drink or to the cinema. Even on the few occasions they had babysat the two children so that Jeffery and Carrie could go out of an evening, Jack had never tried to push her to go further. He was quite happy to sit on the sofa watching television with his arm round her, taking things slowly. The nearest they came to physical intimacy was if they played music on Carrie's record player and danced slowly round the room to the Everly Brothers' *All I have to do is Dream,*

358

Jack holding her close against him. Anna couldn't have been more content, especially since they had heard nothing more from Gilbert or his lawyers.

'Oh, someone at the door,' Carrie said in surprise when the doorbell suddenly rang. 'I'll go. Jeffery's probably forgotten his key.'

'Here you are, Jack,' Anna went on as Carrie went out into the hall. 'Biscuit?'

'No, thanks. I'll pick you up at half seven, then.'

'Yes, great. Should be good. I wanted to see it. I love Dickens. You know I was doing English lit for A level. Oh, Carrie, what's the matter?'

Her friend was standing in the doorway, her face pale. 'There's ... someone to see you, Anna,' she stuttered. 'I've asked her to wait in the sitting room.'

Anna frowned, feeling the blood pumping in her veins. 'Whoever is it?'

'It's ... it's Frankie. Smiling all over her face as if nothing had happened.'

Anna felt herself go cold. She saw Jack's forehead crease into folds and he put his hand on her shoulder. Anna took a deep breath and strode into the other room with Jack behind her.

Frankie jumped up from the chair, as immaculately turned out as ever, but with a perplexed light in her cornflower-blue eyes. 'What's all this about?' she asked, shaking her head in confusion.

'You've got a nerve, coming here–'

'Jack, no.' Anna stepped forward, taking Frankie's outstretched hands and gazing at the puzzlement on her face. 'You ... you don't know, do you, Frankie?'

Frankie's nonplussed expression deepened.

359

'No, I don't. I haven't got a clue what this is all about. Just because I haven't been down to see you for months because–'

'No, it's not that. It's ... it's Gilbert.'

'Gilbert?'

'He found us,' Anna told her flatly. 'Charlie and me. And now he wants custody.'

'What?' Frankie's face was a picture of horrified disbelief. 'You mean–'

'He's tried to force Anna to give Charlie up for adoption. Fortunately it doesn't look as if he has a legal leg to stand on, and he seems to have given up. But he could only have found Anna's whereabouts if *you* had told him.'

Jack's mouth was tight as he spoke, his eyes bright and accusing. But Frankie staggered backwards and sat down hard in the chair again, her lips white and trembling.

'Gilbert?' she mumbled, then raised her head sharply. 'No. I never told him. I swear it. I can ... I can only think he must have followed me. And he's trying to take Charlie away from you? Oh, my God, I'm *so* sorry, Anna. I had no idea. But ... it must be all my fault!'

She burst into tears, burying her head in her hands and weeping inconsolably. Anna sat down and put her arms around her trembling shoulders.

'It's all right, Frankie. I don't blame you. And as Jack said, he seems to have given up, anyway.'

'But it *isn't* all right!' Frankie protested, lifting her tearstained face. 'I always thought I'd been so careful. So, he must have known for some time and never said a word, the conniving...' She paused to sniff, glancing up at Jack. 'I shouldn't

360

say it, but our marriage isn't what it should be. I'd loved him all my life, even after, well, you know. Even now, I think if I could give him the child he wants, things would be OK. But he's obsessed. And it's mainly his mother's fault. She tries to be nice about it and I think she is quite understanding, really, but she's so *strong*–'

'She's had to be,' Anna put in. 'You know she wasn't allowed to marry the man she loved? She was forced to marry Sir Hugh instead because it suited her parents better. That must make you very hard.'

Frankie blinked at her, eyebrows arched. 'I never knew that.'

'She told me once. As a sort of confidence, when she broke it to me that Gilbert was about to marry you. She never said anything about Gilbert and me, but I'm sure she must have known.'

'That's typical.' Frankie gave a bitter laugh. 'Things unspoken. And I never saw through it all. Like I always thought Gilbert was so charming. Perfect, really. But deep down, he's just – I hate to say it – but a mummy's boy. And now this.' She pursed her lips and looked earnestly into Anna's face. 'I truly am sorry.'

'Well, it looks as if no harm's been done. But I'm afraid I must get to my afternoon client.'

'Yes, of course, Jack. I'll see you out. Won't be a moment, Frankie.'

Anna followed Jack out into the hall and he turned to give her a quick kiss. 'See you tonight, then. And Frankie'd better mind herself. Best if she doesn't let on to her husband that she knows what he's been up to.'

'Yes, I think so, too,' Anna agreed with a worried sigh. 'But we mustn't let it spoil our evening. See you at half seven.'

'Yes. And ... I love you, Anna.'

She smiled back, thinking how lucky she was to have such a good man as Jack in her life now. She blew him a kiss as he walked down the path and then turned back into the sitting room.

Frankie kicked off her shoes and then threw her coat and hat onto the bedroom chair. She would have liked to stay for ever and ever with Anna in the comforting atmosphere of Carrie's happy home. But life wasn't like that. She had dreaded coming back to Ashcroft Hall but what choice did she have? There was no way out, at least none that she could think of in her present state of shock. Thank the Lord Anna was so understanding. But then she had experienced life in the Ashcroft circle. Frankie had friends in London, of course she did. But they were all part of the same scene, and she would have been shunned if they'd known how she felt about Gilbert now.

She heard footsteps outside and cringed when the door opened and Gilbert stepped into the room, giving that devil-may-care smile that had once seemed so attractive. Frankie forced a smile in return and sat down at the dressing table to brush her cap of blond waves so that she didn't have to face him.

'Have a nice afternoon in Tavistock?'

Her heart missed a beat. 'Yes, thank you. I went for a walk in the park.' Well, that was true. She had. With Anna.

'You didn't buy anything, then?'

'No, not today.' God, he *knew*, didn't he? And she could feel the sweat on her palms as she put down the brush.

'Frankie, turn round. There's something I want to talk about.'

She swivelled round on the stool, slowly, her pulse wild and erratic. But Gilbert looked perfectly calm as he sat down on the edge of the bed, his hands spread.

'You know we don't seem able to conceive a child of our own,' he began, head bowed. 'But, well, you know I have a son. By Anna Millington. My mother's servant. Well, you were there, and I also know you've been seeing her.'

A shudder of fear and horror spiked through Frankie's muscles and she visibly jerked. Oh, God. But Gilbert looked up now, his face expectant.

'I don't mind. Not now, anyway. In fact, it's a good thing. Because now I know where my son is. And, well, I know it was a shameful thing I did, but now I want to make amends. I want to adopt the boy. Give him the life that should rightly be his and make him my legal heir—'

Frankie sprang to her feet, hot anger thrusting into every nerve, but Gilbert put out his hand.

'Please don't be cross, Frankie love. Of course, if we ever have a child of our own, it will take precedence. But if we don't—'

'You think I'm worried about that?' Frankie spat, her eyes snapping venomously.

'What, then? You think it would cause a scandal? Well, I'm hoping to persuade Anna to give him up so it can all be settled amicably and

363

no one will ever know he's really my son. Only, Anna's refusing to admit that he is, so I need you to persuade her that it's in his best interests.'

'What!'

'Well, he'd have everything he'll ever–'

'And you think it's in his best interests to be torn away from his mother? If you really loved him, you wouldn't even think of it!'

'Oh, come now, surely you can see–'

'No, I can't!' Frankie rounded on him, her teeth bared like a tigress, so that for a moment, Gilbert recoiled at seeing his meek, obedient little Frankie fighting back. 'You refused to help Anna when she was absolutely desperate and now, just because it suits you, you want to take Charlie away from her. Well, I'll have nothing to do with it!'

She went to barge past him towards the wardrobe, but he leapt up, grabbing her arm so that she was swung round to face him. She glared down at his hand, eyes like ice, and opened her mouth to deliver a caustic riposte. But before a sound came from her lips, Gilbert yanked her forward so viciously that she felt her shoulder wrench in its socket and she was flung across the floor with the force of it. She lay for a few seconds, winded with pain and shock. She could hear Gilbert breathing heavily as he stood over her, but she wasn't frightened anymore. Outrage had driven her fear to the back of her mind.

'I'm your husband and you'll do as I say!' she heard his voice above her. 'Swear in court that the child's mine if you have to.'

Frankie lifted her head, her eyes narrowed to dangerous slits. 'Oh no I won't,' she snarled back.

Gilbert scowled down at her, his face purple. First his mother and now his wife. Well, he'd show them who was boss. And his foot shot out in uncontrolled fury.

Frankie didn't react. He must have missed, so he kicked out again and then again, until he stood back, breathless and his face a contorted mask. Surely the bitch had learnt her lesson? But as she dragged herself upwards, she glanced at him with eyes of steel.

'Think you can beat me into submission?' she rasped, her chest burning with each breath.

Gilbert snapped, blinded with rage. Why wouldn't she listen to him? He didn't want to hurt her again, so he grasped her by the shoulders, standing her on her feet. But as he shook her, he lost his grip. As she went down, her head cracked on the sharp corner of the marble coffee table, and she lay lifeless on the thick, luxurious carpet.

The room was filled with a sudden, deafening silence.

'Frankie?'

Gilbert's voice came out as a whisper as he knelt on the floor beside his wife and turned her over. Her eyes were closed in her alabaster face, and crimson liquid was leaking into her hair and trickling down her temple.

Oh, God. Panic gripped Gilbert by the throat and he jumped backwards. He'd killed her. But, no. He could see she was still breathing. But...

He charged out of the room along the landing and then hurtled down the staircase at such speed that he nearly tripped over his own feet. 'Mother!' he yelled. 'Frankie's had an accident! She fell and knocked herself out. Mother! Mummy, where are you?'

Gilbert swaggered along the corridor, trying to react casually to the admiring glances at the massive bouquet in his arms. The hospital had telephoned to say Frankie had regained consciousness in the morning and that she was expected to make a full recovery from the concussion. In some ways it was a relief, but in others...

'Oh, what lovely flowers,' a nurse declared as he reached the door to the private room. 'Shall I put them in water for you? Gorgeous, aren't they, Lady Ashcroft? Won't be a jiffy.' And she relieved Gilbert of his peace offering.

Frankie looked so tiny and frail, her face almost as white as the snowy pillows she was half propped up on. A large bandage swathed her head so that just a curling wisp of hair stuck out from behind each ear.

'How are you feeling, my love?' Gilbert asked, his voice smooth and oily.

'Apart from a thumping headache and feeling as sick as a dog?' Her words were slow and quiet but Gilbert was nevertheless aware of the spark of anger behind them. He gently shut the door and pulled up a chair.

'You ... you haven't said anything? About how it happened?' His heart was hammering now, and he was relieved when Frankie closed her eyes. But he wasn't prepared for what came next, determination glowing behind her near whisper.

'I didn't have to. When they undressed me, they saw all the bruises. Dr Franfield's looking after me. He came to talk to me this morning. He said he knows I've been assaulted and asked who did it. He said I should report it to the police.'

Gilbert began to quiver and his hands balled into fists. Surely she wouldn't?

'But I won't. Not now, anyway. But it's all on file. Just waiting. But I swear that if you ever try to take Charlie away from Anna, legally or otherwise, I'll go to the police. And I'll use it as grounds for divorce and see that it makes national headlines. Oh, one more thing. I won't be giving you a son. Or a daughter for that matter. It'll be separate bedrooms from now on. And if anything suspicious ever happens to me, the doctors here have been instructed to take my file to the police. I've dictated a letter to my solicitor to that effect as well. Now I'm tired, so you can go.'

Gilbert's mouth opened like a goldfish, but before he could utter a word, the nurse came back in with the flowers. 'There we are. Oh dear, your wife's dropped off to sleep. Perhaps you'd better leave.'

And Gilbert couldn't quite read what was behind her smile.

Chapter Thirty-Two

'You were right,' said the voice at the other end of the line. 'She can't afford a place like that. She lodges there, but there's nothing wrong in that. You wanted to know what sort of home she's made for the child. Well, pretty good, I'd say.'

Damn! Gilbert gripped the receiver more tightly as he stood in the London phone box. He had hoped to discover the exact opposite. Then he might have been able to persuade Frankie that it *would* be in the boy's interests for them to adopt him. He would have to tread carefully, mind. Once she had recovered from her accident, Frankie had gone abroad with an old school friend and would be away some time. Hopefully she would have calmed down by the time she returned.

'She works part-time,' the private detective was saying. 'At a solicitors'. The landlady looks after the child. All a perfectly good arrangement.'

Solicitors? No wonder... It seemed the hussy had thwarted him at every turn. Blinding fury clamped him in its hungry tentacles at the fellow's next words.

'It seems she has a boyfriend. Lodges a couple of doors away. Has his own small gardening business. And he's very good with the boy. I've followed them several times in the park.'

Gilbert gulped down his exploding rage. A boyfriend. With his own business! In his head he could see it all unfolding. Marriage – and a legal adoption of *his* son! Well, he'd put a stop to it somehow! He'd go down to Tavistock by train, take a room somewhere under a false name. Buy a car, something unobtrusive, pay cash and use false details for the registration. And then … well, he wasn't quite sure. But the opportunity would arise, it was bound to.

'Thanks,' he mumbled through taut lips. 'Tell

368

me how much I owe you and I'll bring it in cash.'

The voice told him and then the pips went. Gilbert didn't put any more money in the slot.

'Hello, kids. What are you doing?'

'Picture,' Charlie told Jack, scarcely glancing up from his work of art.

'That's very good, both of you,' Jack praised the two children, bending over to inspect the random scrawls of coloured crayons. Charlie beamed up at him and then went back to his masterpiece, tongue stuck out of the side of his mouth in concentration.

'Anyone fancy going up on the moor after lunch?' Jack asked enthusiastically.

'Oh, yes! Blow the cobwebs away!'

'Ooh, not for me, thanks. You two go on your own.'

'You sure, sis? Daniel pointed out a walk to me not far from the hotel. Along an old track. He reckons you can take a pushchair. Just the first bit from where you can park to the track could be a bit tricky. Get the map, Anna love, and I'll show you. The track runs out to the ruins of Eylesbarrow mine. Quite interesting, apparently.'

'Sounds super!' Anna cried. An afternoon on her beloved moor, a beautiful early spring day and, most of all, with her son and the quiet, steadfast man she had come to love. What more could she ask?

'That was lovely,' Anna declared as they bumped the pushchair along the grass towards where the van was parked. 'But I'm exhausted!'

'Great to get out on such an isolated part of the moor, though,' Jack said with a grunt of exertion, negotiating the pushchair over a thick tussock. 'Fantastic on a day like this, but imagine living and working there all year.'

'Yes. It was pretty blowy out there today. I have enjoyed it, mind.'

It had certainly been exhilarating, way out beyond any sign of civilisation, with the bleak moor rolling away in every direction. She was weary after the long walk, but she really didn't want it to end.

'We've worn Charlie out as well,' she chuckled, glancing at her son fast asleep despite being jolted along in the pushchair. 'Shame we've got to wake him up to get him back in the van.'

'We don't have to. We could sit down here for a bit and enjoy the sunshine until he wakes up. It's more out of the wind here.'

'Why didn't I think of that?'

'Because you're not as clever as me?' Jack teased with a roguish lift of his eyebrows.

Anna laughed as they settled down in the shelter of a large boulder. There was even some warmth in the sunshine. 'I love the spring,' she sighed contentedly. 'Everything's so fresh and you've got the promise of the good weather to come.'

'Mmm. It's still pretty cold the minute the sun goes in, mind.'

Jack lay down, hands joined behind his head, and closed his eyes. Anna contemplated him, his strong jawline, the way his hair flopped over his forehead, and she felt herself swell with pleasure. She loved Jack so much. There was that delicious feeling in the pit of her belly whenever she was with him. Gilbert was out of her life now. Even Frankie had disappeared abroad. She'd sent a postcard from the French Alps. *Our first port of call on the Grand Tour,* she'd written, so Anna assumed she and Gilbert had taken a long holiday together. Perhaps it would mend their marriage, and Frankie might even find herself pregnant at last.

Anna hoped so, and her vision swept across the moor. It wasn't the prettiest part, but the sense of timelessness, of being at one with nature, was overwhelming. She snapped off a stem of grass and played with it, all so still, just the whisper of the breeze and Jack breathing beside her. She couldn't resist tickling his nose with the end of the grass. His face twitched and the corners of his mouth curved upwards. Then his eyes flew open, and with a playful roar, he rolled over towards her. She fell back, laughing as she gazed up into the sapphire clarity of his intense eyes, deep pools she felt she could drown in.

'I love you, Anna Millington,' he breathed. 'The business is doing well, and soon—'

She never heard the rest. A shadow fell over her and her gaze moved over his shoulder. She froze, her thoughts spinning in a tortured dance. Gilbert! But surely he was hundreds of miles away? Yet here he was, or some effigy of him, since his face was hideously contorted in violent rage and she could smell the reek of alcohol on his breath. Anna's mind whirled in confusion and she couldn't scream a warning as the menacing figure raised a hand clutching a stone and brought it downwards. A stifled cry caught in Jack's throat and he slumped down on top of her.

Anna's brain roared into action. Dear God in heaven, Charlie! She heaved Jack's dead weight from her just in time to see Gilbert snatch Charlie from the pushchair and start running along the path towards the road. For a split second, Anna glanced back at Jack. He was stumbling to his feet, one hand clamped over his head and blood trickling through his fingers. There was no question. Anna sprang forward with some sudden, superhuman speed and tore after her son.

She was gaining. Gilbert stopped by a small car parked next to the van, fumbling in his pocket, presumably for his keys, but hampered by Charlie who was wailing and kicking at his rude awakening and finding himself in the arms of a stranger. Gilbert's eyes flew across at Anna, his face crazed. She was almost on him. Her foot caught on a stone and she measured her length on the ground.

A shout from behind. Pounding footsteps. Jack raced past her and Gilbert looked up with an unearthly, deranged expression on his face. In his haste, he dropped the keys. No time to retrieve them. Only one answer and that was to run.

Anna saw Jack stagger sideways, holding his head again. But even as she picked herself up, Jack was already in pursuit of Gilbert's fleeing figure and Anna chased after them. Gilbert charged down the road, in his maddened state heading further out onto the moor. It was sheer lunacy. But they *had* to catch him. Jack's long legs were flying over the tarmac, but every so often, Anna saw his knees buckle and he grasped at his head again. Her own lungs burnt in agony as, soon after a bend in the road, she saw Gilbert veer off to the right with Jack hot on his heels. She hurtled after them, tripping on the uneven ground, on and on, splashing through a wide stream and then clambering over a gap in a stone wall.

It was then that Jack came to a standstill. Oh, no. Surely he hadn't given up? Anna wheezed up to him, her eyes shocked at the savage dread on his face.

'For God's sake, stop!' he yelled, his voice roaring across the moor. 'It's Fox Tor Mire!'

Anna turned rigid. Jack bellowed his warning again, but Gilbert paid no heed. Anna could only watch, petrified. And then it all seemed to happen in slow motion. Gilbert floundering in mud up to his knees. He tried to stop, but the momentum of his headlong rush carried him forward, and as he struggled frantically, he disappeared up to his chest.

Anna's heart ruptured and she stared, wild-eyed, at Jack.

'Bloody idiot,' he muttered under his breath, and ran forward.

Anna followed, blundering, her muscles like jelly. The ground became soft and boggy, like standing on a floating cushion. Spray came up at every step, water oozing up and getting deeper, topped by the brackish, oily slick from the peat below. Ahead of her, Jack sank up to his ankles and stopped. He flung his jacket aside, then dropping down, stretched out across the surface and began to wriggle forward on his stomach.

'Jack?' Anna squealed.

'I did this once in the army,' he called back. 'I

think I can reach them.'

She followed, terrified and whimpering. She could feel her entire body sinking into the sludge, and Jack, oh God, he was heavier than her. The mire stank and she felt it seeping through her clothes, slimy and freezing cold.

'Don't come any further. Grab hold of my ankles.'

Her hands shook but she did as he ordered. Everything was so slippery and mud was curdling around Jack's body. But he was only feet from Gilbert who was flailing in the slough with one hand while still clinging onto Charlie with the other.

'Stop struggling or you'll sink further!' Jack shouted. 'Give me the boy!'

Gilbert seemed to stop. What in God's name was going on in his deranged mind?

'Gilbert, please!' Anna screamed. 'He's your son, for God's sake!'

'So, he is, then?' she heard Gilbert crow.

What did it matter? All she cared about was Charlie's safety. 'Yes!'

'Come on, man, quick!'

Jack reached out as far as he could, almost there. Dear God. And then, miraculously, Jack had him, and Charlie's chubby arms appeared out of the mud around Jack's neck. Slowly, inch by inch, they both wriggled backwards, Anna still holding Jack's ankles just in case. The instant it was safe to do so, Jack got up onto his knees and passed Charlie into Anna's trembling arms. Filthy, stinking, shaking with cold and shock, they clung to each other, tears of relief streaming down Anna's cheeks as she clutched Charlie to her.

'Wrap Charlie in my jacket and then get to the hotel and get help.'

Anna stared at Jack. Of course. Fencott Place was back down the road nearly a mile from where the van was parked. Yes, get help, but... Panic seized her again. 'Jack, you won't...?'

'Risk myself to save him? No. He's probably standing on the bedrock anyway.'

'Promise?'

'Promise. Now, go!'

She was bone-weary, ready to drop. She dragged herself back across the moor to the road. Her arms felt like lead from carrying Charlie. He was crying, his little face a picture of misery. Oh, it was so far! But she was nearly back to where the pushchair had been abandoned. She dumped Charlie in the pushchair and, dragging it across the grass until they were back on the road, she hurried along the tarmac, pushing it in front of her, as fast as her wobbling legs would carry her.

When she reached Fencott Place, she grabbed Charlie and flung open the door to the hotel, 'Lily! Daniel!' she screamed at the top of her voice.

A second later, they both came running from the kitchen, Trojan barking at their heels. Anna saw the horrified astonishment on their faces at the desperate, filthy state they were in.

'Gilbert tried to take Charlie!' she gasped. 'He's stuck out on the mire. Jack's with him.'

'I'm on my way. Lily, call 999.'

Daniel was already out of the door and Lily was running to the phone. 'And then I'll get you and Charlie in a nice hot bath,' she called over her shoulder.

Anna stood there, quivering, and then burst into tears.

'It was only mild concussion but William insisted I stay in overnight. Do you know how Gilbert is? He must have been in the mire nearly five hours before they finally got him out. He'd lost consciousness long before. Daniel and I just couldn't shift him, there was so much suction. And the fire engine was out on another call and we had to wait.'

Anna sighed, drained after the day's events and yet with every nerve on edge and ready to leap into action.

'Yes, I know. They're still working on him. They say he should recover from the exposure, though he'd been drinking heavily which didn't help. Alcohol draws the heat from the body core, William said. But they're more worried that he seems to have inhaled some of the putrid water. What'll poor Frankie think when she finds out?'

'That's what I've been thinking. Interpol are trying to find her.'

Anna nodded, and for a minute or two, they sat in silence, each lost in thought.

'But Charlie's safe. That's the main thing.' And Jack squeezed her hand.

'What'll you do now?' Anna asked gently. A light mist hovered over the gardens of Ashcroft Hall, enshrouding the tulips and swathes of delicate forget-me-nots.

'Now Gilbert's dead, you mean?' Frankie's voice was flat, expressionless. 'I still can't believe it.

Pneumonia. Probably from the water that got in his lungs. Or the exposure, or both. Well,' she sighed resignedly, 'probably sell this place. I've got power of attorney over everything. Lady Prue had another stroke, you know. A severe one this time. It's left her like a cabbage. Outwardly, anyway. Who knows what's going on inside her head? I reckon it was the shock of finally accepting what Gilbert was really like.'

'And you?'

Frankie turned to Anna with a wistful sigh. 'My feelings for Gilbert died long ago, I realise that now. I'll survive. I'm a very rich widow. I'll take care of Lady Prue, of course. Employ a couple of nurses. She could go on for years. And perhaps, one day, I'll start to live again.'

But ... we can always be friends? I feel so guilty–'

'Don't be. You've freed me as well.' And she encircled Anna in a warm embrace.

The bride and groom posed for photographs in the glorious August sunshine. Anna had never seen Ethel look as radiant as she did in her gauzy veil and ivory gown. She and Bert were made for each other. Ethel, a broad smile on her face, was lapping up the joy of her special day, but catching Anna's eye, gave her a cheeky wink.

Anna grinned back and gave the thumbs up sign as Jack came over to her, leading Charlie by the hand. A warm tide lulled her in contentment as she smiled at them. Oh, she couldn't be happier! After all that had happened, they had won through in the end. If only her parents had been there to know how happy she was with Jack. A vision of her mum, with the purple roses around her neck, flashed across Anna's mind. But they had all been bruised along the way. Her mum from her unfailing love for the man her dad had once been. Ethel, separated from Bert while he did his National Service. Poor Lady Ashcroft, forced to renounce the man she truly loved and now reduced to such a sorry state. Dear, *dearest* Queenie with her heartbreaking, lifelong secret. Carrie, with her scare over Jeffery's health. And now Frankie, torn apart by sadness and regret.

And herself?

Life had been hard on her. But with Jack by her side, she felt she could climb mountains. He bent down to speak to her and she turned to him, her heart lurching at his closeness.

'Can we make a date for this time next year?' he whispered. 'At the church in Tavistock?'

Anna blinked at him, and elation spiralled up inside her. His eyes held hers, soft and intense with love.

Oh, yes, her heart sang. And the world stood still.

Acknowledgments

As always, I should like to thank my agent and my publishers for their continued support. My gratitude also goes to Paul Rendell, Dartmoor guide and historian and editor of *The Dartmoor News,* who once again checked my manuscript for details on Dartmoor history. A huge thank you must go to Christine Barron, former theatre sister at Tavistock Hospital, for her information on Didworthy Sanatorium, to Dr Marshall Barr, founder of the Berkshire Medical Heritage Centre, for his information on the treatment of tuberculosis in the 1950s, and to my good friend, Sir Michael Willats for his input regarding vehicles of the time. Roger Paul of the Princetown History Club also contributed local facts for this novel, and Mr and Mrs Cribbett kindly shared their memories with me.

Author's Note

Readers who know Dartmoor well may recognise my model for Holly Cottage. The real building was condemned a few years earlier than in my book, but I have changed the date to suit my story. Happily, unlike some of the other buildings mentioned in the novel, the cottage survived by virtue of the fact that it was used as a pigsty by a local farmer but has now been restored to a residential dwelling.

My model for Ashcroft Hall might also be recognised, but I must point out most strongly that the Ashcrofts bear no resemblance whatsoever to the aristocratic family who lived there for a brief period.

The publishers hope that this book has given you enjoyable reading. Large Print Books are especially designed to be as easy to see and hold as possible. If you wish a complete list of our books please ask at your local library or write directly to:

Magna Large Print Books
Magna House, Long Preston,
Skipton, North Yorkshire.
BD23 4ND

This Large Print Book for the partially sighted, who cannot read normal print, is published under the auspices of

THE ULVERSCROFT FOUNDATION